THE
INCOMPLETENESS
THEOREM

MARK McDOWELL

Print ISBN: 978-1-66782-486-4
eBook ISBN: 978-1-66782-487-1

For

Jill, Reilly & Reagan

CONTENTS

1.

PRIME FACTORS | 2021

I STAND ON THE REAR TERRACE OF MY HOME WEARING threadbare boxers and regard the midsummer sky at dawn. In a moment the rising sun will crest the roofs of the McMansions opposite me on this quiet cove of Lake Cooke. I step out of the boxers and now nude walk across the travertine pool deck to the edge of the pool, my toes curling around the coping. It's a soft morning, cool for mid-July in Carolina. The usual din of cicadas and crickets is absent, an indication that today will not be sweltering. I step down onto the first of four steps leading into the shallow end of the pool. The water is also soft, something I attribute to it being saltwater, though you cannot taste the salt and it's okay to open your eyes underwater. I plunge in with a shallow dive and swim across in a dozen strokes.

I don't worry about the neighbors. A buffer of pines, oaks and ruinous sweetgums on either side of my backyard shields me, and the lots are large to begin with. I am aware of Meagan inside, but it's only just past 6 am and she won't stir for hours, her teen brain still gulping in sleep. I swim back to the shallow end, climb out of the pool, and wrap myself in a beach towel that has been draped across a chair for days, maybe weeks. This might be my shower for the day, we'll see.

I'm in decent shape for my age, fifty-five. My belly is flat, though no washer board, making me nearly unique among my peers. I'm about five-ten. My gray brown hair has been thinning since my late thirties so I keep it close cropped. I don't so much comb it now as point it. Last year I quit shampoo entirely, body wash will do. More and more in the summer, the sunrise swim is my shower.

There are other things in the more and more category, and in the last year category. Making my bed more and more, not doing the dishes more and more, keeping music on more and more. I became a widower fifteen months ago, and that has led to more and more, and less and less.

Last night the board of the Club gave me a nice send off - *a laurel, and hearty handshake* - to quote a favorite line. Our chairwoman, porcine Pam, twice divorced, spoke effusively of my service over the past year, my notable election to the post after Diane's death, and my unique form of diplomacy. For these contributions I received a fine bottle of Blanton's bourbon, which Dale and I sampled about an hour later on this very terrace.

I move inside for a cup of coffee. Next I will check the market futures and probably text Dale, who will be doing the same. We're gamblers, Dale and I, co-conspirators in poker, naked puts and Club politics. Some of these things Pam calls diplomacy.

* * *

My name is John Callany and I go by Jack. I'm rebuilding myself. The process started when I was inducted into widowerhood last year, though it probably would have started even if Diane were still among the living simply by virtue of advancing middle age. But the sudden death of a spouse by heart attack on an ordinary Saturday morning is an abrupt event and may accelerate things already advancing on their own accord.

I don't plan to rebuild my new self as my younger self. Recapturing youth is a pathetic struggle that smells of hair dye. I hate tryhards, as my daughter Meagan says. The ripped jeans Diane would buy me were way too tryhard.

But there are inescapable aspects of personality that follow one across the decades. I've had a lot of solitary hours to distill and redistill my identity down to its essentials. My son Jimmy told me when he was in high school that his student number was the product of 157 and 173, both primes. This past year and even now I'm trying to factor myself into primes, the canonical self. There's no easy way to do it, just brute force, like when Jimmy factored 27,161 when he probably should have been doing something else. Jimmy is good at math and I might be too.

One of my prime factors is *smart ass*. In another life on another planet, I was a stand-up comic. In middle school I could burn, roast, fry, flame, crush, char and slam any would-be antagonizer on the school bus. A few years later I was on the high school debate team and damn good, though looking back it was an exercise in sophistry and persuasion without conviction. The gift of words came directly and undiluted from my father, a dinner table pontificator. The man had no athletic ability as a child and so fought with words.

Another prime factor is *defiance*. I chafe under authority, even the benign sort, and I've never been good at having a boss. My military service lasted four years and one day, the exact obligation required to repay my bachelors degree in math from Davidson, except for the extra day, which was due, ironically, to a math error on my part. I appreciate irony, but I assign that to the first prime factor, smart ass. I ascribe the defiance prime to the same man, my father, whose severe nineteenth century discipline birthed it.

I'm still sieving for my other prime factors. Smart ass multiplied by defiance is less than a whole Jack Callany, so there must be other factors.

* * *

I met Dale at Thursday night Men's Poker at the Club more than ten years ago. It could have been even longer - a decade's not what it used to be. Diane and I joined the Club around that time despite misgivings about the country club lifestyle. She wanted to get back into tennis and shed a few pounds. I felt compelled to be a bit more social myself.

Thursday Night Men's Poker caught my attention during the new member social. I enjoy a bit of poker and I had seen the men's lounge with its mahogany paneling and heavily framed paintings of hunting dogs, not to mention its capacious humidor. I saw myself as a Club Man, peering through blue smoke from behind tall stacks of poker chips and enjoying a tumbler of bourbon with a single large clear cube of ice. This was poker as I had envisioned it, not as I had experienced it in the basement of my fraternity house, where we played on the ping pong table. What we lacked in ambiance in my college days we made up for in ruthless game play. At twenty I could smell fear and sense a trap, and it didn't hurt being a math major.

There were eight Club Men the first night I played. They all seemed to know each other well and were only guardedly welcoming toward me. This was not dispiriting. No all men's group is effusive about anything other than sports, and poker is not social the way a backyard barbecue might be. The initial buy-in was $300, so these men were angling for $2,000 and probably quite a bit more. I slow played, better to be underestimated.

By the end of the first hour, I pegged Dale as the boss. He sat directly across from me and I was able to study him without being conspicuous. He had a smooth, youthful face and arched eyebrows that gave him a friendly yet fiendish look that brought to mind the dancing devil on Underwood canned ham. He had a smooth bald head with black fringe that was incongruous with his unlined face. Dale had no tell I could discern, and his nerves were steely. Early in the evening he won big with a boat on the river. He was holding two-nine unsuited. Later he folded a pair of kings in an uncanny move that saved him more than $500. He nursed Blanton's all night. I knew we would be friends.

* * *

I take my coffee, black and teeth curling, to the desk in what had previously been the master bedroom. The first night after Diane died, and ever since, I have slept in the spare bedroom downstairs. I traded our master suite furniture to the lawn man for three months of free service and then set up a ten foot folding table from Costco on the spot our king bed had occupied.

I like to spread out when I work. I have two large monitors that support my options trading habit, and on both sides are unruly stacks of paper with various levels of urgency according to a system I understand but could never articulate. I allow a few inches of space between the monitors so I can take in the view of Lake Cooke that once made this room the obvious choice for a master bedroom.

Options trading is both income and sport for me. Hookes calls it picking up pennies in front of a steamroller. Dale calls it running across the highway for a hotdog. On a good day I will close three or four thousand dollars. On a bad day, like one of those last year when the virus suddenly reared its invisible head and robo traders almost destroyed the US economy, I've lost over a hundred thousand dollars. The steamroller got me that day. No pennies, no hotdog.

Almost all of my net worth, not including this house but most certainly including one million dollars from Diane's life insurance policy, I've turned over to Hookes for cautious custodianship.

He has earmarked part of the total for me to use as collateral in a margin trading account where I mostly sell naked puts, though sometimes naked calls too. Day trading in the nude, I suppose, though by now I have exchanged my sleeping boxers for a pair of running shorts and tee shirt from the Dancing Gnome brewery.

Most people glaze over when they hear about puts and calls, especially naked ones. They consider it too complicated, or too risky, or both. I like it that way. I'm happy to be a wizard of the obscure and it's fine with me when people change the subject. The truth is I am just an insurance salesman, sitting at a Costco table in running shorts, getting paid big fat premiums by traders who can force me to buy their stock if it falls too far. Most of the time I collect the premiums and never have to pay out claims. Of course, every once in a while there's a catastrophe and that's why Hookes has me on a leash.

I got interested in options seven years ago when my father shucked off his mortal coil and made me an adult orphan. My brother Brian and I split the two million dollar estate right down the middle. I handed over my half to Hookes and he suggested selling covered calls on the stock positions to juice the upside and protect the downside. That piqued my curiosity about options and led me to the more arcane sphere of naked calls and puts. It was *terra incognita* for Hookes and made him nervous, but I took to the new math and became a disciple of *McMillan on Options*.

Dale jumped on the options train with me. As a poker maestro he had a natural affinity for it, and I enjoyed having a comrade in arms to share trading strategies with. Most mornings by 7:30 Dale will text me or vice versa, when pre-market trading gives us a hint about what the day holds. He texts me now about Regeneron, saying I can probably close my naked call for a tidy $4,000. Nice. It was one of the stocks that soared beyond rationality while we endured shelter-in-place orders and I've wagered ten thousand share's worth that it's due for a drop. I text him back: "If you're right I'm buying enchiladas on Friday." In reply I get the thumbs up and margarita emojis.

2.

A LITTLE DITTY | **1988**

DIANE AND I WOULD HAVE CELEBRATED OUR THIRTIETH ANNI-
versary the summer after she died. I had planned for us to celebrate in New
York City that September, taking in the US Open, catching a couple Broadway
shows, rambling through lower Manhattan, and then finally sharing a late
night cigar on a park bench. She knew none of this. It was going to be my
surprise for us, and I had already found tickets to the US Open and a nice
condo on Airbnb.

The US Open was definitely for Diane's benefit and not mine. In the
last year of her life, and in fact in the last minute of her life, she was tennis
obsessed in a way I would never have predicted. In the waning years of her
forties, Diane had progressed from being a weekend 2-5 piker to the twice
daily 3-0 striver. She played on the Club team and the community team, and
between matches and practices she would be on the courts by 8:30 most
mornings and not off until 9:00 in the evening, later if there were drinks *apres*
tennis, which there usually were.

I had begun to see our pearl anniversary as an inflection point on a
line whose origin was a dance club in Georgetown, and whose other major
inflection point was in 2000 when we became parents. With a little calculus,
the attentive student can find the area under this line: bliss, career, parenting,

malaise, return to bliss. Except we never reach the final stage. This was a finite integral and the upper bound, as far and Diane and I were concerned, turned out to be malaise.

One summer after college I was working at the Pentagon as butter bar second lieutenant. Most Thursdays and every Friday after work the boys and I would change into civilian khakis and button downs (a jaunty, well paid look), and ease into the twentysomething bars on K or 14th. At one of these, three or four hours past happy hour, the room was being rocked by *Jack and Diane* and we were screaming with abandon. A startled woman with wavy chestnut hair was mashed up against me by two of my boys and dates they had found that evening.

"Hey Jack, meet Diane!" they screamed above the music.

That's how we met, and that's why a little ditty was and still is our anthem.

3.

CASSEROLES | 2020

I WON'T PLACE MY ORDER TO CLOSE THE REGENERON OPTIONS
until after the market opens. It's foolish to place an order before you see the
real time action. I use this quiet hour to scan email and clickbait news headlines. I have an unread email from Pam Loving, the chairwoman of the Club
board, to the rest of the board. My year of service officially ended three weeks
ago, at the end of June, but I will continue to receive board emails until I ask
Pam to unsubscribe me, which I may or may not do. This email recounts the
minutes from last night's meeting, including my own valedictory, along with
an enumeration of upcoming summer events and Clubhouse renovations, all
of which had been canceled or delayed during my year of service. Pam also
includes a list of HOA community standards violations, though the shame
list is now much shorter than it had been a year ago.

The Weltons are cited for having seven cars in their driveway. I know
these do not belong to house guests but are mostly cars that David and his
teenage daughter are repairing and planning to flip. Cyrus Bolton, age 78
and seldom sober, is cited for growing vegetables in his front yard, but his lot
lies in the barbaric territories just beyond the boundary of the HOA and he
flaunts the community standards gleefully from his decrepit golf cart, which
is also parked in the front yard. Cyrus was sweet on my wife and would putter

down to our place in his golf cart throughout the summer with offerings of okra and ripe cantaloupe. The Jones's two tiered mailbox in gold plate and other Trumpian flourishes is not to code and has been sent a final warning.

A Columbia professor, Wallace Sayre, deep in the 1950s declared that "academic politics is the most vicious and bitter form of politics because the stakes are so low." I maintain that Sayre conceived this nugget while serving on a neighborhood HOA board and only later adapted it to faculty meetings. My twelve months of service, to which I had been elected in a misguided act of sympathy, were distracting at a time when I needed distraction, hilarious (at least to me) by my own construction, ribald on many levels, and infuriating in retrospect.

My seat on the board, one of seven, had been occupied by Diane who was duly elected and had served almost one full year before she collapsed on the tennis court. All terms are for two years and are staggered so that every year three of four seats are up for reelection. Last year it was three seats, but then a fourth seat became available, Diane's. The Club by-laws required a special election to fill any vacated seat, and the board had decided to combine the special election for Diane's seat with the general election in June. Four candidates were running, the three incumbents plus Ari Nimrod, and it was assumed, with disgust, that Ari would win Diane's seat.

One week before the elections last June, Pam rang my doorbell and proffered a foil wrapped casserole dish with stout outstretched arms. "I thought you might appreciate a home cooked meal," she said. I thanked her, took the dish, and invited her into my foyer.

"It's Hawaiian chicken," Pam said.

I worked my way through quite a few casseroles after Diane's death. About half were lasagna of some form, vegetarian, pepperoni, gluten free. There was also taco casserole (tasty), several variations of chicken and rice, tuna (awkward), Cajun shrimp alfredo, hamburger tater tot with cheese, and cauliflower with Monterrey Jack. Each of these I tried on days when I was not fasting (Mondays and Thursday) and some I finished entirely. Others I double bagged in plastic and threw away. All these dishes I scrubbed thoroughly with a wire brush, ran through the dishwasher and attempted to return within six months.

One must exercise care when accepting casseroles. Some are wordless expressions of grief and support, some are Trojan Horses with hidden intentions, and some maybe a bit of each. More than half of the casseroles came from the divorced coterie at the Club, some of whom had been traded in for newer models while others were merrily enjoying freedom by their own hands. Some left their dishes at my front door with notes written in sharpie and signed with hearts (I would receive a text a few minutes later), while others would linger at my kitchen counter and probe how very *lonely* I must be.

Of course, as Freud said, sometimes a casserole is just a casserole. Dale, who is single and does not cook, came over one night with carryout enchiladas from Cantina Azteca and ate them with me right out of the styrofoam box.

Pam planted herself in my foyer with the permanence of a fireplug. Please, please Pam, don't say how lonely I must be and reach for my hand (I think but do not say). Pam had separated from her second husband, Gordon, just before the holidays after a two or three year union fraught by his cavalier spending of her money. In truth, a decent amount of my walking around cash came from Pam via Gordon via Thursday night Men's Poker. The boys there say I'll call anything, which is a joke because of my name, but it was really Gordon who would call any bet no matter how pathetic his hand. His profligate spending was on display in the Club parking lot (Maserati convertible), on his dock (Cobalt), on his wrist (Cartier), and on his and Pam's waistlines. In this neighborhood, conspicuous wealth is nothing unusual, but Gordon had been the front desk clerk at Happy Brothers Tires before he married Pam, who was a well heeled VP at the largest insurance company on the east coast. Gordon would drive Happy Brothers customers back to their homes if their repairs were going to take a while. Evidently Pam had a lot of tire trouble.

She looked at me for a too long moment and then said, "Jack, I know it's soon, but …." I may have gulped.

"We can't let Ari Nimrod take Diane's board seat. Would you ever in a million years consider running?"

I was so relieved that Pam's proposition was not carnal that I nodded a faint consent.

Ari Nimrod was a perennial affliction to the Club board. He had stood unsuccessfully for election every year for the past five years, and despite the community's rebuke, would attend every open meeting as a concerned homeowner and drown the proceedings with interjections crafted to comply with Robert's Rules of Order. It was Nimrod who elevated the community standards guidelines to a public shame list, patrolling the neighborhood by day, photographing and annotating infringements. At board meetings he would insist on reading his findings aloud into the minutes, and as soon as the minutes were published he would email a link directly to the Town Herald, which has an unquenchable thirst for breaking news.

On the third Monday of each month, board meeting nights, Diane would return home knotted in frustration. "My God," she said more than once, "we managed to squeeze a one hour meeting into three hours!" She was not planning to run for a second term, having seen enough politics in her ten years of State Department service before we moved here. It was becoming increasingly difficult to find anyone to run for a seat, so thoroughly had Nimrod poisoned the atmosphere. He would win a seat one day through simple attrition, and it looked like Diane was his attrit.

Nimrod is well known to me and I take delight in calling him by his last name, never Ari. By day he is a telemedicine radiologist, which means he sits in front of a high resolution computer monitor in the basement of his substantial house and reviews X-rays, CT scans, and MRIs sent to him from around the globe. He's an independent concierge radiologist available to anyone who can pay his two thousand dollar an image rate. It's the ideal arrangement for a doctor with no bedside manner and a desire for several hours each day to devote to Club politics and neighborhood code violations.

The only reason Nimrod hasn't been run out of town or had his knee-caps busted is an unspoken communal sympathy for his wife Sara, a vulnerable longsuffering wisp devoted to their twin pre-teen girls. Sara is pretty in a vulnerable unmade up way and to onlookers her union with Nimrod is asymmetrical and inexplicable. We all vaguely assume that Nimrod lashes out at her when she interrupts him with a grilled cheese sandwich while he's reading X-rays, or that he forgets her birthday every single year, or that he never notices her shoes. When I picture them *in flagrante delicto* (I wish I didn't but can't not) she is weeping or looking out the window, her head rotated away from Nimrod's heaving face.

* * *

The evening of Pam's visit, probably before I had reheated the Hawaiian chicken, word was spreading by text and Facebook and God knows what else that I would be on the ballot. In the years before Diane was on the board I seldom gave the elections a passing thought, can't recall a single Facebook post on the topic (though I only check my account a couple times each year), and most certainly did not cast a vote myself. But there is a hive mind in the neighborhood that feasts on these matters and follows every development breathlessly.

Just before seven the next morning I received a text from Pam: *it's too late to add your name to the ballot, by-laws say that nominations close 2 weeks before election.* This was followed by a sad face emoji squirting large blue tears from both eyes. Then another text: *fucking nimrod must have memorized the by-laws*, followed by a dozen parrot emojis.

The parrots made me smile.

The Nimrods moved in about eight years ago. They built new on an almost two acre lot next to Cyrus Bolton. Cyrus's place was and is an eyesore, an aluminum mobile home set on a permanent brick foundation and boasting a large vegetable garden in the front yard. The lot next door, which lies entirely within the HOA boundary and has an enviable deep water dock, had been passed over during the housing boom because no buyer wanted to build a dream home next to Cyrus's shithole. Then Nimrod came along.

He got the lot for twenty percent less than asking, and before breaking ground hired a landscaping firm to plant a double line of arborvitaes along the property line. Today those trees tower at thirty feet and separate the properties completely, except for a small stub of land on Cyrus's lot that juts in the lake. When Nimrod's house was finished a year later, the arborvitaes were still fairly short and the DMZ between the Nimrod's and Bolton's was still passable.

One evening that summer, I came home to find Cyrus parked in front of our house in his golf cart speaking with Diane. On his back seat was a six pack of Bud Light, which was customary, and a shotgun which was less customary. Diane was holding a basket of garden tomatoes, a gift from Cyrus, and I heard her saying, "Don't do that Cyrus, you'll only make things worse," and Cyrus replying to the effect that he didn't give two shits.

I parked and joined them, and shortly learned that the Nimrods had a parrot named L'il Girl whose cage they rolled out onto their rear balcony every morning at sunrise. They did this on the very first morning they awoke in their new home, and every morning after, which had been a month's worth at that point. L'il Girl rejoiced each morning at the rising sun with a loud witch's cackle, followed inexplicably by *I pledge allegiance to the flag*. Then more cackling, more pledging, and so on.

Cyrus's bedroom window faced the Nimrod's balcony, and L'il Girl's morning adhan had become Cyrus's unwelcome alarm clock. Like many septuagenarians, Cyrus was usually up shuffling around before 5:00 am. Nonetheless, his indignation had grown daily to the point now that he was preparing to dispatch L'il Girl with his shotgun.

"If I have to listen to the little mothfucker say the goddam Pledge of Allegiance one more time I'll blow her l'il fuckin head right off," he declared solemnly.

Diane was certainly not above obscenity, but Jimmy and Meagan were still impressionable. As Cyrus continued his diatribe, I could see that Diane was trying to discern if the kids were within earshot. I also knew by her body language that she was ready to be extricated.

"Cyrus," I said. "I've got an idea that might work *and* will keep you out of jail."

Then to Diane I added, "Hon, can you give us a minute?"

Diane did not like being dismissed from a conversation and it's something I would ordinarily never do, except in this case I attempted a little wink. Seeing the opportunity, she rose and kissed Cyrus on the cheek, thanked him for the tomatoes, and went inside.

"I'm listening," said Cyrus.

"Use your nut, Cyrus. These birds learn to speak by imitating, right?" I asked.

He nodded.

I went on. "Somebody or some TV show or something taught that bird the Pledge of Allegiance." Another nod. "Well," I continued, "you have a sailor's command of the language. Why don't you teach L'il Girl a few words of your own?"

After a moment Cyrus's lips stretched into a wide loose yellow tooth smile. "Callany, you're a fuckin' genius."

Cyrus Bolton's house is about a mile from mine, so we were not bothered by L'il Girl's morning pledge, nor did I observe firsthand Cyrus's precise method of retraining her. I envisioned him at daybreak, parked in his golf cart among the juvenile arborvitae, croaking out obscenities in a steady but easily memorized repetition. *Suck Cock Bitch. Suck Cock Bitch. Suck Cock Bitch.*

By the time the old man's corn had come in that summer, Li'l Girl had forgotten the Pledge and was greeting the sun each day with a joyful command for oral sex.

At the annual Halloween neighborhood potluck that fall, I found myself in line next to shy Sara Nimrod. I asked her how they were liking their new home. She said they loved it, and were hoping to start a family soon, but they had been forced to get rid of their bird.

I helped myself to some macaroni and cheese and said I was happy for them but it was a shame about the bird.

Cyrus wasn't at the potluck. He had not been invited owing to his property being on the wrong side of the HOA boundary.

I never told Pam the L'il Girl story, but when I saw the parrot emojis I knew she knew. Maybe Diane told her. Probably the hive mind.

You'll think of something, Madame Chair, I texted back.

* * *

Pam Loving did think of something: a write-in campaign.

I told her that if elected I would fill Diane's seat for the remainder of her term, but under no circumstances would I do any stumping or baby kissing for the write-in slot. That would have to be a strictly grass roots movement, and Pam had all of one week for the roots to take hold. She turned to Aristotle Poe.

Aristotle was the longest serving board member and I considered him a friend. He was a veteran of Thursday night Men's Poker (and of an actual war), had been playing there years before me, and in fact was there the night of my original debut. From that evening I can only picture with certainty Dale, because we struck up our friendship shortly after, and Aristotle, because he is such an unforgettable figure.

Aristotle is a large colored man (he prefers this term to African American so I defer) in a club where there are damn few, he is rotund in a firm but not flabby way, and he motors around the sidewalks of our community in an electric wheelchair he calls his Tesla. He looks a bit like James Earl Jones and has a fine baritone voice. I've been told he was a judge in Atlanta before retiring a hundred years ago, and that he had been in the Army JAG corps either during or after Vietnam, where his left leg was blown off.

It's true that I size people up by their poker game, as did Harry S Truman, who selected his cabinet from among his poker regulars, knowing the risk tolerance, sense of humor and overall judgment of each after decades of play. Aristotle I rate top quartile, where I also rate myself, though neither he nor I are top decile. His greatest strength is his stony, inscrutable face. He looks exactly the same (mildly irritated) when he flops a boat as when he flops horseshit. His weakness is that he rarely bluffs. I attribute this to his having been a judge and fair mindedness being deeply coded in his DNA. Of course when he does bluff it wreaks havoc.

The year before Diane joined the board, Aristotle had motioned that our board join the National Club Association and cough up twenty-five hundred dollars in annual dues. The motion carried and we received a hefty three ring binder of national best practices covering all aspects of club administration. I recall that Diane was impressed by it during her new board member indoctrination. Most clubs in the South (I consider us not Deep South but Shallow) are still governed by debutante etiquette and white male community bank board members and golfing buddies. She felt our Club was less clubby as a result of our NCA membership and more likely to thrive after the current old guard relocated to Eternal Autumn Assisted Living.

Aristotle did three things to make the write-in campaign a success, two of them legal. First he walked Pam step by step through the process of designing the ballot and administering the actual election, strictly respecting NCA best practices. This included making decisions on absentee voting (no), electronic voting (no), voting location (the Clubhouse Grand Hall), and voting hours (7 am to 6 pm). Second, he suggested hiring an inexpensive but capable temp who could design and print the ballots, manage the voting process on election day, and oversee the tally.

The third thing Aristotle did (I learned this later) was call Dale that evening with a special request. If he, Aristotle, could provide Dale with copies

of all the warning emails sent by the Club to members found to be in violation of HOA community standards over the past three years, could he, Dale,
send a mass anonymous email to those offenders recommending they write
in my name on the ballot instead of checking the box next to Ari Nimrod's.

"You bet your ass," said Dale.

Fast forward six days. Pam had managed to hire a temp, Brenna Wilder,
who had graduated virtually from Chapel Hill three weeks earlier with a
Master's in Communications. Brenna designed a ballot that read "Vote For
No More Than Four" and then listed four names on four lines, followed by
a fifth line labeled "Write-In: _____."

Of the seven hundred members of our HOA, less than one hundred
would ordinarily turn out to vote for the Club board. But Dale's anonymous
email had reached almost two hundred voters, all of them prime offenders
who had failed to bring in their trash bins promptly after Monday pickup,
or paint their mailbox posts when they began to flake from excessive dog
piss, or move their vegetable gardens from their front yards to their backyards, or any number of other infractions noted and read into the record by
Candidate Nimrod.

Pam Loving phoned me at nine o'clock that evening. Jack Callany, the
first write-in candidate in Club history, was the top vote getter, with more
than one hundred total votes.

"Aristotle might want to notify the National Club Association," I
told her.

4.

THE INFLUENCER | 2021

THE MARKET OPENED LOWER ON FEARS THAT THE FED WOULD raise interest rates, and by 10 am the twenty or so stocks on my watch list are all red. In the options line of work, red can be very good. I have a naked call on Regeneron, which means I'm betting the price will drop. I place an order to close that position when the option price drops another dollar. I also (mainly) use the red days to sell naked puts on stocks I really like. I spend the next hour watching the watch list, looking for irrational sell offs.

Just after eleven I hear the blender roar to life downstairs in the kitchen. Meagan is risen! She mixes frozen mixed berries, organic spinach, protein powder and a trendy milk substitute into a dark green icy mush that looks like the goose shit I find in our backyard. A few minutes later I hear the thud of her bare heels coming down the hallway to my office *slash* former master bedroom I shared with her mother. "Yo Daddio," she says from the doorway.

"How's the frozen goose crap?" I ask her.

"Shut up."

She walks into the room, stands behind me, and presses her chin into the top of my head. It's been just the two of us this past year. Jimmy came home for Meagan's high school graduation in June and then drove back to

Boston for a summer internship at a pharma company in Kendall Square. Meagan will be gone in less than a month. I will drive her to Boston College in August, we'll spend a day or two with Jimmy, and then I'll have thirteen hours on my drive home to contemplate my own prime factorization.

"Was that blender made in North Korea by drunk tank engineers?" I ask Meagan. "It's the loudest piece of machinery we own."

"Dad, you bought it at Target." I know her eyes roll, even though I can't see them.

"Please don't use that thing if I'm taking a nap."

You wouldn't guess that Meagan was the natural offspring of Diane and me. She doesn't look like either of us. Her hair is fine and straight, dark red, not a carrot top but the shade of red that women pay a fortune for in salons. Her eyes are a hazeley green that recalibrate to match her clothing. She has a dancer's lithe body and moves about the house, rarely before noon, with languid indifference. This exquisite package of teen femininity also stomps like a footsoldier and laughs like a hyena when it's just the two of us.

Meagan shares this with her late mother: she is a study in contrasts. Excruciatingly lazy yet wildly ambitious, geeky but hates school, Ben and Jerry's *and* kale.

These days her job title is less lofty, though maybe not. She is an *influencer* on TikTok and has something like one million followers and growing daily. Her schtick is to perform a five or ten second dance featuring flirtatious acrobatic and yoga-inspired body contortions and then finish with a close up of her biting into something grotesquely unhealthy, like an oozing bacon cheeseburger from Five Guys. The videos only show her first bite, which drives her followers insane with curiosity to know if she actually finishes whatever it is.

There's a powerful desire to believe in magic, in this case that a teen girl can absolutely chow down on anything she wants and still move and look the way Meagan does. She has been making that little bit of magic for the world since she was fourteen. Last year, with a boost from isolation and social distancing, she hauled in over fifty thousand dollars in sponsorships, a quarter from athletic wear companies and three quarters from fast food restaurants. I have told her she will be a CEO one day.

Sometimes she does eat the entire cheeseburger.

"What's today's taunt going to be?" I ask her.

"Whaddaya mean?"

"I mean, what greasy carby piece of junk food are you going to taunt your beloved followers with?" I reply.

She smiles. "Not today dad, I made one Sunday. Next one will be Friday."

Sometimes I get to be *best boy* on her videos, which means I run out to buy the taunt while she practices the day's dance. It's not unusual for her to practice for an hour before she starts recording, and even then she'll record and delete a dozen times before she's satisfied. She only does the big bite finale one time, obviously, because that requires no practice. On Friday she might send me to Taco Bell or Chick-fil-A or who knows where. My job is to make sure the food is unwrapped and at the ready the moment she is satisfied with her moves so there won't be any break in the video.

"OK," I say. "You gonna be around the house today?"

"Not really. Shopping with Maddie this afternoon."

And with that I feel her chin lift off my head. She kisses my cheek, glances at the computer screen, says "Boring..." and floats out of the room.

Actually it's not boring at all. My close order on Regeneron has been filled and I pocket $4,700, better than I was expecting. I text Dale enchilada emojis and he replies with margarita emojis. If I actually do buy him a Mexican gut buster lunch on Friday, I'll be sure to bring home a greasy chimichanga for Meagan.

5.

CIGAR | 1989

THE NIGHT I MET DIANE, AFTER WE HAD BEEN SQUEEZED together by my coworkers and a circle of jovial strangers at a dance club, the two of us walked through DC into the small hours of the night. She was just the right size for me, narrow hips, small waist, full round breasts, her forehead at the height of my lips. Her hair was a mousy brownish that would reveal amber highlights on a bright summer day. Her lips were full and smirky. The whole ensemble made me think lustfully of the silver silhouette on the mudflaps of a semi (long haul truckers have hours upon hours to fantasize). I wanted to kiss those lips and feel that body squeeze against me and slide my palms into the back pockets of her jeans.

On that first night - it was June and clear and before the suffocating humidity of late summer in DC - Diane drew me into the web of her mind, which radiated with order and humor and sarcasm. Her intelligence was palpable and elevated mine by inviting me to keep pace. I was simply spellbound by this brilliant mudflap masterpiece.

On our walk I learned Diane was two years younger than me, had just finished her junior year at Georgetown, was from LA, and had just moved off campus. She had spent her freshman year at UCLA but transferred to

Georgetown for the debate team in hopes of another national championship. That summer she had an internship at the State Department.

Electricity arced across the space between us, which diminished block by block until we were happily and carelessly bumping into each other, and in the darkness our voices became detached from our bodies. Diane's words, precise and incisive, and punctuated with self aware giggles, drifted ahead of us on the street. Who knows the topics we covered? Our curricula vitae, favorite burrito places, preferred jogging routes, pet peeves, and anything else that crossed our dizzy minds.

I've read that certain skills like face recognition and language acquisition are so essential to human survival that regions of our brains are hardwired to perform them. Sizing up a mate must also be such a skill, and for adults in their mid-twenties, that cranial region must be large indeed. I found Diane's piercing intelligence refreshing and challenging and alluring, but it was also clear that she would not suffer fools and could be surprisingly abrasive. My mating radar told me this played a role in her leaving one college for another, and moving off campus (alone) after only a year at Georgetown. In the very same instant, I wanted to be smart enough for her. And attractive enough. Pheromones were spewing.

At two or three in the morning we found ourselves at the Jefferson Memorial, backlit, magisterial and vacant. We sat on a Park Service bench looking out over the motionless tidal basin, hip to hip, my arm slung over the bench behind her. It was the first time any silence had settled between us. Lights sparkled on the inky surface of the water.

Diane finally spoke. "Want a cigar?"

I had been thinking of a kiss, actually.

"I guess, sure." I said. "But we won't be able to find one around here."

Diane reached into her tiny handbag and produced a single *Romeo y Julieta Capulet*. Another fact about this woman I simply could not file anywhere.

"I only have one," she said. "We'll share it." It was a declaration, not a question.

With a cigar cutter from the same handbag (what else was in there?) she neatly clipped the cap and then slowly inserted the full length of the cigar into her mouth, sealed her lips around it, and rolled it languorously. My eyes widened despite every effort to play it cool, cool, cool.

"Haven't you ever seen that before?" Diane asked after withdrawing the cigar. "It moistens the leaf, makes it burn slower." Her eyes were playful.

She lit the cigar expertly and took a few short draws so the flame would catch, then blew white smoke towards the water and handed it to me. I took a puff, felt the hot acrid smoke in my mouth, and held the cigar out for Diane. Instead of taking it, she turned her face toward mine and kissed me, first softly, then deeply. The taste was cigar smoke and perfume and perspiration. I pulled her closer with one hand and with the other pointed the cigar towards Tommy J.

6.

McSTOMACHACHE | 2021

ON FRIDAY I MEET DALE AT CANTINA AZTECA FOR LUNCH. We've been coming here for years, every other Friday or so. Diane despised the place for reasons abundant and obvious enough - shabby decor, midday darkness (its few windows are stained glass), and a looping mariachi soundtrack - but I'm rather fond of it and so is Dale. The lunch specials, which include acreage of yellow rice and refried beans, are served on plates the size of manhole covers and the margaritas come in ornate ten pound glass goblets rimmed in salt.

Since we began trading options more than five years ago, Dale and I have had a standing arrangement that whoever makes the most *cha-ching* that week has to buy. I'm expecting this will fall to me after my Regeneron score Wednesday, but Dale has one upped me with a naked put on Disney that he closed this morning. It's a wager I'm happy to lose.

Dale is about my age, maybe a year or two older. The year he turned forty, his wife left him for a woman - an option trade Dale had not foreseen. This was well before I met him but he's shared bits and pieces over the years and I've sketched a composite in my mind. Dale's wife was the lipstick half. Her paramour (I picture her in jeans and boots and a man's haircut) was someone she had known in high school and reconnected with at a reunion Dale failed to attend.

Like me, Dale spent his twenties and thirties heads down, working long hours and traveling almost every week (I did not travel as much). He's a finance weenie, as we used to say in the engineering division, by training and by disposition. As a child I suspect he wore a green eyeshade visor when tallying his paper route returns. By thirty-nine he was the Chief Financial Officer of a public company that made plastic containers of all sizes (some as large as a house) and had offices in Mexico and China. He retired four years ago when a private equity firm took the company private and supplanted him with a whiz kid from McKinsey. His payout was as large as a plastic container as large as a house.

Our margaritas arrive and we each grab the substantial stem of our goblet like baseball bats and raise them to a toast.

"To naked calls," I say.

"To short puts," Dale replies.

I have a phobia about chipping my teeth which activates instantly when I press the thick glass to my lips. If this were my third margarita instead of my first, I could see myself ever so slightly miscalculating the trajectory of the salty rim and cracking it sharply into my front teeth. This unwelcome imagery sends a shudder down my shoulders. If this were to happen it would set me back months in the exploration of dating apps, where Dale has achieved novice-to-intermediate status and I have not yet reached the stage of downloading an app.

The margarita suits the venue and me perfectly. Quaffable, slightly sweet, oversalted, and made with a generous pour of house tequila. "Plans for tonight?" I ask Dale. I'm not specifically asking whether he has a date, but now that dating apps have intruded into my consciousness I decide to run with it.

He turns his face slightly towards the table then arches one eyebrow in my direction with a sheepish look. "Doesn't look like it."

"But you're saying there's a chance?" I ask, a line from a movie we often quote.

"Not a great one," Dale replies. "I'm awkward at texting so I get ghosted before the actual conversation stage."

"You're awkward at that stage, too," I rib.

Dale grins. "Anyway, there's no one I'm that interested in right now. What about you, ready to get on Bumble?"

I'm saved by the arrival of our enormous plates. I'm a *tres enchiladas* man myself. Dale almost always gets the fajitas, which occupy three plates and most of the table top. The server reminds us to be careful, the plates are hot, and in fact they are straight from the core of the Chernobyl nuclear reactor. "The fajitas look mighty fine," I say, nudging our conversation into a different lane. I make one of my standard jokes by pronouncing *fajitas* so that it rhymes (sort of) with *vaginas*.

"Yep, but the portions are skimpy," Dale cracks.

"I'll probably give it a try after Meagan goes to school," I tell Dale, meaning Bumble. "Maybe you can help me set up my profile."

"Sure," he replies. "Maybe you can help me with texting."

Dale prepares his first fajita carefully, equal amounts of chicken and steak, a smear of guacamole and some shredded cheese rolled into the warm tortilla. He takes a bite and chews, then says, "I had a dream last night. Actually this morning. I had already woken up, but fell back to sleep. I was running down a street somewhere. Not being chased, more like jogging except I was in regular clothes. And while I'm running I start pressing my tongue against the back of my teeth, and they aren't tight, they're loose, all of them. I tell myself to be careful and stop pressing them, but I can't stop and pretty soon they're dropping out of my mouth. And I keep running the whole time. I think I should stop and pick them up, but I don't. I just keep running."

Now I'm just staring at Dale, thinking about the margarita goblet shattering my front teeth. Why do we both have teeth issues?

"It's your subconscious telling you it's time to deal with the severe halitosis," I tell him.

"Fuck off."

"Okay, seriously," I say. "What do you think it means?"

"I Googled it after I got up," Dales says. "It's a pretty common dream, actually. It means I'm a shitty communicator, can't get the right words out when I need to."

"Ah," I say. "See exhibit A, no date tonight."

"Right," he says, finishing off his first *vajita*.

* * *

Driving home from lunch I dictate a text message to Jimmy from my car: *OMW what are we doin tonite cya soon.*

I send Jimmy a variation on this same message every Friday. It's a joke we started when he was a senior in high school. By then it was becoming more and more evident he would not be a commuter student, holed up in his dank adolescent bedroom during five or six years of community college. He's a smart kid, and by then he was focused on going to the best college he could get into, probably one many states away. I started telling him how much I would miss him (I really would, terribly) and how no matter where he went I would come hang out with him every Friday night.

"I'll be sitting there in your dorm room on Friday afternoon when you get back from class, playing your guitar and talking with your roommates. We're gonna have so much fun." I would tell him.

"Sounds great, dad," he would always say, and I think he sort of meant it.

Meagan couldn't be more different. I've made the same crack to her a few times and she stops me in my tracks each time, "Shut up, dad, it's not funny." I think she means it, too.

Jimmy is more laid back, Meagan more intense. One time I took Jimmy and his friends through the McDonald's drive-thru line when they were all pre-teens. When it was our turn to order, I asked, "Do you guys still have the McStomachache?" Jimmy and his friends howled.

The hapless girl on the other end of the speaker was silent for a moment, and then said, "No sir, I'm sorry, we don't have that anymore."

This was just the answer I was hoping to hear. "Nooooo," I wailed, "Please don't tell me corporate has canceled the McStomachache! They did the same thing with the McRib a few years ago."

More nervous silence from the girl, then, "I'm sorry sir, would you like to try our crispy buttermilk chicken sandwich?"

Jimmy and the boys hooted and hollered all the way home and Jimmy still asks for a McStomachache from time to time, including at his dining hall at college. He shares my love for a solid stupid joke that can be dragged out of cold stoage at any time.

Meagan, if she senses one of these old jokes coming, or even a distant variation on an old joke, will shout "No, dad, STOP!" It is not easy to get her to laugh, which makes me want to try all the harder. When she was a self-conscious twelve year old, we went to a Chick-fil-A drive thru. The price was something like six dollars and twenty-eight cents. I told the boy at the window I was prepared to offer him five dollars and ninety cents. He stared at me dumbfounded. "Oh God," Meagan said, and crawled into the back seat, curling herself up on the floor.

Later, from Meagan: "Dad, do not ever, EVER, try to negotiate in a drive-thru line again!" (I was actually thinking it would make a good TikTok meme.)

There is a pattern here and I need to think about whether it could be another prime factor of Jack. *Humor as anger?* Doesn't feel right, though I've read that all humor is an expression of anger. *Humor as fear?* Maybe. Maybe fear of my sweet attentive children becoming indifferent adults. *Humor as dominance?* That's possible too. Meagan, like her mother, cannot stand to be dominated, upstaged, or condescended to. Maybe Jimmy sees my fear, my fear of the end of his childhood, and so he goes a little easier on me.

I have not brought a chimichanga home for Meagan. She told me before I left that she was feeling more desserty for today's video. When I walk into the kitchen, I see two containers of ice cream on the counter, lids off, semi-melted. The caramel syrup is out. Upstairs I hear her music and the thump of her bare heels on the carpeted floor of her bedroom.

I put away the ice cream and syrup, then walk upstairs to her door, which is closed. I tap gently. No answer. I open the door slowly and see her posing in front of her cell phone, which is leaning against a window.

"Do you need a best boy?"

"NODAD!"

I continue down the upstairs hallway to my office and begin to feel the stupefying lethargy that only *tres enchiladas* and two goblets of house tequila can bring on.

7.
PINK LINE | 1990

EACH SEMESTER AT GEORGETOWN, JUST BEFORE FINALS, DIANE would put me on ice for a week or two so she could study and write. No visits, no calls unless urgent, definitely no woggling. So I was surprised to get a call from her on Monday of finals week in the last semester of her senior year. "We need to talk," she said.

We met that afternoon at Uncommon Grounds, a coffee shop on campus where you could usually count on finding a two-top. I didn't think I was being dumped. The L-word had entered our couple vocabulary that spring and we were talking about moving in together in the fall.

The talk was, in fact, wordless. Diane was already sitting at a small table when I arrived. She half stood to kiss me, and when she sat down her lips formed a fine straight line, not her usual dimply smile, and her eyes were pleading. She reached into her purse and handed me a plastic pregnancy test stick with a clear as day pink line in the viewing window.

There are the gradual changes in life - developing skills and expertise, accumulating some degree of wealth, watching hair turn gray or vacate the premises altogether - and there are the abrupt ones like a pink line when you least expect it. Abrupt changes, like prime numbers, are packed in tight at the front of the number line, when we're naive and indestructible and short on skills, wealth and gray hair. Mercifully, the primes become less frequent as we lurch further down the number line.

We were married in a civil ceremony four weeks later at the Marriage Bureau of the DC Superior Court. Neither of us told our parents, an omission I regret to this day. The truth is we felt *solved*. Diane had pulled through finals with an almost disturbing degree of composure and graduated *summa* (though her cherished debate team was felled by Wake Forest in early elimination rounds). She had landed an analyst role at the Department of State that would start in August. I had just pinned on First Lieutenant and felt a degree of competence in my job at the Pentagon, and as a married officer my housing allowance bumped up nicely. We felt older and wiser than our peers. We knew something about love that they couldn't understand.

Our honeymoon lasted from that Friday night until the next Tuesday morning, when Diane's bleeding started and we careened in my Honda Civic to Walter Reed. A female Army Major doctor told us Diane had an ectopic pregnancy. The fertilized egg had not completed its journey to the uterus but had stopped short and embedded itself inside a fallopian tube. The pregnancy would have to be terminated or the tube would rupture and could lead to Diane's death. Diane lay in her hospital bed and I sat in a naugahyde chair next to her, holding her left hand, which had a gold band but no diamond yet.

That night we made phone calls from her shared room at Walter Reed. Her roommate was decent enough to feign sleep while we called our parents and cried, and then after we hung up and kept crying and hugging.

We had definitely let go of sixteen.

8.

THE SHALLOW SOUTH | 2020

ON THE THIRD MONDAY OF JUNE LAST YEAR I REPORTED TO THE Clubhouse for my first board meeting and swearing in ceremony. It was a beautiful evening, the sun slanting in golden through the treetops and the pollen affliction having passed, so I decided to walk the mile from my house. Despite valiant efforts to be *present*, my mind was lingering three decades in the past, in an ersatz cheerful municipal chapel in the District of Columbia, holding Diane's hands in my hands. How would she feel if she could see me now, walking into my first board meeting at the Club, preparing to fill her seat? Maybe she would be proud, but more likely amused that I had somehow been roped into it.

Board meetings are held in the Lakefront Room, straight back from the gilded main entrance of the Clubhouse. It's the same room where wee Club members sit on Santa's lap in December and meet the Easter Bunny in the spring while their parents mingle over Old Fashioneds and the vodka drink *de jour*.

Entering I made eye contact immediately with Aristotle Poe, who had positioned his "Tesla" discreetly under the table and had a yellow legal pad placed before him. Aristote exuded Chairman of the board, though it was

Pam who held the title. Aristotle's stern face broke into a wide smile and he extended a pandemic approved fist bump as I rounded the table.

"Welcome to upper management," he said. "You have some big shoes to fill."

"I owe it all to you, Aristotle," I replied with a wink. "And those big shoes come with heels, so I'm slightly off balance." Aristotle emitted a gratifying laugh.

I recognized most of the other board members spread out around the table at a safe social distance from one another. One face belonged to Rick O'Shea, the neighborhood's omnipresent realtor. His shiteating grin beams from signs found on every street in the neighborhood and his "Ricochet Roundup" (ha-ha) goes into all seven hundred mailboxes twice a month. Rick is no taller than five foot eight in his lifters, has an abundant head of golden hair which I suspect is dyed, and his cheeks bear acne scars from an adolescence of championship masturbation. He was talking to a young woman I didn't recognize and leaning uncomfortably close into the conversation. She could have been the daughter of anyone in the room.

A few minutes later we had all taken our seats and Pam Loving, who had filled a plate from the buffet prepared for us, called the meeting to order. She smiled at me and I smiled back. We were co-conspirators, I suppose, though my real allies in this suburban election triumph were Aristotle and Dale, who was not on board and never would be.

Pam rapped the wood and brass gavel on the table with a bit too much vigor, causing ice to tinkle and mouths to shut. "Good evening everyone, our meeting is called to order," she said. "I would like to welcome Mr. Jack Callany to our board. Jack, we're all still in mourning over Diane's passing (solemn nods around the table) and we are deeply, *deeply* grateful that you are willing to serve out the remainder of her term." Polite clapping and head nodding. Ricochet Rick, his teeth as large as dinner plates, was grinning vehemently.

Pam turned to the young woman Rick had been pummeling with conversation. "Brenna, could you please stand at the front here and hold the

Bible and Club Charter for Mr. Callany." I remembered Brenna now as the assistant Pam had hired to help with the election. She was not sitting at the main board table, but in a Clubhouse chair against the wall by the buffet.

Brenna rose and walked toward Pam. She carried a large three ring binder from Staples atop which rested a faux leather bound Bible with gold brushed edges. Here we had two of man's great moral codas as only the Shallow South could render them.

"Jack, will you please stand, place your left hand on the Bible and raise your right hand," Pam asked.

I approached Brenna and prepared to take my oath. I realized for the first time that she was disarmingly attractive. Below the shoulder dark brown hair, large eyes also very dark brown, lightly tanned skin. She was wearing a pale blue summer dress that accentuated everything else. A matching blue facemask hung from her left ear. I made eye contact with her and gave a short, tight smile before placing my ringless left hand on the Bible and turning to face the board.

In this instant the door to the Lakefront Room swung open causing a sudden change in air pressure that makes papers flutter. Ari Nimrod strode into the room and stopped abruptly when we all turned to face him.

"Mr. Nimrod," Pam stated flatly, an unwelcoming acknowledgement.

Nimrod pulled his facemask off dramatically and replied sharply, "*Doctor* Nimrod." We were all silent. My left hand remained on the Bible but I slowly lowered my right hand.

"You can't swear him in. That election was a farce and you all know it." Nimrod's face was red and a vein in his forehead protruded, a poker tell that had cost him dearly over the years.

Pam stood. "*Doctor* Nimrod. We held a well publicized election. We followed the NCA guidelines. *To. The. Letter.* Mr. Callany won as a write-in candidate, fair and square."

"We'll see about that," Nimrod huffed, then cast his gaze around the room. "You people have been using this board to feather your own nests for years. You'd do anything to keep an honest person from getting elected." I thought about Rick O'Shea and what kind of impact his board seat has had on his real estate sales. Nimrod was an assaholic, but he might have a point. I remained silent.

"I demand a recount before Jack Callany or anyone else is sworn in!" Nimrod carried on. "And I have the right to demand it. It's in the Club Charter, Article three, paragraph three." Nimrod waved a piece of paper and I thought about the three ring binder under the Bible in Brenna's arms, which must be getting tired.

Aristotle spoke next. "Jack, please have a seat. Ari, you too." A pause. "Brenna, bring me the Club Charter."

Aristotle took his time. He flipped to the section that Nimrod referenced and read in silence. He turned to a few other pages, checking cross references. At last he looked up. "Madam Chair, *Doctor* Nimrod is correct. Any member of the HOA in good standing can demand a recount within thirty days following an election. It's only been two weeks."

Pam lowered her fork to her plate and looked at Aristotle, then me.

"Very well then," she said, sounding British. "We will have a recount. Mr. Callany, I'm sorry but we can't proceed with your swearing in tonight. You're welcome to stay as an observer and I hope you will."

"I'll be an observer, too," said Nimrod. He walked to the Clubhouse chair that Brenna had been sitting in and dragged it to the main table, to a spot next to Rick. Brenna, who was still standing by Aristotle and holding the Bible, now had no place to sit.

"One moment, please," I said, rising.

I stepped out of the Lakefront Room and found an empty Clubhouse chair near the Grand Hall. I returned and placed the chair near my own, then motioned to a grateful Brenna to sit.

Pam called the meeting back to order and it commenced with a quorum, though down by one director. The high drama for the evening had passed and the board took up the doleful business of managing a social club during a global pandemic: whether it would be safe to reopen the pool by July 4th (probably not), how to improve the restaurant's carry-out business, and how long to delay upgrades to the golf greens and tennis observation deck.

Nimrod demanded to know when and how the recount would happen, to which Aristotle glowered. Nimrod also rose during the community input section to read into the minutes the past month's community standards violations, which included the appearance of a new and fabulously non-compliant double decker mailbox at the Jones's.

I was silent throughout. I tried to refine my disdain for Nimrod, there now being so much new material to choose from, but I was distracted by the presence of Brenna beside me. I wanted to douse the ember of attraction, banish the memory of our eye contact. I was ashamed to feel anything like this. Diane was too recently gone and I was too old and past these kinds of urges.

The meeting adjourned, followed by elbow bumps and well wishes. Nimrod dashed for the door. I fist bumped Brenna as disinterestedly as I could and told her it was nice meeting her. (She was still holding the Bible.)

Moments later I was walking home, my mind ranging across past and present, petty politics and new possibilities. It was a lovely June night, the moon a waning crescent. It was my thirtieth wedding anniversary.

9.

HOLD 'EM HOWARD | 2013

IT TOOK TWO OR THREE YEARS OF THURSDAY NIGHTS AND more than a few testy showdowns on the river before I could comfortably call myself a regular at Men's Poker night. By regular I mean I had *my* chair at the table (between Dale and Aristotle), Enzo at the bar knew my drink (Woodford on ice with a healthy pour of diluting water), and the boys usually wouldn't start playing until I turned up, assuming I was not later than about fifteen minutes.

I have seen many newbies come and go, probably one a month, and it didn't take long for me to learn the rules. On someone's first night they would be welcomed coolly and then largely ignored. All newbies play tight, folding most hands early, so the rest of us would play loose, making large bets pre-flop from early table position. The idea was to shake the new guy's tree until his walnuts fell out. Of course, our own walnuts were at risk with this strategy, and we all got skunked from time to time, but usually the big winner was one of us and not the newbie. As odds men, we knew that over time our payouts would average out and we would get the side benefit of winnowing weak and foolish Hold 'em tourists.

I do not keep a spreadsheet of my weekly wins and losses as some do, including Dale, but I'm certain I'm in the black over my tenure at Men's Poker night. Some are perennial donors and don't realize it or even care because the bourbon and cigar smoke are reward enough.

At some point after I became a Thursday night made man - maybe seven or eight years ago - I showed up a few minutes early only to find my chair occupied. I made eye contact with Dale, who was sitting next to the imposter, and he gave a barely perceptible *I dunno* shrug. I took an open seat opposite my regular spot. The newbie was early forties, thin in an unhealthy way, with strands of pubic like black hair pressed to his oily scalp. His eyes were close set. He wore a luau style shirt in pale orange featuring green martini glasses and sailboats. I nodded gravely without saying a word, prompting him to reach a bony hand across the table and say, "Hi. Ari Nimrod."

We meet at last! This was early fall, maybe September, and I had been hearing about the Nimrods and their godforsaken bird for months. I didn't know if L'il Girl was still on prem by this point (she would eventually enter a bird rescue program), but I did know from Cyrus that she had learned her lines well.

Game play began and I couldn't catch a card. As expected, the boys were betting hard and I was obligated by code to make calls I knew were hopeless. Each time the action came around to me, one or two wiseacres would chant, "Call any, call any!" Dale, despite being my best friend, jumped into the fray with, "Give it to Jackie, he'll Callany thing."

Call I did and lose I did, hand after hand. At one point, I lost a Queen high flush to a full house laid down by a gloating Nimrod. After ninety minutes I had to re-buy, and what irked me (all of us) was that Nimrod had accumulated an enviable stack of chips and was growing more insufferable by the minute. This was not how newbie initiation was supposed to go down.

One of the regulars, Sheriff Steve, finally cracked the code of silence toward newbies and asked, "Ari, whaddaya do?"

"I'm a radiologist," Nimrod replied, looking at his cards instead of Steve, and not inviting further inquiry.

I glanced at Steve as if to say, *This one's prickly.*

Eventually the button came around to Nimrod. Halfway through his deal, while he was concentrating, I asked, "What station do you work at, Nimrod?"

He paused the deal and faced me, annoyed. "What do you mean, 'what station'?"

I widened my eyes in mock innocence. "I mean what *radio station* do you work at?"

Nimrod sneered and returned to the deal. "I'm a *radiologist*. That's a kind of *doctor*. I don't work at a radio station."

Suddenly Aristotle erupted, "*Mis-deal!*"

Nimrod had accidentally flipped a card face up. If one of the regulars had done the same thing, we would have just left the card face up and made it a burn card, but in Nimrod's case we all tossed our cards into the center of the table.

When Nimrod redealt I noticed his bald veiny head was flushed, a tell of embarrassment. I eyed his stacks of chips and decided it was time for me to tighten up and guard my stack.

At one point in the next half hour (and half glass of watery bourbon), everyone folded on fourth street except Nimrod and me. We were head to head for the first time. I had an open ended straight shot, Nine to Queen. The river came up King and Nimrod pushed.

All eyes turned to me. *Callany! Callany!*

I feigned nerves, but I knew I had the nuts. There was no flush or full house possibility, and it was impossible for Nimrod to have a straight to the Ace.

"Call," I said, pushing in everything I had.

Nimrod flipped his hold cards, raised his nose, and announced, "Kings and Queens."

I paused before my reveal and looked at Nimrod, then asked him, "Did you ever meet Howard Stern?"

Instantly his forehead flushed. He half stood with palms down on the table and yelled at me, "NO! I told you I don't work at a radio station. I'm a doctor. I'm a Brown graduate!"

"Sorry," I said meekly. "I misunderstood."

There were snide grins around the table. Nimrod settled back into his chair and began to reach for the chips.

"Hold up," said Steve (that's one of the reasons we call him The Sheriff.) "Whatcha got, Jack?"

I flipped my hold cards, Jack Ten, and said, "Straight to the King."

"Goddammit," says Nimrod, beet red, scalp to neck.

He counted my chips and then pushed an equal number of his own toward me. I had doubled up and Nimrod was on his back heels, chipwise.

Nimrod was flustered and we all knew it. I waved Enzo over and discreetly asked him to bring Nimrod another chardonnay, on me. A conciliatory gesture, but not really.

For the next hour Nimrod's forehead and oily pate stayed red. He started to play impulsively. At one point Dale asked him, "Now what is Brown? Is that a four year college?"

Nimrod looked up in disbelief. "It's an Ivy League university." A pause, then he said, "I think I've had enough."

Nimrod rose and Enzo cashed him out, about half his buy-in. We didn't skunk him, but we inflicted some damage. My guess is he would be back for more. There were unenthusiastic *good nights* and *good meeting ya's* as Nimrod made for the door. Just before it closed I blurted out *suck cock bitch,* rolling the last syllable into a coughing fit.

Nimrod turned and stared holes through me.

10.

YOUNG REPUBLICAN | 2021

SUNDAY LATE AFTERNOON, JIMMY CALLS FOR HIS WEEKLY check in. I'm in the kitchen foraging for dinner possibilities and Meagan is by the pool with country music blaring.

"Father," he says in greeting.

"Son," I reply.

"Holy Ghost," he says. It's one of our longstanding scripts, an artifact of the brief and unsuccessful church tour we made when the kids were younger.

"Dad, taxes really suck. You never told me how much it would be."

Jimmy had evidently gotten his first paycheck for his summer internship at the pharma lab. He landed a prime gig at one of the big firms researching neurological treatments. The way Jimmy told it, he wasn't the best bio-engineering student, and he wasn't the most brilliant coder, but he had the best combination of the two, and with that he scored a thirty thousand dollar summer internship and a fast track to employment if he wanted it.

When he was in middle school, you would never guess Jimmy would one day (soon) be the math brains behind a leading computer model of Alzheimers. He was a desultory student, unmoved by the onset of the school year, and an abject minimalist in the fields of homework, study and reading for fun.

Jimmy clearly had a brain. In elementary school he captained the Rubik's Cube club and could solve a three by three in around thirty seconds. He later tackled the four-by and five-by, and these and many other odd shapes fill a duffle bag that lays in the closet of his bedroom today. But as far as the classroom, teachers and test scores went, Jimmy was indifferent bordering on hostile.

Then in high school something changed. A loose wire in this brain must have made contact with an anode or cathode and fused. He became a young man on fire, especially for math. He would linger at the dinner table and sketch geometry proofs on unused napkins. It wasn't unusual to find scraps of proofs and equations anywhere in the house, on paper towels, on junk mail with enough white space to accommodate a conjecture, and on his bathroom mirror in Sharpie.

Midway through Jimmy's freshman year at the public high school, Diane and I requested a meeting with his guidance counselor, Ms. Moonpenny, in the hopes of elevating Jimmy's (and our own) profile on her overwrought agenda. She would be Jimmy's guidance counselor for all four years, and then Meagan's as well, having been assigned last names A through H. Ms. Moonpenny told us that Jimmy's math teacher, Dr. Sanders, was one of the most well liked teachers in the school. He was the only teacher on faculty with a PhD (in math) and he was known for devoting almost as much classroom time to life and personal stories as he did to math. Kids who hated math blossomed under him. Over more than two decades, he had trained a battalion of mathletes, dominated the state math contests, and sent girls and boys to top colleges. Proofs on napkins and toilet paper? Well, that might be a first.

"No one ever forgets their first paystub," I told Jimmy. I decide not to recite the old line about death and taxes, the former still being too close at hand. "That's how the Republican Party starts recruiting."

Jimmy laughs. He's easygoing and not as obsessed with politics as most college students. "Yeah Dad, but I need to build up some bank so I can start my own options trading!"

Sure sounds like a Republican, I think to myself.

We speak for fifteen minutes. He's getting some recognition for his internship work. They want him to work part time when classes start (that might be a challenge). We discuss me bringing Meagan to Boston College in a month. He can take off work Thursday and Friday of that week. Nothing serious on the girlfriend front (fine with me). Then, "Bye dad, have a great week."

I miss having Jimmy around this summer. The virus last year was a strange blessing because he came home the first week of March for Diane's funeral and didn't go back to Boston until the fall. Jimmy and Meagan and I clung to each other that spring, sometimes all three of us sleeping together in my bed after a Netflix binge. We were good to each other then, no yelling, no sarcasm, no dirty dishes piling up in the sink. The kids thought I was more fragile than I actually was, and they doted on me in a way that was new and sweet.

I got back into trading stock options last summer when the markets settled down and I was able to face the carnage in my portfolio. Jimmy got interested and I showed him my trade history going back six years, to the very beginning. I walked him through the positions I was holding when the virus hit and showed him what happened when the bottom dropped out of the market. It was liberating to be transparent with Jimmy and draw him into my drama.

"Dad, I want to get into this. I want to help you dig out of this hole," he said to me. It was May. We would have the next three months together.

"You're on, Son!" I told him.

"That's Holy Ghost to you," he replied.

11.

SKINNY DIPPING | 1990

DIANE WAS DISCHARGED FROM WALTER REED, CHILDLESS, ON a steamy afternoon in late June and we emerged together blinking into the sun. It was 1990 and we had been abruptly thrust into adulthood only to be yanked sharply back.

None of Diane's friends from Georgetown were in the vicinity of marriage and of the guys at my office in the Pentagon only one, Paul Papadopoulus, was engaged. "Well," Diane said to me one night, "it's like skinny dipping. Someone's got to go first." So we jumped in bare naked and rollicking.

Step one was to show everyone, ourselves included, that we were just as cool, free and spontaneous as we had been before we got hitched. Diane moved into my apartment in Kalorama, which I shared with a friend from my Davidson days, Matt O'Reilly. We would prowl the clubs of Georgetown, K Street and Arlington with our posse on Friday and Saturday nights, return to the apartment to thrust and sweat until we collapsed, and then sleep until the crack of noon. We were manic about fitness, too, notching one or two 10Ks every month, biking the C&O Canal trail until dark, and walking endless miles through the city and across the Potomac's many bridges. Heady stuff, all healthy and inexpensive, and proof to the world that marriage had not altered us one iota.

In retrospect, July was our honeymoon. Diane had not yet started work and I took two weeks of leave. When I finally returned to the Pentagon, Diane played house, watched soaps, and even made pasta from scratch for Matt and me a couple times. It was a domestic side of her I had not anticipated (and would later realize was just an experiment on her part).

August crept up on a Wednesday, the sun blazing orange before seven in the morning. Anyone who has spent a summer in DC knows why Congress and the landed gentry all recess that month. The city becomes a muggy swamp, hotter than Miami (somehow), and miserable for those who rely on public transportation.

Diane started at State that Wednesday with an elite cohort of "Fast Trackers" who would work rotations across several directorates during the first year before settling into the best matched cubicle. Of the dozen recent grads in her program, she already knew three, two others from Georgetown and a guy named Esteban who lived in her same dorm at UCLA when she was a frosh. Diane started in Global Affairs, in the Population, Refugees and Migration office (Esteban landed something in Arms Control).

My lease on the apartment with Matt was due to expire at the end of August, so Diane and I would soon be playing house for real. For two weeks we met after work in the late afternoon to explore neighborhoods, which meant walking everywhere, sweating until our hair was pasted to our fore-heads, and of course sampling the nearby sushi, burritos, coffee and beer that would (if selected) become our daily staples.

In the end we settled on Arlington, walking distance to the Courthouse Metro. We found a tidy three bedroom post-war colonial with a kitchen straight out of a 1952 ad in Life Magazine. The selling point, apart from monthly rent that could not be matched in any decent DC neighborhood, was an airy screen porch in the back, off the kitchen.

The week we moved in, Diane's mother visited from California and spent her days shopping for us at Bed Bath & Beyond and Crate & Barrel, loading us up with the accouterments of suburban living and entertaining. She had been divorced for ten years and was still playing the field, which contributed to her being mercifully nonjudgmental about the turn of events Diane and I had been through over the past few months.

My parents came two weeks later to size us up and generally scold me. They had met Diane a few times while she was still in school, but had never dwelled longer than a bruncheon. My mother had expected her first daughter-in-law to be more girly, a bake-cookies-together type. My father was taken aback by Diane's sharp tongue and opinionated zingers during dinner and the evening news.

Whenever one of my father's provocations led to an argument, Diane would counterattack with a dossier of evidence and logic presented at gradually increasing volume until all us were awed into silence. It wasn't unusual for her to tear off the scab of the day before's topic and salt it further during an otherwise pleasant lunch or walk. It was a side of her I was certainly aware of - I had watched her in many debate rounds at Georgetown - but it was jarring here at home, and especially so when my father was pummeled into silence.

"You don't have to humiliate people when you argue with them," I told her one night in the kitchen after my parents had retired for the evening.

"Well I was *right*," Diane said to me. "And I have a right to express myself."

On the last day of my parents' visit I went for a walk with my father. "You've got your hands full, son," he said to me..

"I know," I replied. "But it's different when it's just the two of us. We're really great together."

Dad looked at me but said nothing.

"Dad, Diane barely knew her father. I think maybe she needs to impress you."

"Or prove to the world that she never needed a father," he said.

It was a fissure that would widen.

12.

RECOUNT | 2020

THREE DAYS AFTER NIMROD STORMED THE CLUB AND USED administrative jiu jitsu to block my swearing in ceremony, I found myself back at the Clubhouse for the recount. It was a Thursday afternoon and Pam sequestered us not in the comfortable Lakefront Room, but in the copier room behind the Club's accounting cubicles. She had scrupulously followed NCA guidelines, inviting both Nimrod and me, as well as the board Secretary, Siobhan Sorcer. Brenna Wilder stood holding what appeared to be a shoebox. We were the Recount Five.

Siobhan is a tall strappy woman who had played D1 field hockey at Indiana University and (years later) weekly tennis matches with Diane. Her husband Doug is a mortgage lender and has probably financed twenty percent of all the homes in our community. He was universally called The Sorcerer for his ability to work magic in the face of unhelpful appraisals, blemished credit, and propped up income. He and Rick O'Shea were like peas and carrots, and his grinning face could be found in every issue of the Ricochet Roundup. Rick no doubt played a role in landing Siobhan on the board. Siobhan, however, is no sorceress, just a reliable and highly literal Euchre playing midwesterner. She had been a casserole bearer two months earlier, a guileless and tasty macaroni and cheese with bacon bits that made a brief appearance in one of Meagan's TikTok videos.

Brenna's shoebox I presumed held the ballots to be recounted. Her dark brown hair was combed back and down past her shoulders, and was damp, probably from a shower in the lady's locker room downstairs. She wore a loose fitting dark purple blouse, bell bottomed twill khakis, and sandals that revealed toenails of the same purple hue. I averted my eyes before the creepy-middle-aged-guy play clock ran out, turning instead to Pam who looked like a slightly overstuffed sofa in a rust colored pantsuit.

"Okay everybody," she said. "Thank you for coming this afternoon. Please have a seat."

We collected ourselves around a folding formica table, maybe the exact Costco model in my former master bedroom from which I now conduct options trading. Pam sat at the head and Brenna opposite her. I sat on one side, opposite Siobhan and Nimrod, who had been austerely silent.

"I'll be recording the meeting," Nimrod said, placing his iPhone on the center of the table.

"There's no need for that, Mr. Nimrod," said Siobhan. "I'm the board secretary and I'll take notes."

Nimrod sniffed and faced Pam. "It's my prerogative to record this meeting and that's what I intend to do."

"Is that allowed?" Pam asked Siobhan.

"I don't know," Siobhan replied. "It's never come up before."

Silence hung in the air for a moment, then Siobhan said, "I could check the By-Laws or the NCA binder." She moved to stand.

"It's fine," Pam said finally. "Everything's on the up and up here. Jack, any objections?"

"None at all," I replied, staring at Nimrod with the faintest hint of amusement on my face.

"Very well then," Pam said. "I call this special meeting to order. We are here to conduct a recount of the ballots of our board election of June the second."

Pam then explained the recount process. Siobhan would remove one completed ballot from the shoebox, examine it for irregularities, and then read aloud the names receiving votes. There could be one, two, three or four names, no more, and one of the names could be written in instead of next to a checkbox. After Siobhan had read the names from one card, she would pass it to Pam for verification, who would then pass it to Nimrod for inspection, and then to me. After that, rinse and repeat.

"Is everything clear? Any objections?" Pam asked. We all nodded assent and Brenna rose from the table and stood next to the marker board, where she would keep a running tally.

The first ballot took almost a minute to move its way through the inspection gauntlet. I grimaced. At this rate we'd be here for three hours.

The saving grace was watching Brenna. She had a sweet face and seemed oddly cheerful under the circumstances, as if this were all a silly game (she would have been right). She faced the marker board and drew tick marks while Siobhan read, then twisted her lithe body to face Pam, Nimrod and me while we triple checked Siobhan. Twisting, turning, twisting again.

Thirty minutes in, Nimrod was leading me fifty votes twenty-two. He began leaning forward. *I'll show you, you lying fools,* his face screamed.

Brenna became less cheerful as the recount progressed. Sometimes when Nimrod's name was read I saw her eyes widen slightly.

The next thirty minutes were decidedly better for Jack Callany. I pulled ahead ninety-five to eighty and there were only a few cards left. Nimrod settled back into his seat and folded his arms, his scalp reddening.

After the last ballot was passed around, we had our answer. All three incumbents had been re-elected, as expected, and I was a lock for the fourth seat with one-hundred two votes against Nimrod's eighty-eight.

Brenna sat down cheerfully, a well deserved rest after more than an hour of playing Twister at the marker board. Nimrod stopped recording and slid his cell phone into his pocket.

Pam wrapped us up with a reading of the final vote totals into the minutes. "That concludes the ballot recount. This meeting is adjourned."

Nimrod was up first without a word or nod to any of us.

"Coming to poker tonight?" I asked the back of his head.

He turned to look at me and sniffed. "I doubt it."

"I could use the money, Nimrod." I cracked.

13.

DEEP POCKETS, SHORT ARMS | 2021

LAST SUMMER WAS ONE OF THE STRANGEST OF MY LIFE. DIANE had been gone three months and a listless melancholy seeped into every quiet moment. It didn't help having a year of lockdown and social distancing begin the week after we buried her.

Salvation took the form of Meagan and Jimmy. We were quarantined together, cooking and eating together, and lounging around the house in a way we hadn't done since before Jimmy was in middle school.

Meagan's national dance competition and Duke Tip summer camp had been canceled. She was allowed to see a few friends, but we all took the distancing and contact restrictions seriously. It wasn't easy, especially for a rising high school senior socialite. That's when Meagan began to pour herself into TikTok, doubling her number of followers month after month and creating a lucrative dancing junk food brand.

And Jimmy was serious about wanting to learn options and help me recover my springtime losses. He had read my two McMillan classics on the topic and watched dozens of YouTube videos at one and half times speed.

"Most of this stuff is about how to hedge actual stock positions," he told me. "But you're not hedging, you're selling insurance to the guy who is."

I nodded; this I understood.

Then he went on, "We're gonna win by studying the order volumes. We care about how many bids and how many asks there are for any given contract."

"Okay," I said. This was new.

By the time the ballot recount was settled, Jimmy had written a computer program that pulled down the entire bid ask order book for any stock we were tracking, and plotted the change in orders over time on a graph in our browser. "Look," he showed me one morning, "there are more than a thousand open contracts on Goldman Sachs for January 2021, fifty opened today alone. Any trader can see this." Then he pointed to his browser. "But look here. There is twenty-five percent more volume for bids than for asks. More people are trying to buy than to sell, Dad. The price on the January 2021 contract is headed up."

I digested this information. "So," I said carefully, "let's sell some insurance to the people who are still worried about the price falling."

"Right!" he said animatedly, "Those insurance policies will most likely never have to pay out."

Jimmy stood behind my chair and leaned toward the screen, his face next to mine. Together we sold ten contracts to open a new position. Less than four hours later we closed the position, up $6,200.

"Son, you're hired." I told him.

That night we made dinner together. Meagan made her now famous sourdough bread with a scored "M" on its crusty top. Jimmy made freakishly long zoodles from three large zucchinis and a plastic contraption we kept in the pantry. I grilled sausages, sliced them, and tossed them into the zoodles with olive oil and parmesan cheese. It was a fine summer feast for the three of us. Diane would have been proud.

"Can we go on the boat after dinner?" Meagan asked. It's something we did one or two nights each week. We had a twenty year old bowrider that we bought used the year we moved to Lake Cooke. I wanted something not too fancy to learn on. We kept it clean and serviced, but the last few times we had gone out there were problems and we had been lucky to limp home without a tow. Battery, spark plugs, and impeller were all starting to go.

"I'd like to but I'm a little worried she's not seaworthy," I replied.

"We don't have to go far," Meagan replied.

"We'll try. Don't get your hopes up, we may not be out long."

Then Jimmy spoke up. "You oughta get a new boat, Dad. You know, new beginnings."

"Do you have a hundred thousand dollars laying around?" I asked him.

"I might in another month," Jimmy said. "If we can keep having days like today."

"You've got enough money anyway, Dad." Meagan piped in. "Treat yourself."

The truth was I did have enough money, but I've been frugal my whole life. Dale called me the Scotsman - *deep, deep pockets and short little arms.* I spent half a day with Hookes Miller when Diane's life insurance paid out. We had taken out a one million dollar policy on her years before when the kids were young and the premium was very low. Between that, my half of my parents' estate, and the payout from the sale of the fiber company I worked at for more than fifteen years, there was enough salted away for me to live off the returns that Hookes produced.

I knew I could warm to the idea of a new boat. I had been on Rick O'Shea's Cobalt a few weeks ago for a lunch outing and had a glimpse of what I was missing. Dual props, quiet engine, robust sound system, color GPS, all the other do-dads.

"You guys might have an idea there," I said. "Jimmy, let's split the difference. If you can rake in fifty-K in options for me, I'll pull another fifty out of the vault."

"Hey, wait a second," said Meagan. "I want a piece of the action, too. I'll throw in all the sponsorship money I earn this month. That could be ten thousand, maybe twice that much."

"Dudes, we got us a summer project," I said.

"Daddio," Meagan screamed with joy and thrust her hands into the air.

* * *

Monday morning dawns, the last week of July. I swim one lap in the pool, but rather than climb out, I lean back on the side with my elbows on the coping. I look out across the pool to Lake Cooke. For a moment my mind is empty. I am perfectly in the present, devoid of memory or plans. I fixate on the glints of light sparkling on the lake as insects touch its mirror surface.

Slowly my consciousness rises.

I will fast today, as I do most Mondays and Thursdays, and the thought pleases me. The day has started calm and quiet, and fasting will prolong the feeling, slowing me, making me more deliberate throughout the day. Sometimes in the evening I feel pangs of hunger, but I satisfy them with a tall glass of cool (but not icy) water. More often there are no pangs at all. I will fall asleep early tonight and rise early tomorrow feeling light and having almost no appetite.

I decide I will drive to the state park on the other side of Lake Cooke and run the trails for four or five miles. Early exertion on a fasting day perfects its effect on my body. After running, even on non-fasting days, I am never hungry, only thirsty. My body craves the water and I satisfy it generously.

A bass boat suddenly tears into our cove sending waves splashing against the line of docks and the shoreline. It passes out of view, but has ended my reverie.

I towel off and go inside, where I start a cup of Peet's Major Dickason's Blend in the Keurig before going to my room to dress for the trail run. I'm back a minute later in lightweight shorts and a sweat wicking tee shirt, and knobby trail running shoes. The Keurig hisses and sighs. The coffee is black, still bubbly on top, and robust. Diane used to say I needed some major dick every morning.

I leave a note for Meagan in case she wakes up before I'm back. Sometimes she'll run with me, but I'm wise enough not to wake her. I put the lid on my coffee mug, fill a water bottle from the filtered water in the fridge, and head to the garage. There are three cars here. Diane's minivan, which will be impressed into service in one month when I drive Meagan to Boston College, my Tesla Model 3 which occupies the middle bay where the charger is, and Meagan's lime green Jeep Wrangler which she bought with cold hard cash from her TikTok sponsors.

I open the door to my Tesla to set my coffee mug and water in the cup holders while I unplug it and coil the charging cable. I really do love this vehicle even though I'm not your typical car guy. I love it the way you love a new cell phone: a shiny gadget that anticipates your every need and exists only to ensure your convenience and comfort at every moment. (Thinking of it this way, it's far better than a new cell phone.)

I drive against the morning traffic, working stiffs who stream into the city on the hated toll road. In fifteen minutes I exit and find myself no longer in suburbia but in honest to God rural North Carolina. There's a gas station and Bojangles near the interstate exit, then only a two lane road that winds past farm land, dense acres of Carolina pine, a mobile home park, and a ranch style home with a hand painted sign advertising "Psychic Advisor and Pet Grooming." In ten minutes the road ends at the entrance to the state park at the northern end of the lake.

I run here in every season, always early in the day. Fall is my favorite, the woods a riot of orange, yellow and red. On a cool October morning the lake is sapphire blue, the woods still and silent, and I feel weightless as I run along the shoreline. In the dead of winter when the trees are bare and the lake a rough hewn pewter, I can see through the terrain a hundred yards ahead. Once in January, on my birthday, I took a sunrise run here and a red fox ran alongside me for a magical minute.

I park in a gravel lot near the trailhead with only two other cars and begin my ritual stretch. The park is full of life today. In the dark hours of the morning spiders have spun webs across the trail which will break across my sweaty forehead. Black snakes and maybe a few rattlers will seek sunny patches along the trail and listen for my footfalls. Beneath and above and around it all will be a chorus of cicadas celebrating their seventeen year release this summer, their low rhythmic hum pulsing night and day.

I start slowly and may remain slow for the entire five miles, I never know. I do not start the chrono on my watch as I once did. I'm past pushing myself. I will simply run at a pace that feels good. Sometimes I finish at a seven minute pace (rarely), sometimes ten (increasingly). This is a prerogative of a man in his fifties who is happy he can still run at all.

The worst way to occupy one's mind while running is to count footsteps. Diane did this on the infrequent occasions that she ran, making it impossible to carry on any sort of chatter with her. I admit that I have been a counter myself at times. It shackles the mind from wandering thoughts and blinds the eyes to the surroundings, which on these trails are magnificent. Counting turns the forest into a treadmill. The other wrong way to run is with earbuds and music. This is more subtly wrong, since the right music will match tempo and pace and propel the runner along. But just like counting, music kidnaps the mind away from nature. I just fling myself into spider webs and sunbathing snakes and cicadas and let nature have her way with me.

Five minutes in I have settled into a tempo and feel light on my feet. I begin to envision Meagan and me arriving at Boston College in a month. I see us consulting a campus map to find her dorm and the parking lot closest to it, which will not be close at all. I see Meagan meeting her Indian roommate Aditi for the first time in person (they have already spoken on Facetime) and

I stand with her parents and try to be cheerful and supportive and protective at the same time. I see myself making dozens of trips from the minivan to the dorm room with Meagan's suitcases and boxes, passing and repassing other red faced fathers doing the same, while Meagan stays in her room and organizes her shoes, sweaters, sheets, towels, chargers, hair curlers, and hair straighteners, all the while chatting up Aditi.

Then I think Jimmy should be helping me move her in. (Note to self: mention this to him next Sunday.)

The whole family moved Jimmy into his dorm two years ago. He had about half the possessions I suspect Meagan will have, and he and I carried them from the minivan to his dorm room while Diane and Meagan set up shop. Jimmy did not care at all which drawer his underwear went in or where his shaving supplies were stashed or where Diane would place the five by seven framed photo of our family. He was primarily interested in how strong the Wifi was (very) and where the outlets were (not enough).

I reach my least favorite stretch of trail, a quarter mile climb across large cumbersome gravel between two power lines. The trees have been scraped from the earth and the sun is directly in my eyes. I admit to counting steps on this stretch, something like three hundred should get me through. Then a sharp turn and I'm back on an needly pine trail again where it is twenty degrees cooler.

My own move-in day at Davidson in '84 couldn't have been more different. I had to be on campus ten days before the other freshmen for Air Force ROTC boot camp. My parents and Brian took me to the bus station in Greensboro where we waited together on plastic chairs under humming fluorescent lights. We were all quiet, no one sure what to say that hadn't already been said about my imminent departure and the change it would bring to the architecture of our little family. When it was time to board, Dad and Brian each carried one suitcase to the luggage loading area and I carried the other two myself. We all hugged, Mom cried, Brian stomped on my foot harder than I think he meant to, so I shoved him. That was it. A few minutes later I was rolling west under a cloud of diesel.

Ninety minutes later the bus came to a stop on Main Street in Davidson, across from the entrance to the college. It was a searing August afternoon and strangely quiet. A few cars idled at the single light in town where I needed to cross. The headache of having four suitcases suddenly dawned on me. I had to transport them and myself to the center of campus, to Chambers Hall for check in, and I could only carry two at a time. After giving it some thought, I left two bags near the bus stop and carried the other two across the street. I dropped them on the sidewalk, then crossed back over to the bus stop for the other two. In this way I inch-wormed myself onto the grassy quad and across campus.

When I reached Chambers for the first time, a fierce black man in an Air Force uniform stood at the top of a dozen granite steps. He stood impassively as I carried my suitcases up the steps and set them down by the entrance. I glanced back down the steps and across the quad to make sure I could still see my other two suitcases.

"Air Force rot-C?" He asked me.

"Yes, sir." I replied, lacking in all confidence.

"Room one ten." He said. "And don't call me, sir. I work for a living."

"Yessir," I said. "I mean no, sir."

Damn. I had already screwed up. My father had warned me not to stand out. If you do, he said, they'll make an example of you.

"I'm sorry," was all I could finally muster.

I began to walk down the steps to retrieve my other two suitcases.

"Where the hell are you going, son?" the soldier asked me.

I pointed into the quad. "I have to get the rest of my stuff," I said.

He looked at me with scorn and said in a commanding voice that would be seared into my consciousness over the next ten days, "Doubletime!"

Scared, I bounded down the steps and sprinted to my luggage. I grabbed a bag in each hand and ran back to Chambers as fast as I could, the bags heavy and swaying. I attempted my second ascent of Chambers two steps at a time and when I finally reached the soldier I had sweat streaming down my face.

"What's your name, Cadet?" He barked.

"Jack, sir."

Oh no, sir again. "I mean … Jack." I had apparently forgotten my own name in addition to how to speak. "Jack Callany."

"I'm gonna remember you, Cadet Callany," he said with a small nod.

Now I turn onto a side trail for the final mile of my run. It's shaded but uphill, rutted and rocky. As I ascend I feel my pace slow, but when I top the small rise I have a wide downward sloping path back to the trailhead. I open up into a long stride, catching two and three footfalls between breaths.

I finish the run feeling vigorous and thirsty. It's now almost 10 am. An excellent way to start a fasting day.

14.

GLONOUS HISTORY AND CULTUAL | **1990**

I CAN ONLY DESCRIBE THE FALL OF 1990 AS *GLONOUS.*

Diane and I found a shabby Chinese restaurant we could walk to from our Arlington house. It was reliably empty most nights thanks to a booming delivery business, and it had a license to sell wine, which we ordered by the carafe. The floor and tables were vaguely sticky, as I suspect were the walls and ceiling, from years of oils vaporizing off woks in the kitchen. We ordered by number and gesture to a longsuffering Chinese woman, undoubtedly the owner and wife of the cook.

Each table at the restaurant had a jar of chopsticks packaged in red paper. One night Diane removed one, but before tearing off the paper she casually read the writing on it and started laughing. "Oh my God," she said, "have you actually ever read the wrapper?"

I arched an eyebrow.

"Okay," she went on, "listen to this." *Welcome to Chinese Restaurant please try your Nice Chinese Food With Chopsticks the traditional and typical of Chinese glonous history and cultual.*

We read it over and over, mirthfully counting the mistakes and debating the capitalization.

"I work at the Department of State because I'm fascinated by *cultual* differences," Diane told me gravely. Then she tossed me a softball, "How's your eggroll?"

"*Glonous*," I replied with a smile.

We slipped into suburban life with surprising ease. We were up by six on weekdays and on the Orange Line together by seven. We would almost always stand, holding onto a seat back or the overhead grab straps. At the first stop, Rosslyn, I would kiss Diane and sometimes cop a feel before transferring to the Blue Line, which delivered me to the Pentagon. She stayed on the Orange Line one more stop to her office. On the way home, usually around six, Diane would get off at Rosslyn and wait for me on the platform so we could ride the final leg together and walk home.

We both put in long days and worked with a sense of fervor that irritated our older and more jaded co-workers. We were still velocitized from demanding college years, and I think we also had a strong desire to prove we were as precocious in adulthood as we had been in childhood.

At State, Diane poured over population data for East Africa, analyzing and cross-checking birth rates, death rates, migration patterns, ethnic centers and disease. In her rotation as a Fast Tracker, she was invited to meetings with senior State Department officials, embassy staff, and occasionally (I think) spooks from unnamed agencies. There was talk of a holiday gala that was the best in DC.

I had already been at the Pentagon in my Air Force job for more than two years. My office was responsible for spec'ing out the avionics for aircraft that wouldn't even be built for another five years, at which point I planned to not be in the Air Force. I liked my job and especially the people I worked with, which included a posse of second and first lieutenants with hot-off-the-presses math and engineering degrees. But progress towards our mission was glacial and the pay was almost half what most of my Davidson buddies in civilian attire were earning.

The holiday party at my office could hardly be called a gala. We worked in a restricted access area and the full bird Colonel who supervised us was a Mormon. My first Christmas there the Colonel took leave on a Friday, leaving Major Tillwell (who would never advance beyond Major) in charge of the shop. At ten that morning he showed us how to make frozen daiquiris in the paper shredder.

Our house gradually became the focal point of our free time. It was a rental, but we pretended it was our own and the landlord was agreeable to almost every improvement we suggested. The kitchen was avocado green and we were approved to repaint it a pale yellow, which immediately pulled it forward a decade or two. We also painted the bedroom a sleepy gray-blue shade and added dark curtains. I labored in the yard throughout the fall, first killing the weedy lawn with Roundup, then replanting it with unadulterated fescue. Each day of labor ended with a few cold beers on our screen porch, to which Diane had added hanging ferns and strings of tiny lights.

We started going out less partly to save money but mainly to enjoy our little nest together. Our meals were simple but we ate regally in the dining room by candlelight, cloth napkins in our laps.

On weekends we hosted friends. One night I suggested poker, a hallmark of my college days, and Diane, who had never played, agreed to give it a try. I invited Matt, a distinguished alumnus of my Davidson poker group and my pre-Diane roommate, and Paul Papadopoulus from the office (we called him Papa) and his fiancee. Diane invited Esteban, her erstwhile UCLA dorm mate and his girlfriend, who was apt to be someone different each time you asked him.

I've always prided myself in being a good poker teacher, and because only Matt and I had played before, we spent the first hour teaching the others the order of hands, how to bet, and a few basic games like five card draw and seven card stud. I insisted that we play with real money, knowing that otherwise the betting would be wild and unserious. The buy in was ten bucks each, just enough to keep everyone on their toes.

Some poker games never come to life, pots never grow and people don't talk. Our game that first night was not one of these. Diane sat next to Papa's fiancé, Athena, and they immediately hit it off. When Athena dealt she named three or four wild cards, a rookie move that would never fly at my fraternity but that created wild chaos and betting in our dining room. Diane would do the same, but would also name her games based on the wild cards. Jacks became *Pimps* and Queens became *Ho's*, so we had *Ho's-Up Pimps-Down*, *Speed Limit (fives wild)*, and *Bitches and Ho's* (Bitches are hearts and diamonds, Ho's are clubs and spades).

It was a raucous night and well lubricated with Jose Cuervo and Jagermeister. Esteban and Athena were the big winners, taking home most of the sixty dollar kitty. I lost early and then kept losing, and Matt also had a poor showing. I was happy for the newcomers to win: it would keep them coming back.

We locked the front door behind the last couple and stumbled into the kitchen for tall glasses of water before bed.

"Want to set up a regular game?" I asked Diane.

"Yes," she said, "that was *glonous*."

"And *cultual*," I replied.

15.

BREAD | 2020

LAST MARCH CAME IN LIKE A LION, AND RATHER THAN GOING out like a lamb contorted itself into a mythical beast of dread and destruction. The weekend before St Paddy's Day, we were all gathered under the same roof. Jimmy has been told not to return to campus for the rest of the semester, Meagan's high school was closed for an indefinite stretch and her teachers were attempting to conduct classes online, Diane was compacted into fine bone ash in an engraved mahogany box on our dining room table, and I was in a fog, sleeping odd hours in the guest room and taking long walks at all hours of the day.

As we were beginning to cope with the cruel sudden death of mother and wife, the rest of the world gawked, ignorant and utterly unprepared, at the onslaught of a bat virus born in Wuhan. A few friends sat Gaelic shiva with us and delivered cards and casseroles, but for the most part our grief, along with all other headlines including a national election, was eclipsed entirely by the story of a microscopic virus.

A week later we were told to *social distance* (now a verb) at precisely the moment we needed social closeness. Then came *stay at home*, *work from home*, and *essential business*. We were isolated, but we were together, and while I never would have guessed it, this was the ideal way to mourn. We did not have pastors or neighbors or beefy ladies from the tennis squad parading into our house each saying "I'm sorry for your loss." We did not have to hug each one and say *thank you* or *we'll be okay* or *Diane loved you so much.* Instead we draped ourselves across one another on the sectional sofa and watched Bill Murray films, or listened to whatever playlist Meagan put on, or just talked and cried at a completely unhurried tempo.

Jimmy or Meagan, but not both together, would go to the grocery store once each week for the mundane - eggs, veggies and fruits, craft beer, and Moose Tracks ice cream - as well as the precious - toilet paper and hand sanitizer. Fortunately Diane was a Costco maven and had stocked us well with TP and Lysol wipes - an unintended but welcome final gesture. When the shopper returned, he or she would wash their hands obsessively with hot water and dish detergent for the required 20 seconds, then wipe down their debit card and cell phone.

One afternoon Cyrus Bolton pulled into our driveway on his golf cart and began honking its unconvincing horn. He had a bandana tied over his nose and mouth and sipped Bud Light through a straw that disappeared under the bottom of the bandana. I opened the front door and waved from a safe social distance. "It's nice to see another human being, Cyrus!"

"Shore is," he replied. Then, "Jack, I got a personal problem I'm hoping maybe you can help me with."

"Is it your prostate?" I asked with a grin. "You need to go see Doctor Longfinger for that."

"You're in the right ballpark," he replied. "But it ain't my prostate. Hadn't had one for years." He paused and grinned. "Jack, I'm outta the very important papers, if you follow my drift. Thought I'd check and see if you guys got any."

"For you, Cyrus," I replied, "I not only have the very important papers, I'll also send one of my kids home with you to apply it."

"Well, make it your daughter then."

"Stand by, Cyrus," I said. I went to the hall closet upstairs and found an unopened twelve pack of Charmin. I returned to the front door, walked down the steps to Cyrus's chariot and tossed the very important papers onto his rear facing back seat.

"Much appreciated," said Cyrus. "I got a little something for you, too."

He produced a mason jar half filled with a yellow doughy liquid. "This here's starter for sourdough bread. You know how to make yore own bread?"

I raised an eyebrow. "Wow Cyrus, I didn't know you baked."

"Shore I do. Been doin it for years. I'd show ya how myself, but you'd probably infect me with bat shit."

I took the Mason jar from him and peered through the glass. It was viscous and bubbly on the surface. "We'll find a recipe, Cyrus. That's what God made the Internet for."

Cyrus flipped his golf cart into drive and continued around our circular drive. With one hand on the steering wheel and the other holding his beer, he nodded his goodbye.

"Thank you, Old Timer," I shouted, then went to the kitchen and washed my hands and the Mason jar vigorously.

As news of infections, deaths and nursing home genocide mounted and the stock market collapsed violently, Meagan and I applied ourselves to the art of sourdough bread. It was a three day process to make two loaves. Our first attempt produced an inedible, tooth cracking loaf which we attributed to the kitchen not being warm enough. We watched the amateur pros on YouTube and made adjustments, pulling and folding long gluteny yellow loops of dough, and by dinnertime Sunday we had two steaming round loaves ready to be torn apart and slathered in butter.

The next day, a fasting Monday (no bread for me), the Dow collapsed below 19,000 and formed what we would later see as the market bottom. But on that day, after the market had given up 11,000 points from its all time high only five weeks earlier, we could only assume the beatings would continue.

I made the mistake of checking my options trading account and saw that I was more than a quarter million dollars underwater on positions I had only hoped to make a quick ten or twenty thousand on.

Hookes called to check on me that afternoon. "How ya doin, Jack?"

"Hookes," I told him, "I was just trying to pick up a few pennies in front of the steamroller. I had no idea it was going so fast."

"No margin call, Jack. That's the good news. This sell-off is not like anything any of us have ever seen." We chatted for a while but I did not ask him for a detailed report on the carnage. I knew I had also lost a lot in the accounts that Hookes managed. We'd get to that another day.

I de-tuned the news and swore off looking at the options account for the rest of the week. Since no one had ever experienced anything like this before, either in the markets or in the world at large, I didn't see much sense in listening to experts. Instead, Meagan and I went parabolic on bread baking. Since each batch took three days from start to finish, we decided to start a new batch every morning. Once our pipeline was operating at capacity, we were cranking out two or four loaves each day. Meagan started experimenting with rosemary (excellent), garlic (meh) and cheddar cheese (nope). Jimmy joined on occasion for some kneading and rolling, and he was always on hand when the loaves came out of the oven.

We endured the final week of March, self isolating in a comfortable home, distancing ourselves from the news and the stock market, and escaping into a few Jimmy Stewart classics. Meagan found a way to feature our bread making in her TikToks, not just tearing off enormous bites in the final frame, but actually dancing while making bread. During March and April, she almost doubled her follower count and her sponsorship dollars.

The sudden shock of death had been absorbed and dampened, and we were left with a dull aching emptiness. The kids talked about Diane every day and began to allow themselves the gradual shift from reverence to humor to sarcasm ("I hated it when Mom …"). The mojo was improving.

The last day of the month was clear and warmer, in the low sixties, so Meagan and I donned hoodies and delivered fresh loaves to Cyrus and Dale. Cyrus waved wildly and gave us a grateful snaggle toothed smile from the front door of his mobile home. At Dale's, Meagan and I formed a football formation, she hiked a loaf to me and I lobbed it high to Dale. "Touchdown!" he muffled through his mask.

The next morning I rose to the smell of fresh bread baking downstairs. Usually we baked in the afternoon so I was puzzled but content. When I came down for coffee, Jimmy and Meagan were both standing by the oven.

"How about a warm slice for breakfast?" asked Jimmy.

"Sure," I said. "You made your own loaf?"

"Yep," He replied. "Got up real early today."

Jimmy opened the oven and withdrew a perfect round loaf, but instead of being golden brown it was a dark blotchy gray.

"That doesn't look so good," I told him.

"Whadja put in it?" asked Meagan.

"Oh," Jimmy replied nonchalantly. "I used the flour in that wooden box in the dining room."

The color drained from my face. "Guys," I said weakly. "That's not flour …."

A pause.

"April Fools!" they both shouted at me. "Jimmy added food coloring to the dough."

I didn't know whether to laugh or cry. But then, I laughed, and the kids laughed, and I kept laughing so hard there were tears running down my face.

16.

SWIPE LEFT | 2021

AFTER THE TRAIL RUN I GRAB THE WATER BOTTLE FROM MY Tesla and walk around the gravel lot to cool down. I have forgotten to bring a hand towel so I pull my shirt off and wipe my forehead and neck. Once I've cooled down, I put the shirt back on and sit down in the front seat with the door open. The shirt is damp but I'd rather deal with that than feel my bare back on the Tesla's pleather.

I check the market from my phone. The Fed will probably raise interest rates by a quarter point tomorrow, but that is now priced in and option prices are fairly stable. I probably won't open or close anything today.

I look at myself in the rearview mirror. My face is still flushed from the run, sweat glistens on my forehead, my hair is damp but pointed in the right direction. I look my age and I think I look okay, and I suddenly wonder how I would fare on Bumble. Dale's been at it for a while and I think he gets matches every week. He just doesn't get past the swipe-right stage.

I don't know what I want. Sex would be great, at least in theory, as an act, but then come the expectations and emotions and explanations. I've already lost my widower virginity and that came in equal parts of pleasure and angst. On the other hand (of a long arm) is remarrying, which I don't seek and cannot begin to visualize. In the middle there is dating, and that's intimidating, worrisome and, goddammit, a little bit enticing.

Without giving it much thought, I download Bumble and click *Open*. In doing so I've just crossed a line that's been looming in my mind for a long time. When I've thought about taking this step over the past few months, I've gotten wrapped around my own thoughts, trapped in scenarios I didn't like, and every time I've stopped short of the download. But today I just breezed across the line. Funny how that is sometimes.

I'm prompted to link my Facebook account and start writing my profile description. I can't do it right now, right here. I rest my phone inside the other cup holder and take another long drink of water. I commit to finishing my profile before the day is over.

Returning home, the house is quiet. Meagan is probably still asleep or at best laying in her bed and scrolling through her phone. I decide to take an actual shower, not just a pool dip, and apply body wash, either *Mahogany* or *Arctic Blast*. Before I step into the shower, I study myself in the mirror and think of adjectives, but then stop. Whatever picture I upload to Bumble will speak for itself. I should be looking at the interior mirror and describing what I see there. Not so easy. That is a man rebuilding himself and searching for prime factors.

I shower and shave, then dress in under fifteen seconds in my summer uniform - khaki shorts, craft beer tee shirt, and Birkenstocks. I smell like Aqua Velva Musk.

In the kitchen I see Meagan. "Morning sweetheart," I say in a higher timber than I would use for anyone else.

"Morning Daddy," she replies. "Watcha doin today?"

"Well, I drove to the state park and ran ten miles on muddy trails before you even woke up."

"Ten miles? Wow," she says.

"Okay, five," I say, then pause. "Okay, fine, four miles. And the trails were dry."

She's preparing a smoothie and not really paying attention.

"How would you describe me?" I ask her.

"You mean to my friends?" she asks. "I don't know."

"No," I say. "To another adult."

"I wouldn't," Meagan says tersely. "Why would I do that?"

I'm not getting anywhere and I don't want to enlist Miss TikTok in helping craft my Bumble profile. I seriously doubt I'll tell either kid I'm even considering it.

"Nevermind." I say, turning with my coffee.

"Hold on, Dad," Meagan says. "How about *retarded*?"

I smile and say, "Stupid is as stupid does."

The blender erupts loudly and I head upstairs to the office.

Whoever designed the Bumble app was cruelly insightful about aging daters. You can't stick your toe in the water, hesitate and retreat. All I really want to do at this point is browse a few profiles and see how other men my age are describing themselves. But before I can do that, I have to sign up with Facebook (no way!) or my cell phone number, which I do despite misgivings. Then I have to specify my gender by scrolling through three screens of options reflecting the most nuanced and sensitive distinctions imaginable. Then upload photos. Then describe what gender I am looking for (three more screens of scrolling).

Bumble won't let me have a simple test drive, so I decide to go rogue. I identify as a *Woman, Seeking Male*, and upload one random picture from the Internet of a white woman who might be in her late forties. For my name I choose *Jennifer*, which Google tells me was the most common female name of 1970. (These days it's the most common Anglo name for Chinese immigrant women, go figure.) I am masquerading because I want to read other men's profiles. God, I hope I can redo my profile later with a new gender, name and

Seeking field. I worry that my cell phone number, which is real, will forever make me Jennifer online.

When I do begin flipping through profiles, I'm careful to only swipe left. If I swipe right, Damian or Chuck or Bruce will think I'm interested and start hounding the shit out of me. The good looking men, all of them Marlboro men with full heads of hair and rugged three day shadow, pose next to motorcycles or private jets and proclaim their interest in *authentic conversation* and *romantic walks*. What a load of crap. I get an inkling of just how hard it must be for a single woman in her late forties to avoid being bamboozled. Then there are the men who take the *awe shucks* approach and feature their beer bellies, above ground pools and pit bulls. These guys post pictures of themselves with Hooters girls, or working underneath their pick-ups, or (in one case) revealing actual buttcrack while attempting a yoga pose.

I could stop now. I've gotten the lay of the land for these profiles and I feel ready to take a stab at Jack Callany's, which will chart a course down the middle between Marlboro Man and Buttcrack Man. But I'm also strangely curious to see how Jennifer might fare, and I'm feeling protective of her in this wild world where *it's hard to get by on just a smile, girl.* So, for fun, I decide to be Jennifer for a day.

17.

SOLSTICE | 1990

THE HERALDED STATE DEPARTMENT HOLIDAY GALA WAS HELD
at the Old Post Office building on Pennsylvania Avenue the weekend before
Christmas. It promised to be the most sophisticated gala I had ever attended,
featuring Secretary of State James Baker and a retinue of Deputy Secretaries,
Undersecretaries, Deputy Undersecretaries, and quite a few actual secretaries. I chose to wear my Air Force mess dress, the military equivalent of a
tuxedo with silver striped First Lieutenant epaulets and a single ribbon over
the breast pocket. My black patent leather shoes shined like mirrors.

Diane commandeered our bedroom for over an hour to dress herself in
secret, relegating me to our tiny guest room where I dressed in four minutes.
I waited for her downstairs, coiffed, buttoned and spit shined on the sofa, a
football game on to pass the time (I seldom watch a whole game). Shortly
after six she appeared on the staircase and slowly glided down. I was appalled
and aroused.

She wore a tight fitting black dress, ankle length with a slit up the front
that revealed dark maroon silk lining, and bell bottom long sleeves, also lined
with maroon silk. Her head appeared to rest in the center of an inverted
umbrella made of the same silk and tipped forward. Her head was crowned

by a black skull cap with a deep widow's peak and two eight inch black horns. She wore black lipstick and stiletto heels. I rose from the coach and gaped.

"Don't touch," she said with a wicked smile, approaching so close her breasts brushed my uniform.

"I feel underdressed," I said meekly.

"You look dashing, Leftenant," she said to me.

"You look ...," and here I was grasping, "... diabolically gorgeous." I paused, then asked, "What in God's name is this outfit?"

Diane stepped back, raised her chin slightly and said, "This is how I celebrate the winter solstice."

I'm not in the habit of tracking solstices and equinoxes, but it was the twenty-second of December and I would never doubt her.

"It's not exactly Christmas-y," I told her.

"The State Department is non-denominational," she smirked. "And besides, this is my chance to make an impression."

"Oh, you will." I told her.

She stepped back and spun a slow three-sixty for me. Diane was sexy in sweatpants and a tee shirt, so I knew the Cruella De Vil cosplay would be enough to turn me and a dozen undersecretaries into whimpering fools. My mind raced ahead five or six hours to the moment we got home and the "don't touch" orders were rescinded.

I called a taxi for our ride in the city. There was no way Diane could walk to the Metro in those heels. We arrived at the Old Post Office just after 7:00 pm. Taxis and limos were lined up to disgorge their payloads of men in tuxes and ladies in glittering gowns. I took Diane's hand and we ascended the steps to the main entrance, a dutiful First Lieutenant and his wiccan wife.

Our first stop was the coat check where I exchanged my Air Force overcoat and Diane's wool shawl for a claim ticket. We eased into the main atrium and I was instantly aware of eyes turning towards us and conversations pausing. I fixed a smile on my face and tried my best to look deliberate. The only soul I knew at State was Esteban. Diane nodded at a few of the people who were looking at us but I steered us toward the bar, which was three deep in tuxes waiting for martinis.

While we waited, Diane nudged me and whispered, "Eagleburger."

"Sure," I said. "With a Coke and fries."

"No, you idiot." She tilted her head toward three o'clock. "Lawrence Eagleburger. He's the number two guy at State." I turned my head casually and saw a fierce looking portly man in tails next to his wife. We made momentary eye contact and I detected the faintest nod. The mess dress uniform can elevate a young man.

Suddenly Diane reached across me and extended her hand toward Eagleburger. "Hi Larry," she said in a familiar tone.

He turned to her, accepted her hand, but appeared to scowl. "Good evening," he said. "I don't believe we've met."

"I'm Diane Callany," she replied brighty. "I'm a Fast Tracker in Global Affairs. East Africa."

Eaglerburger did not move to introduce his wife. "That's wonderful," he said with indifference. "I hope you enjoy the Christmas gala."

He turned slightly toward the bar, gently ending the exchange, but Diane persisted. "You mean the winter solstice gala!" she said cheerfully. Eagleburger ignored her and his wife turned an arched eyebrow toward Diane. It was excruciatingly awkward.

Diane faced me plaintively and I directed us slowly toward the bar at an oblique angle away from the Eagleburgers.

"*Larry?*" I whispered. "Are you guys on a first name basis?" At the Pentagon, junior officers like me addressed all the top brass by their titles and never by first name.

"Well I don't *know* him," Diane replied quietly, "but that's what everyone else calls him."

We finally got our drinks, a chardonnay for Cruella and double gin and tonic for Mr. De Vil. We drifted about the atrium, taking occasional questions about Diane's horns and toasting the winter solstice with strangers I presumed to be ambassadors and spies. I would need to report all these foreign contacts my first day back at the office.

The dinner bells began to chime and we made our way into a formal ballroom with more than a hundred tables set with sparkling glassware and floral centerpieces. We found our assigned table in left field, but here at last was Esteban (no date) and the other Fast Trackers. Being next to other twentysomethings, and far away from the tables where Eaglerburger and Secretary Baker sat, I felt myself relax. I had downed the G&T by then.

Dinner was wonderful, with each course a salute to a different allied nation. Shrimp cocktail from Vietnam, grilled Romaine salad (from Romania?), lamb chops from Ireland, and a chocolate mousse cake from France. Attentive staff moved plates silently on and off the table and kept our wine glasses fully charged. Diane gave the solstice its full tribute in wine and boisterous story telling.

When coffee was served, Secretary Baker walked to a standing microphone and said a few words of Christmas cheer and good tidings for the new year. He was brief, a minute or two, and he returned to his table. Just as the polite applause was drawing to a close, Diane stood, spread her arms wide and shouted "And happy winter solstice to all!"

There was laughter, then murmuring. The Secretary glanced toward our back corner. The Fast Trackers and their hapless dates grimaced and studied the suddenly fascinating tabletop. I grabbed Diane's dress at the waist and pulled her into her chair. "What the hell was that all about?" I whispered harshly.

"Eat shit, Jack," she said loudly and pushed me away.

Guests at the tables near us watched in amused horror while the rest of the room returned to conversation and clinking glass.

"Let's go," I said to Diane. "You've had too much to drink."

We rose from the table and Diane stumbled in her heels. I took her elbow and steadied her as we made our way toward the closest door. Suddenly, and from nowhere, two Capitol police officers appeared next to us and followed us out into the atrium.

"It's time to go home, you two," said one of the officers.

"Who the hell are you?" Diane slurred.

"Now." The second officer said, becoming rigid.

"Happy fucking winter solstice," Diane said to the two them.

"This is the last time we're going to ask," the first officer said. He removed the handcuffs from his belt.

Diane was wide eyed but defiant, "Get our coats, Jack."

"No," the officer said. "I want you out that door right now." He pointed to the main entrance.

I guided Diane toward the door. When we reached it, she turned and flipped off the two Capitol policemen. "Thank you," she said. "Thank you for doing your jobs so well."

I hurried her out the door and down the steps to a line of taxis that had begun to queue. She was snoring loudly by the time we reached the Fourteenth Street bridge.

18.

NAMING RIGHTS | **2020**

LAST JULY BECAME *BOAT MONTH* IN THE CALLANY HOUSE. Jimmy was hell-bent on options trading. He was in my home office every morning by 8:30 to study the extended hours market and plan out the day's trades. Meagan had no need to rise at such an ungodly hour, but every day by noon she was either filming herself or playing hard-to-get with sponsors who clamored for a few seconds with her growing audience of teeny boppers.

Jimmy spent the July Fourth weekend holed up in his room writing Python code to manage our options trading. He would provide the software with a list of stock symbols and it would analyze the most active options contracts in a window of time that started four months in the future and ran for a year. The software would find specific strike prices where there was an imbalance in the number of buyers, or *bids*, and sellers, or *asks*. In cases where the imbalance was big enough, the software would actually make a trade - open a new options position - that favored the momentum.

On the Monday morning after July Fourth, I gave Jimmy thumbs up to go live, but not to open more than five contracts in total. I didn't want the sorcerer's apprentice to run amuck and ruin me. We sat in front of Jimmy's laptop when the market opened and watched columns of green numbers scroll rapidly up the black screen.

"Has it made a trade yet?" I asked after a few minutes.

"Nope," said Jimmy. "Watch this window." He pointed to an empty rectangle on his screen. The setup was unfamiliar to me. His software wasn't running on an Internet browser, it was running in a code developer's window. "When it makes a trade, you'll see it right here."

We watched. Thirty minutes, nothing. I went for another cup of coffee. More watching.

Then it happened. "Bingo," said Jimmy. In the little rectangle I saw the word *COST* followed by some letters and numbers. "Dad, we just sold one put on Costco."

The morning rolled on. It wasn't a particular exciting day on Wall Street. Just before noon the software opened another position, this time Amazon. We ate lunch in front of the scrolling laptop screen.

Just after two in the afternoon, the software closed the Costco position. "How much did we make?" I asked Jimmy.

"The software doesn't show that," Jimmy told me. "Check your account."

I pivoted to one of my monitors and logged in. "Jimmy, we made two hundred and fifty bucks." I told him and high-fived each other. "Not too shabby."

I stayed at my computer and Jimmy stayed at his. Costco stock kept climbing. "Jimmy," I said, "We closed too early. Ten more minutes and we could have made a thousand instead." Jimmy was over my shoulder staring at my screen.

"*Shit*," he said under his breath. "I need to fix something. The software's too conservative."

He clacked away on his laptop for the next hour, then leaned back in his chair. The green numbers were scrolling once again. In the last five minutes of the day, the software closed the Amazon position and paid us twelve hundred dollars.

"Not bad for sitting on our asses all day," I told him.

"I made it a little less conservative, Dad," Jimmy told me. "There's a risk it might hold onto a position too long. Some days you might curse it."

"Some days I curse my own brain," I said. "Hey, do you have a name for your software?"

Jimmy looked at me. "A name?" he asked. "No."

"It needs a name," I said. "The Terminator. Little Boy. Something like that."

"I'll think about it, Dad."

We walked down to the kitchen and found Meagan standing at the sink eating ice cream from the carton. She looked up sheepishly. Diane would have pounced on that kind of behavior, but I was a longtime offender myself (*why dirty a bowl?*) and Meagan knew she could get away with it.

"Hey Meag," Jimmy said. "We ran my new software and bagged almost fifteen hundred bucks today."

"Wow," Meagan replied. "You and your big brain."

Jimmy glowed.

Meagan continued, "All I did was score a four thousand dollar sponsorship from Blue Bunny."

"Meag, are you kidding?" I asked in excitement.

"Nope," she replied. "I get paid as soon as I make four videos that each get at least a hundred thousand views."

"How hard will that be?" I asked her.

"Not." She replied. "It'll be done this month."

That evening I grilled chicken apple sausages and we ate on the terrace.

Jimmy spoke up, "Dad, we might have our fifty-K *this* month if we're lucky."

"Yep," said Meagan. "When are we going to start looking at boats?"

I gave it some thought. "We can look next weekend."

"What're we gonna name the boat, Dad?" Jimmy asked. "Things need names, right?"

"*Touche.*" I replied. "Who has ideas?"

"Let's call it *Tik Dock*," said Meagan. "I'm the one who'll be bringing in most of the money."

"No way, Jose," said Jimmy. "My software's going to crush your videos." He was silent for a moment. "I think we should call it *Open Options.*"

Both kids looked at me.

"Guys, we'll decide on July thirty-first when the stock market closes. That's a Friday, so the timing is perfect. Whichever of you has brought in the most money gets the naming rights. Deal?"

"Deal!" they both said.

19.
JENNIFER | 2021

I AM IN MY OFFICE ONE AFTERNOON DESIGNING JENNIFER MAN bait when I should be paying attention to the stock market. I need more than one picture, so I Google "claire danes look alike" and scroll through pages and pages of faces, full length bodies, and action shots that plausibly belong to the first Jennifer photo I uploaded. It doesn't take me long to assemble a portfolio of five photos, none of them the same woman and none of them actually Claire Danes. It works because Claire Danes is pretty but lacks distinguishing features. I don't know how a sidewalk cartoonist could draw someone with a generic face and get paid for it.

So that's it, generic Jennifer. Mid-forties, college degree of unspecified flavor and pedigree, divorced, one adult child, non-smoker, social drinker, rare pot user, agnostic but Christian curious, into walking, flying kites, and Netflix.

I'm about to write Jennifer's personal statement when Meagan appears at the door. "I'm taking the jetski over to Emil's," she says. "I'll be back before dinner."

"*Email*?" I ask. "I haven't seen him in a while."

"That's because you call him *Email* and he doesn't want to come over anymore."

I snort. "He's awfully thin skinned. I think you should move him to your spam folder."

"Uh huh, okay Dad." And she's gone.

I decide that Jennifer's statement must have a touch of humor. I compose: *Me: Playful. I can make a game out of anything from a leaf to a restaurant menu. Commonly used 4-letter words: SHOE SALE. Annoyed by vegetarians, documentaries, and alerts on cell phones, mine and everyone else's. I do the cooking. Looking for a long term monogamous relationship, but very picky. YOU: Play the games I dream up and play to win (don't dare throw me a game). Notice my shoes. Make me laugh. Fix me coffee and remember how I like it. Clean up after I cook. Put your phone on dnd. Bring a sense of adventure. Picky but don't not pick me.*

I want to show this to Meagan, but she's gone now (checking her Email), and even if she weren't I wouldn't. In keeping with my impulsiveness toward all things Bumble I submit without any more reflection or drama. I'm a voyeur now and I want to see how my competition plays this game.

I watch the market close and none of my orders fill. I'm fine with this. I like my current positions, and as Dale says, *you only need to be right on one day.* My open positions are six months out and I have plenty of time for that one day to arrive.

Fasting days move a bit slower than feeding days. I feel a small pang of hunger and walk to the kitchen to refill my water glass. I end up flushing out my system most Mondays and Thursdays. Lots of water keeps the hunger away and I figure a twice weekly flush can only be good for my pipes.

In the kitchen my phone vibrates. It's Bumble. My first suitor. Less than thirty minutes. Yes, they do know how to hook you. Bachelor number one is Dan. He looks a little bit like me, maybe a couple years younger. Dan is into indoor soccer and has two Newfies. *God, how does he have any room in his house for furniture?* He's in to travel and doesn't drink. I swipe left.

In the next hour I get seven more matches. A guy in his twenties named Rocky asks for a picture of my tits. *Really? Does that work?* I'm tempted to screen scrape a huge rack from YouPorn and send it back to him, but I think better of it. There's an Asian guy who comes across cheerful and obsessed with mountain biking. Swipe left. I don't get any of the Marlboro Men this time. Maybe those are just mannequins to get new users interested when they start their Bumble adventure. Most of the guys are more or less like me, some more sporty, some more romantic, some balder, some more hirsute.

I get the vague feeling that *I can do this*. I'll blend into the middle of the pack and I suspect my *widowed* status will confer trust and sympathy. I'm not looking for sympathy, but I want to fill the funnel with enough prospects that a few good ones drop out the bottom.

Meagan calls to say she's having dinner at Emil's. Fine. I'm not eating anyway.

Later in the evening, as I'm brushing my teeth and getting ready for bed, I get another Bumble alert. (Jennifer would not approve of these alerts, but Jack enjoys having a game afoot.) I unlock my phone and I'm startled to see my latest match: it's Dale.

His main photo is good. He's wearing a baseball hat, which stalls the bald reveal just long enough for him to make a good impression in other ways. Twinkling, intelligent eyes, a crooked Dick Cheney smile (but better), and a certain sincerity I know is real.

I feel guilty reading his profile, like looking through his medicine cabinet. *Looking for companionship and someone to share meals with.* He doesn't oversell himself, and in fact I think he comes across lonely. A better friend would have swiped left, but I swipe right.

Jennifer: *How long have you been using Bumble?*

Dale: *About two weeks. You?*

About two hours.

I like that you cook. What's your specialty?

Enchiladas. (I have no idea why I say this)

I love Mex food. And I'd be happy to do the dishes ;)

Are you the type who washes dishes before putting them in the dishwasher?

Um. Yes. Is that bad?

No, just old school.

I'm old school.

That usually means chivalrous, too.

Call me Lancelot.

Don't call me Guinevere.

Of course not, that would be rushing things ;)

How long have you been divorced?

14 years.

Long term relationships since then?

Not really. Married to work until a couple years ago.

Retired now?

Semi. You really start with hard questions.

I like a hard man ;) Ask me one.

I will. Over lunch. Friday?

I thought you said you weren't rushing things?

Gotta eat.

OK, but I'm not cooking. Where you taking me?

Ever been to Cantina Azteca? They make a nice enchilada.

Never been, but I'll try it.

OK Jennifer, Friday at noon.

See you then, Lancelot.

20.

CAVIAR | 1991

AT THE END OF MY FIRST DAY OF WORK IN 1991, I MET DIANE AT our usual place on the platform of the Rosslyn Metro. I knew immediately that something was wrong. Her small frame slumped and when she smiled to greet me her eyes were fever dull.

"Hey cutie, you okay?" I asked.

She gave a thin smile. "We'll talk at home," she said.

We stood on the train for the short ride to our stop. I held an overhead strap with my left hand and rubbed her back in consoling ellipses with my right. I knew it must be work. Today had been the reckoning for her gala excesses. I winced just thinking about it.

When we got home from the gala, I carried her newlywed style from the taxi, through our front door, and upstairs to our bedroom. I peeled off the horns, the inverted umbrella collar, and the witch's robe and folded them neatly on the chair in the corner of our bedroom, then helped her into her knee length sleeping shirt and made her drink a tall glass of water. It was not the disrobing I had envisioned a few hours earlier.

The next morning I brought her coffee and sat beside her on the bed. Diane spoke first, "God those people are stuffy."

"Which people?" I asked.

She looked at me puzzled. "Every one of them. At the gala. Even my friends. No one seems to have a sense of humor."

It took me a moment to process this. I was expecting her to be contrite, embarrassed.

"You did put on quite a show," I said.

She eyed me skeptically, was I friend or foe?

"It was a gala for chrissake," she said.

That was quintessential Diane. Brilliant, stubborn, unrepentant. A middle finger raised high to the world. I found the entire ensemble oddly enchanting. Maybe it was the contrast to my own calm nature. Maybe it was the shock of such audacity coming from a petite package.

When we reached our house and the door closed behind us, Diane slumped onto the couch and started crying, sucking in lungfuls of air then crying louder, moaning and trembling. I tried to hug her but she didn't lean into me, so I sat next to her, still, with my arm lightly around her shoulders.

"I think," she said, pausing and catching a breath, "I'm being," another pause and a low moan, "being fired."

"They can't fire you," I said. "It's the government. No one ever gets fired."

Diane kept crying.

"Even Caviar can't get fired!" I said.

Diane gave the faintest hint of a smile. Caviar Anderson was the colossally incompetent administrative assistant to Diane's boss at the East Africa desk. Her fingernails were five inches long, making it impossible for her to type, a skill I'm not sure she possessed anyway. She smoked two packs of Menthol Lights every day, creating a thick haze in the anteroom of the Deputy's office where visitors waited. When Caviar wasn't smoking, she was chewing gum and producing ear popping cracks. She had the utmost disdain for Diane and all the Fast Trackers.

Finally Diane caught her breath and settled back on the coach, leaning her head against my shoulder. She looked straight ahead when she spoke. "Eagleburger personally called Leo and told him to fire me." Leo ran the Fast Tracker program.

"Holy shit," I muttered.

"Leo told me he's thinking about it. He can't ignore Eagleburger, but he might be able to save my job somehow."

"How could he do that?" I asked.

Diane released a post cry shudder. "I'm getting kicked out of Fast Trackers," she said. "That's for sure. Leo's talking to some friends to see if there's a place for me somewhere else at State. Somewhere Eagleburger won't notice."

This would hit Diane where it hurt. Her brilliance mattered to her a lot, and being filed away in the *Department of Redundancy Department* at State was a gulag sentence.

We kicked off our shoes and sat for an hour on the couch. She closed her eyes while I twirled my finger in chestnut hair. We fell into a resigned peacefulness.

"What do you think you'll wear for the vernal equinox?" I asked.

She turned and kissed me. "Nothing at all."

21.

NEIDERMEYER | 2020

AT THE JULY CLUB BOARD MEETING I WAS OFFICIALLY SWORN in by Pam Loving. Brenna Wilder held the Bible and Charter with her arms extended toward me and I reached with a straight left arm to place my hand on top. We were still keeping our social distance, though neither woman wore a face mask this time.

Nimrod did not interrupt with a dramatic last minute appearance. In fact, he was nowhere to be seen, a rarity for these meetings. People still weren't resuming exotic vacations, generally just a few days at the beach or mountains, so I assumed Nimrod must be home pouring over MRI scans and seething at Sara and his twin daughters.

I sat next to Rick O'Shea who looked relaxed in a golf shirt and khakis. His face was newly sunburned, except for his eyes and the bridge of his nose, which were pale and made him look raccoonish

"Yard work this weekend?" I asked him, deducing from the sunburn.

Rick turned to me and grinned with large teeth. "Hell no, I outsource that. I spent Sunday on the lake. Mighta overdone things."

"That'd be a first, Rick," I chided.

I was about to ask Rick where he bought his boat when Pam pounded the gavel and called us to order. The Club was managing to stay afloat despite the pandemic. Golf was up, carryout had sustained the dining room budget and now limited seating was allowed, but the pool was still closed and the usual summer barbecues and socials had all been canceled. Club life was muted, along with everything else.

Without Nimrod's ritual reading of community standards violations into the record, the meeting was brief and sober, and wrapped up in an hour.

"Glad to have you on the board at last," Siobhan Sorcer said from across the table. She sat next to Aristotle Poe who had been silent most of the meeting. He nodded solemnly but his eyes twinkled.

"Happy to be here!" I said.

"Where's your nemesis tonight?" Rick asked.

"Dunno," I replied. "Killed by his own troops in Vietnam."

Rick got the joke and erupted, but Brenna looked worried. "Really?" she asked. "Killed?"

"Jack's talking about Douglas C. Neidermeyer," Rick replied.

"Oh," Brenna replied shyly. "I didn't know him."

"Brenna, have you not seen *Animal House*?" I asked.

"No," she said.

"Put that on your list for quarantine," I winked at her.

Rick and I both rose to leave and I asked him where he bought his Cobalt. "The boat show, last February," he said. "I wanted to buy used but I couldn't find anything decent around here."

Pam looked up from her notepad. "A used Cobalt? I've got one I'd love to sell."

I remembered Gordon, her profligate kept man and *ex* as of six months. He had been a reliable source of liquidity at the Men's Poker night, but we hadn't seen him in months since Pam shut off the spigot and forced him to limp back to Happy Brothers, hat in hand.

"I didn't realize you still had the boat, Pam." I said with growing interest. She had sold Gordon's Maserati convertible for a pittance just to piss him off. I figured she had done the same with the boat.

"Yep," she said. "I didn't want to sell a boat in December, and then the virus hit."

"I know it's a Cobalt," I said. "What else do you know about it?"

She gave a shrug. "Just another expensive man toy as far as I'm concerned. I think it's a 2018 or 2017."

Rich chimed in. "It's a 2018. I was on it a few times with Gordon last summer." He looked sheepishly at Pam, though I don't know why. "It's sweet, Jack. An R5, open bow. Probably a hundred-K new."

I looked at Pam. "You really want to sell?"

"Absolutely," she said. "Make me a reasonable offer and get it off my dock the same day."

"I'll call you tomorrow morning after I've looked at prices."

The room was beginning to empty. I saluted Aristotle as he pivoted in his electric wheelchair and rolled out. Rick and I waited with Pam while she packed her notes into a small attache case and then walked with her into the parking lot.

Before we parted ways, I asked Pam, "Did you guys ever name the boat?"

"No," she said. "Gordon wanted to call it *Breaking Wind* but I said no to that. We split up before he ever came up with something more civilized."

"Well," I said. "Gordy always was a mighty wind breaker."

Rick, Pam and I exchanged elbow taps and parted ways.

22.
WATERFALL | 2021

FRIDAY I RISE EARLY, FEELING ALERT. IT'S THE MORNING AFTER a fasting day, and rather than being famished I am calm and light, unhurried to break my fast. I straighten the sheets on my bed, and standing before the window begin my diurnal stretches and unconvincing yoga poses.

I admit that I'm giddy about sucker punching Dale on his lunch date today. He's a good natured fellow, but serious, not the type to think up his own jokes or waste hours constructing an elaborate but futile prank. Not so with me. I've always had an internal homing beacon that zeroes in on people's foibles, phobias and peeves. When I discover one, I subconsciously file it away in my mental armory.

Pre-kids and while we still lived in Arlington, Billy Ray Cyrus released his masterpiece, *Achy Breaky Heart*. Diane absolutely hated that song, not just because she plain hated it, but because she couldn't get it out of her head once she heard it. I would catch her humming it around the house and then wallowing in self loathing the moment she caught herself. One April Fool's Day a decade later, when we all had cell phones, I changed her ringtone to *Achy Breaky Heart*. Diane was terrible at technology and had no idea how to change it back, and I allowed her to suffer for a few weeks.

I chalk up pranksterism to my *smart ass* prime factor. It serves me well at the poker table, among other things. That same homing beacon that activates my prank circuitry also detects tells, bluffs and actual monster hands with profitable accuracy.

I also know something about being the *victim* of a good prank. Victimhood of this sort provokes a waterfall of emotions. They are, in order: shock, confusion, rage, entrapment, resignation, humor (in some) and finally awkward self awareness (in fewer). When I see my kids caught in this waterfall, sometimes of my own creation, I tell them *don't get mad, get Steven.*

I spent the searing middle August days of 1984 in a mini boot camp for ROTC training at Davidson College. Over a ten day stretch, twenty-five of us young men and women learned to wear a uniform, march in formation, address a superior, and respect the chain of command. This information was not imparted through books or lectures at the chalkboard, but by weakening us with fatigue, ripping us open with humiliation, stuffing us with protocol, and suturing us back up in a uniform with a straight gig line. This process was overseen by a masochistic fascist tyrant by the name of Gunnery Sergeant Animalu, the fierce uniformed man who greeted me at the top of the steps to Chambers on my last day as a civilian.

I wished simply to survive the ten day period without vomiting on myself or being expelled from ROTC and stripped of my scholarship. I would venture that twenty-four of us shared this same objective, but there was a twenty-fifth, Steven Murphy, who was wired differently. A few years later I saw a Far Side comic where Gary Larson captured Steven's essence. The single frame comic shows a scene from Hell. Two devils stand together observing an emaciated man pushing a wheelbarrow through flames while whistling cheerfully. One of the devils says to the other, "You know, we're just not reaching that guy." That was Steven, and try as he would, Gunnery Sergeant Animalu just wasn't able to weaken, rip, stuff or suture him. Of course, Steven grew exhausted like the rest of us and bungled his share of the menial but impossible tasks we were given, but he never cracked. He had wild mischievous eyes and seemed to find everything we did slightly ridiculous (and he was right, of course).

Near the end of our training period, the Gunny woke us up at 4:00 am in our primitive barracks by slamming an empty metal garbage can to the floor and rolling it down the aisle between our bunks. The veins in his neck bulged as he ordered us to attention and informed us we were to be in uniform and seated on the bus idling just outside the door in ten minutes. "We don't have all goddamn day!" He told us.

At 4:09 am we filed onto the bus and took our seats, me at a window and Steven next to me on the aisle. We started our field trip to Fort Bragg, a three hour ride mostly in darkness, where we would no doubt have a delightful day and ample opportunities for character development.

We all slept heavily on the bus ride, motionless as cadavers, and when the bus finally stopped inside Fort Bragg, I was groggy and disoriented. The Gunny stood at the front of the bus and barked orders for us to file out and line up by the curb. We did so with order and alacrity, blinking at the morning sun and catching a wave of Carolina August heat as we stepped from the bus. When the Gunnery Sergeant saw me step down his eyes narrowed cruelly.

"Callany, what in the hell's the matter with you?" He roared.

"Nothing, Sergeant," I replied confidently with matching volume.

He glowered at me while I stood at the bus door, blocking the exit for the others. After a moment he pointed to a spot on the pavement apart of the group formation. "Callany, park yourself over there."

"Yes, Sergeant." I replied.

I was somewhere between petrified and indignant. What had I done?

When all the cadets had disembarked, the Gunny walked over to me and put his face inches from my own. He was taller than me and I was staring at his prominent Adam's apple.

"Cadet Callany, I'm going to ask you one last time. What in God's name is wrong with you?"

"Nothing, Sergeant," I replied. There was no other acceptable reply.

He drew in a long breath and glanced sideways toward the formation of other cadets, then said, "Callany, drop and give me fifty push-ups NOW!"

I hit the pavement and felt the hot macadam on my palms. Ten pushups, then twenty. At thirty-five I slowed perceptibly. The final five were grueling.

"On your feet, cadet!" He yelled.

I rose quickly and attempted to collect myself.

"Now, do you know what in the hell is wrong with you?" the Gunny screamed.

"No. Sergeant," I said, this time more resigned.

Animalu became agitated and looked to his left, then right. Finally he pointed to the large side view mirror on the bus, near the door.

"Go look at yourself, Callany."

I broke my rigid stance and walked to the bus. In the mirror I saw my face red and lined with beads of perspiration. My left cheek had been tattooed with a fine blue spiral, drawn by a ball point pen. Beneath the spiral in block letters were the words: I SHAVE MY ASS.

I tumbled into the waterfall of emotions known to all prank victims. *Steven! That motherfucker!* While I had been sleeping on the bus - while every-one had been sleeping - he had stayed awake and made my face his canvas.

I turned to the Gunnery Sergeant with pleading eyes. "I didn't do this, Sergeant." It was a ludicrous defense but I could think of nothing else.

The Gunny ordered me back into formation and would not let me wash my face all day. I marched across Fort Bragg, ran the Recondo Course, and ate two loaded cheeseburgers in the enlisted dining hall while advertising my hairless ass to all.

* * *

I strolled in Cantina Azteca at ten minutes past noon on Friday with an unshaved ass, sporting an obnoxious fruit salad Hawaiian shirt. The hostess greeted me but I spotted Dale at our usual table, seated so he could watch the entrance. I nodded to the hostess and indicated that I saw the person I was meeting.

"Dale," I said cheerfully, approaching his table. "You didn't tell me you were coming here today?"

"Oh," he mumbled, "Hi Jack." Then an awkward silence.

I moved to sit with him in the booth. "Mind if I join you?"

"No," he said. And then added, "Well, yes." Another pause. "Jack, I'm meeting someone."

"No problem," I said cheerfully. "Aristotle?" Aristotle Poe liked this place, too, and sometimes joined us.

"Jack," Dale said, lowering his voice. "I'm meeting a woman. For the first time."

I looked at Dale in mock surprise.

He continued, "I met her on Bumble. She said she likes enchiladas so I suggested this place."

"You know how to treat a girl, Dale," I said.

"Look," Dale said to me seriously, "She's supposed to be here any minute. Do you mind …?"

"Not at all," I said, "I'd love to meet her. What's her name?"

"No," Dale said, lowering his voice further. The mariachi sound track seemed to get louder. "I mean, would you mind leaving us alone?"

I hesitated a moment. "Oh God, Dale, I'm sorry. I'm such a clod! Of course, of course."

"Thanks," he said, relaxing.

"I won't stay long," I continued. "How about we share some guac and then I'll find another table?"

Dale grew agitated and leaned back in his booth seat. "Jack, seriously, I'm about to meet her for the first time. Can you just take a hike … NOW?"

The waitress approached, completely unaware of the mounting tension. "Can I bring you anything? Drinks? An appetizer?"

"Absolutely," I said to Dale's horror. "Two jumbo house margaritas and a large guacamole."

Dale's eyes darted from the waitress to the front door, then to me. He whispered, "What the hell, Jack?"

The waitress stepped away and I grinned at Dale. "Why ya so uptight, *Lancelot*?"

Dale's eyes widened, then narrowed. He had entered the waterfall. I waited.

Finally I said to Dale, "I'm an asshole."

"Yes you are," he replied. He was still reconstructing what must have happened.

"Lunch is on me," I told him. "Dale, don't get mad. Get Steven."

23.

HANDFASTING | 1991

ONE FRESH MORNING IN MAY DIANE AND I DECIDED TO RIDE our bicycles on the paved path along the Potomac River. The embarrassment of the gala and Diane's reassignment were behind us, though still healing, and the spring delivered new projects and diversions. We coasted into an empty Rosslyn early in the morning and wound down a pedestrian ramp that deposited us in a parking lot that connected to the main trail leading south to Mount Vernon.

We pedaled across the mostly empty parking lot toward the bike path, and then stopped near a small footbridge to adjust Diane's seat. While I was fussing with an allen wrench, Diane said, "What's over there?" She pointed to the footbridge, which crossed a narrow finger of the Potomac to a wooded area.

"I have no idea," I replied. "Wanna see?"

When I finished adjusting her seat, we walked our bikes across the footbridge and entered a park that was dark with morning shade. Suddenly I realized this was Teddy Roosevelt Island. I had seen it on maps but every time I had run or biked through the area, I had been too focused on the Key Bridge and Georgetown to realize the island was right here.

We leaned our bicycles against a bike rack that had one other occupant, a dismembered and rusted frame, and walked quietly along a mulch trail toward the center of the island. We crossed an ornate waterless moat from another era and found ourselves in a grotto of granite, a rectangular plaza lined with stone benches oriented worshipfully toward The Bull Moose himself. Teddy Roosevelt in bronze patina stood more than twenty feet above us, his right raised in exhortation to Diane and me alone.

"I love this place," Diane whispered. "I can't believe I never heard about it while I was at Georgetown."

"Me neither," I said. "It's DC's lost memorial."

We stood in silence, then Diane turned to me and said, "Let's get married here. With Uncle Teddy officiating."

I hadn't seen this coming. "I thought we already *were* married," I said, kissing the top of her head.

"No, really," Diane said. "Let's have a real ceremony with your parents, and my mom, and our friends. Right here."

I loved the idea. Our civil ceremony last June had been perfunctory and surreptitious, and I knew our parents, our mothers especially, were saddened and cheated by our choice. The quiet of the soft morning enveloped us.

Suddenly I dropped on one knee and took Diane's hands in mine. "Will you marry me ... again?" I asked.

"Yes," she said, her eyes brimming. I stood and kissed her under Teddy's severe gaze.

Diane had endured three weeks of unpaid leave from State, a merciful maneuver by Leo to lower her profile, and in February she started in her new position in Global Analysis. This department occupied the most distant orbit of the organization, the Pluto of the State Department, known by the Fast Trackers as Glob Anal. In a windowless office most rapidly accessed by the freight elevator, Diane and a wan despondent group of State Department lifers manually entered data from foreign almanacs, registers and census reports into 1970's era computer terminals.

The role was an appalling misuse of Diane's intellect, made all the more punishing because she was intensely verbal, the star (nearly) of the Georgetown debate team. During her first weeks of exile, we discussed a jailbreak that would return her to ground level and natural light. We consoled ourselves in the certain knowledge that she was simply in the penalty box for a while, too bright an asset to be squandered by her country.

Diane divided her work day into modules to mark the time. There was Arrival Module, which started as early as possible, often 6:00 am, and included coffee and reading *The Washington Post*; Work Module #1 lasting no more than one hour; Mail Room Module; Lunch Module; Filene's Basement Module; Work Module #2 (optional); Half Price Bagel Module at Einstein Brothers in the afternoon; Afternoon Coffee Module; and End of Day Tidying Up Module. As the weeks went on, new modules were added, old ones removed.

One morning she ran into Caviar at the mail room and Caviar asked her, "How's life in Glob Anal?" The next day Diane replaced Mail Room Module with Lobby Attractions Module (there were rotating displays for visiting school children).

There were a few social casualties of her reassignment as well. Night out invitations from her Fast Tracker friends became fewer and fewer. We still saw Esteban occasionally, but single life kept him busy. Diane's two Georgetown classmates in the program stopped returning her calls.

The morning we stumbled onto Teddy Roosevelt Island, we were still hopeful that Diane would be released from Global Analysis within the year. Her modularization of each day made the position tolerable, and we had plenty to keep us occupied, exploring DC's trails and restaurants and bars, playing house, and hosting poker. Our days were predictable and stable, and it seemed like a perfectly natural time for a proper wedding ceremony.

Diane threw herself into wedding planning, adding a Wedding Planning Module to her work day and talking on the phone at night with her mother and friends in California. We took an after dinner walk through our neighborhood one evening and she said to me, "I'd like our wedding to be a handfasting."

I looked at her. "Does that mean we can't eat with our hands?"

"It's something I just learned about," she said, ignoring me. "It's an ancient Celtic tradition where the bride and groom have their hands tied together with rope symbolizing their union. After one year, if they both agree, they have a wedding ceremony."

"What happens if they don't agree after a year?" I asked.

"They go their separate ways. It's like they were never married," she replied.

"So we'll get our hands tied this year and push the wedding off another year?" I asked.

"No," Diane said. "That's what happened last year. The Justice of the Peace was our handfasting. This year we'll make it official in front of everyone."

I liked the idea.

Diane continued, "I want our hands to be tied when the ceremony begins. Then, when we're pronounced man and wife, we'll untie them."

"So we're *untying* the knot?" I asked playfully. Diane ignored the comment.

"I want the whole thing to be casual with a Celtic flair," she said. "Don't laugh, but I want to wear a toga instead of a wedding dress. And a garland in my hair."

"Are you going to wear the horns?" I asked. Diane narrowed her eyes and let this pass, too.

"I want you to wear your uniform tux. The mess dress," she said.

"Sure," I told her. I certainly couldn't see myself in a toga and garland. "But I might lose my security clearance if the boys from the office tell the Colonel I was seen in uniform with a Celtic goddess."

Diane smiled and added, "At a pagan wedding ceremony officiated by Teddy Roosevelt."

24.

THAT'S HOW MUCH I LOVE YOU | 2020

WHEN THE MARKET CLOSED ON JULY 31 LAST YEAR, I CALLED A family meeting in my home office. This was the hour reckoning: had the kids raised half the money we needed for a new boat? The goal had been twenty-five K each, with naming rights going to the winner.

I knew where Jimmy stood since his software had been making trades on my personal options account. I kept a close eye on his trading. The software worked beautifully when the market was gently rolling hills, less so when there were cliffs. The previous week he found himself on the edge of one of those cliffs and wiped out about half of his gains for the month. Jimmy's haul stood at almost twelve thousand dollars, a more than decent wage, but not sustainable for him or anyone without the benefit of a large account to allow margin trading.

I called down the hall for Meagan to join us, but there was no reply.

"Text her, Dad," said Jimmy. "She probably has her earbuds in."

Call me old school, but texting people in the same house just doesn't seem right. On the bright side, when she's away at school our communication won't change all that much. I texted her. "OMW," she replied.

"Dad, I want to make some adjustments to the code," Jimmy said while we waited. I raised an eyebrow. "I want to study these things called the Greeks to see if there's some kind of early warning indicator for the kind of sell off we just had."

"You'll be well on your way to running a hedge fund," I said.

A few minutes later we heard Meagan coming down the hall. She walked into the home office *on her hands*, auburn hair grazing the floor and necklaces dangling in her face. She stood in the doorway, inverted, and said, "Hi guys."

I exchanged glances with Jimmy, who rolled his eyes.

"Pretty impressive, Meag," I said.

She rolled her feet away from us, her back arched freakishly into a human bridge, then popped up and spun around, her face beet red. "I came as fast as I could," she said smiling.

"Okay slackers," I said. "Now's the moment of truth. Did we make enough money to buy a boat?"

Jimmy grimaced. "I don't know, Dad. I closed eleven thousand eight hundred. Probably not enough."

We both turned to Meagan.

"I guess I win," she said, lifting a leg straight into the air alongside her cheek. "Put me down for twenty-K."

"Dang," Jimmy said.

I was impressed, maybe stunned. "I know you had the Blue Bunny deal," I said. "What else?"

Meagan smiled, "I got another four-K from Blue Bunny, and a twelve-K from Lululemon."

Jimmy narrowed his eyes. "Hey, how much have you actually received as of right now?"

"Um," Meagan paused. "Only two-K. The contracts pay out over the next three months."

Jimmy turned to me, "Dad, my money is in your account right now. That's what should count. I won this thing."

I rubbed my chin and looked them both over. "Guys, your total haul was about thirty-two-K. Very impressive, unbelievable in fact." I continued, "But a new boat requires cash on the barrelhead. We only have fourteen-K in real cash."

"And most of that came from me," Jimmy said triumphantly.

"Go ahead and name it, bruh," said Meagan. "I didn't like my name anyway. *Tik Dock*. How dumb."

"I thought it was pretty good," I said.

Meagan ignored me and cartwheeled her body into another handstand.

"That's it," Jimmy said. "I win and we'll name her *Open Options*."

I looked at Meagan. "Meag, you okay with that?"

"Sure," she said. "It's clever."

Then I said, "There's just one little problem. We don't have nearly enough money. We need at least another month, maybe two."

"But Dad," Jimmy said, "I'm heading back to Boston in a few weeks and I want to at least *see* the boat I named."

"We'll discuss it over dinner," I said. "You guys want to go out?"

Meagan righted herself. "With you?" she asked. "Dad, I have a life. Emil and I are going out."

"I'm down for it," said Jimmy.

Meagan formed an "L" on her forehead and glared at him.

"Well," I said. "I need to run an errand before dinner and I need help from both of you. We'll leave in half an hour and I'll have you home by six, Meagan."

Jimmy rolled his office chair back and stood, scratching his stomach. "I'll be ready at five," he said, and walked down the hall toward his room.

Meagan slumped into Jimmy's chair and began arching her eyebrows and alternately sticking her tongue out at me. I responded by rolling my lower lip out and folding my tongue over my upper lip, then raising my eyebrows. It was a spectacle strictly reserved for the family.

"How much do you love me, Dad," she asked.

I pulled my lips back to their normal position and looked out the window with my best faraway contemplative gaze.

"Well," I said carefully, preparing to play a game we had invented years before. "Let me put it this way."

Meagan adjusted in her chair, suddenly intent.

"Let's just say that I was in the Swiss Alps, standing on the very tip of the Matterhorn, and I was strapped to a hang glider made of the lightest material on earth - some sort of nanotube technology - so light that it was invisible, and it was handmade by Elon Musk for his personal use on Mars one day, but he loaned it to me because he owed me money. And while I'm standing there, the sun begins to rise and washes over the mountain tops in pure gold, and I'm waiting for just the perfect moment to leap off and glide for hours down to a soft Alpine meadow filled with new spring flowers."

Meagan was nodding along, buying into the visual.

"And then a warm breeze blows from behind me. I hear it first, before I actually feel it. I make one last check of my harness, and I look at the massive wing of the hang glider, but I can't even see it because it's invisible, but I can see the sun glinting off its surface so I know it's there. And everything is just perfect for my launch, so I take one step to the edge, and I'm almost at the point of no return, but then all of a sudden…."

Meagan beamed, she knew what was coming.

I continued, "My cell phone rings, and I look down and it's you calling, so I answer."

I paused and looked at Meagan. It was her turn now, according to the rules of our game.

She sat up straight and said, "And I say, 'Daddy, I'm in bed and I forgot to turn off my light. Can you come turn it off for me?'"

My face brightened and I said, "'Of course, doll, I'll be right there.' And I tear off the hang glider and toss it off the mountain, and I start hiking down the mountain, slowly at first since it's very steep at the top, but as soon as I can I start running. And I run all the way to the bottom and I hitchhike along the highway until some unsafe-at-any speed Citroen picks me up and takes me to the Geneva airport, and there's a plane about to leave for North Carolina so I buy the last seat, which is in row ninety-nine, and it's a middle seat between the President and Vice President of the Swiss Obesity Society, and as soon as we land in North Carolina I run all the way home without any water, further than a marathon, and I run into your room, and I see you there in bed with your sheets pulled up, and I turn off your light."

Meagan finished the story for us, "And I say 'Thank you, Daddy.'"

"That's how much I love you," I said.

"I don't feel like going on an errand," Meagan said abruptly, standing.

"After everything I did for you?" I asked. "I raced across the globe just to turn off your light."

"Not really," she said. "I need to get ready for my date."

I made a low rumble in my throat and glowered at her.

"Okay," she said at last. "But can it be quick?"

"It'll be quick," I said to her. "Be in the kitchen at five."

I walked down to the kitchen, eyed the accumulating dirty dishes, and sent a text to Pam Loving.

At five we rolled out of the garage in my Tesla. Meagan took shotgun, pulled the visor down and opened the mirror so she could bat her eyelashes and apply lip gloss. I steered us through the neighborhood but not onto the main road that leads into our small town. Instead I wound deeper into our peninsula and eventually pulled into Pam's driveway.

"Whose house is this?" Jimmy asked.

"This is not an errand," Meagan added indignantly.

"Come on," I said.

I walked down Pam's driveway, but rather than approaching her front door I walked through the gate leading into her back yard. Pam's place is on the lake, too, and I walked across the back yard toward her dock.

"Dad, this is trespassing," Meagan said. "Where are we?"

I saw Pam standing at the end of her dock in a black summer dress with white polka dots. Her round cheeks shone and she waved. The kids follow me in awkward silence.

When we got close enough, I shouted, "Hey Pam! Do you remember Jimmy and Meagan?"

She looked at them, smiled broadly, and replied, "Oh my God, Meagan is gorgeous. And Jimmy, you're taller than your father."

Pam looked at me, then motioned to the boat in the slip attached to her dock. "How do you guys like your new boat?"

"*Our* new boat?" Jimmy asked.

"I let your dad steal it from me," said Pam. "It belonged to my ex and there's no way I'm letting him keep it. It's almost brand new, less than twenty hours on the engine."

We walked down the ramp and boarded the boat one at a time. Pam stood on the dock.

"It's perfect, Pam," I said smiling.

The kids examined the boat in shocked silence, admiring the shining gel coat, chrome fixtures and wide, clean seating. I winked at Pam.

"It's all yours, Jack," she said. "Drive her home. You can leave your car here and get it later."

I turned the ignition key and the inboard motor started, a nearly silent hum in the stern. We backed out of the slip, waved at Pam, and smoothly accelerated into the main channel towards our house.

"How much was it?" Jimmy asked.

"She really did give me a great deal," I replied. "I don't even want to say what the price was."

"So how much do we owe you," Meagan asked.

"Nothing," I replied with a smile. "I'm really proud of how hard you guys worked to save up this summer. Mom would be proud, too." I throttled up and we left a tall foamy wake in our tracks. "You guys save that money. You'll need it at college."

"Thanks, Dad," said Jimmy.

Meagan kissed my cheek. "Thank you, Daddy."

"That's how much I love you," I said.

25.

STOOGES | 2021

IT'S FRIDAY THE 13TH, AUGUST, AND I'M LYING AWAKE IN A Marriott in Providence, Rhode Island, while Meagan slumbers in the other bed. The curtains are opaque, heavy and I have drawn them together, but a shocking ray of sunlight pierces a vertical slit where they don't quite meet. It's just past seven and I decide to let her sleep. I will rouse her at nine, fetch coffee from the Starbucks two blocks away (black for me, exotic latte of some sort for her), and then scroll through clickbait on my smartphone while she gets ready. We should roll into Boston around noon.

We've been on the road since Wednesday morning, following the nearly identical route we made two years ago when we deposited Jimmy in Cambridge: Arlington on night one, where we stayed with Paul and Athena, then Providence on night two, where we don't know a soul but enjoy the vibe of College Hill. Only last time we were four. Diane kept us on schedule, fussing with Jimmy to keep his "travel things" separate from his "dorm things" so we wouldn't have to unpack and repack the van each day, and generally ordering us around like the Von Trapps. Now we are two, and Meagan has her shit together far better than Jimmy ever did, and even if she didn't, I couldn't be as regimental as Diane.

On Tuesday afternoon I carried Meagan's two suitcases and four lidless plastic bins from Target down to the foyer. She had been packing diligently for the past week and I noticed checklists on her bed and vanity, written in pencil in her dense left-slanting style. Meagan's preparation is probably not much different from what it would have been if Diane were here, though Diane would know where the bin lids were and there would have been bouts of shouting between mother and daughter, followed by a détente. As it was, I hadn't been able to help Meagan much at all.

"Let's just double check the less obvious stuff," I had said. "Sheets and towels?"

"Right there," Meagan said, pointing to an open bin.

"Your heavy coat? Gloves?"

"Yes, Dad, in the blue suitcase."

"What about chargers?" I was met with an eye roll.

"Come on," I said, "Let's just walk through the house and see if there's anything else."

We begin upstairs in my office. Meagan ignored my Costco desktop but walked to the nightstand that remained on the spot it had occupied when my marital bed was here. On it was an untidy stack of books and two framed pictures, one of Diane and me in the bow of our boat looking relaxed and cheerfully drunk. The other was the family picture we had sent as a Christmas card the year before Diane died. Meagan considered both pictures, then asked if she could take the one of Diane and me on the boat.

"Of course," I said.

We walked down the hall to Jimmy's room, which has been empty since his last visit, Meagan's graduation in June. She walked through his room, running her fingers across the top of his bed, his desk, his bookcase.

"Remember how we used to sleep in here together on Christmas Eve?" she asked wistfully.

My eyes suddenly brim with tears. Even as teenagers they would sleep in Jimmy's room on Christmas Eve. Diane and I would enjoy eggnog with nutmeg and a fine Kentucky additive downstairs until their hushed voices stopped, then fill the stockings and stack gifts next to the tree. When Diane went upstairs to get ready for bed, it was my duty to take a bite or two from the hard, vaguely snowman shaped homemade sugar cookies that had been left out, and then leave a few shreds of carrot (chewed in haste by a reindeer) at the threshold of Jimmy's bedroom door. It was a detail gleefully noticed every Christmas morning.

I blink back tears and turn my head away slightly. I don't believe Meagan notices, or else she has suddenly become merciful. She picks up a small framed photo on Jimmy's nightstand and studies it. It's the two of them in Halloween costumes, Jimmy is six and wearing a cardboard box painted like a Rubik's cube, his obsession that year, and Meagan is four, dressed in German lederhosen and a tiny porkpie hat with a small brown feather in its band.

I think to myself, *Please don't take that one*. It's been in Jimmy's room forever, a witness to countless bedtime stories and tuck-ins. It's an artifact from when there were four of us and childhood was never ending.

She set it back down carefully and said simply, "Cute."

Downstairs Meagan paused in the dining room. The elegant wooden box containing Diane's remains sat on the dining room table, exactly where I placed it eighteen months earlier. I didn't want to move her - the box radiated a presence, at least for me - and I wasn't ready to allow myself to think of spreading her ashes. Meagan placed her hands on both sides of the box, leaned to kiss it, and then rested her forehead on its lid for a long, silent moment. Then she kissed it again, stood and faced me, dry eyed.

"Mom would be proud of you ... *is proud of you*," I said.

"I always thought she'd be helping me move into college," Meagan said, her eyes still on the box.

Meagan moved slowly from the dining room and I waited behind. She walked softly through rooms on the first floor, the kitchen, our family room, the formal living room where we hoisted our Christmas tree every year on the Saturday after Thanksgiving. She returned to me after a few minutes and hugged me, putting her head against my chest. Fine auburn strands tickled my nose.

"Going out tonight for a last hurrah?" I asked.

"No," she said pensively. "Ava's at the beach and Maddie and Shannon have already left for school."

"What about Emil?" I asked.

Meagan stepped back and looked at me. "That's the first time you've said his name right."

"Oh sorry," I quipped. "I meant *Email*."

"Whew," she said. "That's a relief. I thought maybe you had a mini stroke or something."

I arched an eyebrow.

"No," she said, and then paused. "I moved him to the spam folder. Isn't that what you suggested a few weeks ago?"

"Well, that would be the first time you took one of my suggestions," I replied. "I thought you liked him."

"Meh," Meagan replied. "I don't want to start college with a long distance relationship."

I regarded her for a moment, then said, "My wise and wrinkled grandmother always said, 'Absence makes the heart grow fonder … *for someone else*.'"

Meagan smiled, then asked, "Dad, can you take me wakeboarding?"

"I'd love to," I said. "Here's to *Open Options*."

* * *

The next morning Meagan and I rolled out of the garage at ten in a minivan that was washed, gassed and groaning under the weight of her worldly possessions. Meagan sat beside me drinking a gooseshit green smoothie.

As the garage door rolled down she asked, "When can I take my Jeep to Boston?"

"Never," I said. "You haven't been trained to drive with Yankees." Meagan slapped my arm playfully.

"Maybe in the spring, maybe next year," I added. "Let's wait and see what it's like up there. You'll end up being the chauffeur for your entire dorm."

I did all the driving on day one. Meagan commandeered the stereo, connected to her iPhone with Bluetooth, and took us on a two hour odyssey beginning with her current favorites - Zac Brown, Sam Smith, and Mt. Joy - and then inched back through her childhood with Taylor Swift, One Direction, and Pharrel Williams, and then concluded in a burst of third grade enthusiasm with Hannah Montana.

Meagan and I were the two music lovers in the family. If we were in the car, or on the boat, or in the kitchen, we were listening to music. If Diane or Jimmy walked into the room, the first thing they did was turn the music down, or off. Now, as we put interstate miles behind us, the music was a scrapbook of eighteen years.

At five in the afternoon we exited the Shirley Highway and navigated into Arlington. Glebe Road was seedy and steaming, perpetually under repair, and afternoon traffic was heavy. Meagan had reclined the passenger seat all the way back. Her eyes were closed and her earbuds were in, and I decided to let her be.

Without planning it, I navigated down Wilson Boulevard, past Clarendon, and then turned onto a neighborhood street shaded by dark sentinel oaks. Quiet descended suddenly. I slowed to a crawl and rolled my window down. This was the neighborhood where our little ditty began. Instinctively I knew the streets, the turns that would come, but the dimensions were off, the homes smaller, trees taller, the afternoon light off hue.

Many things were unremembered: older homes we must have passed many times. Others, mundane, were strangely in place. A basketball hoop on the street in exactly the spot it had been thirty years ago. A gaudy metal daisy by the front door of the house on Oxford Street.

I turned onto Jackson and there, midway down, was the home Diane and I had rented after college and poured ourselves into. It was still a tidy, compact two level colonial. The brick had been whitewashed, a frosting that made it more dignified. The sapling red maple I had planted in the front yard thirty years before towered over the home, spreading a fine canopy of deep green leaves. I stopped the minivan short of the house, an unsuspicious distance to observe and remember.

Visitation of places past is both sacred and mundane. In one glance I see four years compressed into a single frame, a palimpsest of aspirations, hopes and defeats. Here we experienced the onset of adulthood, breathlessly bold and hopelessly naive. Sitting there I was swept into a riptide of nostalgia for the innocence and potential that defined us in those days, but to which we had been completely blind. I shifted into park and let the riptide carry me.

After a minute, maybe ten, a teenage boy emerged from behind *my* house rolling a dark green trash can down the drive. He could have been Meagan's age. He was dressed in black sport shorts, an Atari tee shirt, and flip flops. His hair was a tangled brown mess that hung over his eyes. He deposited the trash can at the end of the driveway, glanced at my van indifferently, and loped back up the drive and disappeared behind the house. I could glimpse a corner of the screen porch.

Suddenly I was back on shore in the present. I became aware that I had stopped too long on this street, though no car had passed. I looked at Meagan, who was clearly asleep and not just zoned out on a playlist. For an instant I considered waking her, showing her this place, telling her a few stories. Two years ago when we passed through with Jimmy we did not stop here. We were past due to Paul and Athena's, and besides, we knew there would always be another chance for the four of us to knock politely on this door and ask to have a look around. I shifted into drive and continued slowly down the street.

I took the interior route through the neighborhood, south toward Ballston, to reach Paul and Athena's place. Paul Papadopoulus was one of the OGs. He had been a butter bar with me at the Pentagon, but unlike me had stayed in for twenty-some years and retired as full bird Colonel. Paul had retained a teenager's body into his early thirties, skinny in a boney unhealthy way, and prone to getting angry red zits on his nose and temples. He had boundless energy, then as now. There was always time for another game, another prank, another all nighter. He was excruciatingly fun to be around, and utterly exhausting.

Athena was custom made for Paul. She was his height but thinner and had painfully straight black hair and full lips that were naturally red. She also suffered from errant zits well past the normal age, and I used to wonder if they infected each other during lovemaking or by unchecked sharing of pillow cases. They had met at Brandeis as freshmen and neither had ever dated anyone else.

Athena was treacherously brilliant and had a sharp, playful mind. Diane loved her immediately and the two of them presided loudly over our regular poker nights with arcane and shifting rules and rituals. When I called them with terrible news last March, they packed their car and drove to Carolina immediately. They checked into a hotel a few miles from our house at three in the morning, exactly seven hours after my call, and were at my front door at eight the next morning with a bag of warm bagels.

Paul and Athena were married two years after Diane and me, and they bought a bungalow in Arlington about one mile from the house we were renting. There were weeks, especially in the summer, when we saw them every day. On warm evenings we would walk to their house and sit on their front steps sipping wine, or they would walk to our place and sit with us on the screen porch enjoying what passed for craft beer in those days (Sierra

Nevada and Sam Adams). More than once we walked them back to their house, or they walked us back to ours.

Diane and I had settled into the knowledge that we were a couple with only a small circle of friends. (*She's a strong flavor*, my father had said of Diane.) Paul and Athena were at the center of our circle. The arrangement suited Paul and me - we were fellow lieutenants with the even keeled dispositions of an engineer and a math major - but for Diane and Athena the connection was more electric. They were both brilliant, opinionated, argumentative and sarcastic. They could have just as easily been arch enemies if one chromosome or quark had been toggled, but as it was they adored each other and piled fuel onto one another's fires.

As the minivan neared Paul and Athena's home - the very same bungalow, now paid off and worth multiples of their original price - I tugged the earbud from Meagan's ear, waking her.

"Stopdad," she slurred.

"Rise and shine," I chirped. "We're less than a minute away from Uncle Papa and Aunt Athena's." We had asked Paul and Athena to be godparents to Meagan and they had agreed with enthusiasm. Diane, as a God-curious pagan, was indifferent to their godparent status but liked the *aunt* and *uncle* monikers.

Meagan raised her seat, arched her back, opened her eyes wide and blinked. "How long have I been asleep?" she asked.

"At least an hour," I replied. I handed her earbud back to her and she put them away, saving me the effort of telling her to do so.

"Will Chloe be there?" Meagan asked me.

Chloe was Paul and Athena's only child. She came along after they had been married four years, which was four years before Jimmy. Chloe was pure Papadopoulus: gawky, oily, enthusiastic, precocious. She had graduated from UVA in three years, worked at NIH in Maryland for a couple years, and is now in medical school in the Bronx at Albert Einstein.

"I don't think so," I told Meagan. "I think she's in New York. We'll ask."

I parked on the curb in front of Paul and Athena's house, then stepped out stiffly, rolling my shoulders and rotating my neck. The front door opened and two enormous Newfoundlands bounded out and charged us, a combined three hundred pounds of lumbering, slobbering canine.

Paul appeared on the porch and shouted, "Larry! Moe! Get back here!"

I leapt back into the minivan and closed the driver's door with one Mississippi to spare before Larry (I think) reached me. He stood on his hind legs and placed his baseball mitt paws on the window, his wide red tongue lolling from the side of his mouth. Moe, in a coordinated movement, ran to Meagan's side of the minivan. She did not climb back in like I did, but knelt and embraced Moe, letting him lick her cheek and almost topple her over.

In an instant Paul was at my door subduing Larry onto all fours and grinning through my window, which was still rolled up. There was a zit on the side of his nose, a waxing gibbous. I rolled my window down.

"Heeeyyyyy," said Paul jubilantly. "I think Moe's even happier to see you than I am!" (Evidently it hadn't been Larry.)

"Howdy, Colonel Papa," I replied with a smile. "You're going to have to pay for a car wash to get this slobber off."

Paul let out a belly laugh.

Paul, Meagan and I made our way into the house, squeezing alongside the exuberant dogs through the front door. Athena appeared, embraced us vigorously, and led us into her bright and chaotic kitchen.

I noticed on the refrigerator a photo of a newfie, Curly, recently deceased. Athena held Meagan by the shoulders and was speaking in conspiratorial tones. Paul proffered a frosty mug of beer.

I pointed to the picture on the refrigerator and said to Paul, "I sure am sorry about Curly. Things must not be the same around here."

"No," he admitted, casting his look down. "The stooges just aren't the same."

We were silent for a moment. Then I offered, "Papa, there actually was a fourth stooge, you know. Shemp."

Paul's face livened. "*You're* telling *me* about the stooges?" he roared. "Shemp was one of the original three. Curly came later when Shemp left to pursue a solo career."

"That's what the best ones always do!" I said. We clinked our mugs.

"So, is there a puppy Shemp in your future?" I asked.

Paul rolled his eyes and gave me a maniacal look, his trademark since Second Lieutenant days. "Ask Athena."

* * *

A perfect evening followed. Paul grilled salmon and we ate on their shaded back deck. The evening was mercifully cool for August in DC. Plates were cleared, another bottle of wine was opened. The conversation wandered with digressions on digressions until we were delightfully lost. It has always been like this with Paul and Athena, both of them (and especially Diane) turning conversation into tackle football. I was proud of Meagan, who took to the sport with ease that would have made her mother proud. I played my usual role as referee, largely silent, just like the slumbering beasts spread at our feet on the deck, but occasionally forced to call out unnecessary roughness or targeting (at which the players jeered).

As dusk fell, we became aware of the pulsing throb of cicadas that filled the night air, returned from exile. The last time they appeared, Diane and l lived only a few blocks away and Meagan was one, Jimmy four.

I paused to ask myself, *How many cicada cycles will I get?*

At last we said goodnight, Meagan in Chloe's room and me in the guest room. I cracked the window open and fell asleep to the eerie rhythmic lullaby.

On Thursday morning Meagan, Athena and I walked the dogs through the neighborhood. We made our way to Garfield Street, to the house Diane and I had purchased after I left the Air Force and we decided to put down roots here. It was a red and white Sears Roebuck house, charming when we bought it and more so now.

"Do you remember living here?" Athena asked Meagan.

"A little," Meagan replied. "I remember it more from visiting after we moved." Meagan had been five when we left Arlington and moved to Lake Cooke.

We called it the red and white house. Diane and I spent our thirties here, burrowing into our careers, mine broadening, hers narrowing. In 2000 we brought Jimmy home from Fairfax Hospital, and Meagan followed two and half years later. We sold the place in early 2008 a few months before the collateral debt obligation shit hit the fan and walked away with almost three quarters of a million dollars in equity. In this way, and others, Virginia had been good to us.

When we returned to Paul and Athena's house, Meagan staged a TikTok video. It began with a close up of her in scorpion pose - balanced on one foot and canted forward, her arms extended over and behind her head to grasp her other foot midair - followed by a slow zoom out that revealed Larry and Moe lounging indifferently beneath her. I asked Meagan later in the car if she planned to go after dog food companies for sponsorships. "Nodad," she said.

After a sensible lunch with Paul and Athena, we reloaded the minivan, hugged Paul and Athena with glorious disregard for social distance, and rolled down Jackson Street as they watched from their curb holding Larry and Moe by belt sized collars.

We made it to Providence in reasonable time, Meagan at the wheel (to gain some Yankee driving experience) and me placing a few option trades from my iPhone. I let Meagan choose our road trip music, which was alternative chill punctuated with gratuitous f-bombs. I stopped commenting on it after a while and attempted some chill of my own.

We arrived in Providence late afternoon, checked into the Marriott where I now find myself, showered and dressed, sitting in the lone armchair in artificial darkness, waiting to wake Meagan. Today we stage our assault on Boston with reinforcement from Jimmy, who is taking the day off work.

I stand quietly, move toward the window, and grasp the curtains at the seam where they meet. Like a marathon runner crossing the finish line in triumph, I spread my arms wide and white sun instantly fills our room.

26.

MILLENNIUM | 1999

DIANE AND I SPENT THE LAST WEEK OF THE MILLENNIUM IN A stuccoed salmon colored mansion built into a bluff on the north side of Saint Croix. Our bedroom was large with a tile floor cool to the touch and a small private mirador overlooking the sparkling Caribbean Sea. I had rented the home more than a year earlier when Y2K fears were at their peak and rental rates were enticing. Paul and Athena joined us (without Chloe, who was three and welcomed the new year with her grandparents) along with my brother Brian and his girlfriend at the time, a hardbody yoga instructor named K'arma.

Diane had been pushing for Egypt, hoping to climb a pyramid, slip away from the guided tour, and sleep on a stone ledge somewhere near the top. She told me she wanted to greet the rising sun of the new millennium like the Da Vinci man, buck naked with hands at two and ten. I did enough research to convince myself, and a reluctant Diane, that we'd probably spend Millennium Eve in a foul Egyptian jail cell eating camel stew if we attempted this, though she was welcome to practice the pose around our house any time she liked.

I made the case that Saint Croix was one time zone to the east of Eastern Standard Time, which meant we could celebrate twice: first on Saint

Croix time and then again when the ball dropped in New York. Diane was excited by the prospect of welcoming the new millennium under Caribbean starlight, and then a few hours later greeting the rising sun an hour ahead of the unwashed masses on the east coast.

We were each ready for a new decade in our own way. I was thirty-four and Diane was thirty-two. My career had been gliding along with unexpected ease, doors opening as I neared them. I left the Air Force after my four year commitment (I gave them one extra day as an act of good citizenship and poor calendar skills) and stumbled into an engineering and design job at a tiny fiber company, American Fiber Network, headquartered on K Street in DC. An Air Force major I had known casually at the Pentagon had left mid-career the year before to join AFN. When word got out that I was trading in polyester blue for khakis and button downs, he encouraged me to apply. I didn't know anything about fiber optics or what they were used for, but I had a degree in math that wasn't too dusty and they needed to bulk up their network design team. The fact that I could also do some rudimentary computer programming clinched the deal. In the land of the blind, the one eyed man is king. By the time I stepped foot on Saint Croix, eight years into the job, I was head of engineering, a direct report to the CEO, and in possession of stock options that had me dreaming about a Porsche 911.

The same decade had been crueler to Diane. While I had doors swinging open, she encountered doors locked and unanswered, sometimes hearing the slide-click of deadbolts being turned from inside. She stayed on at State in Global Analysis hoping that Lawrence Eagleburger would retire or drop dead, but instead he was elevated to *acting* Secretary of State when James Baker left to run George H.W.'s reelection campaign.

"I'm screwed," Diane told me when she heard the news of Eagleburger's interim appointment.

"Come on, Diane," I said. "Do you think that guy has a personal vendetta against you? I doubt he even remembers you."

"Then explain why I can't get a single department head to interview me," she retorted.

I was silent. This was the sound of deadbolts turning.

"He's such a narcissistic ass," she went on. "Did you know he has three sons and they're all named Larry Eagleburger?"

"You're kidding," I said.

"Nope. Look it up." I did, later, and it's true. (They have different middle names.)

Diane hunkered down in Global Analysis, certain that Eagleburger was a short timer. She was right, sort of. He was elevated to *actual* Secretary of State a few months later by George H.W., but served as lame duck until Clinton was inaugurated two months later. Diane was elated to have a Dem in office and she was swept up in Bill Clinton euphoria, so it made sense for her to remain at State and see if the new administration would afford her the opportunity to move upstairs (to the ground floor).

I had left the Air Force six months earlier, and even though my civilian prospects were bright, it didn't feel prudent for Diane to leave her job, too. So she stayed, and suffered. Her work in Global Analysis was painstaking and thorough. Nightly she would tell me about new data sources she had discovered that changed basic assumptions on foreign policy. Often she would find mistakes in the data others in her office had entered into the databases. But around the office she was a scold, drawing attention to the mistakes of others during staff meetings, trumpeting her own successes too vociferously. Her performance reviews became more lopsided each year, with high marks for knowledge and accuracy, and irrecoverably low marks for teamwork and communication. I knew from my Air Force days that a B+ on a performance review spelled doom. When Diane showed me her reviews I saw career suicide where she saw only ignorant reviewers.

Christopher Warren, the next Secretary of State, did not come to Diane's rescue (nor ever visited Global Analysis as far as I knew), despite Diane's fervent hopes that her work would be noticed. In the middle of

Clinton's first term we decided to buy a house in the neighborhood where we were renting. I had quietly crossed the six figure income threshold, something that would have been years away had I remained in blue, and home ownership drifted within reach. Diane remained at State to keep our employment history stable and ease the mortgage application process. She was also hopeful that things would be different under Madeleine Albright, who was ushered in for Clinton's second term.

Diane waited and waited for her just deserts, strangely loyal to an organization that had marginalized her. I remember a Japanese movie in college about a dog named Hachi who waited at the train station every afternoon for ten years for the return of his master, who had died. Sometimes I thought Diane was the the State Department's Hachi, but I couldn't bring myself to tell her.

When we moved into the Red and White House, we pulled the goalie and decided to start a family. That gave Diane another reason to stay at State. She could milk maternity leave (so to speak) and then decide whether to stay or go. We applied ourselves vigorously to the plan, but a year, and then two, and then three, yielded no results. We were both shaken, worried about our plumbing, and wondering whether Diane's ectopic pregnancy had wrought silent havoc. And so, when Diane stepped foot onto Saint Croix, she was thirty-two, stuck in a career cul-de-sac, and (we thought) barren as the Sahara.

New Year's Eve 1999 fell on a Friday, which I found cosmically satisfying, not because it was the perfect night for a party, or because it was the Sabbath, but because I just could not let my favorite (so far) millennium end with a whimper on a Wednesday. Diane and I landed at the airport in Christiansted around noon on the Tuesday before New Year's Eve. My brother Brian and his girlfriend K'arma were scheduled to land within the hour. We collected our bags and waited for them so we could ride to the house together. Paul and Athena would arrive the next day.

We had not yet met K'arma. She and Brian had been dating six months, since K'arma dethroned her predecessor, Amy, after a record-breaking four

year reign. Diane liked Brian (everyone did). He's easygoing, offers an affirm-
ing laugh at others' jokes, and plucks the banjo in an ambling, desultory way
that draws people in. She had never cared for Amy, who was doe eyed, gull-
ible and exuded sexuality. I don't think Amy understood a single joke Diane
made, or even realized she was joking. For Diane, whose trademark was her
acerbic wit, Amy was a total write off from the beginning.

We waited in the tiny humid airport watching tribes of pale, blinking
Ohioans and Minnesotans and Mainers wander past, eventually locate their
bags, and then file towards the rental car counters and taxi lines. Half an hour
later a large group arrived, filling the concourse, and Diane and I scanned
the faces for Brian and K'arma.

Suddenly Diane raised her arms and began waving. I followed her gaze
and saw Brian grinning brightly. Next to him was a striking, rail thin woman
with absolutely straight black hair that hung below her waist. She had at least
four inches on him, and he's five-ten or eleven.

"Oh God," Diane said under her breath to me before they were close
enough to hear.

Brian reached us first and K'arma hung back a half step to await
her introduction. Brian wore khaki shorts, Birkenstocks and an alarming
Hawaiian shirt. His banjo case was strapped across his back. Diane opened
her arms and embraced Brian, kissing him on the cheek. I made eye contact
with K'arma and gave a brief smile before Diane released Brian. He and I
shook hands, then leaned into a hug with vigorous back slapping.

"Guys, this is K'arma," Brian said, stepping back to enlarge our circle.

I extended my hand to her. "It's great to finally meet you," I said.

"So you're Jack," she said airily. "Nice to meet you, too," and after a
short pause added, "Peace."

"Peace," I replied, though I had never said that before in a greeting.

Diane leaned in. "Hi K'arma, I'm Diane." She pronounced K'arma with
two syllables, *kuh-arma*.

"It's so nice to meet you, Diane," said K'arma. "Brian adores you. My name is K'arma, pronounced like *karma*."

"Oh, I'm sorry, " said Diane. "Usually an apostrophe means there are letters missing."

K'arma looked puzzled and my early warning radar activated.

"You know," Diane said. "Like *can't* means *can not* and *don't* means *do not*. Is there supposed to be a letter between the *K* and the *a* in your name?"

The faintest sneer appeared on K'arma's face. Her extraordinary height, especially in relation to Diane who was eye level with her nipples, gave K'arma a natural aloofness which she employed now, looking ahead over Diane's head. "No," she said calmly. "Just *karma*."

An awkwardness rose within me. This was vintage Diane, to draw first blood, especially from an attractive female newcomer.

Brian rescued us with a boisterous laugh. He stepped forward in the direction of baggage claim, put his arm around Diane's shoulder and said, "This way *Duh-iane*." K'arma and I followed.

The ride to our house on the bluff was peaceful enough, and Brian and K'arma marveled at the opulent limestone staircase, the breezy foyer and the spectacular views from every room. They chose the bedroom on the first level, directly below ours, with French doors that opened onto the pool.

"This is magnificent," said K'arma. "I'll do yoga by the pool every morning."

Diane looked at me and rolled her eyes. She was not the yoga type.

Brian was two years younger than me, more popular and probably smarter, but he lacked ambition, maybe because I had absorbed all our mother's womb had to offer. When I went to Davidson on an ROTC scholarship, Brian called me a *dreamchaser*. When I left the Air Force to work at the fiber company he said I was a *climber*. Brian went to UNC Greensboro and graduated in five years with a degree in cartography.

"I didn't know you were so interested in maps," I said when he declared his major.

"I'm not," he shrugged.

After graduation he landed a job in pharmaceutical sales and within six months was pulling in twice what I made as a First Lieutenant. He was a natural for sales, cheerful and chatty. He quickly learned the doctors' lunch preferences and dietary restrictions, and had lunch delivered twice each month alongside his drug samples. Brian faithfully over ordered, ensuring there would be enough food for the front desk and staff. He made a name for himself quickly, and a few years later he was recruited by Pfizer to become one of the first Viagra reps in the Carolinas. The little blue pill put Brian in a BMW convertible on his thirtieth birthday and then into a million dollar home on his thirty-second. A map maker with no ambition done good.

The graph of Brian's love life was a lot of dots in the *fun quadrant*, whereas mine was basically one dot in the *serious meet-the-parents quadrant*. Girls gravitated toward Brian in every setting and there always seems to be room for one more, like clowns in a Volkswagen. When he danced at parties it was with three or four girls, or more, and he kept them all gyrating and grinding. Sitting around campfires, which we did a lot in our high school and college years, Brian ruled the night with his twangy banjo. He had a way of making eye contact with people while he played that made each of them feel like they were the only other person there.

More than anything else, Brian was a rare natural listener. He didn't have the need to speak (as Diane did) and he was content to let others carry on. If there was a pause in conversation, he allowed it to linger, and in his presence the quiet could be comfortable. He nodded attentively and would almost always pose a question to the speaker that would invite more enlightenment, detail and confession. I learned from Brian by watching him in action, and I admit to trying to channel his style.

There were times, including the very moment on the veranda in Saint Croix where we sat drinking Red Stripes together, that I wondered if Brian lacked an attachment gene. Everyone loved him because he presented an agreeable blank canvas, but for him dating was crowd surfing, elevated by adoring hands, gliding from person to person. Amy had not struck Diane or me, or my parents for that matter, as *the one*, but she had shattered previous dating records on their second anniversary and we started to treat her like family. Now we knew she was just another raised hand in the crowd, lofting him along.

I wondered if the little blue pill had anything to do with Brian upgrading from Amy to K'arma. Not because he himself needed the assistance, though I know he tried a few samples (so did I), but because he spent every single work day and God knows how many dinners and parties talking in his particularly effective way about erections.

"So where the hell is Saint Croix anyway?" Brian asked me on the veranda.

"I'm not really sure," I said. "We need to ask a cartographer."

* * *

The next morning I woke before seven, the sky pale blue outside our bedroom window. Diane was sleeping heavily. I pulled the sheets back gently and stepped onto the tile floor. From our window I saw the slate sea, calm and flat at this hour. I came closer to the window, drawing into view the grounds around our house and the spa on the far side of our pool deck, perched on the steep slope of the bluff. At that moment, K'arma appeared from her room below ours and walked languidly onto the pool deck. She was nude, shaved smooth, and tan as peanut butter. I watched her unroll her yoga mat on the pool deck, face the yellow glow to the east with a hands-to-heart gesture, and then drop into a graceful and revealing downward dog.

Diane stirred in the bed behind me, "How's the day look?" she asked.

"Glorious," I replied, smiling to myself as I crawled back into bed.

Paul and Athena arrived by taxi at noon and gaped at the house and grounds as we had. Brian knew Paul and Athena from his visits to Arlington. He introduced K'arma with a flourish as she stood by regally, and Paul took her hand warmly. I saw Athena glance at Diane and receive the tiniest smirk in reply. The two of them were soul sisters and could communicate an encyclopedia of emotional content in a single blink.

"Lovely to meet you, K'arma," said Athena, smiling. I knew *lovely* was the kiss of death. "Have you enjoyed Saint Croix so far?"

K'arma spoke with her eyelids half closed. "I love it here, the warm breeze, the sunrise." She paused, "I practiced yoga by the pool this morning as the sun rose. You must join me tomorrow morning."

"I don't know," said Athena. "I could try. I've never gotten past child's pose."

"I could give a class," said K'arma. "I'm a part time instructor." She looked around at the group. "Who wants to practice yoga with me in the morning? Seven o'clock."

"I don't have the right kind of clothes," I said, a private joke to myself.

"Don't be silly," K'arma replied. "You can wear anything."

"Okay, I'm in," I said, raising my hand.

"Me too," said Brian.

"Count me in, too," said Paul.

Diane folded her arms and Athena put her hand on her hips. "We'll see," said Athena.

Brian had taken my cartography quip to heart and planned an afternoon excursion for us. The first stop was Cheeseburgers in Paradise, a shantytown of tents and Quonset huts arranged around a central kitchen where thick handmade burgers were burned crisp and topped with American cheese, grilled onions, and mayonnaise. We found an empty picnic table and ordered a round of the island's most famous libation, the painkiller, made with Cruzan 151, tropical juices and a dusting of nutmeg.

When the drinks arrived, Paul slapped the table loudly and proclaimed, "This really is paradise!" which led to a round of toasts, cheers, and proclamations about the coming millennium.

Our server was a wiry Rastaman with mangey dreadlocks and a broad toothy smile. "What can I getcha, mon?" he asked.

"Are there any vegetarian options?" asked K'arma.

The waiter arched an eyebrow. "You mean vegetable toppings, Luv?" he asked.

"No," said K'arma with a hint of disdain. "I don't eat burgers."

The Rastaman was dumbfounded. "This here be Cheeseburgers in Paradise, luv."

K'arma glowered while he looked at her quizzically.

"Why don't you just get fries?" offered Brian, the peacemaker.

"Are they cooked in lard?" K'arma asked the server.

"Oh no, madam," he said. "Day be deep fried."

K'arma rolled her eyes. "Fine," she said, "an order of fries."

The rest of us ordered burgers, driven half mad by the smell of smoke pouring off the grills, along with another round of painkillers. The Cruzan rum was our best chance to transcend the increasingly awkward group dynamic, in which Diane and Athena were a combo, the three guys were a clique, and K'arma stood alone. At least she drank, and with zeal, and that loosened her up enough to keep lunch enjoyable. She ate a prodigious amount of fries.

The next stop on Brian's itinerary was a jungle bar called the Domino Club. Nestled in a rainforest and accessed by a washer board gravel road, it made Cheesburgers look like haut cuisine. There were three hand hewn buildings, open air with thatched roofs, two of which were bars serving only painkillers and a local canned lager. The third structure was a sty housing two filthy five-hundred pound pigs. We went to the bar first, where Brian ordered a round of painkillers and a six pack of beer.

"Why bother with the beer, Brian?" Paul aked.

"The pigs can't have painkillers," Brian replied.

Paul hesitated. "But they *can* have beer?" he asked.

Brian flashed a winsome grin and said to us, "Come with me." This was Brian at his best, a showman with an audience.

We followed him to the sty and as we neared, one of the pigs, Buster, stood on his hind legs and draped his front feet over the top of a wooden gate. He jutted his snout into the air in a rooting motion and snorted, eyeing Brian and the beers.

"I think this is how it's done," said Brian. He held an unopened beer can by the bottom with two fingers, stretched out his arm, and gingerly approached Buster. In a flash the enormous pig snatched the can from Brian's hand, clenched it in its jaws, and tipped its head back to drain the beer. In less than two seconds the beer was gone and the mangled can fell to the ground among a pile of others inside the sty.

Diane and K'arma stood in stunned silence, repulsed, but Athena was gleeful and said, "I want to do the next one."

Brian handed her a beer can and she approached the sty as he had. This time Buster's companion, Miss Piggy, rose for the treat. Athena let out a thrilled shriek when Miss Piggy plucked the beer from her fingers and drained it. Athena hopped back to our group in a single deft motion.

"Do those pigs get drunk?" K'arma asked warily.

"Absolutely not," said Brian.

"Uh huh," said Diane, "and neither do we! Another round anyone?"

* * *

We rolled back to the house in a large Jeep taxi late in the afternoon. I felt like a fried egg, buzzed, burned and salty. We all plunged into the pool, which was inexplicably cold, and then dispersed to napping hideaways around the house.

I was up early again on Thursday, not specifically to see K'arma's nude form in yoga poses, but certainly open to the possibility. I pulled on gym shorts and a tee shirt and padded out to the pool deck for my first ever yoga lesson. No one else was there, so I stretched and watched the sky slowly lighten.

The prior evening had been a bust. I had napped fitfully on a chaise lounge near the pool until eight in the evening. I woke with a headache and a gnawing hunger, and found Diane and Athena talking in the kitchen, drinking water and nursing their own painkiller aftereffects. I roused Brian from his drooling nap on one of the couches and we watched a few quarters of the Peach Bowl. Paul and K'arma made no appearance at all. It was a pity to waste a great island night, but we had thoroughly overdone it in the afternoon with painkillers and pigs, and it was probably best that we had a recovery night before Friday.

I heard the door to Brian and K'arma's room open and I turned to see K'arma's stately figure wrapped in a white bath towel.

"Morning," I said in a hoarse whisper.

She mouthed a silent reply, *morning*.

"Is Brian coming?" I asked.

K'arma shook her head. "Still sleeping."

I thought Paul, with his boundless energy, might post for the occasion.

"Shall we begin?" asked K'arma.

A wave of intimidation came over me. I knew in a moment she would drop her robe. It would be only the two of us, K'arma silky and naked and me paralyzed by involuntary mental adultery and wondering if yoga protocol required me to remove my own clothes. The situation wasn't eased by the knowledge that we were on full display to everyone else in the house, and on top of that, I had grave doubts about my ability to perform a single yoga pose.

"Be gentle," I said grinning. "I'm a yoga virgin." I regretted it the moment I said it, but the sex lobe of my brain had hijacked the metaphor lobe.

"Do you have a mat?" she asked, nearing me.

"No." I said meekly. I didn't travel with one, unlike K'arma.

"You can use my towel," she said, removing it in a fluid motion.

I turned my face away, uneasy with her frank nudity, but an instant later I faced her and saw she was wearing a two piece strapless bathing suit. Mercy and disappointment, an uncommon combination, washed over me.

"We'll begin in child's pose," she said, and I modeled her pose (the only one I knew). We held the pose in silence for a full minute, allowing blood to flow into our morning muscles. As I relaxed, I felt an unexpected gratitude toward K'arma. She was detached, otherworldly, but also generous and non-judgemental.

Just as I began to enter a proper yoga state of mind, I heard a door open onto a balcony above us and an exuberant Paul shouted down to us, "Who's ready for a painkiller?"

Thursday proved to be another debauch. Cartography Brian led an expedition to the Cruzan rum distillery where samples were free and generous, and then to a series of beaches and tiki bars. On the drive home we bought an enormous whole salmon from fishermen in a battered truck parked on the side of the road that led to our house. We managed to clean and grill the magnificent fish for dinner, washing it down with painkillers made from the half dozen bottles of Cruzan rum we bought at the distillery.

It was a wonderful boisterous evening with drunken charades and an attempt at Trivial Pursuit, which we found in a cabinet at the house. We had played many cutthroat rounds with Paul and Athena over the years, and Diane was the formidable champion. On this night we dispensed with the board and pieces and just passed around the box of questions as we sat by the pool. Paul suggested a new variant, Strip Trivial Pursuit, which I wholeheartedly supported, but the ladies shouted it down. Instead, every wrong answer was punished with a plunge in the icy pool.

After half an hour, only Diane was bone dry. We had each missed at least one question, but K'arma had missed every single question that came her way. Brian, ever attentive, turned on the spa and modified the punishment to a plunge in it rather than the pool. Soon we were all giving wrong answers on purpose and one by one we filled the large hot tub.

Midnight crept around and we were a tangle of drunken arms and legs in the hot tub, shouting over one another about politics, New Year's resolutions, and Y2K.

Suddenly Brian stood, looked around, and asked, "Where's K'arma?"

I hadn't seen her leave. We were all here in the hot tub together, but I couldn't remember how long it had been since I had actually been aware of her. We all felt the same way. She was here - with us - yet somehow not memorable at all.

Athena finally spoke. "I remember her sitting on the edge, right there." She pointed to the side of the hot tub that bordered our steeply sloping property, dense with tall tropical landscaping.

Brain leaned over the ledge and peered into the darkness. "It drops off really fast," he said. His voice was worried.

I turned off the bubbles and suddenly we were in silence.

"Karm?" Brian called down the slope. "K'arma, are you there?"

For a long moment there was silence. Then, faintly, we heard a rustle of leaves and branches. "Brian?" came K'arma's halting voice. "I'm down here."

We all leapt from the spa and Brian, Paul and I made our way through the back fence and down around behind the spa. We found K'arma standing barefoot on the uneven ground. She seemed OK, but was quiet and passive. We led her gently up the hill and back onto the pool deck.

"What happened?" asked Brian, worried.

"I fell, I guess," said K'arma.

"How long were you down there?" Paul asked.

"I'm not sure," she replied. "A while."

"Karm, why didn't you call for help?" asked Brian.

"I don't know," K'arma replied, her voice trailing off.

We disbanded, shaken, and went to our rooms. Diane and I showered together in the large dual head shower in our en suite. While I was washing her back Diane tilted her head and asked, "Is Brian really serious about *kuh arma*?"

"It'd be hard to believe," I replied.

"She's a total airhead," said Diane.

We collapsed into bed for a night of chaste sleep, the last of the millennium.

Friday morning we slept late, and if K'arma had practiced yoga at sunrise, clothed or otherwise, I wouldn't know. We made it a lazy day, scattering ourselves around the house and pool, and taking in a few Bowl games. (We were pulling for the Hokies, but they wouldn't play until the national championship a few days later.)

After lunch Brian and I took a walk, following the road further up the bluff toward the few homes that overlooked ours. The road was poorly graded and the walk became strenuous almost immediately. We lean forward into our strides.

"Is K'arma okay?" I asked. "She's been quiet."

Brian took a few steps to collect his breath, then said, "She's fine." Another breath. "She can be spacey sometimes."

"How long do you think she would've stayed down there if we hadn't looked for her?" I asked.

"Dunno. She gets confused."

We walked along in silence, broad views of the sea opening beneath us.

"So, are you guys serious?" I asked.

Brian looked at me, then turned to face the road. "No," he said.

Then he continued, " A few weeks ago we were out to dinner. She went to the bathroom and was gone a long time." He took a few labored breaths. "After a while I started looking around the restaurant. I saw her sitting in the booth directly behind me, by herself."

"Huh?" I asked.

"Jack, she got lost in a restaurant."

I took a few strides, considering this. "Brian, did you tell me she went to UNCG?"

"Fuckoff," he said, grinning.

We came to the end of the road, which was also the beginning of the driveway to the house on the summit of the bluff. The house was out of view but undoubtedly magnificent.

"After the restaurant episode I knew we had no future. I just didn't want to be the guy who dumped his girlfriend a few days before the greatest party on earth." Silence for a moment. "Anyway, I think she knows, and she's okay with it. She's not clingy."

We began the walk back downhill. "Need a painkiller?" I asked.

* * *

The six of us stood together at sunset on the west facing balcony upstairs. As the orange sun melted into the Caribbean, we clinked our wine glasses (mine containing painkiller) and toasted the receding year. That night, at Diane's insistence, the ladies wore party dresses and the men wore slacks and blazers. We were not going to slouch into the new millennium in flip flops and leis.

At ten we took pictures in every combination and permutation possible with six people. In one we lined up from tallest (K'arma) to shortest (Diane), and I think the separation suited them. For our couples shot, Diane insisted on a full blown ballroom dance dip, her leg kicked up in a serious thigh reveal and her face turned to the camera in a gleeful open mouth smile.

That night we reveled at the Buccaneer Hotel, which Diane had discovered, researched and booked months earlier. Its massive ballroom and terrace glittered with tinsel and lights, and we danced to the carefree notes of steel drums and imbibed the drinks offered by passing waiters. A few minutes before midnight the band summoned everyone to the center of the ballroom for the ersatz ball drop, but Diane corralled us away from the crowd and onto the terrace, which had emptied. We stood together at the balustrades overlooking the ocean, arms locked and swaying slowly. From the ballroom we heard jovial voices counting down, and at the stroke of midnight the six of us circled into a chaotic group hug, followed by indiscriminate kissing, and then at last paired off as couples.

"Happy new millennium," I said to Diane.

She kissed me and said, "Technically the new millennium doesn't start for another year."

"Why did I have to marry the captain of the debate team?" I replied.

We made it back to the house in time to watch the ball drop in New York and celebrate again. This second New Year's we celebrated in sweatpants and pajamas around a television in the main living room. As Dick Clark heralded the new year and two million people crowded the streets of New York, I felt a pang of melancholy and remembered the lyrics of a Peggy Lee song that amused me as a child. *Is that all there is?*

That night Diane and I made love, as I'm sure the other couples did too, and in the wee hours of the new millennium, unknown to us at the time, a new soul arrived in our family.

27.

SURPRISE | 2020

THE BACK HALF OF AUGUST LAST YEAR WAS MY FIRST TASTE OF the new normal, with Jimmy back in college and Meagan in her senior year at high school. The night before he left, Jimmy showed me how to run his options trading software. I wasn't sure I'd use it.

"Can you turn off the actual trading?" I asked. "I'd like to know what it recommends, but I'd rather make the trades myself."

"Of course," Jimmy replied. "I use it that way, too." He showed me a checkbox in the *Settings* menu called *Enable Trade Execution* and he unchecked it.

"Thanks," I said smiling. "Not that I don't trust your code."

"Oh by the way," Jimmy said. "My code has a name."

I arched an eyebrow. "Yes?"

"I call it *Lion Oil*," he said.

"What does that mean?" I asked.

Jimmy smiled. "It's as powerful as a lion and as slick as oil."

"That's a little weird," I replied.

"And," he continued dramatically, "it's a palindrome."

I thought about this for a second and grinned. "I like how your mind works," I said.

On Saturday morning Jimmy left to start his sophomore year after the abrupt departure in March. Classes would be virtual, he explained to me, and he'd be attending from the comfort of a room in his fraternity house until further notice. He caught a ride with a shaggy and tatted boy he knew from Scouts who was headed to Boston in an avocado green VW bus for his fifth (I think) year at BU.

On Monday I was up at six to make Meagan a veggie omelet and a lovingly sectioned grapefruit, as Diane had done every year on the first day of school. Meagan breezed into the kitchen at twenty past in oversized sweatpants and a wrinkled Wofford College tee shirt from Goodwill. *Homeless chic.*

"I think you've overdressed," I said, smiling at her.

"Not for an all day Zoom call," she replied. "And besides, most of my friends probably won't even get out of bed for class."

I winced, sad that Meagan would have to spend her senior year in her bedroom, online.

She sat at the counter bar and devoured the omelet. She pushed her empty plate across the countertop toward me so I could add it to the pile of dishes to be washed later.

"Eat some pamplemousse, sweetie," I said.

"I'm full, Dad," she replied. "And I want to fix my hair before class starts."

I nodded and said, "You gotta look good for the webcam."

Megan pushed her barstool back and began to slide off.

"Hang on," I said. "First day of school picture." I grinned and snapped a picture with my iPhone.

She walked around the island to examine the picture on my screen. "Gross," she said.

I thought she looked adorable.

Meagan began to walk from the kitchen to the back staircase leading to her room.

"I'm going to eat your pamplemousse," I called after her.

"Fine," she said, disappearing.

I stood quietly for a moment, then bagged the grapefruit, which I could not eat anyway since it was a fasting day.

Monday night was the Club board meeting, another part of my new normal, at least for the next nine months. Surprisingly, we had a full house. I had expected more members to be away on vacation, but the lingering effects of the virus and the tentative start of school must have prevailed to keep everyone at home. Nimrod was there, sitting in one of the chairs reserved for visitors and observers. He wore blue hospital scrubs, not because he made rounds at a hospital (he didn't), but because he wanted to make sure everyone knew he was a doctor. He had a small briefcase on his lap.

The primary order of business was the budget, which was shaping up to be fairly miserable. The virus had ravaged our revenue forecast, with virtually every summer event canceled and the Club's two restaurants operating at social distance capacity. It was becoming evident that long hoped for improvements to the golf course would need to wait another year, maybe more, and Aristotle raised the unwelcome notion of a member assessment at the end of the year.

"That's a good way not to get re-elected," Pam commented.

"Ha!" barked Aristotle, "Then let's do it for sure. A ten thousand dollar assessment just before Christmas."

When we reached the point in the agenda for public comments, Nimrod rose and cleared his throat.

"Three minutes," said Siobhan Sorcer, board secretary and enforcer of time limits. Of course, there hadn't been a three minute limit on public comments until Nimrod made it essential.

Nimrod opened his briefcase and withdrew a few sheets of photo paper.

"I need to report six violations of the community standards code," he said officiously.

"First, the Howards on Sailview. They have a garden in their backyard that exceeds the six-by-eight foot dimensions permitted." He slid a large color photo onto the center of the table. The Howards had plowed up at least half of their lakefront backyard to plant a garden. The photo revealed corn stalks five feet tall.

"Second, the Weltons on Sunset Shores have a decommissioned police car in their backyard, and you will see it is literally up on cinder blocks." He paused for effect. "How do you think this affects our property values?" He slid another photo across the table.

"Next up," Nimrod continued, "Cyrus Bolton." He paused for dramatic effect, raising his chin and slowly sweeping the room with his gaze.

Cyrus was a perennial target of Nimrod's, not to mention his immediate next door neighbor. It was long ago established that Cyrus's property was not subject to HOA rules, but Nimrod persisted.

"Mr. Bolton has a seven foot tall Bob's Big Boy statue in his backyard. I can't hazard a guess as to where he obtained it, or why."

This at last did perk the board's interest. Nimrod slid the photo to the center of the table and I picked it up to examine it more closely. "Where did you take this photo, Nimrod?" I asked.

"From my dock," he sniffed.

The photo was shot across a small stretch of water, from Nimrod's dock into Cyrus's backyard. On a spit of land at the rear corner of Cyrus's lot, precisely at the property line he shared with Nimrod, was a large cracked and faded statue of Bob's Big Boy holding a plate with a burger overhead in its right hand. I hadn't seen one in years.

I passed the photo to Rick O'Shea who gave a low whistle. The photo made its way around the table, causing some heads to shake in amusement.

"What's Bob's Big Boy?" asked Brenna.

We all turned to face her, equally amazed that she was so young and we were so old. Pam responded, "Brenna, honey, Shoney's used to have one of these Big Boy statues in front at every location."

Suddenly I was curious to know when the last statue had come down and I made a mental note to Google it later. It must have been in the 90s, but who the hell knows.

Brenna frowned and asked, "What's Shoney's?"

Nimrod cleared his throat again. "May I continue?"

Siobhan nodded gravely. I think she had forgotten to start the timer in the first place.

Nimrod ran through his final three violations, each with photographic evidence. The Warner's dockside flag not taken down at dusk. The Hugland's orange and blue sunshade (not authorized). Three beer kegs strewn across the Zinheiss's backyard.

Nimrod gave a slight nod as he finished, then sat primly as if to say *I rest my case.*

"Thank you, Mr. Nimrod," Pam said. "We'll look into these and send out notices as needed."

I knew that few if any notices would be sent. I also knew that most of these pictures would be in the *Town Herald* on Thursday.

After a few other business items, Pam adjourned the meeting and we rose to leave.

"Anyone want to grab a drink or a nibble downstairs?" Pam asked. The grill downstairs served half price wings on Mondays. I hadn't been in years because of my fasting regimen.

"I could use a drink," said Rick.

"Sorry Pam," I said, "today's a fasting day for me."

She frowned and said, "At least come and sit with us."

"Come on, Jack," Rick echoed.

Meagan was at home, probably doing homework or on her phone. She had already given me a rundown on her first day of online classes before I left for the board meeting.

"Sure," I said. "I can stay for a while."

Brenna collected Nimrod's photos and the single page agendas that had been left behind on the table. She stood by Pam, uncertain where to go.

"Brenna, care to join us?" Pam asked.

"Thanks, I'd love to," she said.

"Are you twenty-one?" Rick asked.

"Of course she is, Rick," said Pam. "Brenna finished *grad school* in May."

"I'm twenty-six," Brenna said, fixing an eye on Rick.

We made our way to the dimly lit bar and grill and the Club's lower level.

"Can we sit outside?" I asked the hostess, mindful of social distancing.

"People have been coming in," she replied. "We're seating at every other booth. It looks like it might storm."

I hadn't noticed, but ominous clouds were rolling in. August in Carolina.

We took a booth near the bar. I slid in first and Rick sat next to me. Brenna and Pam sat opposite us. A server approached almost immediately and Pam, unabashed, ordered thirty-six wings for the table and three different sauces. Chardonnay for Pam and Brenna, Stella for Rick, and water-no-ice for me, Mr. Austere.

Rick opened things up. "What in the hell is Cyrus doing with that statue?"

I shook my head, unable to supply an explanation.

"It must weigh a ton, literally," said Pam. "How could he have even moved it there?"

"He's got more heavy equipment than any person on the lake," I said.

Behind his mobile home Cyrus had a Bobcat front loader, an enormous rusted John Deere tractor with attachments for snow removal and grass cutting, and God only knows how many derelict jetskis and boat trailers. He had rigged a tow hitch to his golf cart and sometimes pulled a small flatbed trailer around the neighborhood piled with scrap he collected from construction sites.

Drinks arrived and Brenna proposed the toast, "To Bob's Big Boy!" Glasses clinked, including my tap water.

"Were they good?" asked Brenna. "The burgers, I mean."

"I would say they were pretty *forgettable*," Rick chimed. "But they were never *bad*, so Shoney's would do in a pinch."

"I liked them," said Pam.

"What about you, Mr. Callany?" Brenna asked. She looked straight at me and held her gaze. I may have detected a playful smirk.

"It's Jack. Please." I said. "Mr. Callany was my dad."

She smiled and continued to hold her gaze.

I added, "I'm with Rick on this one. *Edible but forgettable.*"

The wings arrived and plates covered the table. I moved my modest water to the only remaining unoccupied surface, near the wall. Pam and Rick loaded up, but Brenna took only a plain celery stick and crunched it between her teeth.

In this situation, where I'm at a restaurant with friends on a fasting day, I inevitably do most of the talking because my mouth is not otherwise occupied. Most of the time it's a mini lecture on fasting, since the others regard me as an oddity requiring explanation. I wasn't surprised when Brenna asked, "Why do you fast, Jack?"

It's a topic I can expound on, and which Diane and Meagan had long ago tired of hearing. I offered the abridged version to my companions.

"I started about four years ago," I said. "My pants were getting too tight and I decided to drop a few pounds. Diane had heard about it on NPR and was giving it a try, so I decided to try it too. It really wasn't too hard to fast two days each week. I chose Mondays and Thursdays so I could eat whatever I wanted on the weekends. I lost the weight in less than two months, but by then I had learned about the other health benefits and I decided to keep doing it."

All three were looking at me, chewing, so I went on. "There have been a lot of lab studies in the past few years about the benefits of fasting. Improved immunity, delayed onset of cancer and chronic diseases. In lab tests, anyway, rats lived thirty percent longer when they were on intermittent fasting diets. No serious side effects as long as you drink plenty of water."

"So that's your anti-aging trick, Jack?" asked Pam.

"We'll see about that," I said.

Brenna smiled at me again, "I would say you're very well preserved, Jack."

As she said this, I felt a toe gently brush the inside of my calf beneath the table. Instinctively I pulled my leg back. There wasn't much legroom in the booth, so my leg was pressed against the back of my bench seat.

A moment later I felt the toe again. It was a bare toe. It was Brenna's, and it touched my calf and moved upwards slowly. She was looking directly at me. I reached for my water.

Brenna turned to Pam and asked, "Pam, why does Mr. Nimrod spend so much time on the violations?" Brenna watched Pam, waiting for her to finish chewing, but under the table she resumed the soft caress with her toe. Her question was a decoy to divert attention from the wildfire blazing at our end of the booth.

No one had played footsie with me since college and even that single incident had led nowhere. But here was a very attractive woman only a few years older than Meagan putting me in sexual checkmate in a booth with no escape.

The instant I realized the touch of Brenna's toe was intentional, long dormant corridors in my mind illuminated in blinding light.

My first wave of thoughts: *she's coming onto me, to me! an attractive woman sees me and wants me! I have been invisible so long, a dad, a dad with a dad bod, and this painfully beautiful woman who exudes soft sexuality is choosing me.*

And in an instant these thoughts were overrun: *it can't be, I'm misunderstanding, I'm going to humiliate myself, get away now, shut down, control-alt-delete.*

And then just as quickly my mind formed uninvited images: *Brenna writhing beneath me, her dark hair splayed across a pillow, but her face morphs into Diane's, young Diane's.* I turn my head imperceptibly to clear the thought.

And then finally: *I'm old, this is wrong, I'm almost thirty years older than her, stop, STOP!*

Pam was holding forth on Nimrod. Rick was piling wing bones high on a tiny white dish. I felt Brenna's toe trace its way to my left knee and then inch forward along my thigh to the edge of my khaki shorts. In another second her foot would be in my crotch, which has begun to swell. I took a drink of water and looked at her awkwardly as if to say: *do you have any idea what you're doing?*

"Jack? Earth to Jack." I heard Pam's voice and realized she had been speaking to me. I had been facing her but completely oblivious.

I caught her saying, "... name the boat yet?"

I smiled, trying to appear casual, but my mind was stampeding bulls. "No. Well. Yes." I was stumbling. "We've decided on a name but I haven't had it stenciled on yet."

"Whatcha gonna call her?" asked Rick.

"Um." I stalled. Brenna traced ovals on my thigh with her toe. "Jimmy got the naming rights. He chose 'Open Options.'"

"So you're keeping your options open, Jack?" Brenna said in a tone only I realized was fraught with meaning.

I looked at her for a moment, then turned to Rick. "Not like that, really. It's a play on words with my stock options trading. Jimmy helps with it."

Pam leaned toward Rick, "I sold Gordon's Cobalt to Jack a couple weeks ago."

Rick smiled and said, "Sweet."

At last Brenna withdrew her foot. I didn't realize how shallow my breathing had become until I took a full breath and began to settle down. She turned her attention to the teriyaki wings. Watching her eat one, then two, I realized how much she looked like a child. *What in the hell was going on here?*

"I still haven't been out on the lake," Brenna said casually.

Pam turned in disbelief, "Brenna, you're missing out on the best thing about this area. I'm sure Rick or Jack would take you out any time."

Rick nodded, chewing. I gave a thin smile and nodded.

"Jack, Meagan's a senior in high school right?" asked Pam. "I bet she and Brenna would get along."

Brenna nodded brightly. "Pam, everyone knows Meagan Callany. She's the most famous TikTok'er in the state."

This information hit me like an unpainted speed bump at night. It was surreal that Brenna followed Meagan on TikTok. That meant she had seen the inside of my house. She had seen my hand passing slices of pizza and greasy paper-wrapped cheeseburgers to Meagan in the final frames of her posts.

"What's TikTok?" asked Pam blankly.

"I'll explain when you tell me what Bob's Big Boy is," Brenna teased.

We sat in the booth for another hour and had two more rounds of drinks. For most of the hour, Brenna kept her toes to herself and I began to wonder if I had fantasized the whole thing. But when Pam signed the bill,

I felt her toe again, on my calf, tapping gently. She didn't make eye contact, but she kept tapping until we slid out of the booth.

We made our way to the parking lot, which was still steaming from the thunderstorm that had rolled overhead while we were inside, and said our goodnights. Brenna followed me toward my car as Pam and Rick peeled off in different directions. I hoped fervently that Brenna's car was somewhere near mine in the parking lot. I wasn't ready for anything else.

"I'd love to see the lake sometime, Jack." She said. No mention of Meagan.

I knew that what I said next was critical. Would I open a door, or close one? I took a few steps, then turned to face her.

" I'd like to show it to you," I said. I didn't know I would say this until I actually did.

I was standing by my Tesla. Brenna motioned to a Honda Civic three slots down. "I'm right here," she said. Then she added, "I had fun tonight."

"Me too," I said quietly. I gave a nod and we parted ways.

That night I lay in bed for hours, replaying the evening over and over. The touch of Brenna's bare toe had made me seventeen again, filled me with raging excitement for the possible. I cycled violently between teenage and middle age, unable to rest, horny and guilt ridden.

At one in the morning I walked upstairs to my office and mindlessly opened a browser window. The room was dark and blue light washed over my face. I began typing into the search bar.

From the doorway behind me came Meagan's voice, "What're you working on, Dad?" I was startled and turned to face her.

"Oh, I'm just looking something up," I said. "Shouldn't you be asleep? You have to be up in five hours."

"I know," she replied. "So what're you looking up."

"I'm trying to find out when Shoney's dropped the Bob's Big Boy statue."

"Huh?" Meagan said. She looked profoundly bored.

"I'll explain another time. It's not something the TikTok generation would understand."

"Deep," she said. "Can you meet with me and my guidance counselor on Friday at school, *in person?*"

I checked my calendar. I preferred to be at the computer in the last couple hours before the market closed for the week, but I said, "Sure, honey."

"Good night, Daddy," she said from the door.

"G'night," I replied softly. I could hear her bare feet walking down the hall to her room.

I looked over the search results. 1984. That's the year I graduated from high school. I didn't realize the Big Boy had been gone so long. Brenna must have been born ten years after Bob was decommissioned.

* * *

Wednesday after lunch at my desk I decided to take the kayak over to Cyrus Bolton's place. He's actually closer by water than by asphalt, and it was a pristine silent day in Lake Cooke. I walked onto our dock in running shorts, flip flops, and a tattered Davidson tee shirt that was actual vintage (1987), not faux vintage like they sell in the bookstore now. I rolled the kayak into the water, sat on the side of the dock to steady the vessel with my feet, and then slowly lowered myself into the rear seat. The lake's surface was glassy, broken only by the figure of a duck as if added by a painter with two short strokes as a finishing touch. I pushed off the dock and the kayak glided silently and with surprising speed out into the lake.

I had purchased the two-seater years ago expecting that Diane and I would make this an early morning ritual. I had pictured myself preparing a thermos of hot coffee in the dark dawn and us gliding soundlessly to the center of our cove, or perhaps to one of the heavily treed islands nearby, and drinking coffee at sunrise. That never happened. Diane had gradually cut out coffee after Meagan was born (and in keeping with universal laws of conservation, I had started drinking more). Diane's weight had also become a factor. I could count on one hand the number of times she had been on the kayak. I'm sure she was uncomfortable, pinched, and unsteady. My carefully laid kayak plan was reduced to just me, a solitary figure with a mug of coffee, on a lake painted gold by the morning sun.

Lately I had been using the kayak more often, rediscovering the beauty of silence on water. The Cobalt, and our old bowrider as well, were roaring monsters that shattered the surface of quiet coves and brought distrubed neighbors to the ends of their docks with hands on hips.

I paddled rhythmically into the main channel where I could see two miles across into the next county. In the distance was a sailboat, and beyond it a jetski spewing a rooster tail of water. I passed the tips of two fingers of land, one with a tasteful and pricey Nantucket style home, the other with an older brick ranch, both enjoying panoramic views of the water from sunrise to sunset. I turned into the cove beyond the ranch and followed the line of docks and gazebos. Nimrod's home was nestled in the back of the cove, the vertex of the parabola, and had a commanding view of the main channel.

The far side of Nimrod's lot marked the edge of the developed neighborhood and the outer limit of the homeowner association's jurisdiction. Here curbs and sidewalks ended abruptly and city water and sewer gave way to wells and septic fields. This *terra incognita* was, and had been for many years, the home of Cyrus Bolton.

As I neared Nimrod's home I immediately saw the Bob's Big Boy statue. Cyrus had placed it precisely at the edge of his lot on a picnic table sized peninsula that protruded into the lake. The statue was angled to face the Nimrod's expansive rear terrace, which included a pool and outdoor kitchen. Most of the property line that Nimrod shared with Cyrus was demarcated with a double row of arborvitae that had grown tall and wide in the eight or so years they had been neighbors, but the treeline did not extend to the spit of land where Bob stood grinning cheerfully.

I pulled my kayak alongside Cyrus's decrepit wooden dock and tied it off on a loose cleat. I was happy that I tossed my flip flops into the kayak - walking barefoot on his dock was an invitation for debilitating splinters. Cyrus had no less than five fishing rods on his dock, a few laying on the dock and a few standing in PVC tubes he had nailed to the side of the dock. The old timer was nowhere to be seen.

I reached the end of Cyrus's dock and stepped into the backyard, a private junkyard littered with boat trailers, defunct jetskis, Cyrus's tractors and earth moving equipment and tires in various states of decay. I called out his name, knowing that to accidentally surprise Cyrus on his own property was to invite a shotgun blast. As the first syllable of his name left my mouth, I heard the explosive bloodthirsty roar of a doberman. *Oh shit,* I had completely forgotten that Cyrus had a dog, an "outside dog" who spent day and night guarding Cyrus's detritus.

The dog appeared from nowhere and bounded murderously toward me. Fear flooded my mind and I felt helpless standing at the edge of the yard in flip flops. I may as well have doused myself in A1 steak sauce. As he neared me, the dog leapt into the air, its porcelain teeth bared and ribbons of saliva streaming back across its cheeks. I held my hands out toward the attacking dog, a hopeless but involuntary gesture.

In the final instant before my throat was ripped open and my jugular severed, the doberman slammed to the ground with a violent lurching thud. I realized the dog was chained to an iron stake in the center of the backyard. The chain was long enough for the dog to reach the water, but it had become wrapped around a tractor tire and shortened just enough feet to spare my life.

"Peaches," I heard Cyrus shout from his back porch. "Leave Mr. Callany alone."

The dog stood slowly, dazed, and growled menacingly toward me. I didn't move.

Cyrus walked down from his porch and moved slowly across the obstacles in his yard until he reached Peaches. He extended a hand to rub her neck and scratch behind her ear.

"Good girl," he said tenderly.

Then Cyrus looked at me, sizing me up. "Jack, Peaches here wouldn't hurt a fly." He gave a grin revealing his fragmented yellow teeth.

Peaches was still fixated on me, a low growl building in the back of her throat.

I didn't move any closer to Cyrus or Peaches, and I tried to settle my fear, which I'm sure to Peaches was being broadcast like an amber alert.

"Howdy Cyrus," I waved. "Thought I'd kayak over and say hello."

"I'm shore glad you did, Jack." He replied genially. "Come on up to the porch and I'll getcha beer."

"That'd be great," I said dispiritedly. Between me and the porch was the small matter of a homicidal dog.

Tentatively I approached Cyrus. Peaches stood beside him, alert and emitting a low guttural growl. With his left hand Cyrus pulled the dog's chain and brought her to heel, and he extended his right for a fist bump. When I was close enough I bumped Cyrus's fist and resolved not to make eye contact with the dog. The moment our fists touched, Peaches relaxed. Cyrus released the chain and the dog turned from us and wandered to the shade of the tractor.

I took a seat on a rusted glider on Cyrus's back porch. He slumped into his stained upholstered Lazy Boy, and we saluted one another with cans of Bud Light. The previous summer I brought Cyrus a four pack of Charlotte's finest hazy IPA, a *thank you* for a box of his garden tomatoes and okra he had given us. He eyed the can suspiciously, then popped one open and took a sip. He twisted his face in disgust and said, "This shit tastes like pine resin." True enough, I thought. The next day I brought him a twelve pack of Bud Light, silently ending any attempt to reform him.

"Tell me about the Big Boy statue," I said, motioning toward the corner of his lot.

Cyrus beamed and was about to laugh but instead lurched into a phlegmy bronchial cough. When he recovered he asked, "How 'bout that? Like it?"

"I love it, Cyrus. It's the reason I kayaked over here. You serving burgers?"

"Well," he said. "Yore pal Nimrod cain't stand it."

"I have a sneaking suspicion," I said, "that's exactly why you put it there."

"Damn straight," Cyrus responded. "That motherfucker takes his boat out every afternoon to spy on his neighbors. Peaches dern near jumps out of her skin when he comes slinking back to his dock after dark."

I regarded this comment. "He's looking for community standards violations, Cyrus."

"Then why the hell's he spying on me? I don't live in the HOA and I can do whatever the hell I want."

"You go right on doing what you want," I told Cyrus. "He can't touch you."

"I know that, Jack," Cyrus retorted with a note of irritation. "That's why I put Bob there. I want that a-hole to know I've got eyes on him, too."

I smiled. "I think you put a blemish on his sunset view."

Cyrus howled and this time did not fall into a coughing fit.

"You know what I'ma do with that statue?" Cyrus asked. He leaned towards me and gave a bleary conspiratorial wink.

"Oh God," I said, shaking my head in mock dismay.

"I'm gonna saw off his right hand - the one holding the plate - and replace it with a new hand giving Nimrod the finger."

I could visualize it instantly. "I like it," I said.

"Well," he replied, "Ain't you the one who tole me to train his bird to curse? I learned from the best."

I drained my Bud Light and smiled. "How you planning to make a concrete hand giving the bird?" I asked.

"Come wid me," Cyrus said, rising from his Lazy Boy.

I followed him across the backyard toward one of his ramshackle storage sheds. He opened the door and propped it open with a stone. Inside, on a small table, was a wide wooden log standing on end. It was being carved into the shape of a fist with a fat middle finger sticking straight up.

I marveled. It was a work in progress, but very well done. "You did this, Cyrus?"

"Damn right," he said. "I used to carve totem poles for the Scout camp years ago. I know a thing or two about woodwork."

I put my hands on my hips and studied his creation. I would most definitely be hearing about it at a board meeting one of these days.

"It's done right to scale," Cyrus told me proudly. "I measured the hand on the statue."

"What are you going to do with the hand and plate after you saw them off?" I asked.

"Dunno," he said. "Probably give it to Peaches. You want it?"

"That's mighty generous of you, Cyrus," I said. "But no, give it to Peaches. It'll keep her off my windpipe for a while."

We left the shed and I turned toward his dilapidated dock and my kayak. "Cyrus, I just wanted to give you a heads up that Nimrod did complain to the board and he's probably already sent pictures to the *Town Herald*."

"You think I give a rat's ass?" he replied.

"Nope," I said, shaking my head and smiling.

We shook hands again and I gave a short military salute. "Thanks for the cold one, Old Timer."

"Watch out for the dog," he replied, chuckling as he returned to his porch.

* * *

Friday morning Meagan opened my bedroom door and woke me, "Dad, don't forget. Meeting with Ms. Moonpenny at two-thirty."

"Righto," I said groggily. I heard Meagan's bare footsteps land heavily as she walked back to her bedroom for another day of online classes. I drifted back to sleep.

When the market opened that morning I was determined to close the two positions I had open. Most of the stocks I followed were near all time highs despite ongoing pandemic fears and weak consumer spending. I launched Lion Oil, careful to make sure that *Enable Trade Execution* was unchecked. This way, Jimmy's software would alert me when it uncovered an opportunity to open or close a position, but it would be up to me to pull the trigger.

Next I loped into the kitchen to make an apple and banana smoothie, breaking my Thursday fast. When I came back to the office fifteen minutes later Lion Oil had popped open a dozen windows telling me to close both positions. *Way to go, Jimmy*, I thought. Your software can read my mind.

I logged into my trading account and placed mid-market buy orders to close both naked puts. Within a minute the orders were filled and I was $8,200 better off. And I still had half of my smoothie left. Lion Oil really was slick.

At twenty minutes past two I pulled my Model 3 into one of the many open spaces in the teacher's parking lot at the high school and buzzed my way into the office. Entering, I felt a nostalgic anxiety as I always do in such places. *Reporting to the principal's office* was simply never a good thing (even if he or she was your *pal*, which he or she never was). First come the smells. In my day it was the toxic duplicating fluid from the mimeograph machine that produced stacks of damp reproductions in a disconcerting shade of purple. These days it's a slightly more pleasant blend of Febreeze (laid on too thick) and soy latte from the Circle K up the street. (In the days before remote learning, the smell of hot grease from the cafeteria would permeate the corridors, the tailings of chicken fried steak and fries.). After the smells comes the rest of the office gestalt: the call bell and its accompanying slip of pink paper stating "Press Only Once," hermetically sealed with scotch tape to the countertop; inspirational posters (*You are free to choose but you are not free from the consequences of your choices, I can explain it to you but I can't understand it for you,* and so on); and of course the gum chewing, sometimes cheerful, sometimes insolent, but never helpful front office assistant (I involuntarily think of Caviar Anderson).

I did not see Meagan, who I was hoping would be here waiting for me, nor did I see Ms. Moonpenny. I waited for the present day Caviar to look up from her phone, which she did not do until I tapped the call bell. She turned her head toward me but said nothing.

"I have an appointment with Ms. Moonpenny?" I said-asked.

Caviar returned her gaze to her phone and said, "She's in her office."

I knew where her office was. Diane and I had met with her each year while Jimmy was in high school, and again for the past three years while Meagan was here. I exited the front office, having evidently checked in to their satisfaction, and turned down a narrow corridor leading the administrative offices. Ms. Moonpenny's office was on the right, near the end of the corridor, looking out on the teacher's parking lot. Her door was open. Meagan was already seated, chatting with her. Both were maskless.

I stepped in. "Hi Ms. Moonpenny," I said, unsure if I should extend a hand or an elbow. Pandemic countermeasures were everywhere, and inconsistent. "Jack Callany."

She rose and offered an air elbow. "Hello Mr. Callany, please have a seat."

"I'm so sorry you lost your wife," Ms. Moonpenny said with genuine sadness. I had not met with her since the prior fall. I would have liked to have seen her in the spring to discuss the impact of Diane's death on Meagan's high school experience, but the school closure in March made that and just about everything else impossible.

"I appreciate you saying that, Ms. Moonpenny," I said, seated. "It's been a surreal year."

Ms. Moonpenny did not reply immediately. A quiet filled the room and the word *surreal* lingered over the three of us. It seemed that Ms. Moonpenny's clear blue eyes began to glisten. A year that was meant to invoke perfect vision had become myopic and cloudy.

"How have you and your family been?" I asked after a moment.

"Oh we're fine," she said, and then corrected herself. "Well, I'm by myself. My kids are grown and out of the house. My brother in Georgia had a scare but he tested negative."

I nodded.

"Let's talk about Miss Meagan," Ms. Moonpenny said, back in her professional posture and turning to Meagan. "You have an impressive daughter, Mr. Callany. She's number fifteen in her class of five hundred."

I knew Meagan was making good grades, but I didn't realize she had pulled so far ahead of the pack. She did most of her school work while I was asleep, so I rarely saw her working and admittedly didn't appreciate the extent of her effort.

Meagan spoke. "I'd like to be top ten," she said with excitement.

"That's absolutely possible," Ms. Moonpenny said. "You need to load up on AP classes in the second semester. That's not something a lot of seniors want to do."

"I do," Meagan said with conviction. "I can handle it."

Ms. Moonpenny typed on her keyboard and studied a computer screen. I wondered idly if there was some sort of Lion Oil for guidance counselors. (Note to self - ask Jimmy about this.)

"You could take Calculus BC in the spring," she said, peering over her monitor at Meagan to gauge her reaction. "Dr. Sanders is teaching it."

Diane and I credited Graham Sanders with Jimmy's remarkable blossoming in high school. He was probably the most popular teacher in the school, which is seldom true for math teachers. Kids who hated math started liking it, and kids who were good in math became great.

"Dr. Sanders?" Meagan said with excitement. "I'd love to have him again. Can I register?"

"I've just put you in for it," said Ms. Moonpenny. "You need to make an A in Calc AB this semester. If you don't master AB, you'll struggle in BC and end up hurting your GPA instead of helping it."

"I like AB so far," said Meagan.

Ms. Moonpenny studied her, then asked. "What are you thinking about for college?"

Meagan glanced at me instinctually, then faced Ms. Moonpenny. "Well, Chapel Hill would be great." She paused. "I'm also thinking about Boston College and BU."

Ms. Moonpenny smiled and said, "Ah, you want to follow Jimmy to Boston?" I wish she hadn't brought up Jimmy. Meagan had followed in his academic shadow for a long time. I knew she was every bit as brilliant as he was, just less inclined to pour herself into school. This was *her* year, not a Jimmy retrospective.

"Not really," Meagan said forthrightly. "I just love the New England vibe. And Chapel Hill seems like thirteenth grade for kids at this school."

"Chapel Hill is a great school, Meagan. Less than ten percent of the class will be admitted."

Meagan demurred for a moment. "I know. I shouldn't have said that." She paused. "I just want to do something different. Get a little further away."

Ms. Moonpenny glanced at me with a faint smile on her lips and I retorted with a shrug and a sideways glance at Meagan.

"Good for you, Meagan." Ms Moonpenny said. "We've sent a few students to BC and BU over the years, and you will be an excellent candidate."

Meagan beamed, and Ms. Moonpenny continued, "I don't know if social media helps with college admissions, but you're one of the best known kids in the state right now."

"Ms. Moonpenny," I said with a mock surprise. "Do you follow Meagan on TikTok?"

"I sure do," she replied while smiling at Meagan. "I can't let myself eat those cheeseburgers and hot fudge sundaes, so I get them vicariously from Meagan."

Ms. Moonpenny was soft looking, but slender. I would guess she was in her late forties. Past the age of regular trips to Five Guys.

"I'll tell you a secret," Meagan said to her. "Most people don't know this, but I only take one bite. The bite you see on the video."

Ms. Moonpenny narrowed her eyes and wagged a finger in Meagan's direction.

Meagan continued, "Then Dad eats the rest."

"It's possible," I said meekly. Sometimes I did, if it wasn't a Monday or Thursday.

We spoke for a few more minutes about college essays (get started) and whether or not the SAT would be required. Again, this was a surreal year.

Meagan and I rose to leave and Ms. Moonpenny stood at the same time. "Come see me anytime," she said to Meagan.

Then she approached me and extended her hand. Instinctively I reached to shake it, even though that old protocol was still off limits. When I did, she clasped my hand in both of hers and looked up into my face. "You have a lot to be proud of, Mr. Callany." she said.

"Thank you. Thank you, Ms. Moonpenny," I said.

"Claire," she responded.

"Thank you, Claire." I said quietly.

Meagan and I walked together down the hallway and out the main entrance to the school.

Meagan turned toward the senior parking lot and said, "See ya at home."

"See ya there," I replied. I walked toward the car in the teacher's lot. Unwittingly, I had parked directly in front of Ms. Moonpenny's office. As I got into my car, I could see the back of her head as she studied her computer screen.

28.

WHAT ON THE HELL | 2021

MEAGAN HAS BEEN ASSIGNED TO XAVIER HALL ON THE "UPPER campus" of Boston College at Chestnut Hill. She and I and Jimmy, who has joined us for the afternoon, drive up Comm Ave in our Odyssey and turn onto Hammond Street. In a moment we have exchanged a chaotic Boston thoroughfare for a bosky suburban street bordering the gothic New England campus.

Meagan, who is sitting up front with me, rolls down her window despite the heat to take in the sights and smells of her new home, which she has visited only once before, this past spring for Admitted Students Weekend.

"Dad," Jimmy says from the back seat, "She's like a dog with her head out the window, blowing in the wind."

Instead of replying, Meagan sticks her head and hands out the window and begins panting.

I slow as we approach the campus. I had worried that the crippling sadness of bidding adieu to my youngest child would strike without warning and make me jelly kneed, but the actual feeling gripping me in this moment is a prosaic annoyance that I will not be able to park anywhere near Xavier Hall.

Meagan continues her dog routine through the open window longer than I consider normal. "Jimmy, she's definitely ready for college," I say.

"I wouldn't go that far," he quips.

With one hand I rifle through the info papers stacked on the center console of the minivan. "Meagan, where is the Commonwealth Avenue parking garage?" I ask.

She pulls her head in and immediately begins staring at her phone. "I'll find it, Daddio," she says.

I pull to the curb and rummage through papers until I find an analog map printed in ink. I spot the garage and ease back onto Hammond.

After a few minutes Meagan asks, "What's the name of the parking garage again?"

I grimace. "I'm on it, honey," I said. Analog killed the digital star (again).

The only spaces available at the Comm Ave garage are on the top level, which compounds the problem of the garage being half a mile walk uphill to Xavier Hall. I just don't see this happening. I could have a heart attack (like Diane, only I don't get to play tennis) and collapse on a quad somewhere.

"Plan B," I say, and maneuver back onto College Road with the laughable plan of finding street parking. To my amazement, we find a space on Tudor Road within sight of Xavier Hall.

Move in is well organized and proceeds almost exactly as I had envisioned it. Jimmy and I trudge back and forth from the minivan to Meagan's unairconditioned room on the second floor. Meagan, who has arrived before Aditi, chooses her side of the room, immediately makes her bed, and begins to organize her clothes in the dresser and closet.

Jimmy and I are sitting on the bare mattress of the other bed, recovering for a few minutes before our next and hopefully last trip to the minivan, when Aditi's family appears at the door. Aditi is a wiry flat chested girl with round glasses and shoulder length wavy black hair. She sees Jimmy and me first, sitting sweaty on her bed, and then turns to Meagan. Jimmy and I jump up and I instinctively reach to smooth over the part of the mattress we had been sitting on.

"Meagan?" Aditi asks. She speaks in fast clipped syllables.

"Aditi!" Meagan exclaims. They immediately hug in the way of teen girls where they barely touch.

"Oh my God," Aditi says, "It's happening!"

Meagan beams.

Jimmy and I look at each other. Soon, maybe now, this place will not be for us.

Aditi's parents stand at the door. Her father is a well fed man of forty with a modified mullet haircut and a proud mustache. He wears tight navy slacks and a short sleeve dress shirt with a green and gold windowpane design. I see a bead of sweat at his hairline and I know that in half an hour, after hauling Aditi's boxes and suitcases into this room, he will be drenched. Aditi's mother is an older version of her, stringy in running shorts and a Bitcoin tee shirt.

"Oh hi," she says to me. "I'm Geeta." Her words are crisp and well formed. Her intelligence shines. This is Debaditya." She motions to her husband, who extends a moist hand.

"Debaditya Bhattacharjee," he says with a formal nod. "Nice to meet you."

"Jack Callany," I say with a smile. Then I hesitate, wanting to repeat his name but unable to unravel the syllables.

"Call me DB!" he says with a broad smile.

"That's what everyone calls him," Geeta says.

"Thank you," I say. "Thank you, DB."

We stand in silence, unsure what we can say without embarrassing our daughters. Finally I ask, "DB, do you need some help with Aditi's things?" I have no idea why I ask this.

"Oh that would be extremely, extremely nice of you," he says with obvious relief. "We had to park so far away. The Commonwealth Avenue parking garage."

I glance at Jimmy and he imperceptibly raises an eyebrow.

I agree to walk with DB to the parking garage. Jimmy will make another trip to our van for Meagan's things, and then wait in the van so he can vacate the parking space when DB and I return in his car.

The plan works well, but after DB eases his oversized BMW into our parking space, Jimmy and I need to repark the van. "Put the hazards on, son." I say to him. "I'll walk back to Meagan's room and see what she wants to do next."

DB removes an enormous suitcase from his trunk and I offer to take a box from the backseat. We labor the short distance to Xavier and up the flight of steps. DB struggles, banging the suitcase on each step and wiping his forehead repeatedly with the shoulder of his shirtsleeve. *What on the hell*, I hear him mutter to himself.

When we get to the room, Meagan and Aditi are glued to Meagan's cell phone and I guess they are browsing TikTok together.

"Aditi," I say, "You'll need to take over my job of handing Meagan something greasy to eat at the end of her videos."

Aditi turns to Meagan and says earnestly, "I could do that."

"Hey Meag," I continue. "Jimmy's double parked. We gave our parking space to Mr." I pause for a moment. I will not attempt the last name. "To DB. Would you like us to stay?"

Meagan looks at me blankly.

"Or we can come back in a couple hours and pick you up for dinner."

"Dad," Meagan says to me (I detect a note of condescension), "there's a first year orientation and party tonight."

I realize I am being dismissed and it lands hard. This is the precise moment that Meagan truly leaves home and I become an empty nester (truly empty, unlike empty nester couples). I'm about to pass a major milestone here in Meagan's hot dorm room with this Indian family for an audience. Fortunately Geeta is fussing with Aditi's suitcase, which DB has hoisted onto her mattress.

Meagan and I hold eye contact. She sees the moment for what it is, too, but she's opening a door and I'm closing one. She is filled with excitement for the new and I am a relic of the old.

She steps to me and offers a wide hug, pressing her head into my chest and holding me tight. It's not a teen hug at all, it's a father daughter goodbye hug. Over her head I focus on the framed photo of Diane and me that Meagan has placed on the top of her dresser. We are sitting in the bow of our old boat. Diane is holding a glass of white wine at a careless angle and her lips are parted. She was probably saying something when Meagan snapped the photo. I am next to Diane, leaning back, legs crossed, barefoot, a contentedly buzzed look on my face.

Meagan took that picture hastily three or four summers ago, one of probably a hundred she snapped the same day. How strange that this particular moment, which wasn't especially fraught with meaning or emotion, would become the still frame that watches over her for the next four years, maybe many more. I wonder to myself, *What if I could have leaned over to Diane in the boat and told her that I would be the lone ambassador from our marriage here in Meagan's room today? Could I have warned her not to play tennis on Leap Day? To move up that doctor's appointment by one month?*

Meagan pulls away and says to me, "I'll walk you down to the van." Then to Aditi, she offered a cheerful, "Be right back."

She holds my hand as we walk down the corridor to the stairwell. When we reach the van she motions for Jimmy to lower the passenger side window, which he does.

"Hey bruh, thanks for helping me move in," she says.

"Anything for you, sissy." He replies. "I guess we'll be seeing a lot more of each other?"

Meagan considers this, then says, "Gross." Jimmy rolls his eyes.

Meagan turns to me. "Thank you Daddy. I'm going to text you every day."

"Will I see you in the morning?" I ask. I am still clinging to something and I regret asking the question.

"Daddio, my idea of morning is not the same as yours."

I realize it's time to let go. "Hon, I'm so proud of you. I hope you love it here."

I give her another hug and she doesn't rush it.

"Love you, Dad," she says at last, then "Bye" which she drags into two syllables.

And just like that, she turns and strides back to Xavier, her fine auburn hair trailing behind her. I am torn between the mundane and the profound, and as is often the case, mundane wins the day. I climb into the passenger seat of the minivan and Jimmy eases onto Tudor.

Jimmy follows Comm Ave back into town, passing Fenway Park and the Citgo sign.

"You too tired for an urban hike, Dad?" he asks.

I'm more hot than tired. "Sure," I say. "You know your way around?"

"I've done some cool runs over here. I can keep us out of trouble."

We find a parking place near Mass Ave and Marlborough Street, our second stroke of parking luck today. We stroll down a brick sidewalk lined with the city's last true gas burning streetlights. The feeling is *old money and privilege.* Inside the brick and limestone townhomes no doubt hang pennants from the Harvard-Yale games of the roaring twenties. I pretend I am Jay Gatsby.

"How was your summer, Dad," Jimmy asks me. I'm touched he would ask. I realize Jimmy's showing signs of empathy.

"I have my routines down pretty well," I tell him. "Trying to stay healthy, still fasting. Trail running at least once a week."

"Do you ever fire up Lion Oil?," he asks.

"Every single morning," I reply. "I keep the auto trading off so your sorcerer's apprentice doesn't run amuck, but I almost always do what it tells me."

Jimmy is clearly pleased.

"Dale asked me if he could run it, too."

"Yeah, I guess," Jimmy replies. "He'd need to give me his account password."

"I'll ask him when I see him next," I reply.

"How is Dale?" Jimmy asks.

"Tired of being single," I say. I decide not to mention Bumble and Jennifer. Jimmy may not appreciate that I'm still a college prankster at heart. "He was a *yuge* help in my battle with Nimrod."

Jimmy chuckles. He knows the whole story. "They're not going to forget you at the Club, Dad." We take a few steps, then he asks, "No interest in staying on the board? It seemed to do you good."

"None!" I say emphatically. "My term was up in June and my work there is done."

Jimmy steers us right onto Gloucester Street ("It's *Glowster*, Dad," he says when I mispronounce it) and then left onto Comm Ave again. It's the same Comm Ave that leads to Boston College, but now we're in the heart of Back Bay and the atmosphere is completely different. The homes on either side are grand nineteenth century sentinels, dwellings of the Brahmin class.

We stroll along the shady path of the linear park that divides Comm Ave. It's a thoroughfare of runners, dog walkers in Lululemon, and summer loves.

I'm impressed that Jimmy knows the city so well. He points out landmarks as we approach the Boston Public Garden.

"That's where they filmed Cheers," he tells me, motioning to a building near the Gardens. We continue into the Boston Common and pick up the red stripe of the Freedom Trail. He shows me the world's first subway station ("There must have been two stations," I tell him) and the site of the Boston Massacre ("Only five people died there," he says. News to me. I thought a massacre has to be a hundred or more). We wind through Quincy Market, hot and sticky and bookended with buskers, and then cross into the Italian North End.

"There's the Old North Church," Jimmy said pointing. "You know, *one if by land, two if by sea*? That's the steeple where the signal was sent."

I am genuinely impressed by Jimmy's tour. "What did they call it back then, Jimmy," I ask. "Just the North Church."

He grants me a laugh. Actually, we have the same sense of humor but he doesn't realize it yet.

We have dinner in the North End at a *ristorante* where all the wait staff are men, brusque Italian Bostonians. Jimmy tells me about his job at the pharmaceutical company in Kendall Square. He likes it for the summer, but he says he may look for something at a start-up next year. He tells me about his fraternity house and the room he'll get this fall.

As he speaks I am twenty again. I remember that summer vividly. I had no job that summer on account of mandatory Air Force cadet training in the middle of July. I squandered June and August gloriously with high school buddies in Greensboro, playing poker, getting girls' phone numbers, driving to Myrtle Beach six to a car. I lived with my parents that summer, but was more boarder than son. I did not particularly want to invite them into my new adult life.

I am sensitive to this now, and while I'm happy he's talking, I want to respect boundaries. We concentrate on tender homemade pasta.

"What's next for you, Popsie," Jimmy asks. "You're an empty nester now."

I know this and have known it, of course, but tomorrow when I roll south out of Boston it will be my inescapable reality. I give myself a bye for the past eighteen months. I buried my wife (well, cremated her), endured a global pandemic, and launched my youngest child into college. But if I'm being honest, I've been on a slow descent into acedia for much longer. In my twenties and thirties I was on fire. I had the brains, luck and personality (I list these in alphabetical order only) to ride the fiber optic broadband wave; the burning desire to achieve more, earn more and own more than my parents; and the deep motivation to be an all-star father. Now here I am at fifty-five with all boxes checked and my son is asking me *what's next*. Damn good question.

"Dale and I are going to start a hedge fund and make Lion Oil our secret weapon," I say. I don't mean it and I'm not sure why I say it. But I can't very well say, *I have no idea.*

Jimmy looks me straight in the eye and asks, "Would you date, Dad?"

He hasn't taken the Lion Oil line and I wait a moment before replying. A moonlit scene from nearly a year ago flashes unbidden across my mind, but I suppress it before Jimmy can sense anything.

"I'm not sure," I say, then realize I am nodding gently. "How would *you* feel about that?"

"Well," Jimmy replied, setting his fork on his plate, "it'd be a little weird, I guess." He waits a moment, "But it'd be fine, you should, you really should."

"How do you think Meagan would feel?" I ask.

"Who knows?" Jimmy replied. "Just please don't date anyone *her* age."

Nope, that's for damn sure. Not again, anyway. Can Jimmy read my mind? Then I say, "No risk of that happening. I'm nearing my *use by* date."

"Don't sell yourself short, Dad," Jimmy says, and I appreciate the compliment more than he realizes.

"How 'bout you, Jimmy?" I ask, sensing the door is open. "Anyone special?"

Jimmy studies his plate, which only has a few strands of pasta and sauce remaining. "There *is* someone," he says to me. "I call her the woman of ultimate depression." He gives a pained smile, then takes the last piece of bread from the small basket and mops up his sauce.

"That sounds promising," I say. It is my lot to make inane comments in the presence of profundity.

"She's been in half my classes since freshman year."

I wait for more.

"I can't bring myself to ask her out, Dad." Jimmy says. "She's just too..." He trails off.

I *get* Jimmy. At twenty, some guys have no compunction about asking a beautiful woman out. If they get rejected, they shrug it off and move along to the next prospect. But sometimes - and more often than we nice guys realize - they don't get rejected. I was never that guy and I guess Jimmy isn't either. I tended towards being worshipful, admiring from afar and waiting for the perfect moment for a display of chivalry.

"That's why she's the woman of ultimate depression. It's not that *she* depresses me, it's that *I* depress myself."

A comfortable masculine quiet settles between us. I could opine on love and its pompatusness, but somehow the silence says more. That, and the fact that I would be wrong anyway.

"Maybe I'll venture out this year," I say to Jimmy.

"Maybe I'll ask the *WUD* out," he replies.

* * *

Boston is in my rear-view mirror by 7:00 am Sunday. I have a tall black Dunkin Donuts coffee in the cup holder and I'm listening to my *Boating* playlist, a redneck blend of Buffett, Zac Brown and Kelly Mcguire. I'm in high spirits, buoyed by a sense of potential. I can't put my finger on it exactly, but I go with it. Maybe it's Jimmy's tacit blessing to date. Maybe it's me projecting my middle age self onto his twenty year old self and knowing I would ask the woman of ultimate depression out the next instant I saw her. Evidently I'm still vital enough to be stirred by the hunt.

My phone chirps as I approach Philly and I see it's Meagan calling.

"Callany Pizza Delivery," I say cheerfully. "*Callany* time, day or night." It's an old joke I haven't made in a long time.

"Hi Daddy," Meagan says. *Daddy* means she's feeling vulnerable. *Daddio* means she wants something.

"Hi Sweetie," I say, "Did you flunk out?"

"Not yet," she snickers. "I miss you."

"I miss you, too, Meag. I started missing you the second I said goodbye yesterday."

She doesn't reply.

"Hon, are you okay," I ask.

I hear a sniff, then "Yeah I'm fine."

"How was the orientation party?" I ask.

"Oh my God, Dad," she says. "Everyone here knows me from TikTok. It's crazy."

I'm happy to hear her pep up.

"There's one girl here from Korea who says everybody at her high school follows me."

"Be sure to tell them it's me handing you the junk food," I say smiling to myself.

"When will you get home?" she asks.

"I'm gonna motor all the way through," I say. "It'll be like 13 hours. I'm hoping to get home around eight."

Meagan becomes quiet again, then says, "Daddy?"

"Yes," I reply gently.

"How much do you love me?" she asks.

My heart soars. "Well," I say. "Imagine I'm driving the minivan all the way from Boston to Charlotte."

"Mmmm hmmm," she replies.

"And imagine it's a sweltering hot day in the middle of August. "And my air conditioner is broken …."

"Really?" Meagan asks.

"No," I say, "but just imagine."

"Okay."

"And I've had to suffer through morning rush hour in New York, lunchtime rush hour in Philly, and two afternoon rush hours, one in DC and one in Richmond."

"Mmmm hmmm."

"And I can't stop for food because I'm fasting. And when I stop for gas I accidentally drive the wrong way over one of those *severe tire damage* things and get four flat tires. And when I finally get started again a cop pulls me over for doing sixty in a fifty-five and I get a ticket."

"Mmmm hmmm."

"Oh yeah, and my radio's broken. And my cell phone battery is dead and I don't have a charger. And a bird flies in through an open window and craps all over the inside of the car, including in my hair."

"You don't have any hair," she says.

"Yes I do." I reply. "Shut up."

Then I continue. "And I've had to pee like a racehorse for, like, the past four hours. But I finally get home and pull into our garage. And I'm about to go inside and cool down in the nice air conditioning and take a twenty minute long whiz."

"Mmmm hmmm."

"But just then my phone rings."

"You said your battery was dead," Meagan corrects me.

"Well," I say. "There was just one molecule of electricity left and I was saving it for an emergency."

"Okay," she says with skepticism (the story must be airtight). Then she picks up the story line. "Well, it's me calling," Meagan said. "And I say, 'Daddy, I think I left my toothbrush in the minivan.'"

This is my cue to continue, "And I say, 'Oh doll baby, don't worry. I'll be right back with your toothbrush.' And I walk out of the bathroom without using it, and into the garage, and I back the minivan out and drive all night long to Boston. And when I finally get there at nine the next morning you come running out of Xavier Hall and give me a big hug."

Meagan jumps in, "And I say, 'Daddy, nevermind, I found my toothbrush. It was here the whole time. I tried to call, but I guess your battery really did run out.'"

I pick up from here, "I say, 'That's okay doll, I don't mind one bit.' And then we hug a huge hug and I drive home again."

Meagan waits for the finale.

"That's how much I love you," I say.

29.
WHAT TO EXPECT | 2001

JIMMY TURNED ONE ON THE SECOND MONDAY IN SEPTEMBER. We did most of our celebrating the weekend before. My folks drove up to Arlington from Greensboro and Diane's mother flew in from California the week before. On Sunday afternoon a small happy group gathered on our back deck. It was a *cracking* day, Paul Papadopoulus announced in an ersatz Scottish accent when he and Athena and Chloe, then four, arrived. And it was. Nice and warm but not quite hot, the sky a cloudless robin's eggshell blue. Matt O'Reilly from my Davidson days, still single, turned up along with two other young families we had met at the Lyon Park playground.

Jimmy was the center of attention, perched in his Graco high chair at the center of the deck and ringed by wine drinking adults and sticky faced children. Diane emerged from the screen porch holding a single plate on outstretched arms with an enormous slice of homemade chocolate cake (courtesy of Athena, such productions were not in Diane's repertoire) topped with a single burning candle. The circle parted as Diane approached and we belted out *Happy Birthday*.

At *Dear Jimmy* Diane placed the plate onto the high chair table. Jimmy's eyes widened and a worried look formed on his face. Chloe and three children from the neighborhood pressed in close, prepared to assist in any manner required. Diane stepped back to rejoin the adults and see how Jimmy would approach his cake.

I heard Gina Troiano, a Lyon Park mother, lean to Diane and ask, "Chocolate? I thought it was supposed to be carrot cake?"

This was straight out of *What to Expect …*, the staple gift of all baby showers (we received copies from both sets of parents) and the leading source of parental misery and neurosis in the new millennium. Diane and I diligently read a few chapters together while she was pregnant, but soon enough we realized it was bunk. I later asked my parents if they had read it. "No, it wasn't around in our day," my mother had said. "But there were stacks of them at BuyBuyBaby."

I knew Diane would be peeved at Gina, not just for mentioning a fascist recommendation from the book, but for intruding on this moment with Jimmy.

"Did you read that in *What to Expect*?" Diane asked Gina, not taking her gaze from Jimmy.

"I think so. Yes," she replied. "They're not supposed to have chocolate at twelve months."

Diane turned to Gina and said sharply, "Gina, that's a bunch of horse-shit. Do what we did and burn that book."

Gina's face sagged. She didn't really know Diane. They had pushed strollers together and chatted about diaper rash. Now she had gotten her first real taste. Maybe that's when she began to wonder why there weren't more people on our deck.

Jimmy sat respectfully in front of his slice of cake, his small fists on the Graco tray. He saw a sea of smiling faces and gesturing hands encouraging him to attack the chocolate cake, but he would not do it. Instead he grinned brightly and turned to face whoever was making the most noise. With a nod from Diane, eager Chloe blew out this candle, which created a swirl of smoke that made Jimmy blink. More chanting and mime eating still did not inspire the cautious one year old.

Finally Diane approached, knelt down in front of Jimmy, and ran her finger through the dark icing. She touched it to Jimmy's lips. First he grimaced, but then he brightened and grabbed her finger, sucking the chocolate off it. He looked at the crowd and was met with approval, and as if finally understanding he grabbed the cake with both hands and mashed it into his face. The crowd erupted in cheers and Chloe and the other young children started bouncing on invisible pogo sticks. I was busy filming with our camcorder, but when I scanned the footage that evening I saw Gina and another mother (I can't remember her name) in furtive conversation, arms crossed, near the screen door. *How dare they feed chocolate to that baby?*

* * *

I was supposed to fly to San Diego on Monday morning for a trade show, but my boss at AFN granted me a one day reprieve so I could be home on Jimmy's actual birthday. It was not a big production, just Diane and her mother, and my folks. I grilled burgers, dogs, sweet onions slathered in olive oil, and a couple sheafs of romaine lettuce.

While I was standing by the grill, my father trundled up with two hotdog buns prepared the way he likes them, with mayonnaise, diced onions and pickle spears.

"Jack, how 'bout a pre-hamburger hotdog?" he asked. It was a grilling tradition that went back as far as I could remember. I may have been four the first time my father offered me a *PhD*, as we called them. By now I had enlarged the tradition to include a pre-hamburger beer as well.

We stood by the grill, just the two of us, expertly consuming our PhDs as savory burger smoke seeped from the Weber.

"How are things with you and Diane," my father asked.

I was afraid this might be on the agenda. The two of them operated under an uneasy truce. Both had keen minds and sharp tongues, and I believe they sensed one another as predators, the mongoose and cobra, though I'll never say who was which.

"Pretty good," I began, though my father would never let this stand for an answer.

The truth is that things weren't great. We were in a fairly common post-first-child rut. Diane devoted every moment and every thought to Jimmy, neglecting me and herself. She had not lost her baby fat and in fact seemed to be cultivating more. How many times had we had sex in the past year? I could count on one hand.

At the end of her first trimester, when fears of an early loss subsided and we started to share our news, Diane told me she had no intention of returning to State. Financially we were comfortable - more than comfortable - on what I earned at AFN. But more importantly, State had drained her. Her sassy and provocative brilliance had gone to seed, yielding bitterness. I think Jimmy was her shot at redemption.

"Our marriage is solid, Dad." I supposed it was. I was sometimes lonely in our house, but I was committed to fatherhood and hunkered down for the long haul. Much of the unhappiness we felt was not over big existential issues but rather mundane things like sleeplessness and a woeful lack of adult contact. I added, "It's just a tough phase right now."

My father finished his hot dog and took a draw on his beer.

"Your mother snapped right back after she had you. And Brian," he said with import.

I had no idea how to respond. I flipped the burgers.

"It wouldn't hurt her to get some exercise," he went on. "Maybe get her one of the jogging strollers."

We had one, actually. Brand new, collecting dust.

I gave a long sigh and looked at my father with a thin smile. He patted me vigorously on the center of my back. Enough had been said. I would enlist Diane in the Marine Corps in the morning and send her fat ass to Quantico.

* * *

On Tuesday morning I left our house before sunrise to drive to the Baltimore Washington International airport. Our travel department had booked me on Continental with a stop in Houston en route to San Diego. It would be a long day, starting with a drive to the furthest airport in our metro area, eight hours of travel time, and then three hours of glad handing at hospitality suites near the convention center. Not to mention a three hour time difference. I had pleaded with the travel desk to book me a direct flight out of Dulles, but they found a way to save two hundred bucks instead. *Is that what I'm worth to you a-holes?* I thought to myself when they dropped off my ticket.

I was cruising along at thirty thousand feet, absorbed in an eight-hundred page tome on the history of discovery, when the pilot announced we would be landing in Atlanta on FAA orders. There had been terrorist activity in New York. My first thought: *someone called in a bomb threat, what a pain in the ass, my day just got a whole lot longer.* I returned to my book.

At Hartsfield the full horror of the morning came rushing at me. Some passengers were watching the scene unfold on the Today Show from televisions suspended from the ceiling. That's when I saw the twin towers melt down over and over on a continuous loop. Most passengers were queued in long lines at the gates to rebook their flights. *What are they thinking?* I asked myself. *The last place I want to be right now is on another airplane.* Then: *I've got to call Diane and get the hell away from the airport.*

I didn't have a cell phone, few people did. I found a wall of pay phones in the terminal with people lined up five deep behind each one. I waited fifteen minutes. Most people who made it to one of the phones stepped away after a minute or two, shaking their heads. All lines were busy, only one in ten calls were getting through.

I decided to start walking toward baggage claim with no plan, no destination. I could not understand what I was seeing around me. Business people and families were streaming towards the gates. Most of them were acting like everything was perfectly normal. Others were visibly angry, not because of a terrorist attack on US soil, but because their travel plans were disrupted. The scene was surreal and I moved through the crowd in my own silent bubble. Finally I saw signs for MARTA and decided to take the train into the city. I did not know Atlanta but I would figure something out.

An hour and half later I was checked into the Grand Hyatt at Buckhead. I stood at the window in my room, the curtain drawn open, and watched traffic crawl along Peachtree. I kept imagining a jet diving from the sky and tearing into the Buckhead skyline.

I called home and Diane's mother answered on the first ring. *It's Jack*, I heard her say to the room. I told her I was okay, in Atlanta. *Oh thank God.*

A moment later Diane took the phone. She released a loud heaving moan, and then cried and cried into the handset, unable to form a single word. I began crying too, overcome at last with raw emotion.

Finally she formed her words. "I just knew you were gone," she said. "All I knew was you were flying to California. I never thought to ask what flight you were on."

She heaved and cried some more.

"Do you have news on?" she asked.

"No," I replied. "I'll put it on now," I said, walking to the dresser for the remote.

"Jack, there was a flight from Dulles to LA that hit the Pentagon."

I felt ice water rush through my veins. That's the flight I had been pleading for. Those a-holes in travel had done me the greatest favor of my life. I slumped into the upholstered chair near the window with the remote in my hand.

"How many planes so far?" I asked.

"Four," she said in a small voice. "They say there could be more. One might be heading toward the White House."

We spoke for a few more minutes. Diane held the phone to Jimmy's face and I listened to him babble.

"I love you so much," Diane said. "Don't you die on me."

"I love you, too," I said. "And I'm not planning to."

After a moment we ended the call, not wanting to tie up circuits.

I kicked off my shoes and remained in the chair. Waves of emotion and thought washed over me. *Nothing will ever be the same again, we're going to war, I've got to re-join the Air Force, we've got to get out of DC, what if I had died today, thank God we had Jimmy, what the hell kind of world have we brought a new baby into, how am I going to get home?*

On Friday morning I rented a car and drove ten hours to BWI. The weather was flawless, bright and warm, and virtually every overpass on the highway was draped in American flags. Everywhere people waved. I kept the radio off. I had had enough news for a lifetime and music seemed too trivial for this moment. I let the miles roll away and I basked in the budding sense of patriotism and unity that seemed to emanate from the world around me.

It was dark when I pulled into the driveway at the red and white house. Our parents were still there, a godsend for all involved, and I sensed for once that the tension between Diane and my father had been broken. We were all staring down one of the greatest disasters of the century and a truce had been called on internecine warfare.

That night Diane and I lay in our bed with little Jimmy between us. I was overwhelmed with gratitude to be holding them close in the nest. When words had been exhausted, I lay on my back, eyes open, and listened to the surreal roar of fighter jets patrolling overhead.

30.
CLASS | 2020

I INVITED DALE TO SUNDAY DINNER WITH MEAGAN AND ME. Jimmy had been back at college for two weeks, and Meagan had been scarce all weekend, sleeping her mornings away and heading out with friends by late afternoon. When Sunday afternoon rolled around I was feeling domestic and ordered her to stay home for dinner with Dale and me.

"I like Dale," she said unprompted.

"Me too," I replied.

"He's classier than you, Dad."

"What does that mean?" I asked.

"I don't know," she said. "Refined."

"And I'm not?" I asked.

"Well," she paused, reflecting. "You make a lot of stupid jokes that most adults your age wouldn't make."

I regarded her with a stern eye, then said, "Please don't tell me you want a normal father." I hesitated for a moment, then exclaimed, "Oh God, please don't tell me *you're* becoming normal!"

"Don't worry, Daddio. I'm weirder than you." She contorted her face and started beating her eyelashes rapidly.

"You had me worried for a second," I said. "I like having Dale over every now and then to keep us from getting too weird."

"Dad," she said, "that's what I mean by classy."

At five Dale walked around to our back terrace with a four-pack of hazy IPAs. I was sitting in a low chair by the pool with my feet in the water listening to Jimmy Buffettt and Alan Jackson.

"Jack," he called out, waving.

"Hey Dale," I replied, "pull up a chair. Whatcha got there?"

He sat in the other low chair next to me and opened a beer for each of us. "Low cal hazy," he said. "It's the new thing."

The beer was actually great. The hazies in my fridge were tasty but each one had the carb load of a loaf of bread.

It had been a blistering afternoon, but now the sun had dipped behind the tall trees next to my house and a wedge of shade fell across our chairs. We looked out over the pool at my little cove on Lake Cooke and watched the wake surfers in the distance plow mountainous wakes through the water. We sat in silence and took in the scene.

After a comfortable moment Dale spoke, still looking ahead at the lake. "You've been pulling ahead of me on the options leaderboard," he said. "That's gonna cost you a few lunches at the Cantina."

I hadn't told Dale about Lion Oil yet. Not that it was a secret (though maybe it should have been), I just hadn't taken it too seriously until recently.

"Jimmy wrote some software for me over the summer," I told him.

Dale's eyes narrowed. "You cheating *sonabitch*," he said with a smile.

"It's pretty slick," I told him. *Oily*, I thought. "Come on up, I'll show it to you."

We rose to walk inside when Meagan appeared at the slider. "Dad, Mr. Bolton's out front." She glanced at Dale, "Hi Mr. Dale," she said cheerfully.

Dale and I walked through the house to the front door and saw Cyrus on his dilapidated golf cart in the circular drive.

I came out the front door and saluted, "Cyrus."

He returned the salute with a hand holding an open can of Bud Light.

"Cyrus, you remember Dale?" I asked.

Cyrus nodded gravely toward Dale. I actually can't recall if they've met.

"Got somethin' to show ya," Cyrus said.

There was no way to miss it. In the small bed at the back of the golf cart was an enormous plaster cheeseburger on a dinner plate three feet across.

"Is that what I think it is?" Dale asked me.

I turned to him, "I dunno. Were you thinking Cyrus had sawed the arm off a Bob's Big Boy statue?" I asked.

Dale's eyes widened. "You read my mind."

"Cyrus," I asked, "What're your plans for this cheeseburger?"

Cyrus took a long draw on a can of Bud Light and then cleared his throat dramatically. "Jack, I'd like to mount it on the roof of this here golf cart."

I nodded solemnly. "Cyrus, you really know how to make a statement."

Cyrus grinned, showing his remaining yellow teeth. "Damn straight," he said.

"Yep," I continued with a wink toward Dale, "it's a statement all right, loud but not clear."

"Loud is good," Dale said, then added, "sometimes."

"How do you propose we mount this thing?" I asked Cyrus.

"Well," he chewed, "I sunk two pieces o' rebar into the bottom of the plate and drilled two holes in my roof here. I think we just need to set her up there, but it's too damn heavy for one person."

Dale and I examined Cyrus's handiwork. He had mortarted two pieces of rebar, about twelve inches apart, into the bottom of the plate. I gripped the rebar bars with both hands and found they were cemented solidly in place.

Dale looked up through the roof of the golf cart and then eyed the rebar. "This could work," he said to both of us.

"Course it's gonna work," Cyrus said, annoyed but clearly amused with himself.

I had Cyrus pull his golf cart in front of a garage bay where I could set up two step ladders on one side of the golf cart. Dale and I hoisted the enormous plate and cheeseburger from the bed of the golf cart and gingerly climbed the stepladders. When we were high enough, we rested both rebar rods on the roof of Dale's golf cart, next to the holes Cyrus had drilled. Dale remained on his step ladder while I moved mine to the opposite side. In another moment, we maneuvered the rebar in the two holes Cyrus had drilled, and *voila*, Cyrus had a fine looking Brobdingnagian plated cheeseburger on his roof.

Cyrus himself had not moved from the driver's seat. He gazed up at the two pieces of rusted rebar that now pointed down at his head.

"Cyrus," I said, "don't take the speed bumps too fast. Either you'll bounce off your seat and impale your skull, or you'll send this cheeseburger flying."

"Or both," Dale said.

Cyrus climbed out and admired the new accessory on his roof. "Thank ye, boys," Cyrus said, ignoring our advice. "I like it. I like it a lot."

As we stood by the golf cart, Cyrus eyed the Tesla in my garage with suspicion. I'm not sure he knew I owned one. "One a them fancy Jap electric cars?" he asked with disdain.

"Electric, yes," I said to Cyrus, "Just like your Yamaha golf cart. Which is Japanese, by the way. My car was made in the USA."

Cyrus shook his head as though I were spewing propaganda. "*She-it*," he said, dragging the word out for seconds.

I turned to Cyrus. "Why don't you stay for dinner, old timer. I'm planning to grill some Costco steaks."

Cyrus quite literally licked his chops and nodded. "Why thank ye, Jack. I'd love to."

Over dinner I told Dale about the Bob's Big Boy statue and how Cyrus had positioned it as a sentinel at the edge of his property to antagonize Nimrod. Cyrus aided the storytelling with guffaws and obscenities when he wasn't busy chewing. Dale and I enjoyed a cabernet with the steak, though Cyrus stuck with Bud Light. Meagan sat in silence, turning her head from speaker to speaker, appalled (I think) by our juvenile hijynx.

"So how's the new hand coming along?" Dale asked Cyrus.

"Done," Cyrus said, nodding. "Just gotta paint it." He chewed and swallowed, then continued. "I'm stringing up some low low voltage lighting, too."

Dale and I nodded in appreciation. Meagan asked, "What's that?"

Cyrus turned to her and grinned. "I'm gonna put three spotlights on the Big Boy," he said. "I wanna make sure the Nimrods can see him at night, too."

After dinner Dale and I poured Cyrus back into his golf cart and pointed him home. He had a full belly and our hearty approval for his lawn art.

When he came back inside, Dale asked me, "Is he going to be allowed to drive that thing on public roads?"

"I think the cops have given up on Cyrus," I said. "As long as he keeps it under fifteen miles an hour, they just look the other way."

"You oughta see if the old man can find you another Bob statue. Send it up to Jimmy for his frat house."

The mention of Jimmy's name reminded me to show Dale Jimmy's options trading software. I led Dale upstairs to my office and gave him a thirty minute crash course on Lion Oil.

"I'd like to run this, too," Dale said when I wrapped up the demonstration.

"Fine by me," I replied. "But this version is hard coded to my brokerage account."

"Even better," Dale said.

I smiled. "I'll talk to Jimmy. It might be a while before he has the time."

Dale stayed for a two finger pour of Blanton's, neat for him, on the rocks for me, and then bid farewell as night fell. I moved to the kitchen to wash our dishes and clean up - my least favorite chore around the house - but I couldn't very well pin this one on Meagan, and I *did* like a clean kitchen start to the new week.

Meagan appeared and sat in one of the bar stools opposite the sink where I was working. "That's what I mean by *classy*," she said unprompted.

"Pray tell," I replied.

"Well," she started, "There's Mr. Bolton. He has absolutely no class at all. But he's proud of it, if you know what I mean."

I nodded and thought to myself, *that boy is a P-I-G pig.*

"Then there's Mr. Dale," she continued. "He was nodding politely, but I could tell he was shocked. He would never do something like that to his next door neighbor. He wouldn't even be able to *think* of something like that."

"True," I said. But only *maybe* true. Dale had a devious streak, and it was all the more nefarious because of his classy exterior. Meagan needs to become a bit more discerning about the character of man before she slips away to college.

"But Dad, you're right in the middle, maybe closer to the Mr. Bolton side. You were laughing so hard at the part about the big middle finger I thought you were going to choke." I hadn't realized. Time to enroll in Pranksters Anonymous.

"*That's* why I said Mr. Dale is classier than you," she continued.

I looked at her and arched my left eyebrow several times in shock. "Why am I doing these dishes when there's a teenager in the house?"

She ignored my question entirely. "Dad," Meagan continued, "What did mom think about all your pranks and jokes?"

I looked up at Meagan. Yesterday had been the six month anniversary. We talked about Diane often, though it had been a while since I had cried or seen Meagan cry. In many of our private moments, especially everyday moments like this when it would have been so natural for Diane to be standing with us, I made lighthearted cracks to prevent loss and sadness from seeping in. Maybe I was doing a disservice to the grieving process. I decided Meagan needed a real answer whether she was expecting one or not.

"Honestly, Meag," I said, "she thought they were juvenile and she told me more than a few times to act my age." I paused. "But every once in a while she would burst out laughing. She couldn't help herself. You know how serious mom was about everything. It made me *so* happy to see her crack up despite herself."

Suddenly I felt my eyes brimming. I saw young Diane in my mind's eye, a spontaneous giggle escaping her mouth like a burp. It was gratifying. "I guess I just kept up with the silliness for all those years to help her lighten up."

Meagan looked at me with a sad smile.

"Neither of us could suffer fools very well," I continued. "Mom was so … verbal. She could tongue lash someone so fast and so hard they didn't know what hit them. It wasn't her best quality." Meagan nodded her head knowingly. "Me, I'm different. My weapons are sarcasm and irony. When someone really gets my goat, I set a trap for them. I cover 'em with honey and let the wasps get 'em."

"Are you covering Mr. Nimrod with honey?" she asked, a devious light returning to her eyes.

"Didn't need to," I replied. "Cyrus is taking care of Nimrod with no subtlety at all."

"I wanna be just like you, Dad," Meagan said. She had a Mona Lisa look on her face. Did she really mean it? Or was she employing sarcasm, just like me?

I dried my hands on a dish towel and walked around the island to hug her. "And *I* wanna be just like *you*," I said.

"We'll trade then," she said. "You be me and I'll be you."

"Deal," I replied.

"That means you won't be home Wednesday night," Meagan said.

"I won't?" I asked.

"No, you're going over to Maddie's to work on an AP Biology project and you're gonna sleep over."

I snapped back to first person. "Who else will be sleeping over?" I asked.

"No one," she said. "Just me."

"No boys?" I asked, confirming. "No Email?"

"Gross, Dad," she said. "No boys."

I kissed her on the forehead and said goodnight.

I walked upstairs to the home office for a final check of messages and overseas markets. As I sat in front of the screens, my phone vibrated with a text. It was Brenna Wilder: *still waiting for that boat ride.*

I certainly hadn't forgotten about our game of footsie, but at the same time I may have been pretending it never happened. Was she really pursuing *me*? It felt all wrong - a recent widower, a disastrous October-May pairing, ample opportunities for humiliation. But my inner primitive male was on red alert.

I checked the ten day forecast on Accuweather, then texted her back: *Wed 7:30?*

Her reply came in seconds. Two emojis - thumbs up and a sailboat.

Great, I thought. *Just a boat ride.*

31.

SUPERLATIVES | 2021

WITH PHILLY BEHIND ME I HAVE ANOTHER EIGHT HOURS before I'm back at Lake Cooke. The tingling optimism I felt when leaving Boston at sunrise has mellowed and suddenly I feel the need for quiet. I turn the radio off, silencing *A Pirate Looks Forty*, and yield to a small interior voice.

As the interstate unspools before me I realize I have no place to be, no spouse, no progeny requiring attention, and no job. The last time I was so unencumbered was more than three decades ago when I graduated from college and had a glorious month of freedom before I had to report for duty at the Pentagon. I had frittered away those weeks completely unaware of how precious and rare they were.

I squandered two pristine June afternoons with a high school buddy named Steve trying to toss an aerobie frisbee onto one of the goal posts on our vacant high school football field. The aerobie was shaped like a large flat donut, more hole than frisbee, and we must have made a thousand attempts to ring it around the goal post. On the second afternoon, in stupefying Carolina heat, Steve suddenly made the winning toss and we watched the aerobie settle into the elbow of the goal post. We looked at each other dumbfounded and then did a spontaneous belly bump that sent us each to the ground. There we lay, laughing and looking up into the summer sky between the goal posts.

"How ya plan to get it down?" I asked Steve.

"That's the loser's job," he replied. Again we burst into laughter.

I don't remember how we got it down. Maybe it's still there today, a taunting puzzle for generations, or more likely a cautionary tale for today's over scheduled high schoolers who wouldn't dare piss away that kind of time when they should be cramming for the SAT. As for Steve and me, we were joyful as labradors chasing a tennis ball.

Why was now different? Why not find Steve on Facebook, tell him to meet at the football field this evening, tell him I had a brand new aerobie, tell him the game had always been best of three?

I think of Meagan. At this very moment she is discovering an uncharted world at BC. Virtually everything she encounters today and in the coming weeks will be entirely new for her - the people, the buildings, the classes, but also the situations, the emotions, the pressures. Her synapses are crackling and her brain is gulping it all in with excitement and roving curiosity. (I suppose my whole purpose as a parent was to prepare her for this moment when she's shot out of the cannon of childhood into the fraught skies of adulthood.)

I remember the glaring newness of everything when I left home and showed up on the green lawns of Davidson College. To my underdeveloped cerebral cortex, the things I saw and experienced were not only new to me, they were new to the whole world. Some mornings I felt like I was the first freshman to step foot on campus - the place has been waiting patiently for a hundred and forty some years for me to arrive. I tended towards superlatives in those first few weeks. He was the funniest person ever, she was the most gorgeous girl ever, that was the best burger of all time. At Parents Weekend a month into my first semester, I escorted my folks proudly around campus, showing them what I presumed to be the first library, the first science center and the first dining hall they had ever seen.

My mind surfaces a forgotten memory of forty years past that illuminates the newness fallacy in the most awkward terms. One afternoon when I was twelve years old, I was looking under my bed for something. I had to crawl and shimmy on the floor to get far enough under the bed. Without warning my groin began to tingle. Instinctively I rocked my body on the carpet until the tingling erupted into my first orgasm. I hadn't been told about such things and I thought I had made a major new discovery.

The quest for novelty and discovery must run deep in our genes. The greatest tales of civilization are those of new frontiers - the New World (Breaking News: it wasn't actually new), Lewis and Clark and their Corps of Discovery (passing through territory that had been discovered many times in the preceding five thousand years), and of course space flight (possibly truly new, we'll see).

This is Meagan's world today, this very day. She is the first girl ever to move into Xavier Hall, its worn floorboards and ancient radiators well placed props for her arrival. I will fly to see her in October for parents weekend and she will show me the very first college football stadium I have ever seen.

Will I ever find something truly shiny and new again? Diane once commented that you're old when everyone you meet reminds you of some-one you already know. Or bits and pieces of different people. She was in her late twenties, I think, when she made that proclamation and I agreed with it even then. The trouble is, Diane's comment doesn't just apply to people - it applies to everything.

My mood has slumped. I want the world to be all new again. I want to stand at the edge of a new frontier and peer into the unknown.

I study the exits on I-95 as I approach Baltimore and seriously consider swerving west for a road trip - Pittsburgh tonight, deep dish pizza in Chicago tomorrow. Then I decide *no major cities*, and *no interstates* either. I'll take the blue highways and stay in motels with names like the Dew Drop Inn. This is my Jack Kerouac moment, or maybe my John Steinbeck *Travels with Charley* moment. (I should get a dog.)

I enter a small town in Illinois named after a remote character in the Old Testament. At the edge of town, near a white clapboard church with a tall piercing steeple, I see a woman standing next to an old sky blue Plymouth

Scamp that clearly has a flat tire. She's wearing a white sundress and has tangled strawberry blond hair. She looks flustered. I ease my minivan to the curb behind her and open the door.

"Need a hand?" I ask.

Gratitude washes over her face. "Yes," she says, "Oh thank you so much. I've never been able to change a tire."

She opens the large trunk of the Scamp and I remove the spare tire and jack. She hovers nearby, chatting while I take off the flat tire (I see a nail in the sidewall) and replace it with her full size spare (this vehicle must be twenty-five years old).

"Where you from?" she asks. "I see the North Carolina license plate."

"Near Charlotte," I say, but offer nothing further.

"I'm from right here," she says, and she pronounces the name of the town. "I've never been to North Carolina. I hear it's nice."

"It has its charms," I say. "I've never been to …," and I say the name of her little town.

When I finish changing the tire I stand and wipe my hands on a small towel she's handed me. I take in her face, which I hadn't studied closely before. She's stunning. Maybe early forties. Fine lines around her eyes. Her hair is a dirty shade of blond and her eyes are like dark chocolate. She is sensual in her light sundress.

"Thank you so much," she says. "You're such a gentleman." She extends her hand and says, "I'm …," and she says her name.

"Jack Callany," I reply with a grin I hope she finds winsome.

"You've never been to …?" she asks, again saying the town's name and registering disbelief.

I shake my head. *Nope, hard to believe.*

"Please. Let me buy you lunch at Millie's," she says. "They have the best meatloaf in the whole world."

I look at my watch, but the truth is I have nowhere to be. Just another blue highway leading to another motel somewhere.

"Jack, I won't let you say no," she insists after a moment.

"Well thank you very much," I say, tossing the towel back into her trunk before closing it.

"Just follow me," she says. "It's about three minutes away."

At Millie's she orders meatloaf for both of us. It is in fact the best meatloaf I've ever tasted. The slices are thick and saucy. The mashed potatoes and green beans are hot, and real. She tells me all about Millie, who was her great aunt, and the little town, and how a famous author was born here. I'm charmed through and through. I love this place. I don't think we passed a single stoplight on our way through town and we parked right in front of Millie's with no hassle.

Then she says to me, "I lost my husband about eighteen months ago."

I swallow hard and look directly into her eyes.

"It's not easy being a widow in a little town like this," she continues.

"No," I reply softly. "I imagine not."

"Where ya headed, Jack?" she asks me, and her voice is sweet. I think of Olivia Newton-John.

"Not sure," I say. "I might stay here for a while."

Her face brightens and it's captivating.

The traffic on I-95 in Baltimore grinds to a halt, an iron snake of tail lights, and I snap from my reverie. Shimmering waves of heat rise from asphalt and refract the images of the cars in front of me. Industrial smoke-stacks rise from the gritty side of Baltimore. It's midday so this delay must be from an accident or construction. I want to be back at Millie's, but it's impossible. Daydreams are one way streets.

Still, it's not too late to swing west on 70 or east 50 towards the eastern shore. There's no exact reason I need to follow this dreary ribbon on I-95 and I-85 inevitably through DC and Richmond.

It's depressing, what Diane said, about everyone you meet reminding you of someone you've already know. It's not just faces and situations, either. It's houses, towns, lakes, mountains, plates of enchiladas. Everything and every experience is just a recombination of previous things and experiences. I'm fifty-five and maybe by now I've accumulated all my canonical experiences. How do the old folks manage? How do they plod on another twenty or thirty or more years beyond my age with nothing new under the sun, nothing to do but rearrange the furniture?

I remember my grandmother at 85, the last year she came to my parents' house for Christmas. She walked with difficulty and generally poured herself into a recliner whenever possible. She had her wits about her and would regale Brian and me with family lore, some of it interesting, much of it repetitive, most of it (I'm sorry to say) forgotten now.

"Oma," I said to her one day, "why don't you read more?" Her mind was active and curious. It seemed like the ideal pastime. "I'll go to the book store and buy you a few mysteries, or whatever you want."

"Jack," she said, wearily. "All I do is read when I'm home. There's absolutely nothing else to do. All my friends are gone now. I can't walk. I can't drive. I watch a little TV but I get sick of it." She sized me up for a moment. "Getting old is hell. I never wanted to live past eighty."

In those days I never knew when to shut up and let words simply hang in the air. I had to solve everyone's problems for them.

"What do you want to do, Oma?" I asked her on the day after Christmas. "Anything. You name it and I'll make it happen."

She smiled and looked up. "Well," she said, "What I would really like is a cigarette." A pause. "But Dave won't let me smoke, says it's bad for me. Ha!"

Here again, in my youth, I didn't know the old-timers had vices. Now I realize they have them aplenty, as do I.

"I'll get you some, Oma. Right now."

She didn't resist. She winked at me and said, "Pall Mall."

I bought them for her that day, and in the evening while Dave, her second husband, was watching football in the basement I wheeled her onto our back patio and we lit up together, Pall Malls for her, Swisher Sweets for me. I wish I could transport myself back to that cold night and ask her the real questions about life. *How did you manage when Opa died? Have you always felt a sense of purpose? What happens when purpose dies? What's the point of living when every person, place and thing reminds you of bits and pieces of people, places and things from your past?*

Now of course it's too late to ask. Maybe I'll hammer these things into my kids' heads when they come home for Thanksgiving. They would listen politely for a few minutes and then check their phones. I suppose Oma saw me the same way while we were smoking like chimneys on the patio.

I pass a three car pile up and make sure to slow down and get a good look, just like everyone in front of me has been doing for the past half hour. It doesn't look like anyone has been hurt. A few teens are slouching by a jersey wall and a team of police and highway patrol are nicely blocking traffic.

I accelerate finally when the road opens and continue along my route back to Lake Cooke, back to my house, my pool and my home office, née marital bedchamber, like a moth to the flame.

32.

SARANAC | 2003

IN THE SUMMER '03 WE RENTED A CAMP ON SARANAC LAKE IN the Adirondacks for two weeks. Neither Diane nor I had been to the Adirondacks, but we needed to unplug from DC life and we both liked Adirondack chairs and Saranac Pale Ale (ideally together), so that settled it. Meagan was four months old and Jimmy was fast approaching three.

Our camp was a rambler, probably fifty years old, set on three or four acres with frontage on Saranac Lake. It had been an arduous nine hour drive with Diane climbing into the backseat every hour to comfort or breastfeed Meagan while Jimmy alternated between incessant chatter, sleep, Wiggles videos, and scribbling.

When we pulled onto the grass and gravel parking pad next to the camp, Diane looked at me with disapproval and said, "This is *it*? It's so shabby."

I took a deep breath. It was shabby, but that was the idea of an Adirondack camp - quiet, remote, restful. "Let's take a look," I replied.

Diane carried Meagan in her carseat and Jimmy held my finger as we approached what would be our home for the next two weeks. The front door opened into a spacious but dark great room with wood paneled walls and a low, paneled ceiling. There was a modest fireplace with a wood burning stove insert. The walls were covered with decades of Adirondack memorabilia - ancient snowshoes and skis, fishing rods, mounted fish, three mounted deer heads watching from above, and original oil paintings of the lake, undistinguished but homey. Directly opposite the front door was a wall of windows looking out through a screen porch onto the quiet, still surface of Saranac Lake.

"Flea market chic," Diane commented.

"Oh come on," I said cheerfully, "this is what camps are like." I learned later this was partially true. Our camp was old school, an original, similar to most camps pre-1980. Beginning in the *Greed is Good* 80's, a new class of camp began to appear on venerable family lots. Their exteriors paid homage to the simple camp tradition, but their interiors boasted air conditioning, granite countertops, jacuzzi tubs, and flat screen TVs. They also managed to be four or five times the square footage..

Jimmy and I explored the screen porch (it had an inviting hammock) and the backyard with its narrow mulch trail leading to a long wooden dock. There was a primitive canoe rack built onto a tree near the edge of the lake with a single battered aluminum canoe mounted upside down.

"Daddy fish!" Jimmy exclaimed, pointing over the side of the dock.

"You wanna go fishing?" I asked.

"Yes Daddy, can we?"

"Of course, Jimmy," I said, "that's what we do here."

He beamed.

"And we eat the fish, too," I said gravely.

Jimmy's cherubic face contorted. "Eat them?" he asked with incredulity.

I smacked my lips together and said, "Yummy yummy."

Jimmy studied me and then repeated, "Yummy yummy."

We settled into our camp that evening. I made a grocery run, an expensive undertaking for bare necessities that consumed an hour, while Diane unpacked our suitcases and set up shop. When I returned with groceries, I found the three of them on the screen porch watching as dusk settled over the lake. Meagan was strapped into a swinging seat Diane had hung from a rafter in the porch ceiling. Jimmy was twisting her seat so it would spin and she cry-laughed the whole time.

I plopped down next to Diane on the well worn wicker sofa and put my arm around her shoulder. "How's the flea market?" I asked.

"It'll do," she replied with a smile.

Later that evening, when Jimmy was tucked into his single bed and Meagan was down in the Pack 'n Play in our bedroom, we returned to the sofa with our adult treats. For me, a tumbler of bourbon with a splash of water and ice. For Diane, a bowl of Moose Tracks ice cream with a wee dram poured over it. We sat peacefully on the sofa, looking out over the black lake surface and taking in a symphony of cicadas, crickets and frogs.

We were both in desperate need of time together and a break from the press of DC life. The preceding spring had been one of the busiest stretches of my career, to include two or three nights of travel almost every week. I had been home for Meagan's birth - thank God - but I was only able to take two vacation days after we brought her home. Paternity leave was absolutely out of the question. Diane was left to fend for herself most days with terrible twos Jimmy and newborn Meagan.

"I've pumped four bottles," Diane said to me. "Will you keep your promise and take the night feedings?"

"A hundred and ten percent," I said gently. I eyed the hammock on the screen porch where we were sitting. It would come in handy tomorrow afternoon when I needed to recover a lost night.

I had been with American Fiber now for more than ten years and was at full stride. I continued to run engineering, and since the bursting of the dotcom bubble I had become part of the CEO's inner circle. He had a Wall Street background and had been able to navigate the boom and bust deftly. He steered us away from an IPO in 1999 which would have made me rich on paper for a few minutes, then left me with a tax bill far beyond the value of my stock in only a few quarters. Instead, he shrewdly took on debt at very good terms and built the war chest we had been using over the past year to buy distressed competitors in desirable markets. Because he was a finance whiz and not a techie, I held sway over my own domain. I loved the independence of my role, but I also paid the price in endless travel, overseeing our now far flung assets.

I can't exactly say my success made Diane jealous - she had little interest in technology and engineering - but the pattern of my career's ascendancy and her career's decline was now firmly established. There was no avenue back into the State Department for her, and I don't think she would have wanted it anyway. She was a fiercely devoted mother, but her contact with the outside world was reduced to play dates and wine drinking with the Papadopoulus's. When I called home from business trips and mentioned the names of the cities I was in and the fine meals I was enjoying on the AFN expense account, she would say *sounds nice*. I learned to become more vague.

Diane made every moment with Jimmy a teaching moment. She spoke to him like an adult, in complex sentences with a rich vocabulary. She read labels to him, held forth on politics, nutrition and global warming, all to his wondering and adoring eyes. He spoke early, shocking us with full sentences before he turned one. She was nourishing his mind but neglecting her own.

Diane's nourishment over the past few years had been more the edible variety. She tried hard to lose the baby fat she gained with Jimmy, but at some point the lack of results and weariness from the long days weakened her resolve. The doctor said she was overweight when she went for her first check-up after becoming pregnant with Meagan, and as of this month she was solidly in the obese column. I didn't ask her what she weighed, but I was worried she would be overtaking my 165 pound scrawny self. Intimacy between us had been reduced to hugs and goodnight kisses.

We picked the Adirondacks for remoteness, sleep, and a total lack of structure. When I mentioned canoeing and hiking, Diane had been interested, even hopeful, and as we sat on the wicker sofa that night (she scraping Moose Tracks from the bottom of her bowl) I made a silent invocation that she would enjoy the physical activity and decide to get on a fitness kick.

That night I bottle fed Meagan at midnight and 3:00 am. Both times my eyes opened as soon as Meagan began to stir and I was able to steal her away from the room without waking Diane. I had become a light sleeper when Jimmy was born, and I also had the advantage of being able to fall back asleep almost instantly. On the midnight shift, when I sat with Meagan on the screen porch, I realized I should have been helping more with overnight feedings. Diane usually struggled to awaken and then struggled even more to get back to sleep.

The 3:00 am shift was remarkable. The night air was surprisingly cool (I shouldn't have been surprised) and hinted at approaching autumn. From the screen porch I could see brilliant stars in the sky, so I decided to cradle Meagan in my arms and walk to the dock. She was still wrapped up like a burrito and I figured she would stay warm enough despite the temperature. The night sky was a riot of stars and for the first time in my adult memory I could make out the white smear of the Milky Way.

When Meagan finished her bottle, I lay on my back and placed her face up on my stomach. Together we gazed into the star theater. We were rewarded with a brilliant shooting star drawn directly overhead. Meagan celebrated with a burp and within minutes she drifted into sleep, her breathing soft and rhythmic. I lay there, content and very much awake, staring into the sky and watching what I would later learn was the summer's Perseid meteor shower.

When I woke in our bed, the sun was fully risen and Diane and Meagan were out of the room. So much for being a light sleeper. I found them on the screen porch, Meagan feeding.

Diane looked at me serenely. "Thank you," she said. "I can't remember the last time I slept like that."

"It wasn't that hard for me, Hon," I said to her. "I can fall right back to sleep."

"You're lucky," she replied, turning to Meagan.

"Hey," I said. "My vacation gift to you. I'll take the night feedings every night we're here."

Diane looked at me with incredulity. "God you're a sexy man," she said smiling.

It was nice to hear that, especially in my extended celibacy.

We took our first hike that day after lunch, up and down Baker Mountain. I carried Meagan in a backpack carrier and Jimmy scrambled ahead of us on the trail. Diane labored, her face red and damp. On one break, she sat on a fallen tree and collected her breath.

"I've got to get back into shape," she said frankly.

Suddenly I was filled with compassion for her. She was here doing her best, really trying, and my quiet resentment about her weight gain hadn't helped her or me. If this was *for better or for worse*, it was time for me to step up and be a better partner.

Diane gave me a slanted smile. "You didn't sign up for a fat wife," she said.

"I signed up for you," I said, "no matter what."

She smiled at me.

"Let me help you," I said. "Use this vacation to sleep and recover. No dieting. Just relax and build up your strength. When we get back, if you're ready, we'll start a diet together."

"I'd like that," she said meekly.

"Will you share the Moose Tracks?" I asked.

"Don't push it, Jack."

That night around ten, after the kids were down, I led Diane out onto the dock. The moon was rising and the stars were faint. We walked to the very end.

"I brought Meagan out here last night for her bottle," I said.

Diane looked at me.

"The moon had set and the stars were just incredible. Meagan saw her first shooting star."

Diane faced me and raised her open palms towards me. I responded, touching my fingertips to hers. We stood like this in silence for a long moment, then she lifted her chin to kiss me.

"Turn around," she said.

"Why?" I asked.

"Just turn around."

I turned to face the house. I heard Diane slip out of her clothes and then ease quietly into the water.

"Marco," she said playfully.

I turned and saw her head in the water, her white breasts floating up just below the surface.

"Polo," I replied with a smile, stepping out of my shorts and Birkenstocks.

* * *

We found our groove on Saranac. I took the nighttime feedings - usually two of them - and Diane took over at sunrise while I slept with one pillow under my head and one over it to block the insistent morning sun. We cooked, ambled, canoed and napped. Diane called the hammock my office because I spent so much time there.

One morning at the breakfast table, the morning sun struck Meagan's bald baby head at just the right angle to reveal fine shoots of hair.

"See this?" Diane asked me, running her palm across Meagan's scalp.

"Her hair's starting to come in?" I asked.

Diane nodded."Look closer."

"Is that red?" I exclaimed. "She's gonna be a redhead?"

"I think so," Diane replied.

"Where in the hootin' hollerin' hell did red come from?" I asked. We were both shades of brown.

"I think it's your side," Diane replied. "Go look at your beard."

I walked to the bathroom. I had five days of growth on my chin, unusual for me. It must have been my military training, but I shaved every morning, even on weekends. I regarded myself in the mirror, angling my chin up and around under the light above the mirror. What I saw was mainly black, but at certain angles I caught a glimpse of red.

I walked back to the kitchen where I stood behind Diane and started running my fingers through her long, thick hair, inspecting her scalp, looking for evidence of red. What I found instead were strands of gray.

"Um, Diane?" I asked. "You're thirty-five and going gray."

She seemed bored. "Your powers of observation never cease to amaze me," she said. "Have you ever seen my mom?"

Diane's mother was in her early sixties and had been gray since the day I met her fourteen years earlier.

"She was totally gray at forty," Diane said.

I sat down again at the table. "Sounds like I'll have a red headed daughter and gray haired wife then."

Meagan cooed and Diane arched an eyebrow in my direction. I didn't have the finest head of hair myself.

A few days later we loaded up the minivan and locked up the camp. The kids were strapped into their harnesses and I told Diane I wanted to take one last look at the lake. She joined me on a short walk to the back yard, where we stood at the base of the dock and looked out over the serene lake surface. Diane took my hand.

"This place was good for me," she said.

We stood quietly, then she added, "Let's live on a lake."

"That's not easy to find in DC," I remarked.

"Then let's move," she said. "Let's move here."

"It's gonna be a long time before they string fiber out to these camps," I said. "How do you propose we make a living?"

"You'll think of something," she said. "You're Jack Callany."

33.

NO WOMAN, NO CRY | 2020

I ROSE EARLY ON THE FIRST WEDNESDAY OF SEPTEMBER. MY sleep had been fitful and by a quarter to six I abandoned all hope of sleep and walked outside to the back terrace to stretch. The travertine pool surround was cool and damp. The grass beyond sparkled with overnight dew and I remembered something from Jimmy's Scouting days, *when the dew is on the grass, rain will never come to pass.* It would be a dry day followed by a dry, clear night. Perfect for a boat ride.

I stepped out of my sleeping boxers and waded slowly into the pool for a morning lap. I pulled a deep breath into my lungs and pushed off underwater, swam to the far end, executed a decent flip turn, then swam back, fully submerged the entire time. I dried myself, redressed into my single article of clothing, and sat on the orchard stone terrace and contemplated Lake Cook's dark glassy surface.

Later today I would clean the boat and ready it for my guest. It had only been a month since I bought it from Pam, but already Meagan's hair ties had found their way into every cup holder. Corks and koozies, too, had accumulated quietly. My mental checklist: *vacuum, wipe down, check fuel, clean the removable teak table top. Fluffy towels.*

This last one - the towels - created a bolt of angst. Would the lake tour include a swim? Probably not. But if it did for any reason towels would be a necessity. The water temperature was delightful on these Indian summer days.

Without forethought I lowered my head and folded my hands. At first my mind was perfectly blank, but then the words of a prayer - a prayer directly to Diane - filled my mind. *I miss you, Hon. I hope you can hear me now. I have a date tonight. Well maybe, I don't know. So much about it seems wrong. But I want to live, get on with life, you know. I don't know what will happen. Maybe nothing. Probably nothing. I will always be a decent guy. I pray for your blessing. I miss you. I love you.*

Another thought, unbidden, came to my mind: *I would want you to do the same if the situation were reversed.* I fought back the imagery of Diane - not as she had looked these past few years but as she had looked *before* - on a date with another man while I rested as cool pile of ashes in a box on the dining room table.

I raised my head and cleared my mind. We're all meant to keep pressing ahead, doing whatever we do. Parenting, working, running, fasting, joking around. Life really is for the living. My brooding dissolved as quickly as it had come on. A fish jumped on the lake and disappeared before I could glimpse it, sending concentric ripples toward the shore.

At eleven, when the dew had dried from the grass and the boat cover, I made my way down the dock with a vacuum and other cleaning supplies. I've always enjoyed putzing around on the dock, doing light maintenance on the boat and tidying up. Unlike our old boat, *Open Options* had a bluetooth stereo, so I connected my iPhone and started streaming Buffett, Marley and random assorted island tunes.

The weather was mild - mid-eighties and sunny - but on the boat there was no escape from the sun's penetrating rays. After a few minutes of work I peeled off my Resident Culture tee-shirt, which was already damp with sweat. The boat cleaned up easily. Apart from a few scuff marks and cracker crumbs, it was still almost pristine. At a quarter to noon, I laid a towel on the bench seat opposite the Captain's chair and sat facing the stern with a fine view across the lake, quiet and undisturbed in midweek.

As I roasted in the sun, *No Woman, No Cry* queued up on the playlist. Diane had hated this song, which I always found inexplicable.

"It doesn't mean you shouldn't cry because you aren't getting laid," Diane had said to me years ago. "He's telling the women in his audience not to cry because everything's gonna be alright."

"How the hell do you know what he meant?" I had replied.

"Everyone knows that," she said.

When the song ended, I hoisted the vacuum and my bucket of cleaning supplies and walked back to the house. When I reached the pool, I dove in wearing only my gym shorts. The water was deliciously cool and I realized I had probably burned myself to crisp on the boat.

While I stood in the shallow end of the pool, facing out over the lake, I heard the back door slide open.

"Dad?" I heard Meagan say. "Lunchtime swim?"

"Hey Doll," I replied.

Meagan was wearing shorts, a tee shirt and flip flops. She was on lunch break from her online classes, socially distanced from her entire senior class here on our terrace.

"I was just cleaning up the boat," I said. "Had to cool down."

"Why are you cleaning the boat right now?" she asked.

She had me there. *Because I'm giving a sunset lake tour to a woman who's barely ten years older than you.* Oh God.

"I'm taking a few people from the board out tonight," I said casually. By *few* I meant *one*.

Meagan became interested. "Oh really?" she said with import. "A little booze cruise with Pam Loving?"

I swept my hand across the surface of the pool and sent a wide scoop of water flying at Meagan. None of it hit her, but she covered her face and stepped back.

"Maybe, maybe not." I said playfully.

"Okay Daddio," Meagan said. "I'm making a burrito. Want anything?"

"Sure," I replied. "Make me one, too."

When her online classes ended at three, Meagan walked into my office. "I'm heading to Maddie's," she said. "Remember? I'm spending the night. I might do first block at her house since we both have APES." *AP Environmental Science.*

"Okay, Doll," I said. "Wear your mask."

"Roger," she replied.

"And no boys tonight at Maddie's," I added.

"Surely," she said.

"And especially wear your mask if there are any boys," I said.

She contorted her face at me.

"And don't call me Shirley," I said.

"Roger," she replied. "Have fun on the boat with your Club nerd friends."

"Don't worry, I will," I said. Then I added: "Am-scray."

* * *

Brenna pulled into my driveway promptly fifteen minutes late in a Chrysler Pacifica that had seen better days. From inside my front door I watched her park near the side of the house and approach. She was wearing white shorts and a navy blouse, and dressy white and gold sandals with a two inch cork sole. The whole ensemble was casual but striking, all the more so with her tanned arms and legs and flowing brown hair. The only puzzle piece that didn't fit was the minivan, but such is life in one's twenties.

I opened the door as she reached the top step of the entryway.

"Miss Wilder," I said in greeting.

"Mr. Callany," she replied, measuring each syllable. Her dark eyes flashed a flirtatious smile.

"Come on in," I said. "Welcome."

"Are we wearing masks?" she asked. I glanced down and saw she held a purple face mask in one hand.

"Isn't everyone?" I replied. "All the time?"

She looked at me, puzzled.

"I'm just kidding," I said, flashing a smile. "No mask needed here."

Brenna's smile returned and she stepped inside. She took in the foyer and the view through the back of the house of the pool and lake. "This is beautiful," she said.

"Thank you," I replied. "It's just me and Meagan these days but we love it here."

"Oh," she said, half excited, half concerned. "Is Meagan here? I've been wanting to meet her."

"No, she's at a friend's." I couldn't tell if Brenna was disappointed or relieved. Maybe both.

"Can I get you a glass of wine?" I asked. "Chardonnay?"

"That'd be perfect," she said.

She followed me into the kitchen where I had two wine glasses at the ready on the countertop. I opened a Rombauer - my favorite chard - and filled each glass.

"To your first official tour of Lake Cooke," I said, lifting my glass.

"Cheers to that," she said.

"Let's head down to the boat," I said. "I've already packed a few drinks and nibbles for us. If we leave now we can catch a nice sunset."

As we walked across the backyard and down the stone path to the dock, Brenna studied the surroundings with feigned nonchalance. A home like this was new for her, fascinating and probably intimidating. She hid it well.

I climbed onto the boat first and offered my hand to her. She took it and stepped gingerly from the dock to the bow, raising her wine glass high in her other hand for balance. When she was onboard she held onto my hand for a moment longer, then released it to brush her hair back behind her ear.

"What do you like to listen to?" I asked.

"Oh, I like everything," she said. "Do you have any Khalid?"

I had no idea what she was talking about and I'm afraid it showed. "Maybe," I said, stalling. "Would you settle for Mt. Joy?"

"I love them, sure," she replied.

I started streaming the station and backed the boat out into our cove. Brenna sat opposite my captain's chair on the bench seat, facing me. She kicked off her sandals and tucked her bare feet under herself like a cat. The boat gilded slowly over the still lake surface, just fast enough to stir her hair.

"I don't even know where you live," I said.

"In Davidson," she replied casually. "I've been staying with my mom since the lockdown started."

We were both quiet for a moment. The boat engine was almost imperceptible at low RPMs and we took in the black and gold surface of the water. To my mind we were on opposite shores: Brenna was living with her mother, probably in her childhood home and driving the same minivan she has been shuttled to middle school in, and I was living almost alone in a huge empty house.

"Probably not what you were expecting as your first stop after grad school?" I said gently.

"No, not exactly," she said. "I had interviews lined up in Boston and DC, and then … *poof*." She made a starburst with the fingers of both hands, holding her nearly empty wine glass with only her thumb and forefinger.

"That stinks," I said. We glided quietly for a moment, then I said, "Think you'll make a career at the Club?" I attempted a wink just in case.

"Most definitely," Brenna said with a light laugh.

Then she nodded toward my empty wine glass. "More vino?" she asked. I smiled and nodded and she refilled our glasses.

We tooled across the main channel while the descending sun slowly turned red orange. I pointed out a few homes on the shoreline as we passed - Rick O'Shea's on a coveted point, acquired long before the current madness to be on Lake Cooke, Aristotle Poe's wheelchair adapted post modern glass and concrete cube.

I guided the boat into a wide empty cove not far from my house by car but quite a distance by boat. Lake residents have two mental maps - one for terra firma and one *aqua firma*. I brought the boat to stop at the back of the cove and used the windlass to anchor us. Brenna watched as I removed the teak table top from the hold and set it in place in the bow. I opened the cooler and removed a few sushi rolls and a small shrimp cocktail platter, and placed them on the table.

"Sunset picnic?" I said, motioning her to join me in the bow.

"Enchanted," Brenna replied in a French accent, *on-shon-tay*.

She slid onto the cushioned bench seat in the bow and I slid onto the seat opposite her, the table between us. Brenna looked at me for a moment, then curled her lower lip out in a pout.

"I don't want to be over here all by myself," she said. She cocked her head to accentuate her injury, then slid to her left and patted the seat beside her. "And besides, this side has the sunset view."

I smiled and complied, moving around the table to sit by her. She stretched her legs under the table and rested her bare feet on the bench opposite. I slid off my Birkenstocks and did the same. Brenna leaned her head on my shoulder and instinctively I put my arm around her. Her brown hair was fragrant and fell haphazardly onto my chest.

The sun was deep red now and kissed the watery horizon. For a moment I had no history, no sadness, no plans. Every part of me mustered into the extreme present, making me intensely alert and profoundly calm all at once.

"So peaceful," Brenna murmured. I traced slow circles on her shoulder.

The sun dipped below the horizon but its rays illuminated the sky and high clouds above us, creating a dome of orange and blue and purple. We picked at the sushi and began to work our way through another bottle of wine.

"I've been doing my homework, Mr. Board Member," Brenna said to me.

"Oh really?" I asked. "What homework is that?"

She pulled away slightly so that she could make eye contact with me. "Well for one thing," she said, "I watched Animal House. The other night. With my mom."

"Oh God," I said. "With your mom? No one ever watches that movie with their mom."

Brenna gave a small laugh. "She liked it. So did I." A moment passed, "I mean, it was kind of slow and juvenile, but I liked it. I liked the toga party. And the parade at the end."

"Classics," I said with an appreciative nod.

"And Neidermeyer," she said. "I hated that guy."

"Do you see why Rick and I call Nimrod Neidermeyer?" I asked.

"Sort of," she said. "But Nimrod's not the military type."

"Yeah, but he might be killed by his own troops, just like Neidermeyer was."

"What's up with that guy anyway?" Brenna asked.

"You tell me," I replied. We sank deeper into the seat, her head on my shoulder, my arm around her. "A-plus on the homework, Brenna."

The sky grew darker, a few early stars shone. We slouched into each other and listened to the music. Small waves from unseen boats on the main channel lapped against our hull. I glanced at Brenna and saw her eyes were closed.

Ten minutes passed, maybe longer, before I felt her stir. She nuzzled her head into my chest, and then raised her mouth to mine and kissed me. First a tentative kiss, then another, firm and willing. I drank in the moment. It had been a very long time.

"Come on," Brenna said to me, sliding off of the bench and taking my hand. I complied.

She led me to the stern and out onto the teak swim platform. She sat on the edge and lowered her bare feet into the water.

"It's so nice," she said. "The temperature is perfect."

I sat next to her.

We caught a glimpse of the moon behind the tall trees standing in silhouette along the shore. It was enormous, reflecting its silver light across the sky. Brenna leaned in to kiss me again.

"You're so cute," she said softly.

I didn't think of myself as cute. I thought of myself as a bit wiry and wrinkled. I wanted to ask her *why me? What the hell is going on?* But I decided to shut up and keep being cute. I was still mostly in the extreme present and not letting myself get too existential.

"Can you get our wine?" she asked.

"Sure," I replied. I rose slowly, not wanting to rock the boat, and made my way to the bow.

"I'll open another bottle," I called back to her.

When I returned to the swim platform, I saw Brenna's clothes in a small pile. *All* of her clothes. Her head bobbed in the water, her hair wet and pulled back.

"You're very stealthy," I said.

She smiled at me. I could make out the form of her breasts just beneath the surface as she treaded water.

"Marco," she said, and disappeared beneath the surface.

I unbuttoned my shirt and stepped out of my shorts and boxers. Brenna's head reappeared ten feet away and she smiled at me, her white teeth gleaming. I dove into the water and swam toward her. When I reached her I placed my hands on her nude hips for a moment and then surfaced, treading water next to her.

"Polo," I said. I fought back a flash of memory from Saranac Lake.

We treaded water together, then dove one after the other, resurfacing a few yards away, each time touching under the veil of the water. Finally I side stroked to the swim platform and lowered the stainless steel ladder so we could hold it and take a respite from treading. Brenna joined me, lacing one leg around mine and allowing her breasts to graze me. We kissed again as we held onto the ladder.

Suddenly Brenna stopped. She was looking around my head at the stern of the boat.

"I forgot I was aboard *Open Options*," she said. "Is that what I am? An option?"

I looked at her, not certain whether this was a trap. Her face was inscrutable.

"Do you want to be?" I asked.

She reached her hand behind my head and pulled my face to hers. With her lips pressed full into mine, I felt as much as heard her say, *Mmmmm hmmmmm.*

When we separated at last, I climbed the small ladder and stepped into the boat to retrieve the two towels I had left tentatively in the afternoon. I carried both to the swim platform and standing there, watched Brenna ascend the ladder. We stood for a moment face to face, naked and dripping, nothing between us but the two folded towels I was holding. The moon had climbed above the tree lines and spilled like quicksilver onto the lake.

"Brrrr," she said suddenly, folding her arms across her chest. I tossed one towel onto the rear-facing bench seat and unrolled the other, wrapping it around her shoulders like a cape. She took it gratefully and before I could wrap myself, she leaned in for another kiss.

We dried ourselves unhurriedly, making eye contact and drinking in casual glimpses of one another. The sexual tension was electric and unwilling to wait.

I adjusted the back of the bench seat, folding it down to form a tanning pad about the size of a double bed. I spread my towel across the surface and sat waiting. Brenna approached, wrapped in her towel, and sat next to me. I put my arm around her shoulders and we rolled gently onto our sides, face to face, knee to knee, caressing each other.

Brenna's towel loosened and her body was revealed to me again. I felt her shallow breathing on my neck, tasted her soft winey lips. We became a tangle of limbs and wet hair under the moonlight.

"Are we safe?" she whispered to me.

"Yes," I said softly into her ear. I had seen Dr. Snip Snip a year after Meagan came along. We were safe.

And there on glassy Lake Cooke, on a warm night in September, the pale priestly guardian of my widower's celibacy removed his vestments, mopped his troubled brow, and left the building. When we were finished I lay on the tanning pad next to Brenna, her fingers caressing my chest, and felt adored, masculine, at peace. We lay there for a long time, allowing our eyes to close.

34.

THE OBSERVER EFFECT | 2021

IT'S THURSDAY MORNING, DAY FOUR OF LIVING IN A TRULY empty nest. There's *knowing* logically that you're alone in place - I have no problem with that and I've prepared myself for it - and then there's *feeling* that you're alone, and that's harder.

The most stark reminder of the emptiness of the nest is that every single thing is exactly where it's supposed to be. For thirty years I've been shouting across our houses to Diane or the kids, *Where's the remote? Where's my charger? Who ate the leftover pad thai?* Every movable and edible object on prem was up for grabs, a maddening chaos that I now sorely miss.

These days things remain exactly where I leave them. It's depressing to see my iPhone charger plugged into the exact same outlet on the kitchen counter day in and day out, its thin cable twisted exactly as I left it. Who ate the leftover pad thai? No mystery there either.

I consider a business idea: empty nesters and widowers could hire gig economy workers to shuffle around their houses for an hour each day, putting the dishes away in the wrong places, hiding the scotch tape, burying the TV remote under cushions. It'd be an app like Uber and you could specify your desired chaos level on a scale of one to ten. (Actually, make that eleven.)

For some reason I begin to patrol the house. Maybe it's an urge to take inventory, even though I know exactly what I have. Maybe I'm looking for something that's slightly out of place, a clue that supernatural forces or vestigial gestures from higher dimensions exist. My large empty home is the perfect control group for a scientific study of these phenomena. Since it's only me here, anything even slightly out of place is proof positive of unseen forces.

I pause in the formal dining room. It's the room we always walk *past*, never *in*. There on the long polished table is the elegant mahogany box containing Diane's earthly remains. I placed it there after her memorial service last March and haven't touched it since. I don't know why. I don't ascribe any meaning to its being there. But after a year and a half it has legitimized its presence, a sterling example of squatter's rights.

Then suddenly for no reason I lift the box in my hands, surprised (again) by its weight, and carry it through the kitchen and into our family room. There are built-in shelves on either side of the fireplace with framed photos, art books, and other ephemera accumulated over the years. I place Diane on top of a volume of Edward Hopper prints that has laid there for a decade, maybe longer.

This will be my first experiment: to see if Diane moves herself back to the dining room table.

I make my way upstairs to the office and laconically jiggle the mouse, summoning my monitors to life. The market won't open for almost two hours, but I check the futures (*meh*) and scroll through headlines. I haven't had any open positions for a while - my favorite stocks all feel fully priced and I'm not sure I want to sell insurance against any price drops.

My phone vibrates with a text and I know it will be Dale. This is about the time of day we start swapping options tactics.

poker tonight? he's asking.

It's fair to say I've been in a low grade funk since dropping Meagan off at BC. Not because of Meagan being gone. I'm thrilled for her.

No, it's because I feel rudderless.

Last summer I was intent on rebuilding myself. The kids were both home and we leaned on each other for mutual support, slogging through the grief of Diane's death and then in almost the very next instant the arrival of the pandemic. The hardships became a wall we scaled together.

This summer I began the search for my own prime factors. I need them now. I need to restore my sense of purpose, I need to be brutally honest about who I am. I gaze through the window at a gray morning. The surface of Lake Cooke is choppy.

One of the best questions ever put to me came during an on-campus interview when Microsoft came to Davidson College. I had no business going to that interview - my next four years belonged to the US Air Force - but I was fascinated by Microsoft and young Bill Gates in 1987 so I signed up. It was a twenty minute interview, a lot of name, vitals and course load, but near the end, the recruiter, a young severe woman, asked me, *"When you're not doing anything at all, what are you thinking about?"*

I had never actually thought about what I was thinking about (this was before the age of *meta*). I remember telling her, *I'm sort of a daydreamer. When I'm just sitting around, I play through different situations in my life a million different ways to see all the possible outcomes. I break up with my girl-friend and see what that feels like. Then I imagine her dating my roommate. Then I drop on one knee and propose to her. I imagine my advisor not getting tenure and leaving me hanging with an incomplete thesis. Then I imagine him meeting me off campus after he's been fired and together we make a major breakthrough - we prove Fermat's Last Theorem, or something like that - and he gets rehired and I get my degree. Or I imagine running into him one night, homeless, behind the Soda Shop on Main Street, rheumy and helpless. That's what I'm thinking. I'm thinking through a thousand tiny scenarios about my everyday life.*

When I was finished she looked up from her clipboard and said, *Okay.*

And that was that. I did not get invited to Redmond like the more promising candidates. But for some reason I never forgot that question. It opened my mind *to* my mind.

So I ask myself, *Jack, when you're not doing anything at all (like right now), what are you thinking about?*

Money, for one thing. I haven't had a regular paycheck since my early forties. I'm a one-percenter, I suppose, or maybe a two-percenter. I'm not sure what the cutoff is, but I'm on the bottom ledge of whichever it is. My money guy and friend (but a busy friend), Hookes, wires me walking around money every month, the interest and dividends thrown off by my account, but he will not let me touch the principal.

Around the time my father died, I tiptoed into the world of options trading and that has more or less become my job these days. Most people would scoff at the notion that this is a job (it's like saying you're a professional poker player, and a second rate one at that), but I've had a strong work ethic all my life and the options trading gives me the feeling and satisfaction of work. I do it every day (just about), I set goals, I measure my performance. If the Microsoft HR weenie were here in my office with her edgy glasses and clipboard, she would be nodding her approval.

The problem with options trading is that it occupies too much of my present tense. At any given moment, I'm either stalking prey with the certain knowledge I will need to react instantly when the opportunity arises, or I *am* the prey, scampering up trees to get just beyond the slashing claws of a sharp sell-off. I don't actually work very much on any given day, but between 9:30 and 4:00 I need to be vigilant. The result is that my mental foreground is fully occupied even when I'm not actually doing anything, and the background part of my brain reserved for pondering and philosophy is in an alarming state of atrophy.

When I lay this out explicitly for myself, I don't like it one bit.

I thought the Microsoft lady was nodding approval but now I see she's scowling at me and notating something - it could be the shape of an "X" - on her clipboard.

After money the next thing would have to be women. Not sex (most of the time, anyway), but something more ephemeral. Something having to do with *completeness*.

In one of my philosophy classes at Davidson I read *The Symposium* by Plato, his great exhortation on love featuring noted thinkers of the day. Aristophanes, the comic poet, proclaimed that in the remote past each human was in fact two, grafted onto one another back to back. Zeus ordered each person split in half to enfeeble the growing power of the species and in doing so condemned us to forever spend our days searching for our other half.

For most of my life I've been part of a couple. There was a monogamous (and short) train of girlfriends in high school and college, and then of course there was Diane for thirty years. *JackandDiane* was practically a single word among friends, at parties, on Christmas cards, on *everything*. When Diane died there was suddenly no more *andDiane*. Zeus has cleaved us in half.

It's not that I'm in a hurry to remarry, or that I even want to remarry *ever*. It's that I've never fully come to terms with my singularity.

On business trips I was often alone in the evenings. I despised going out by myself, though I did from time to time when I was curious about a highly recommended restaurant, or when I didn't feel like skipping dinner or shoveling down carry-out Chinese in my hotel room.

Everything about dining alone was dreadful, beginning with the hostess's question, *How many?* I would reply meekly, *One*. She (it was almost always a she) would inevitably cock her pretty head and double check, *Just one?* I would nod. *Okay, table for one.* She would lead me to a four top in the center of the restaurant, usually directly under a light, and while I was being seated she would loudly remove the other place settings. Attractive couples at the tables around me would stop their conversation to study me, speculate on my aloneness, and discreetly check my ankle for a child predator tracking device. After an eternal moment a handsome, shallow waiter who was almost certainly banging the hostess would approach and ask, *Are you expecting anyone else?*

In the first few months after Diane's death I was in a fog of grief and self pity, buoyed along by friends and Club ladies bearing casseroles. The wave of sympathy gradually subsided and soon everyone retreated into the lockdown. When the world finally began its tentative reopening, I felt like the lonely diner everywhere I went. Not just at restaurants, but everywhere - the grocery store, Lowe's, the craft beers shop.

Table for one, that was me.

I knew then and now that the lonely diner phenomenon was mostly in my head. Those other couples at the restaurant weren't looking at me. They didn't give a crap about me. The same goes for the mushroom headed middle aged moms at the grocery store and the bleary day drinkers at the Pour House. But all the same I had (and still have) an uncomfortable self consciousness about singledom.

The Callany Incompleteness Theorem states that Jack Callany is incomplete, ambiguous, fractional and ineffectual without a woman.

I recite this theorem with authority to the Microsoft human resources robot and she visibly recoils, shaking her head almost imperceptibly. She says nothing but scribbles further notations on her clipboard. I'm losing her, I feel the interview collapsing in slow motion. Desperate, I reach across the table and touch her left hand, which has no ring, and say, *You and me, babe, how about it?*

I am dismissed from the interview and find myself standing dazed in a hallway of venerable Chambers Hall. I will simply never be invited to Redmond.

Have I surfaced another prime factor? Is the *Callany Incompleteness Theorem* an essential part of me? As with money, I hope not, I don't like it. I want to be whole, in and of myself, without the need for another person. My prime factors should be intrinsic - here within me - yielding my whole self when multiplied together.

I ignore Dale's text and instead pad downstairs for another cup of coffee. The plastic cartridge from my first cup is still in the machine, further evidence that nothing ever changes around here. I glance into the family room and verify that Diane remains prostrate atop Edward Hopper.

When my second cup is ready I head upstairs. I'm still thinking about the lonely diner and decide to capitalize it, *Lonely Diner*. Idea for the future (soon): open a chain of restaurants that cater to solo diners. The tables will be arranged humanely so that diners don't face one another and each will be set with a single place setting. The staff will be trained to be friendly and flirtatious, never judgemental about the singularity of the clientele.

Should the *Lonely Diner* have a bar? Probably, that's where the profits are. But with that line of reasoning, I realize that bars actually are the present day solution for the lonely diner. In my mind I pivot the idea to *Lonely Diner (Alcohol Free)* and suddenly it sounds dreadful. I've experienced an entire episode of *Shark Tank* entirely in my own mind before reaching the top of the staircase.

Still, I feel I am making headway on prime factors. I decide to stick with it a bit longer. Anyway, the markets still aren't open.

The role of women and the curse of Aristophanes requires more reflection, but I want to park it for now. I need to get to the bottom of the Brenna episode, for one thing. *What on the hell was I thinking?* to quote the perspiring Debaditya Bhattacharjee.

There's this business of mental *Shark Tank*. I've done it all my life, even before *Shark Tank* or the rise of venture capital. When something annoys the shit out of me, I become young Tom Edison and try to fix it, defeat it or neutralize it. This skill probably helped me in my career as a fiber engineer. I was never an inventor *per se*, meaning I never applied for a patent (maybe I should have), but I was constantly figuring out fiber routes, capacity loads, upgrades, uptime and God only knows what else for our clients all over the country.

It's fair to say I have an inventor's mind. That's not exactly the same as being creative. I can't draw, can't write poetry (or prose for that matter), can't fold origami swans, but I am creative in a way that lets me solve practical problems. I can turn a bucket of bolts into something.

Okay, so where am I with the prime factors? When I first started down this path of introspection, I assigned myself *smart ass* and *defiance*. Now I'm (maybe) adding *money obsessed* and *in need of continuous female companionship*, and possibly *possessing an inventor's mind*. Not a very flattering portrait. But at this stage I won't toss anything out - I need to be brutally honest with myself if I'm going to get anywhere.

I turn to the physical. We are not just *mens* but *manus*, as Jimmy has reminded me. I care about my health and fitness, and though I can't say I treat my body like a temple, I run every week, fast one or two days each week, and keep a close eye on my waistline. I'm thought to be a lean healthy guy by the people who know me. That in itself is probably the kiss of death. How many times have you heard, *he was so healthy and then he just dropped dead, he was the last guy you'd expect to have a … stroke … heart attack … pulmonary embolism …* the list is endless.

Is health and fitness a prime factor or am I kidding myself? Am I intrinsically driven to be healthy, or is it vanity? (All is vanity.) Is health and fitness just a support beam under my need for female companionship, a lemma to the *Callany Incompleteness Theorem*? I reflect on this. If I were doomed to be the Lonely Diner for the rest of my days, would I care how I looked? Would the Lonely Diner be picking at a kale salad, intent to eat only half, or would he surrender to the wings, flatbreads and death by chocolate?

I lean back in my chair and try to think honestly and deeply about this silly question. What comes to me is that I am *calm*, always have been. I have a steady way of looking at people despite whatever inner turmoil I may be feeling. I credit my modest poker winnings to this characteristic. Big Slick, pair of Kings, unsuited two-seven, doesn't matter. My face remains impassive. Even when I have the absolute right to freak out, when in fact it's weird *not* to freak out, I don't. When my cell phone rang on Leap Day and Siobhan told me Diane was face down on the clay court, unresponsive, and they had called 9-1-1, I had eased my car into the left turn lane and waited patiently for a green arrow so I could make a U-turn and drive to the Club.

I feel certain that my calmness is linked to my health and fitness, though I don't know the direction of causality. Trail running and fasting require mental toughness, the ability to press on when the physical body is wailing for relief. Do those things long enough and you can press on when the emotional mind is wailing for relief, too.

I settle on the word *fortitude* to capture all of it: health, fitness and interior calm. It feels honest to me. I have fortitude. I think of my lanky sophomore year roommate Joe from Amarillo. He was fond of the phrase *testicular fortitude*, the most resolute form of fortitude. For a moment I pause and think about Joe. In my mind he's ageless, a snapshot, reclining in a bean bag chair, his long skinny legs taking up too much floorspace in our tiny room, aimlessly plucking at guitar strings when he should have been studying.

Rock on, Joe.

That's another thing, these snapshots. None of us are snapshots, we're feature length films. But we remember others and even our own pasts in snapshots, single frames extracted from the reel. So what is a person? A collection of freeze frames, or a continuous arc?

My mind drifts to a physics class, sophomore or junior year, the double slit experiment (why do I remember this?). It's a disarmingly simple demonstration that light is both a particle and a wave *at the same time*. What matters is what the observer is looking for. If the observer is looking for particles, they see particles. If they're looking for waves, they see waves. *The Observer Effect.*

I'm the observer of Jack Callany (maybe not the least critical, I admit, but certainly the most familiar). What am I looking for, a particle or a wave?

A freeze frame or a film? Can I find my prime factors by examining each frame, or are they only revealed in the continuous whole?

There's an allure to peering closely at individual freeze frames in a life. We can choose the best moments, the prettiest smiles, the best lighting, and then convince ourselves that these moments represent our essence, our very best selves. Unfortunately it doesn't ring true for me, any more than Meagan's TikTok videos ring true, and they're not true because she never eats the entire hamburger or banana split, or whatever, at the end.

Say we outlawed airbrushing and took the ugly moments along with the perfect ones, would that bring us closer to the truth about who someone is? I don't know. Take the case of Meagan at this very instant - she is luxuriating in the newness of college life, passing out superlative awards to everyone she meets, and none of them remind her of anyone she already knows. Do these moments she is experiencing right now, the good and bad together, sum up Meagan? It doesn't feel right. Particle analysis doesn't tell the whole story. If I do particle analysis on myself, I'm afraid the effort would not surface any primes.

So the right answer must be the wave. We need to watch the whole movie, in IMAX, follow the full arc of a person's story if we want to tease out prime factors. The sum of the particles is less than the wave. Quod erat demonstratum.

Except maybe I'm just falling prey to the Observer Effect, seeing the exact thing I'm looking for. QED under reconsideration.

What could be revealed in the full arc of a person's story that can't be gleaned from some well chosen moments? What comes to me now is: *wisdom*. When all the particles - all the episodes - of a lifetime are observed as a wave, an emergent property appears and we call it wisdom. Every new face reminding us of someone we already know, every situation informed by shards of past situations, this is the sort of wisdom that yields hidden prime factors.

I spin around in my office chair feeling smug, a eureka moment has crystallized in my head. Wisdom. I'll go hunting in *this* jungle and I'll figure out Jack Callany.

I clear my mind and focus on the computer screen. The markets have been open for ten minutes and I now need to get on the ball. I make the mistake of glancing at a stack of books on the nightstand that I've either read or intend to read. On top of the stack is *Time Enough for Love*, an old Heinlein sci fi novel. I say this is a mistake because I now remember a quote from the book's leading character, a two thousand year old man named Lazarus Long.

"... age does not bring wisdom. Often it merely changes simple stupidity into arrogant conceit. Its only advantage, so far as I have been able to see, is that it spans change. A young person sees the world as a still picture, immutable. An old person has had his nose rubbed in changes and more changes and still more changes so many times that he knows it is a moving picture, forever changing."

I should have started here rather than digging a mental hole and filling it right back up again. *Arrogant conceit.* Those are my prime factors, wisdom be damned. I'm my own bucket of bolts.

Yep I'll be there, I reply to Dale.

35.

I'M SORRY FOR YOUR LOSS
| 2009

WE BURIED MY MOTHER ON THE FIRST SUNDAY OF 2009. IT WAS a cheerless day, the sky ashen and the temperature made colder by the mid-Atlantic winter humidity. She had come up just short of seventy years, a victim of R. J. Reynolds. She smoked Pall Malls, *her* mother's brand, though Oma had somehow evaded small cell carcinoma and lived to see eighty-five.

The burial was brief and my father stood throughout the service, ignoring the graveside chair that had been placed there for him. His face was grim and tense, and he issued rough, throat clearing coughs without parting his lips. I did not see him cry.

They had celebrated their forty-second anniversary five months earlier, though by that time mom's prognosis was dim. Dad had taken her to the Grove Park Inn in Asheville for two nights, where she had a massage both days and an early dinner both nights. Dad told me later that she slept most of the time. He had sat in the armchair beside her bed reading Patrick O'Brian on the Kindle I had bought for him.

My parents had lived their own fine yet unremarkable American dream. Dad had gone through the Navy ROTC program at Chapel Hill and that landed him an eighteen month tour in Vietnam. He served on a supply vessel, rarely in harm's way, and he resigned his commission after four years. He returned to his native North Carolina, married, and launched a career in textiles, which along with tobacco was the lifeblood of the state in those days.

Mom was a middle school math teacher in the Guilford County school district, though in those days middle school was called junior high school and ran through ninth grade. (I think *junior high school* is the better term, more aspirational.) I attended the school where my mother taught, though I never had her as a teacher. I was on the "gifted and talented" track (now a vanquished term) and Mom taught the regular classes. She was not popular, though I believe now it was the math that was unpopular and Mom was just the unfortunate messenger. Kids I didn't know said horrible things to me about her. *Don't you hate your mother?* I heard over and over. *Do you hate yours?* I would reply.

My mother was a terrible cook though I didn't know it until I left home. She cooked strictly according to recipes, many gleaned from the back of a seasoning pouch or the side of a box. She used only the exact ingredients specified, and in the exact amounts. If the instructions on Hamburger Helper said *Serves 3-4* she deemed that adequate for our family. Her repertoire consisted of a half dozen items that she prepared in regular rotation - spaghetti with meat sauce, Polish sausages, chili, Hawaiian Chicken, hotdogs stuffed with cheese, and fish sticks with tater tots. Brian and I loved these meals and we drifted into the kitchen every evening just before six to see which treat was in store.

Dad ruled the family dinner table sternly, demanding daily reports from Brian and me, quizzing us on history and vocabulary words he thought we should have learned by that point. He ate intently, chewed hard, and helped himself to seconds if there were any (rarely). As a teen I challenged Dad for the second helping, racing through my first serving and then slowly savoring my second under his glare.

On occasion he would challenge Brian or me to name a word he didn't know. It was impossible - the man had a prodigious vocabulary, though how he acquired it we never knew. One night I challenged him weakly with *numerator*. It gave the old officer pause. *It's part of a fraction*, he had said thoughtfully, then added, *it's the top of a fraction. The denominator is on the bottom - that's why we have the phrase least common denominator.* He had a fifty-fifty chance and damn if he didn't get it right. That's the closest either of us came to stumping him.

The reports and pop quizzes and competitive eating made our family meal a thoroughly unrelaxing affair, though in retrospect I realize it prepared Brian and me for many things that lay ahead - the military mess hall, for one, but also confidence when speaking with adults and an appreciation for precise language. I'm also certain that my father's severe nature made me both defiant and gentle.

I watched as Mom's casket was lowered slowly into the ground. Jimmy, eight years old, held my left hand, and Meagan, five, held my right. Diane stood on the other side of Meagan. Suddenly grief washed over me. I pictured my mother's wasted and lifeless body inside the dark casket. Then I pictured that very casket in the earth under six feet of a damp Carolina clay. I didn't want these images in my mind and rushed to replace them with others from happier times - Mom at Wrightsville beach, her hair soft and natural after a week in the ocean and no visit to the beauty shop; Mom in the kitchen, bending with oven mitts to remove a cookie sheet of tater tots; Mom in the car, smoking, the windows rolled up despite the summer heat so the wind would not disturb her hairdo; Mom on Christmas morning sitting in an armchair while Brian and I tore into presents. Tears rolled down my face.

"Come on," Diane said, gently taking my hand.

I looked one last time at the rectangular hole in the earth. Staff from the funeral home stood by soberly, ready to encourage us to move along if we should linger. I was struck by how perfectly straight and smooth the sides of the hole were. As Diane began to move toward our minivan, I reached into the breast pocket of my suit coat and removed a new unopened packet of McCormick's chili seasoning and flicked it like a small square frisbee into the grave. The funeral director watched impassively. He'd seen everything over the years.

Brian led the slow procession of cars from the cemetery. Dad sat in the front seat with him, his sole passenger. Brian had not married, not to K'arma, not to any of the other contestants.

"If you're gay just come out and tell us," I had joked with Brian recently.

"I bet I've had sex more recently than you," he replied. I'm pretty sure he was right. Bastard.

"That doesn't mean you aren't gay," I said.

We followed the procession down Friendly Avenue to my parent's house on Starmount Drive, their home of forty years and the backdrop of my childhood. As kids Brian and I had tended the wide lawn meticulously under orders from Dad. We mowed and edged the grass, trimmed the shrubs and raked up every clipping, and piled leaves high in the fall. In every season and without warning Dad would send us on *leaf patrol* to collect the stray leaves that blemished his neat green turf. On this January day the yard was spare and shabby, the shameful result of a year of neglect by Dad and me.

Brian pulled into the carport and I parked behind him. Other cars parked along the curb on both sides of Starmount. Somber black clad figures emerged from them, frail and frosty couples mainly, husbands supporting their wives' elbows as they gingerly made their way up the drive to the side door off the carport. Friends never used the front door.

We gathered in the kitchen and Dad stood in front of the refrigerator, a vantage point that allowed him to greet each guest as they entered. He seemed to grow more stern, more military in his posture, as each couple entered. He was steeling himself for the next few hours of caterwauling. I knew him well enough to know this was a deeply private time for him. He would endure the reception, the reminiscing, the fawning, but already he wanted it to be over.

Maylem and gaylem, he called this sort of thing. I never knew if he made the term up or if it was a Gaelic fragment from his own Irish mother.

Diane busied herself in the kitchen, removing foil and Saran wrap from the plates and casserole dishes that had been dropped off that morning. She had grown larger and today she dressed, as she almost always did, in a loose flowing dress and a long wide scarf, an attempt to make her girth seem an illusion. She floated around the kitchen like a sailboat in black, her long hair, now completely gray, a flowing pennon behind her.

Diane approached my father while he was greeting the Weavers and gently touched his shoulder. "Excuse me, John," she said, "I need to get a few things out of the fridge."

He turned to her and on his face I caught a flash of simultaneous annoyance and confusion. I don't know if Diane saw it, or would have even recognized it. I was so highly tuned to the man's moods from my childhood.

He stepped forward, allowing Diane to reach into the refrigerator and withdraw the cheese plate, a bowl of grapes, and coffee creamer.

"Come on, Dad," I said. "Let's move into the living room and let Diane set up in here."

He nodded, grateful to hear my voice, and walked with me into the next room. He continued to stand, shoulders rolled back, chin high. I recognized almost everyone though it has been twenty or thirty years since I had seen many of them. Once full and fleshy faces were now lined and sagging. Mrs. Weaver, a bawdy reveler who never stopped at just one martini was now a sober and taciturn church mouse. Mr. Weaver had somehow become shorter than her, apologetic and lost in his own thoughts.

It was the eyes that helped me to recognize everyone, even when the names eluded me. I thought at the time, *eyes don't age.* The sockets deepen, the lids become creased hoods, but the irises are unchanging in both color and sparkle. Mr. Fike, single then and now, still had a way of smiling with his eyes that drew me to him. He winked at me from across the room, a signal from him to me only. I tried to return the wink, but I'm an average to poor winker and he probably thought I had just been stung on the cheek by a bee. He returned his attention to a bourbon on ice, which I found to be a singularly good idea myself.

Diane stood at the threshold between the kitchen and the living room and announced that lunch was ready. The din of conversation continued but I sensed a slight gravitational shift toward the food. It was good to have a clear and simple mission under these gloomy ambiguous circumstances.

Go. Now. Make a plate of food. Occupy your mouth with an earnest bite. Give yourself a reprieve from the awkward, untrained process of expressing grief.

Thank God for admin, I thought to myself. When Dad called on New Year's Day late in the afternoon with the news that Mom was gone, shock and sadness filled my mind alongside unbidden thoughts of the clerical duties ahead. Funeral arrangements, phone calls, an obituary, cheese plates. The death industry is like a car wash - you take your hands off the gas pedal and steering wheel and it pulls you along slowly and inexorably until you pop out the other side clean and shiny, the job complete. Grief and loss and the deep questions of purpose and meaning retreat under the press of admin and ritual.

The Jews have probably had it right all along, covering mirrors and sitting shiva. A different kind of car wash.

I helped Jimmy and Meagan make plates of food and led them to my childhood bedroom, which was still largely intact. My parents had used it as a guest room but left in place my desk and bookcase and the MIT poster on the wall across from my bed. The kids sat on the floor and picked at their carrots and pigs-in-a-blanket and potato chips in the disinterested way of children.

"This was my room when I was a kid," I told them.

"We know, Dad," Jimmy said. "We sleep in here every time we visit Grandma and Grandpa."

"Well maybe Meagan doesn't know that," I said to Jimmy.

"She knows, Dad," he replied.

Meagan let out a whimper and hung her head low, her forehead almost touching her crossed legs. I sat on the floor beside her and rubbed her back.

"Why'd Grandma have to die?" she asked.

"She was sick, Meagan," Jimmy said. "She smoked too many cigarettes."

I kept rubbing Meagan's back and glanced at Jimmy. *From the mouths of babes*, I thought to myself.

After a moment I broke the silence and said, "Let's play a little game." Jimmy looked at me skeptically, Meagan kept her head down. "You can each pick out one thing in my old room - anything you want - and I'll tell you a story about it."

Jimmy stood and began walking around the room, inspecting everything like a detective. He went to my desk and eyed an unsolved Rubik's cube. Then he fingered the dried yellow boutonniere I wore to prom. It was pinned to the corkboard on the wall behind my desk with the same pin that pierced the lapel of my rented prom tux. I started to formulate a version of my prom story that would be suitable for an eight and five year old.

But then Jimmy turned and pointed to the MIT poster on the wall. "What's *mitt*?" he asked in a tone of mild defiance.

"That's M-I-T," I said. "It stands for Massachusetts Institute of Technology." The poster was a stylized image of the Great Dome, the centerpiece of campus, with *MIT* written across the top in the low-res robotic Westminster font that in the 1960s heralded the future.

"What's that?" he asked.

"It's a college, one of the best in the world," I said, then added, "I wanted to go there."

"Why didn't you," he asked, staring into me.

The old bolus of rejection rose inside me. "I didn't get in," I said.

"You weren't smart enough?" Jimmy asked.

"No, I guess not," I replied.

Meagan looked up and sniffed.

"Well that's where I'm gonna go," Jimmy said. He fixed his eyes on the poster.

"I bet you will," I said. "That would make me very proud."

"I'm going there, too, Daddy," said Meagan. She slipped into my lap and rested her head on my chest.

I smiled and kissed the top of her head.

"Mom and I will be there for both graduations," I said.

"You go now, Meagan," said Jimmy. "Pick out something and Dad will tell you the story."

Meagan climbed from my lap and inexplicably began crawling on the carpeted floor, sniffing.

"Anything you want, Meagan," I said. "Just point to it and I'll tell the story."

Meagan suddenly released a loud bark and stared at me. I barked back at her. In the next instant Jimmy was on all fours barking. Meagan barked again, louder, and I rolled onto all fours and barked back. Jimmy barked again. We all started barking.

The door opened and Diane stood looking at us in wonder. I made eye contact with her and barked.

She rolled her eyes. "What's going on in here?"

"Your kids are both going to MIT," I said.

She arched an eyebrow. "That's obvious," she said.

Diane stayed in my old bedroom with the kids so I could return to the reception. Dad was still on his feet, ramrod straight. Brian stood with him attentively while friends chatted and drifted on.

"I hear ya struck it rich," a voice said from behind. I turned to see Mr. Weaver, now detached from his wife. His entire spotted scalp was visible through oily strands of gray hair, though the most striking aspect of his face were his eyebrows, dense and thick. He had normal eyebrows twenty-five years ago when I saw him here regularly. What bug in the human source code causes the hair on the head to grow sparse while the brows become Amazonian? For an instant I envisioned myself as a follicle surgeon, dressed in a lab coat, slicing away thin strips of Mr. Weaver's eyebrows and sewing them carefully onto the top of his head. In my daydream he is under general anesthesia so I don't have to chat.

"Filthy," I replied with one of my half-ass winks. Mr. Weaver - I knew his first name was Roger but he had never invited me to use his first name, and I'm not even sure I could retrain my brain if he did - was not holding a drink like almost everyone else in the room. He clasped his hands together, kneading his fingers as though greedy for my story and perhaps my money, too. "I've got my jet warming up on the tarmac right now. Want to go for a ride later tonight?"

Mr. Weaver leaned back and raised both eyebrows ever so slightly. His small eyes probed my face. I flashed a smile and could feel it was crooked, asymmetrical, slightly pained. Mr. Weaver smiled back at me and leaned forward again, relieved that I was still good ole Jackie, a regular guy, John and Linda's whiz kid. He unclasped his hands and slapped me on the shoulder.

"Nothing would surprise me, Jackie," he said, slightly ingratiating.

I had in fact become a little bit rich. On Leap Day the year before - it was a Friday - around three in the afternoon, just over four million dollars was deposited into my savings account by a law firm representing the mid-western telecommunications company that had purchased American Fiber Network. I had been there fifteen years and had been quietly and steadily accumulating stock options along the way.

We knew exactly what the amount would be. It had been disclosed in exhibits to the dense legal documents I had been required to sign on the last day of 2007. It was in those exhibits that I learned I was getting the smallest payday of any member of the executive team. The CEO would haul in sixty million, the CFO forty million. I felt like a patsy - obviously I had not advocated hard enough for myself or been greedy enough. But on the other hand, four million dollars and no requirement to stay on or move to Chicago was more than I imagined or knew what to do with.

I had been working two or three hours each day during January and February as part of a short term consulting contract to train my counterpart in Chicago. My counterpart was, in fact, a posse of Pakistani engineers with degrees from Champaign-Urbana and H1-B visas. They weren't particularly interested in my engineering skills since they had developed software that did everything I did, and more. The arrangement suited me just fine.

My contract expired at the end of February, which of course had one extra day that year. I thought briefly of my separation from the Air Force years before, when I had given them one extra day, too. The original management team's final payouts were released from escrow that morning and mine posted to my bank account at three. Just like that, I was retired. My CEO and other cronies had all left immediately after the sale, or after much shorter transition contracts. On this day, I was the last member of the old guard. I left the office with no fanfare and drove immediately to our wine shop in Clarendon, where I paid two hundred bucks for a bottle of Dom Perignon, already chilled.

"We did pretty well," I said to Mr. Weaver. "The money made it possible for us to get out of DC and buy our place on Lake Cooke." He nodded, pleased he was getting the inside scoop. "Diane and I want the kids to grow up slowly. Lake Cooke seems perfect."

"That's great, Jackie, just great," Mr. Weaver said. He was kneading his hands together again. "So are you retired? Both of you?"

"I haven't figured that out, Mr. Weaver," I replied to him. "I'm not really the retiring type. God knows I'm not much of a golfer. I need to figure out what I'm going to do next."

Mr. Weaver seemed disappointed.

"I'm glad to be close to Dad now," I added. "I've been back and forth a lot since the summer."

Diane and I had made a few house hunting trips to Lake Cooke last spring. My mother had been diagnosed at that point, and we wanted to be close. Lake Cooke was less than two hours away from my folks and had everything we were looking for - nice homes on the water, good schools, and proximity to Charlotte. We decided to rent for one year so we could get the lay of the land. In April we found a modest place off the water but perfect for our transition year. In June we sold the red and white house in Arlington for more than three times what we had paid fourteen years earlier. The cash would go a long way at Lake Cooke (and further than I could have ever imagined in June of 2008, moments before the catastrophic housing bust).

I spent that summer beating a trail between Lake Cooke and Greensboro. I spent two or three days each week with Mom, telling stories and talking, and helping Dad around the house. Mom especially liked hearing my tall tales - college days, Air Force days, hijinx at the office. I admitted to supplying Oma with cigarettes on our back porch at Christmas (Mom said the story made her want one, but she demurred when she realized I was ready to make it happen). I fine tuned my storytelling skills, embellishing the beautiful and the dastardly, and circling in slowly on punchlines. *That didn't really happen!* she exclaimed over and over, unless she had dozed off, which became increasingly common as autumn advanced. Mom was able to stay at home through Christmas Day, but on December 26 we moved her to hospice. She lived to see the sun rise on 2009, but just barely.

Mrs. Weaver materialized and Mr. Weaver shrunk visibly in her presence.

"I'm sorry for your loss, Jackie," she said to me.

"Yes," said Mr. Weaver, "we're sorry for your loss."

I hate the phrase *I'm sorry for your loss*. And I feel the same way about *thank you for your service*. Both feel perfunctory, cardboard, and yet I've relied on them many times myself. Their saving grace is simplicity and absence of maudlin sentimentality. They're like boiled noodles, limp and flavorless, but useful for the delivery of sauce. These phrases are useful for the delivery of well meaning smiles and firm handshakes.

Mrs. Weaver offered one such smile now. "We're heading out," she said. "Let us know if there's anything we can do for John."

"Of course," I agreed, nodding. "Thank you for being here today."

Thank you for your service, I thought to myself.

Mr. Weaver gave me a final look of mixed envy and puzzlement, then turned to follow his wife.

Two hours later the final guests, two couples I did not know at all, were out the door. Neither couple wanted to be the last to leave, so they became entangled particles, collecting their purses and coats in a synchronized but wordless manner. They left through the front door, which was my clue they were not close friends.

Brian locked the door behind them and we turned to face Dad, who was still standing and looked haggard. Without a word he moved to his armchair and lowered himself heavily. He toed off one shoe, flipped it onto the floor, then toed off the other. It was a casual act I cannot remember ever seeing him do before. He was the Mr. Rogers type, crossing one leg over the opposite knee and carefully unlacing a shoe, then methodically repeating on the other side. He lifted his stocking feet to the ottoman, crossed his hands over his sternum, and released a long sigh. His eyelids closed for a moment, then reopened, but his eyes were dull and resigned.

"I'm sorry for your loss," I said to him.

"I'm sorry for *your* loss," he replied.

"Thank you for your service," I said.

Dad regarded me for a moment. I may have detected the faintest flash of playfulness in his eyes.

"Thank *YOU* for *YOUR* service," he said.

"Why the hell can't anyone think of anything else to say?" Brian asked.

Dad let out something like a chuckle and low growl.

"When I die, I want people to tell it like it is," he said. "I want them to say I was an irascible bastard."

"I can attest to that," I said reassuringly. "I'll be sure to emphasize it in my eulogy." I grinned, Dad grinned back.

"Can I fix you a drink?" asked Brian.

He didn't answer and we sat quietly. Then he said, "No." A pause. "No, I just need to …." His voice trailed off.

We sat together in silence and the room darkened in the late afternoon gloom. Dad's eyes closed and his breathing became heavy and rhythmic. I closed my eyes too, but did not sleep. My mind replayed scenes from the day - our somber arrival at the cemetery, Dad standing stonily through the service, the creased, pained faces that had filled this room. Faces that had been familiar to me years before, faces that had been busy aging just like my own.

The room was almost dark when I heard Diane's footsteps coming down the hall. She stopped at the entrance to the living room and peered into the darkness while her eyes adjusted.

"Jack?" she whispered.

I rose and stepped to her. "Dad and Brian are asleep," I said.

We eased back down the hall toward my old bedroom.

"I think I'll take the kids now," Diane said to me. I had come in my own car so I could spend a few days with Dad. Diane would drive home with Jimmy and Meagan so they could get back to the school the next day.

We opened the door to my room. Meagan was sprawled across my bed, asleep. Jimmy was on the floor, legs crossed, holding my old Rubik's cube.

Jimmy looked up at me. "Dad, could you solve this?"

I nodded. "At one point, yeah," I said. "I don't think I could solve it anymore."

"Can I have it?" he asked me. I smiled and nodded.

"Come with me," Diane said to Jimmy. "I'm gonna take you and Meagan home." Jimmy was content with his Rubik's cube and stood compliantly. I lifted Meagan into my arms.

"Should we wake your father to say goodbye?" Diane asked.

"No," I said, "Let's let him rest."

Diane and Jimmy walked toward the living room. I carried Meagan and with a free finger turned off the light in the bedroom. I heard Jimmy turning the Rubik's cube, its plastic facets squeaking and scratching. I make a note to add some WD-40 when I got home.

Dad switched on the floor lamp near his chair as we entered the living room. He had woken, maybe to the sounds of the Rubik's cube. For a moment he looked at us blankly.

"I'm sorry we woke you, John," Diane said.

"I wasn't asleep," he replied. But it wasn't true.

"Jack and Brian are staying for a couple days," Diane said. "I'm taking the kids back to Lake Cooke. They have school tomorrow."

Dad gave a single serious nod. "Come here Jimmy," he said. "What've ya got there?"

Jimmy approached him, extending his hand that held the Rubik's cube. "It was Dad's," he said. "It's called a Rubik's cube."

"So it is," my father said.

"I'm going to learn how to solve it," Jimmy said proudly.

"That would be highly efficacious," my father replied. Jimmy beamed.

"Do you know what *efficacious* means, Jimmy?" Diane asked.

"It means smart," he replied.

"That's right," my father said. "You're a highly efficacious young man."

When I was Jimmy's age Dad would've pounced on an erroneous definition. Today he let it slide.

Diane and Jimmy hugged my father and said goodbye, and then left through the kitchen. I followed with Meagan still in my arms. She woke as I positioned her into her car seat and was suddenly wide awake, curious and on full alert.

Diane and Jimmy were already seated up front, Jimmy in his booster seat.

"Daddy," Meagan said inquisitively, "Why did you throw trash in Grandma's grave?"

Diane turned in the driver's seat and looked at me quizzically.

I was amused that Meagan had noticed my private parting act at the cemetery. "That wasn't trash, Honey," I said to her.

"Yes it was," she said with defiance. "I saw you throw paper in Grandma's grave."

"That was a package of McCormick's chili seasoning," I said. A small smile appeared on Diane's face. She understood.

A few years earlier, Mom had placed first in the Guilford County chili cook-off. Not once, but two years running. In the kitchen of this very home hung two blue ribbons marking her culinary skill. I didn't attend the competition the first year she won, but I did the next year to see for myself what sort of competition she faced. It was no amateur event. There were a couple dozen entrants, some were chefs at local restaurants, and they ran the gamut from bison to cinghiale to pressed tofu. Mom had come with the sturdy and unimaginative chili of my childhood - browned ground beef, a can of tomato sauce and a package of McCormick's chili seasoning. For the competition she had employed the entire package whereas for our family she would only use half a package per meal. Scottish thrift.

Mom called me jubilantly after winning her first blue ribbon. Brian and I (and Dad) were speechless, but Mom felt deeply and profoundly vindicated. I went the next year, never imagining she could win two years in a row, and she did exactly that. It was an open and shut case - mom was a great cook after all, and the undisputed chili master of Guilford County.

"Mom will explain on the ride home," I said to Meagan. I kissed her on the forehead and made my way around the minivan, saying goodbye to Jimmy and Diane. Diane squeezed my hand, then rolled up her window and backed out onto Starmount Drive.

When I entered my parent's house, Dad was standing at the fridge surveying the leftover casseroles.

"Hungry?" I asked him.

He emitted a gruff affirmation. I hadn't seen him eat a bite during the reception.

"Have a seat at the table, Dad," I said to him. "I'll get Brian and we'll warm up a few things."

"Let's have some of these," he said, handing me a Tupperware container of pigs-in-blankets. All those years of Mom's cooking had truly ruined his palate.

"Excellent choice," I said to him..

"Highly efficacious," he replied.

36.

HOWL AT THE MOON | 2020

MY EYES OPENED SUDDENLY AND DRANK IN THE SILVER MOON-light. The Lumineers played through the boat's speakers. I was instantly and fully awake and had no idea if I had dozed for two minutes or sixty. The moon was much higher now, well above the treetops.

Quietly I rolled onto my side to face Brenna, my head resting in my raised palm. She lay on her back, her damp wavy hair splayed across the towel. Her face was smooth and unlined, her lips dark and full. The towel covered her body haphazardly.

Brenna blinked once, then twice. She did not turn toward me but she saw me in her peripheral vision.

"That moon," she said softly, and smiled.

I rolled onto my back. We were parallel bodies moonbathing.

"Do you give a lot of lake tours?" Brenna asked playfully.

"I keep my options open," I replied.

"Ah yes," she said. "Options." Her voice trailed off.

"Brenna," I said after an unhurried silence. "You surprised me that night. At the grill. With your footsie."

A small laugh escaped her lips. "Oh my God," she said. "The look on your face!"

"*What?*" I asked sharply. I hadn't revealed anything. When her toe had traced its way slowly up my calf, I was as inscrutable as a face on Mount Rushmore. I had employed my best poker face, unmoved even at the sight of pocket aces.

"Well," she said. "You didn't show it on your face, I guess. But your eyes drilled holes into me. I thought you were hypnotized."

I had no idea. No memory whatsoever of locking onto her that way. Had Pam noticed? Rick?

Brenna rolled onto her side and placed her palm on my chest. "Oh, don't worry about it so much, Mr. Callany. No one saw a thing."

I must have been holding my breath. I released the air and felt myself relax.

"Brenna," I said, looking at her, "Why? Why me?"

She smiled sweetly and waited a moment. Water lapped against the side of the boat. "Pam asked me to. She said you needed to get laid."

No way in hell.

"You're pulling my leg," I said.

"Oh Jack," Brenna said. "You're so mister serious." She moved her hand down my torso. After a moment she continued, "It wasn't Pam. It was all me. I think you're cute. You have a great smile. And the worst wink I've ever seen."

We grew quiet again, both of us content.

Brenna went on, "You're. You know. Sort of…." A pause. "Tragic. Cute tragic."

I closed my eyes. I was resisting the temptation - the overwhelming temptation - to launch a blistering reply. *Tragic? Fuckyou tragic! Is this a sympathy house call?*

But I said nothing. Her words were like an unwelcome roller on the lake that passes under the boat, spills drinks, and moves on, replaced again by still water.

"I don't mean it mean," she said softly. "Last year, in grad school, I dated an older guy. He was really kind, and smart. Guys my age are such asses. They're either flat out assholes, or they're porn addicts. This guy was … real. He had been through some rough times. Tragedy can make a man good."

We lay in silence and I contemplated the most obtuse compliment I had ever received. Tragic is good now. *Tragic is sexy.*

"I don't want to be tragic," I said finally, staring up into the night sky.

Brenna brought her face close to mine and kissed me with her full open mouth. She stroked the side of my face and kissed me again, deeply.

"I'm sorry," she said with a small voice. "You're not tragic. You're handsome. And kind." A pause. "I'm sorry."

Whether it was anger or embarrassment, it subsided with her caress and soft words. We entwined ourselves, towels be damned.

"You really know how to make a girl howl at the moon," she said playfully. Her eyes flashed.

"I didn't hear you howl," I said.

Brenna looked at me curiously, then pulled away and sat back with her legs under her. She was gloriously nude, as smooth as alabaster under the moon. She placed her hands on her thighs, rolled her shoulders back and pointed her chin towards the moon, then released a mournful ascending howl like a lonely coyote in the desert.

When her lungs emptied - and she held the final note impressively - she turned to me, took a deep breath, and smiled broadly. "Did you hear *that*?" she asked.

I smiled and shook my head in disbelief. "I think the whole neighborhood did," I said.

The cove I had anchored in was undeveloped, a rare parcel lined only with trees. But on either end of the cove were prominent homes facing the main channel. I doubted anyone was out, especially on a weeknight, but I could see illuminated windows and the occasional blue flash of a distant television.

Suddenly we heard the loud roar of an engine on the water. A white halogen light washed over us. It was a boat, probably the size of my own, arcing into the cove and plowing high through the water straight toward us. *What the hell?*

"Brenna," I said abruptly, "get into the head." I opened the door to the small bathroom opposite the captain's chair.

She looked at me in terror, then crawled from the tanning pad to the head with a towel in her hand.

"It's just some drunk," I told her, pulling on my boxers. "He'll be gone in a second." Very few boat operators on Lake Cooke were stone cold sober, me included. I used to joke with Diane that I couldn't operate the boat without a beer. Brenna crawled into the head and sat meekly on the closed toilet lid. I shut the door gently.

It wasn't a police boat, that much I know. The few we had on the lake cruised day and night under a distinctive blue light.

In a second the approaching boat slowed and lowered off its plane, sending a deep wave rolling directly toward me. It was about thirty feet away. Its blinding docking lights were still on, but gratefully they were pointed off angle. I was able to make out a lone figure at the helm.

"Everything ok?" a man's voice called across the water. It was a familiar voice, but I couldn't place it.

"Everything's fine," I called back.

There was a moment of silence. The other boat continued to float closer to me. I could almost make out the driver's face in the moonlight.

"I heard a scream," he said, this time with less of a shout. I definitely knew the voice.

"Nimrod?" I called out.

"Who's that?" came the reply.

"Jack," I said. "Callany."

Nimrod's boat, a sleek Chaparral, continued to float closer. My boat rocked in the wake he had created on his approach. I thought of Brenna in the head, tossing and turning. I *really* hoped she would keep quiet, otherwise I would have a lot of 'splaining to do at the Club. *Oh Hi Pam, Hi Aristotle. I was just showing Brenna around the lake. Late on a Wednesday night. Naked.*

"What's going on Jack?" he said accusingly. His boat was suddenly very close to mine. I worried they might make contact.

"Nimrod," I said, "I'm anchored. Do you mind backing off?"

He shifted into reverse, holding his position and not getting any closer.

"I heard a woman screaming," he said. "Are you alone?"

"Yes I'm alone," I said irritably. I don't know why I lied. It wasn't any of his business anyway. I just wasn't ready for anyone, especially Nimrod, to know I was out with a woman, much less that I was making her howl at the moon.

From the head I heard Brenna release a faint mocking howl. It was too low for Nimrod to possibly hear. *This girl is nuts,* I thought to myself. *And I like it.*

"Well I thought I heard something," Nimrod said, his resolve fading.

In the moonlight I could make out his shorts and a white deep sea fishing shirt. There was something hanging around his neck and down his chest. It could have been a pair of binoculars, but it seemed too bulky.

"It was probably a heron," I said. "I heard it too." Herons are beautiful but they have the most god awful banshee shriek. "What about you, Nimrod?" I asked. "Midnight fishing?"

I heard a rare low chuckle from his boat. "Sort of," he said. There was silence. "Fishing for stars. I'm an amateur astronomer."

Who'da thunk?

"Okay, Nimrod," I said. "I'm about to head in. Good luck stargazing."

"Good luck bird watching, Callany," he called back. He spun away from me, engine roaring, and sent another massive wave into the side of my boat. *A born asshole, I thought.*

When the rocking subsided, Brenna emerged from the head, wrapped in her towel. She gave me a goofy smile.

"Is howling at a moon a violation of the community standards?" she asked.

"Absolutely not," I said. "It's encouraged."

She tipped her chin up and drew in a deep breath.

"No," I said, stopping her. "No more howling. Not with Nimrod lurking out there."

She gazed at me. "Oh Jack, don't worry so much."

Brenna let her towel drop and stood before me, once again nude and bathed in the moonlight. She stepped purposefully onto the swim platform where her clothes remained in a tidy pile. I watched her dress unselfconsciously. *It's a good thing Nimrod's wake didn't wash her clothes overboard,* I thought to myself. That would have been interesting. I suppose I could have given her a pair of Meagan's sweats and a tee shirt and sent her home to her mother.

"Ya think Nimrod saw my clothes?" she asked.

Shit. I hadn't even thought about that. He would have said something, he's way too unsubtle.

"I wouldn't worry," I said. "I'll just tell him I'm a cross dressing night-time heron watcher."

Brenna walked to the bow and sat on the seat where we had started the evening. Her tall gold sandals lay on the carpet besider her. From the helm I could make out the glow of her cell phone.

I dressed quickly, pulling on my shorts and shirt. It was nearly midnight and I could feel the enchantment of the evening begin to fade. I activated the windlass and raised the anchor.

We trawled slowly back to my dock. The lake was pristine, inky black, and the moon hung high overhead. I turned the music up and stood at the helm, one finger hooked to the steering wheel, at peace but strangely alone. Brenna worked her phone furiously, unaware of the music, unaware of the grand silhouetted homes we glided past.

"Getting a lot of emails?" I asked over the windshield.

For a moment there was no reply. Brenna was engrossed in her device. "Huh?" she said, and then, "Oh, no, nothing. Just catching up on a few things."

As I stood in the cockpit, I could see the back of her head and catch glimpses of her screen. She was cocking her head and rotating the phone. When Meagan did this sort of thing - and she did often - she was either using the phone as a mirror to check herself out, or taking a selfie with some ridiculous filters applied.

"Are you taking selfies?" I asked Brenna. I really couldn't believe that was what she was doing.

She jumped up and walked through the transom to stand by me.

"Oh my God," Brenna said excitedly. "Check this out."

She held her phone in front me and I saw a short video of her cocking her head and sticking her tongue out. Behind her the moon spilled silver onto the lake. I was not in the video (*thank God*). After five seconds it looped to the beginning.

"It's sooo beautiful out here," she said.

I nodded but said nothing.

She returned to her phone, both thumbs working quickly. "There," she said. "It's live."

"Facebook?" I asked. *Please don't tag me.*

Brenna looked at me curiously. "No," she said. "I don't use Facebook. TikTok."

That's just grand, I thought. Maybe Meagan will get a chance to see it.

I thought Brenna might stand with me for our last few minutes on the water, but she returned to her seat in the bow and continued to swipe her phone.

My dock stands at the back of a shallow cove surrounded by tall trees. At my angle of approach the moon was obscured by the trees and I relied on the dim low voltage lighting on my dock to illuminate the approach. I cut the engine to idle, glided, then shifted into gear for a short thrust toward the slip. I repeated idle, thrust, idle until *Open Options* was centered neatly between the two fingers of the floating dock.

Brenna hadn't looked up from her phone and seemed unaware we had docked. I decided to take it as a compliment of my graceful navigational skills, but I knew that wasn't the case. My docking the boat in pitch blackness was not nearly as interesting as whatever was streaming across her screen.

In high school my posse of friends and I had a rule about the girls we took on dates. When you picked a girl up at home, you opened the passenger door of your car for her. If she leaned across the front seat to unlock your door while you walked around the car, she was a keeper. Otherwise, make it a short night and move on. I have a variant on this rule for docking the boat. If a guest watches attentively as I dock and offers to help tie up, they're a keeper. Otherwise, otherwise. A harsh rule and I don't apply it consistently.

Brenna looked up. "Oh my God," she said. "We're back. That was so smooth I didn't realize we were here."

I was silent.

Brenna turned her face toward me and smiled. She had a beautiful smile and it disarmed me immediately. I gave her a thin smile in return.

"Guess what?" she asked with a hint of excitement.

"What's that?" I asked.

"Guess how many likes I've gotten on that post?"

"Zero?" I replied frankly.

"One hundred and twelve," she said, a social media triumph.

I was genuinely surprised. "You've got to be kidding me," I said. "On a Wednesday at midnight?"

She put her face back into her phone and did not reply.

I gathered up our towels and picnic items and set them on the dock, then tied the boat to the cleats and turned off the battery. My usual docking ritual. I would wait until morning to cover the boat.

"Let's head up," I said to Brenna. She was still sitting in the bow.

I stood on the dock and offered my hand. Once she stepped from the boat, Brenna put her phone into her pocket and slipped her feet into the sexy cork-soled sandals. She exuded sensuality as she leaned over to fasten the tiny gold buckles and her blouse liberally fanned open. But unlike earlier in the evening, I found her sexy in the abstract, not the specific. There was a gulf between us that I had not seen before but which now seemed impassable. She had never known a car without power locks.

We walked toward my house. I carried the towels and the canvas tote containing our empty wine bottles and picnic remnants. She carried nothing.

"I could stay," she said softly.

Images filled my mind. We would step into the pool together. The water temperature would be mild and the cool night air would revive us. We would towel off and stumble into the guest room - now my everyday bedroom - and get tangled in the sheets for an hour. Sleep would descend like a coma. In the morning I would bring a tray with coffee, sugar and creamer into the bedroom. I didn't know how she liked her coffee, or if she liked it at all. She was a stranger that way, but not in other ways. She would be sitting up in bed, the top sheet pulled unconvincingly over her breasts, filming another TikTok video.

"Meagan might be home early," I lied. "Probably best to call it a night."

I thought she might protest, maybe show her pouty lower lip as she had earlier on the boat. But she didn't.

"That's fine," she said. She was chipper. "I've got a big day tomorrow."

Instead of walking to the back door of my house we instinctively turned toward the side of the house where her Pacifica was parked. When we reached it, I sat the towels and the picnic bag down on the driveway and faced Brenna. She surprised me with a hug around my neck, gently pulling my face down to hers and kissing me fully on the lips. I reached my arms around her and pulled the small of her back upward and toward me. I felt erotic confusion. It was a lover's kiss, but in my heart it was over. I had no idea if she felt the same way.

"Good night, Mr. Callany," she said at last. It was *goodnight*, not *goodbye*.

"Good night, Miss Wilder," I replied.

She climbed into her minivan and before she closed the door she asked, "Are there other parts of the lake?"

"Lots," I said, grinning. I was sending the wrong message by grinning. I guess I was keeping my options open.

She turned her ignition key, backed up, and with a small wave she was gone. I stood at the end of the driveway and looked at the dark bend in the road where her van had disappeared. Night sounds washed over me, crickets and tree frogs and cicadas.

I had just slept with someone new after more than thirty years of monogamy, and she had drifted from this sacred moment to her TikTok account with depressing ease.

37.
LADY LUCK | **2021**

BY EARLY AFTERNOON I REALIZE I'M GENUINELY LOOKING FOR-
ward to poker this evening, the scowling faces around the felt table, the
blue haze of smoke from illicit Cuban cigars, the clink of clear ice cubes in
bourbon glasses. Each man will have his roll of cash, Jacksons and Franklins
ready to rumble.

It's been a good day for me despite its rather lonesome and pensive
start. Lion Oil surfaced some strange activity on the January 2022 Google
contracts. Somebody - a person or a bank or a bot - was trying to buy puts
way out of the money and wasn't getting their order filled. Lion Oil flagged
two different price points where the buyer was only able to buy one or two
contracts despite wanting to buy twenty or twenty-five. This buyer was evidently worried that Google was going to crash hard sometime in the next
five months.

I decided to take the bet. I placed orders to sell naked puts on exactly
the contracts the buyer wanted. Bang! My order filled in less than a minute.
I had sold an insurance policy that Google would not fall to the level the
buyer feared. For this, I was paid a premium of almost two hundred and fifty
thousand dollars. That is my money, but not really. I will need to use most of
it to close the position, but any excess I could keep.

Google traded mostly flat through the morning, but just after 12:30 it spiked four percent. I check the headlines and find the reason - Google has prevailed in a court ruling on consumer privacy. I know this will eventually find its way to the Supreme Court, but as for today, I am able to close my naked puts and keep almost sixty thousand dollars of the premium. Not too shabby for three hours of work.

I lean back in my chair and text Jimmy, *Lion Oil's best day yet ;)*

I wait for his reply but none comes. He's probably in class. Or asleep. Or both.

It will be a good night for poker. I think Lady Luck will stay close, but even if she slips away with one of the other boys, I can afford it.

I pad downstairs to make a small lunch. I fast on Thursdays unless I'm playing poker, in which case I can't resist the mixed nuts and cocktails. Those little goodies prevent me from reaching autophagy, so I might as well eat throughout the day and fortify myself for the evening.

I decide on tuna salad. When it's ready, I take it to the kitchen table with a box of crackers and enjoy my lunch with no utensils. I rise to get a napkin, which I have forgotten, and then rise again to get a glass of water, which I have now forgotten twice. There's no one else fussing in the kitchen that I can ask to bring whatever it is I've forgotten. I glance into the family room and see that Diane is still lying in state with Edwin Hopper.

My phone vibrates. Jimmy.

"Son," I say, picking up the phone.

"Father," he replies.

"Holy Ghost." We say this simultaneously.

"Did the lion do something good?" Jimmy asks me.

"Very good," I say. "Best trade ever."

Silence on the line. Then Jimmy says, "Yessss?"

"Fifty-eight grand in three hours," I reply.

"Oh my God," Jimmy replies, "What was the trade?"

"Google." I say. "They won a court decision today. Popped four percent."

"You gonna celebrate?" he asks me.

"Absolutely," I reply. "Poker tonight at the Club, and I'm going to throw caution to the wind."

"That's great, Dad," Jimmy says. "Can I have your Tesla?"

"Nice try," I reply. "But no."

"Gotta dash, Dad," Jimmy says. "Combinatorics in three minutes."

"Mind your matrices," I say. "Bye son, love you."

"Love you too, dad."

Click.

I scoop more tuna onto a cracker, making sure to sweep up the pieces of the last cracker that broke off. In this manner I polish off more tuna salad than I had planned (all of it).

* * *

I enter the men's lounge a few minutes before seven. Aristotle and Dale are already in their positions and the vacant seat between them is mine. Aristotle looks at me with a stern face but his eyes twinkle. Dale gives a limp Cub Scout salute. (I need to talk to him about this.)

Steve is standing at the bar while Enzo prepares his drink, an Old Fashioned with Makers.

"Evening Sheriff," I say, approaching the bar.

Steve regards me with utmost skepticism.

"We missed ya last week, *Call Any*," he says to me.

"Well I didn't miss you," I reply. "I dropped Meagan off at BC and spent the weekend in Boston."

Steve shook his head gravely. "Red's in college already?" he says with wonder.

"Tell me about it," I reply.

"What can I get you, Mr. Callany," Enzo says brightly from behind the bar. "Woodford?"

"I'm upgrading tonight," I reply. "Two fingers of Blantons on the rocks with a splash of water."

"Yessir," he replies.

I take my seat at the table. The ponderous drapes are mostly drawn but a few rays of late August sunlight pierce the masculine gloom and illuminate the smoke from Steve's first cigar. A few other regulars filter in along with one or two new members. (By *new* I mean they've been coming for ten years or less.)

When eight men are seated, the Sheriff deals one card face down to each player. I flip a Queen, the highest card on the table, so I deal first.

I'm feeling lucky, as the Google search bar would say. (Google's been good to me today.)

I carefully lift the corners of my hold cards. Nine, Three unsuited. Not a very lucky start.

One of the other old timers - Darren Zinheiss - lays down one hundred dollars pre-flop. The players after him fold, fold, fold. When the bet reaches me, I know I should absolutely fold. On any other night, that's exactly what I would do.

"Raise a hundred," I say solemnly to Zinheiss.

The little and big blind after me both fold, and it's only Zinheiss and me, head to head.

Darren studies me through the smoke. He's a good poker player and has taken home plenty of my money over the years. I don't believe I have a tell, but maybe I do. Maybe I've developed one. I remember Brenna saying *the look on your face!* when we discussed the footsie episode on my boat last year.

"Call," says Zinheiss. He drops another hundred in chips into the pot.

I deal the flop - Nine, King, Three.

I've got two pair, Nines and Threes, and suddenly I feel better about this hand. I try to project calm boredom.

"All in," Zinheiss says boldly. He adds another hundred to the pot. He's got his whole wad in play and it's the first hand of the night.

The faces turn toward me and begin the low familiar chant, "Call any, call any, call any."

"Call," I say. I push my last hundred in chips to the center of the table and stand at my seat.

Zinheiss also rises.

This is dueling in the digital age. Two middle aged men stand at the poker table facing one another. The others lean back in their chairs and watch intently.

Zinheiss flips his hold cards - a pair of Aces.

I've got two pair and he's got the Aces. I'm favored, but another King or Ace will kill me. I see Lady Luck lace her arm through Darren's and whisper in his ear. *Fickle whore*, I think to myself.

The Turn comes up Jack - no help for either of us.

Enzo has come around from the bar to watch. He quietly dries a martini shaker.

I place the River card face down on the felt and the tension rises. With my index finger I flip it quickly.

Three of clubs.

I've got the boat - Threes full of Nines - and Zinheiss has two pair, Aces and Threes. Zinheiss reaches across the table to shake my hand. He's solid. It's tough to go down with pocket Aces but it happens all the time and he takes it well.

"Enzo," I say. "Mr. Zinheiss's drinks tonight go on my tab."

"Yessir," he replies.

"Thank you, Jack," Darren says. "In that case, I'm staying." He hands two Benjamins to the Sheriff for more chips and sits back down.

Lady Luck slinks around the table to sit in my lap, cooing her apology and kissing my cheek. *Fine*, I think to myself, *I'll take you back this one last time.*

I play tight for the next hour. I've got the largest stack by far, and if I'm too aggressive the boys will keep folding. I also know all eyes are on my stack, each man quietly summing the value in his mind and plotting my downfall. By playing tight I slowly neutralize myself. Memories can be short around the poker table.

Dale is having a decent night. He separated Aristotle and Dave Welton each from fifty bucks with an unexpected straight to the Eight. The Sheriff is bleeding to death one bad call at a time, his fate as the bluff caller.

At nine thirty, Enzo announces last call from behind that bar. Men's poker is not usually a late night affair since the Club closes at ten on sleepy suburban Thursdays. I order another Blantons, watered down a bit to preserve my wits, my fourth that evening. Dale has the same.

"Still have that Pappy?" Zinheiss asks.

"Yessir," Enzo replies.

"I'll take a two ounce pour," says Zinheiss. "With two ice cubes."

Enzo looks at me. This will be going on my tab, probably a hundred and fifty bucks. I give him a small nod, then turn to Zinheiss. "Dammit Darren, sure you don't want a ten ounce Wagyu filet to go with that?"

"No. No thank you," Zinheiss replies with a smile. "I'm not hungry anymore."

I'm still the big winner for the night, even with the bloated bar tab. I think briefly about the options windfall I made today and release a breath.

At five minutes to ten Aristotle deals the final hand. I'm holding the King and Ten of hearts, and sitting to Aristotle's right, I'm last to bet. I raise twenty. Aristotle calls, Dales calls, the Sheriff calls. Everyone else folds.

The flop comes Ace, King, Four. Now I've got a pair of Kings. Jack Queen will give me a straight to the Ace. The only heart in the flop is the Four, so I would need runner runner for a flush. I like my position - lots of outs.

I'm expecting checks around the table since I was last to act, but Sheriff Steve surprises me with a hundred dollar bet. I call, Aristotle and Dale fold. It's just me and the bleeding Sheriff. He's got about fifty bucks left.

The Turn is Queen of Hearts. A heart on the River gives me a King high flush. Any Jack completes my straight. I resolve to put Steve all in if he doesn't do it himself.

Enzo has come around to watch again. We should ask him to play sometime. He seems to know the game.

"Queen of Hearts on the table," Aristotle says solemnly, his eyes on Enzo.

Enzo nods but makes no expression. I'm ready for Aristotle to lay down the River, but he holds the deck in his hand and lets the tension build.

"Enzo," Aristotle says. "You still got your Queen of Hearts?"

Enzo pales slightly. "No, sir," he says, faintly shaking his head. "We couldn't swing the long distance thing."

"Absence makes the heart grow fonder," Aristotle says, and I remember my grandmother's rejoinder: *for someone else.*

"Yessir. I guess, sir," Enzo replies.

"Who was your Queen of Hearts?" Zinheiss asks. It's just like him to insert his nose deep into the poor bastard's business.

"She used to work here," Enzo says. "Upstairs in the office."

Silence falls heavily in the room. I don't know if the others sense it. I become aware of a high pitched buzzing in my ears and I wonder if it's been there all along. Somehow I know what the next spoken word will be.

"Brenna," Enzo says. "Wilder."

"Ha!" Zinheiss exclaims. "The wild one! Good for you, Enzo. Good for you."

"Thank you, sir," Enzo says. He steps quietly back to the bar, hoping to end the inquiry.

I suddenly develop tunnel vision, my peripheral vision goes black. The buzzing in my ears is more pronounced. Brenna and Enzo. *Brenna and Enzo.* Did that start before or after our little lake tour? Why do I even care?

"Jack!" I hear Aristotle's voice. His tone is sharp. "Are you with us? Steve's all in."

I raise my eyes and the present tense rushes in.

"I'm all in, Jack," says Steve. "Fifty-five bucks."

"Call," I reply. But my voice is a whisper. I clear my throat. I see Brenna on the swim platform of my boat, moonlight painting her body. But I'm not there with her. It's Enzo, his youthful Italian body pressed against her.

"Call," I say again, audibly this time. I move fifty-five dollars in chips into play.

"Call any," Zinheiss smirks. Chuckles around the table.

Steve rises from his seat. He's all in, and he's been called. I decide to stand too. I'm violating protocol by standing since I'm not all in. But, it's the last hand of the night, and besides, I respect the hell out of the Sheriff and he's been kicked around pretty good.

Aristotle reveals the River card. Eight of hearts. Flush made it and I've got the King high.

"Whatcha got, Jack," Welton asks.

"I called Steve. He's got to show first," I say.

I like a dramatic ending, though I hate that I'm going to nuke Steve. Lady Luck is standing on a chair behind me, kneading my shoulders and nibbling my earlobe.

Steve flips his hold cards and says, "Ace high flush." He reveals the Ace and Five of hearts. I'm beat.

Lady Luck abruptly climbs down from the chair and runs gleefully around the table to Steve. She jumps on him without breaking her stride and wraps her legs around his hips, casting a brief scornful look my way.

I blow out a long breath and flip my hold cards. "King high flush." I let the bad beat sink in. "Nice cards, Steve."

There are groans around the table. Steve is beaming and the others rise to slap his back. Aristotle reverses his *"Tesla"* out from the table and offers the Sheriff a robust high five.

"What a night," Dale says. There's general agreement. All the drama on the first and last hands, bookends for the evening.

We slowly collect our wallets, cell phones and unsmoked cigars and prepare to leave. Each man drops a few bills into the glass jar at the bar for Enzo. He can usually count on a hundred and fifty bucks in tips on Men's Poker night, maybe more.

I approach the bar and drop a Benjamin into the jar. Enzo sees it and gives me a grateful look.

"I'm sorry about your Queen of Hearts, Enzo."

"Thanks, Mr. Callany," he says. We hold eye contact. I wonder if Brenna told him about me. I study his face but see no sign of that carnal knowledge.

"I'm sorry Lady Luck left you high and dry," Enzo adds.

I grimace.

"Women," I say flatly, and then offer an awkward wink.

I follow Dale to the parking lot and we stand together in the humid night air.

"I'm not sure I should be driving," Dale says to me.

"Me neither," I reply. It has been four bourbons. Or maybe five. "Want to walk back to my place and sober up?"

"I could call an Uber," Dale says noncommittally. "They're back in operation now, right?"

"Nah, come on and walk with me," I reply. "You need to get your steps in today."

He gives me a small smile and we begin walking, hands in pockets.

"You had a great night, Jack," Dale says. "Until the last hand anyway."

I smile. I'm still processing images of Brenna and me, and Brenna and Enzo. It doesn't mean a thing really, just a stirring of awkward memories and the realization that there are layers and layers to everything.

"Zinheiss's taste for Pappy Van Winkle hurt me more than the Sheriff." I say. "Hell, I'm happy to make a donation to Steve every now and then. He holds the bullshitters at bay."

We walk for a few minutes in comfortable silence. Dale is probably my best friend, though I have never told him so.

Dale breaks the silence. "Speaking of holding the bullshiiters at bay," he says, "has Jennifer met any other nice boys?"

I turn to look at Dale as we walk. I have no idea what he's talking about.

"Jennifer?" I ask.

He doesn't answer, doesn't look at me. We keep walking.

Then it explodes in my head. *Oh God*, I thought. *Bumble Jennifer.* The fictitious Claire Danes doppelganger I cooked up for Dale.

"Oh *that* Jennifer," I say to him. "She gets around, you know. I think she's got a thing for Enzo."

Dale gives a wry smile. "I think he's still attached to his Queen of Hearts."

Dale knows about Brenna and me. He's classy enough not to press the point.

We turn onto my street. The moon is bright tonight and the pavement looks white. Cicadas throb. Most of the homes are dark. The blue glow of televisions emanates from a few upstairs windows.

I realize I haven't seen Dale in person since our lunch at Cantina Azteca when I sprung the Jennifer prank.

"I can't believe it's been a month since I bought you lunch," I say to Dale.

"I guess that's about right," he says. "You've been busy getting Meagan squared away at BC."

"True that," I say. We walk in silence for a while.

"I'm a little nervous about whatever payback you have planned for my Bumble prank," I say to Dale.

"As you should be," he replies. "It will be devastating."

We reach my house and walk to the kitchen. "How about a glass of ice water?" I ask. "We can sit out back."

"Perfect," Dale replies.

I fill two tall glasses as Dale looks around. "How do you like living in a truly empty house?" he asks.

Dale's been alone in his cavernous place for years. For a moment it overwhelms me to think of my next ten years, and then ten more, all alone with nothing but my computer monitors in this place.

"I'm not sure I like it," I say. "Everything stays exactly where I put it."

"I know that feeling," Dale said. "Get a dog. That'll stir things up."

Dale had a yellow lab when we first met - Tucker, a champion beast - but Tucker had been gone for years at this point.

"That's right," I say. "You had Tucker to keep you company at first."

Dale nods. He's thinking about Tucker, I can tell.

"But you never got another dog?" I comment.

"I think about it sometimes," he says. "Maybe I will."

I hand Dale his water, then point to the shelf occupied by Diane and Edwin Hopper. "I moved Diane over there this morning," I say for no reason in particular. "If she doesn't like it, she can move herself back to the dining room."

Dale looks at me and faintly arches one eyebrow. That's his trademark. Dale has high precision control over his eyebrows (both of them). He's also not quite as weird as I am, so my comment about Diane moving herself is puzzling to him.

"Does she move around often?" he asks.

"Rarely," I say. "Very rarely."

We step out onto the terrace and sit on the low slung chairs by the edge of the pool. The ice water is refreshing and an excellent complement to the walk we just completed. We sit quietly.

I'm looking straight ahead, my gaze passing over the pool and out across the dark, still lake. "Dale," I ask, "how have you managed for so long? I mean, by yourself, alone in your house."

He is silent for a long time.

"The truth is, I'm kind of a loner," he says. "It doesn't bother me to be alone. I have my regimen, you know. Elliptical, Netflix, options, poker, all that stuff."

We let this sink in.

Dale continues, "I see my brother and his wife fairly often, and their two kids. Jack, I'm your basic INTJ. This is the sort of life we choose."

I'm new to Dale's world. Even if Meagan and I only exchanged a few words on any given day, I still knew she was in the house, or on her way home, or whatever. Now there's a new kind of silence hanging over this place.

"I'm an ENTP, Dale," I say. "I'm not sure this is going to work for me for a decade."

Dale turns his head toward me. "Ah," he says. "You've discovered the Noonday Demon."

"I have?" I ask.

Dales gazes ahead once again. "The silent, deadly demon that kills you from within. First it makes you listless and sleepy. It beckons you to the couch for a nap, or even worse, to your bed, under the covers. It tells you to pull the curtains closed at noon."

"I like a nap every now and then, pardner," I say to Dale. "Don't be telling me those are off limits."

"Mind the nap!" Dale says sharply in a British accent. I know he's referencing the London Underground. When the kids were little we took them to London one Christmas and Jimmy almost fell into the yawning gap between the platform and the train.

Dale continues, "First it's a nap. Then it's a nap every day. The Noonday Demon drains a man's sense of purpose slowly, drop by drop. And then one day, there is no purpose. The curtains don't open. Even when it's high noon."

I sense that Dale has been there, has seen the Noonday Demon. I've seen it, too, or at least heard its soft prowling footsteps.

"You've slain the demon," I say to Dale. A statement and question at the same time.

Dale gives a slow, sober nod. "Habits and hobbies, Jack," he says. "You gotta have them. Even if they seem silly, even if it feels forced. Habits and hobbies are not an end in themselves. They're a gateway to the mind. They keep you creative."

"Is options trading a hobby?" I ask, then add, "Seriously, does that count?"

"Sure, of course it does," Dales says. "But you need more. Learn to play the ukulele. Sign up for Habitat for Humanity. Adopt a Guatemalan kid. Go to church, for chrissake."

Church. Now there's a distant memory. Diane and I were both raised Catholic, she less so than me. By the time I was in high school, our family skipped Mass more than we attended. At Davidson I found other ways to occupy Saturday afternoons and Sunday mornings, and by the time I graduated I was a flimsy agnostic, another disaffected Catholic in the Shallow South.

Diane was baptized, I know that much. Her mother was Catholic and her father was some flavor of Protestant. They split up before she started kindergarten and I think that fracture was the final blow to her mother's (and her own) churchgoing. Diane drifted to a form of earthy paganism during high school, culminating in our Celtic handfasting ceremony at the feet of Teddy Roosevelt.

We never had Jimmy and Meagan baptized - hadn't even thought about it, to be honest - though my parents occasionally inquired. When Jimmy was in fifth or sixth grade, he asked us about religion and for a few months we took the kids to churches of various denominations. We never made it to the Mormon church, or a Mosque, though we did get to a synagogue. The tour of Christianity was limited to an Episcopal church, which Meagan chose for its dark red door. There was no Catholic church on the itinerary.

Diane and I thought vaguely that the *tour de worship* would instill a sense of respect for religion and awareness of the greater universe. I didn't work. Jimmy and Meagan were bombarded with rituals and chants during the *tour* and the primary focus of each visit became the lunch that followed.

Now, thinking about it, the old reliable Catholic guilt stirs. Diane and I had not delivered even "replacement level" religious education to the planet.

"You religious?" I ask Dale.

He is quiet for a long moment. "Not sure," he says finally.

"Let me ask it another way," I say. "Are you a particle or a wave?"

Dale looks at me with an odd smile. "Are we talking about religion or physics?" he asks. "This conversation reminds me of college, sitting on the floor passing a joint around."

"Are you saying you're ready for another bourbon?" I ask. I don't have any pot in the house. In fact, I'm sheepish to admit I've never partaken. The stakes were too high when I was in college - I could have lost my ROTC scholarship - and the stakes got even higher when I was on active duty at the Pentagon. I had opted for the liquid form of escape.

"Thought you'd never ask," Dale replies, arching an eyebrow.

"I'll get us something," I say rising.

"I'll come in, too," Dale says. "Gotta use the little boy's room."

A few minutes later I return to our chairs with two tumblers. Dale is not back yet, so I fold my hands across my waist and look out over the lake's surface, black now since the moon has moved behind the tall surrounding trees.

When Dale returns I hand him a tumbler and we clink our glasses, a simple wordless toast between longtime friends.

Dale smacks his lips, "Nice. Very nice."

"Nothing like a water course to prepare the palate," I say.

After a silence Dale says, "Particle."

"How can you be sure?" I ask.

"I told you already. I'm a loner. I'm a particle."

"That's sort of depressing isn't it?" I ask.

"Not to me," Dale says. "I don't need other particles to define my essence. I'm an element, not a compound."

"You're a noble gas," I say, grinning at him.

After a brief silence I continue, "This morning I decided I must be a wave. My life seems to be more than just a bunch of particles strung together. The wave is more than the sum of the particles."

"Now you're the one full of noble gas," Dale says.

It crosses my mind that I shouldn't bring up my existential ramblings to Dale. He's an intelligent guy but not inclined toward the abstract.

All the same, *in bourbon veritas.*

"I'll give you this much," Dales continues. "Life is an arc. Beginning, middle and end. Like a short story. One moment causes the next." He pauses and collects his thoughts. "These … moments. They're not grains of sand scattered in the ground. They're connected."

"You're sounding like a wave, Dale," I say.

He thinks for a moment.

"No," he says at last. "I am an *arc-ist.* I think our lives form an arc."

"If I disagree, does that make me an an-archist?" I ask Dale. He cracks a lopsided smile and raises his glass.

I'm an arc-ist, too, I suppose. Waves can be arc-ists just as easily as particles can. Where am I on my arc? The apex? That's probably behind me at this point. Am I near the end of my arc? If so, see my earlier point on reconsidering religion. My mind wanders to Diane. Was her arc complete, just brief? Or was it broken midway, a semi-arc?

"So you're saying God is an arc-angel?" I asked Dale. He groans.

We drain our tumblers and sit longer in contented silence.

Finally Dale stands. "I need to roll," he says.

"You're welcome to stay here," I reply. "Plenty of room."

"Thanks," he says, "but no. I need to get my contacts out. I want to wake up at home."

Dale calls an Uber and we stand together at my front door. At this hour and in this neighborhood, it will be a while.

"Am I ever going to get my own version of that trading software Jimmy wrote," Dale asks.

"Lion Oil," I say. I've dropped the ball on this. I keep meaning to ask Jimmy to make a version with Dale's account information.

"I'll have Jimmy give you a call." I say. "Remember, he's going to need your trading password."

Dale arches an eyebrow. "You want me to give my password to a Dark Web hacker?"

He laughs before I can answer. "Tell him to call me anytime," he says. "Except when the markets are open."

I nod and smile.

Dale becomes serious. "Watch that Noonday Demon, Jack." He regards me closely. "He's an arc-breaker. I'm not kidding."

I am moved by Dale. He might be the only person left in the world who actually worries about me. I want to hug him like a brother, but I don't. Particles don't go for that sort of thing.

After a few minutes headlights appear around the bend on my street. Dale's ride is here.

Dales stretches his right hand toward me. I grasp it and pull him toward me. We slap each other's backs. It's a good enough hug.

Dale takes one step down toward the drive and turns to me. "Hey Jack," he says. "One more thing."

I look at him and raise my eyebrows expectantly.

"I've met someone," Dales says, then turns and approaches the waiting car. As he opens the rear door, he raises his hand in the Cub Scout salute.

Dale is acting more and more like a wave, I think to myself.

38.
PI | 2019

PI DAY BECAME A TRADITION IN OUR FAMILY DURING JIMMY'S freshman year in high school, the year the lights came on in his brain. That year, it fell on a Monday and, as usual, I was up a few minutes before six to drive him to school. The bus could have been an option, but it took a tortured route from our neighborhood to the high school and would have required Jimmy to be out the front door by 5:30 every morning. By driving him, Jimmy got an extra hour of sleep, important for the teen cerebral cortex (I'm told), and I got to spend twenty-five uninterrupted minutes with him on the way to school. He was chatty most mornings and I grew to cherish the commute.

I came downstairs in jeans, a fleece pullover and moccasins and found Jimmy peering into the stove.

"Did you make a souffle for breakfast?" I asked him.

"Nope," Jimmy replied. "Apple pie."

I took in the full sensory load - the sweet smell of baking apples and cinnamon, the hum of the oven fan, the sight of mixing bowls, measuring cups, and butter wrappers strewn across the counter top.

"*You're* baking an apple pie?" I asked.

"Yep. For Dr. Sanders' class.

"Pray tell," I asked.

Jimmy stood and looked at me as though I were helpless.

"Really, Dad?" he asked.

"Did you flunk your midterm?" I asked in reply. "Trying to bribe your way out of trouble?"

"Dad, it's Pi Day," Jimmy replied.

March fourteenth, of course. We had talked about this before, but when I was a kid, Pi Day wasn't *a thing* and I hadn't made it a red letter day in my mind.

"Ah yes," I said. "It's also Einstein's birthday." I view this fact as a little wink from the universe. Then I added, "I didn't know you knew how to make a pie."

"It's my first," he admitted. "But that's why God made YouTube."

Thank God God made YouTube, I thought to myself.

"Well, it smells about right."

Jimmy held the pie in his lap as I drove him to school. He also brought a grocery bag filled with paper plates and plastic spoons.

"Spoons were a weird choice," I said to Jimmy while we waited at an interminable light.

"They were closer," he replied. I wasn't sure what he meant, but I assumed he would have had to reach two inches further into the pantry to get plastic forks. The combination of industriousness and crushing laziness in a teenage boy is difficult to fathom.

"Does everyone have to bring a pie to school?" I asked.

"Oh no," Jimmy replied. "I just decided to surprise the class."

"You're a good kid, Jimmy." I said.

We were mostly quiet that morning, both of us enjoying the aroma that filled the car.

Diane rarely did the morning drive to school. I was the early riser, annoyingly chipper to those around me. Diane was our night owl. After the rest of us turned in at ten or eleven, she would clean up the kitchen, surf the Web (usually comparison shopping online), and then watch TV on the couch until she fell asleep. Some nights she would awaken cold on the couch and slip upstairs into our bed, others she would spend the duration on the couch. In the early mornings I would reliably find an ice cream dish and a drained wine glass on the coffee table. These I would rinse in the sink while I waited for Jimmy to appear.

The only thing that would cause Diane to stir before 8:00 am was tennis. She was a member of the Club's Ladies 3-0 team, a cheerful tireless catty squadron of women from the neighborhood who carted voluminous tennis bags and luggage sized purses to matches at clubs around Lake Cooke. Diane joined the Ladies team the same day we joined the Club. At first she was slotted onto the 2-5 "B" team, which is the absolute bottom of the totem pole. She had to lob, volley and smash her way to the 3-0 "A" team, and that itself required three years. Her eventual elevation had less to do with her skill and more to do with one of the 3-0 lifers dropping out for a hip replacement.

Diane and I both understood, though did not discuss, that her primary motivation in joining tennis was to shed some of the weight that had dogged her since the kids came along. She had been up and down, up and down, over the nearly two decades since Jimmy was born. There were stretches, like the months following Saranac, when she made visible progress. She applied her substantial intellect to the study of diets, trying Zone, Atkins, South Beach, Zero Sugar, Paleo and later Keto. She was nothing short of promiscuous when it came to trendy diets, and in fact it was Diane who later piqued my interest in intermittent fasting.

Her weaknesses were ice cream and wine, and she celebrated every weight loss milestone with a binge of both. By the time we were settled at Lake Cooke, Diane had evolved a complex set of rituals to mask her weight. There were the flowing pup tent dresses and shawls, of course, but in the intimacy of our home she went to lengths to hide her body. If she was taking a shower, she would lock the bathroom door. She insisted on coming to bed after me, when the lights were out. She had been a night owl since I met her, but it served a dual purpose as her weight crept up. Intercourse (almost as rare as her driving the kids to school) was strictly under the cover of darkness.

I did see her nude body on occasions when it was inescapable, or by accident. Occasionally I would glimpse her stomach, a dimpled pale loaf, when she leaned forward in one of her flowing blouses. The girl on the mud-flaps had somehow become mudflaps on the girl.

As a young man, I swore I would never have a fat wife. I would marry a skinny one to begin with, and we would take a blood oath to both stay that way. If she did start to thicken, I would point it out to her, remind her of our oath, enroll her in a marathon training program, and demand that she make weight every Friday like a wrestler.

Thankfully, my certainty about things (all things), my quickness to judge, and my tone deaf arrogance gradually yielded to compassion and empathy. Jimmy and Meagan, the light and purpose of our lives, were sweet and tender and perfect and Diane had baked them in her oven. If I was unhappy about Diane's baby fat, she was more so.

Deal with it, Callany.

I dealt with it by keeping myself in shape. Running, weightlifting, pull-ups, and later, fasting. As Diane widened and softened, I narrowed and hardened. I felt good about myself and I supposed I wanted to send a message to Diane, *you can do this too*. She picked up on the message, not as encouragement but as judgment. When I applauded her tennis endeavors a bit too enthusiastically, she heard: *go fix yourself.*

The first great dysfunction of our marriage was my breezy career success contrasted with Diane's persistent struggle to be recognized and appreciated. The irony known to us and our closest friends was that Diane was smarter - much smarter - than me. This is not false modesty on my part. I'm no fool, but sit us down for an IQ test and she would crush me. It was her sharp, cheeky confidence that attracted me to her in the first place. But therein lay the problem, too. Diane could be so pointed, so hurtful. She made people feel stupid, including the people who could quietly shut the doors to her future. My path was easier, I think, because I was easier. I didn't try to score points during arguments and I didn't mind laughing at someone else's stupid joke.

The other great dysfunction was her weight, my unvoiced scolding of it, her jealousy of my weight, my resentment of her fading attractiveness, her resentment of my resentment, and so on.

There wasn't much we could do about these dysfunctions. Talking about them was hardly an option. On the rare times we tried to talk about them, Diane verbalized me into a stupor. In my mind these were not problems that could be solved by talking. These problems were like ugly pieces of furniture you live with because you're used to them, and they're too heavy to move, and no one would buy them, even on Craigslist.

Some guys in my situation would have strayed. I knew plenty who did. The more innocent path, if you can call it that, was the anonymous quickie on a business trip. When I traveled for AFN, there was a regular group that made a beeline for the strip joints in whatever city we happened to be in. Some of the guys were married, some not. It had no bearing on which ones accepted the offer to go into a back room. When I tagged along, which was rare and later became never, I stayed by the stage and drank the ten dollar Bud Lights. Some of the girls were gorgeous, or at least had been, but I couldn't get myself past the complete patheticness of the other men around me - their eager eyes, their tapping feet, their hands gripping wads of cash. They were such willing fools, gladly surrendering to manipulation, so very lonely.

The other path, far more fraught, was the affair and its inevitable emotional entanglement. I had seen it enough times to know the stages. First was build up of erotic tension - two planets entering mutual orbit, then drifting inexhorably toward collison. Second was the illicit thrill of consummation and the balm it applied to the long simmering wounds carried by each. Third was the weaving of the web as one or both attempted to carry on two lives. Then came the breach, the breaking point, the discovery, the confession, the eruption. The fifth and final stage took many forms - counseling, healing and rebuilding; separation, justification, and division; acknowledgement, bitterness, and isolation inside marriage.

I never strayed. For one thing, few opportunities presented themselves. My career field - fiber network engineering - does not offer a broad selection of candidates. For another, I have tended to project *cheerful family man* at the office and everywhere else. I had pictures of the kids and Diane all over my office at AFN. I chatted about my wife and family when people asked me how I was doing. I wore *happily married guy* on my sleeve, and in fact was true. When I had erotic dreams - not often - I could never seem to close the deal. Whenever I neared my willing prey, I would begin to move in slow motion, or I became distracted by something. I never actually crossed the threshold. There was always an invisible wall I couldn't pass through, or over, or around.

In my late thirties I remember an older colleague telling me that men become invisible at sixty. Even if you're in good shape, even if your hair has held on tight for all those years, attractive younger women simply don't see you. Heads don't turn. They just don't think of you *that way*. This colleague was married, happily and for a long time. He wasn't one of the strip club guys. He wasn't looking to have an affair. He simply wanted to know he was attractive to someone attractive. He wanted to be thought of *in that way*.

At the time I didn't think too much about becoming invisible. The prospects for me were distant. But then, at some point in my late forties, I realized it had happened. Not that it was in the process of happening - it had already happened, fully and irreversibly and I hadn't noticed a thing. I was invisible.

If Diane and I had our dysfunctions, we also had our magic. Our best magic was that we talked everyday about everything. Diane was intensely verbal. She thought by talking. She observed everything and commented on it immediately. If she had an idea, she intoned it. This included observing me and having ideas about me. If I was down, or up, or sideways, she would call it out and together, in conversation, we would dissect whatever was going on. Diane was the conversation starter, but I was a willing participant and my contribution was often to color her observations with stories and anecdotes that supported them. After moving to Lake Cooke, we would sit together most nights on the terrace (or in the family room if it was too cold outside) and rehash the day's events, analyze and deconstruct the cast of characters we had met, and share our thoughts on all things upcoming, anticipated or feared.

If there was an infidelity brewing or underway in one of our circles, we would discuss it. There was always some level of drama with the tennis ladies. They were, by and large, pragmatic and stout women who wore visors throughout the day and drove SUVs the size of aircraft carriers. One of them, a lesbian incongruously named Priscilla, kept a Husqvarna leaf blower in the back of her Escalade to clear pine cones and leaves from the tennis courts. To a one they adored wine, and most carried a few bottles in Yeti coolers in their SUVs to be hauled onto the courts after matches.

"We're a drinking club with a tennis problem," Siobhan Sorcer often cracked.

Every year or so, a marital upheaval would ripple through the Ladies 3-0 team. Many of the husbands were tennis widowers (as I would become figuratively and then, one day, literally), giving them license, I suppose, for improprieties in and around the Club. One was spotted by his wife *in flagrante delicto* with the cute pro shop attendant on the eighteenth green after the Fourth of July fireworks a few years ago. Another managed to get the family's housekeeper pregnant, conferring long elusive United States citizenship upon their offspring.

When one of these acts of indiscretion rocked the tennis ladies, they would circle their wagons around their wronged teammate, drink wine late into the evening, and work through scenarios of retribution. On our back terrace, Diane would regale me with these stories, and the next day when I saw Debbie of Gina or another of the named protagonists at the grocery store or the Post Office, I would smile and play dumb. I came to view our community as a seven layer dip of deception.

One night our family was returning home on our boat and Diane and the kids had fallen asleep in the bow. As I skimmed over the black surface of the lake, I looked into the windows of the passing homes. I envisioned an angel flying overhead, able to lift off each roof like a lid and peer inside. The angel would see fine, comfortable homes filled with sad people, wrecked by deceit, alcohol and the other ills of too much money.

Diane and I were actually holding things together pretty well. We were faithful to one another and we hashed out issues grand and petty on the terrace late into the night. Our kids were reasonably well adjusted, at least by the standards of the neighborhood. I liked to think the passing angel would lower the lid back down on our house and give us a passing grade.

"Don't accidentally throw that pie in Dr. Sanders' face," I said to Jimmy when we reached the drop off point at the high school.

"He's my favorite teacher, Dad," he said. "Don't worry."

I smiled at him and he opened the passenger door.

"But," he said, casting me a final glance, "you never know who I might bump into on the way to class."

The passenger door closed and Jimmy entered the main doors of the school, backpack on, carefully holding the apple pie.

* * *

Three years later, to the day, Diane and I sat nonchalantly in the kitchen at a quarter past six in the evening. It was a Thursday, warm for the season, and the sun had not yet set.

"Explain this Tau thing one more time," Diane said to me.

I thought we had been over enough times over the past month. "You know what Pi is, right?" I asked.

Diane nodded. "Three point one four," she said. "The circumference of a circle divided by its diameter."

"Right," I said. "Tau is just two times pi." I looked at her to see if she was following. "You can think of it as the circumference of a circle divided by its radius instead of its diameter."

"I know all *that*," Diane said. "Why is it so important?"

"Honey," I said. "Don't you remember what Jimmy drew for us last week?" I paused. "There are infinitely many shapes with a constant *diameter*. Remember the Reuleaux triangle? That was one example. But there's only one shape with a constant *radius*. The circle."

"And what's the big deal again?" she asked.

"Well," I said, "the ratio of a circle's circumference to its radius is arguably more meaningful than the ratio of its circumference to its diameter."

"And that's Tau?" she asked. She was bored again, probably wishing she hadn't brought up the topic, but allowing the conversation to limp along so she could pass the time.

"Right," I said, "exactly. Six point two eight."

"And that's why Jimmy has to check his email at exactly six twenty-eight today?"

"Bingo," I said dramatically. "On Pi Day, at Tau o'clock, Jimmy will find out if he got into MIT."

We sat in silence at the kitchen table, waiting. I turned the pages of the *Luxury Homes* magazine that had been sitting on our kitchen table for a week, waiting to be thrown out.

At last we heard Jimmy's heavy footsteps on the staircase. I was just past six thirty. Whatever the decision, he knew it now.

Jimmy walked into the kitchen with an inscrutable look on his face, then cast his eyes downward. I rose from my seat, but Diane remained in hers.

"Well," Jimmy said, "I have some bad news."

Silence filled the room.

After a moment Diane sniffed and said, "I'm sorry, Honey."

Jimmy faced us and gave a grim nod.

"Yep," he said, "*Really* bad news." He paused. "Tuition at MIT is going to cost you a fortune!"

A wide smile broke across his face. I took two long steps toward him and embraced him in a bear hug. Diane was on her feet and moving in for a family hug.

"You did it, Jimmy!" I exclaimed, slapping his back.

The three of us hugged and high fived and shoulder punched. It was a joyful moment. I wish I could have bottled it to mete out in drops for years to follow.

The front door opened and Meagan, glowing with perspiration from a run, sloped into the kitchen. She was wearing ear buds and we could hear the tinny sound of music playing at full volume.

"What's going on?" she asked way too loudly.

I gestured for her to remove her ear buds.

"Jimmy got into MIT," Diane said gleefully after the first ear bud came out.

Meagan looked at Jimmy. "Cool, bruh," she said. "Happy Pi Day."

39.

THE ONION | 2020

IT WAS ALMOST ONE IN THE MORNING WHEN BRENNA'S PACIFICA disappeared into the night. I remained in the driveway as the sound of her tires on the road gave way to the ever present throbbing of cicadas and crickets. It was a beautiful night, warm with a touch of humidity.

I was tired but not sleepy. I needed time to spin down and process the past few hours. I walked around the side of my house and into the backyard, where the surface of the pool glimmered under the waxing moon. I stepped out of my clothes and lowered myself in the water, sitting on the ledge that runs the length of the pool. I stretched my arms out along the coping and looked across the lake and up into the night sky.

I had worried, abstractly, that when I met another woman I would be crippled with feelings of infidelity and guilt. But now it had happened (there was nothing abstract about it) I didn't have those feelings at all. I felt an interior calm, a knowing that Diane was okay with this, that she wanted me to live, to soldier on, to roll forward in the untidy business of life.

What tinged my thoughts was not infidelity and guilt, but the low grade melancholy that comes when something long anticipated turns out to be ordinary, not just in the moment, but in retrospect as well. You realize that something had been ordinary the whole time but you had dressed it grandly and elevated it. The stoics had it right (or maybe it was the Buddhists). Call me Epitectus.

After an episode of deeply affecting sexual healing on the stern of his fearsome trireme, Epitectus turned to see Cleopatra (or was it Athena, or Chloe?) tapping distractedly on that flat rectangular stone she held in one hand. He let out a long, low sigh of resignation and watched the ancient stars circle overhead.

The stars over my head were not particularly dramatic. The bright full moon had whitewashed the sky and reduced noble suns and planets to pinpricks. I slid beneath the surface of the water, and pushing off the side of the pool, torpedoed my body across, then back, then again, all without surfacing. When my head finally emerged from the water I gulped in the night air and took long strides underwater to the shallow end of the pool.

Maybe it was the half minute of oxygen deprivation, but I realized I was weary and ready for bed. The spinning gyroscope inside my head slowed perceptibly. I climbed the steps at the shallow end of the pool and toweled off.

I was in bed minutes later, lying on my back, still and meditative. Images played in my mind. Brenna's damp hair on the tanning pad, our bodies entwined. Nimrod's unwelcome intrusion. The lights of lakefront homes gliding past as I navigated *Open Options* quietly homeward. Brenna's van disappearing around the bend in the street. Then, at last, sleep.

I woke earlier than I had hoped - a stabbing ray of sun found its way through the leaf canopy on the east side of my house and struck my eyelids like an evil child frying ants under a magnifying glass. I rolled away and pulled the extra pillow over my head, but it was too late. My consciousness had sprung to life and commenced with jumping jacks.

I kicked one leg out from under the sheets and began to focus on my room. Meagan was at Maddie's doing online classes. She would be home in a few hours. The boat. I hadn't put the cover on last night. Had we left anything behind that would need explaining?

Then suddenly my mind alighted on Nimrod. There was something unsettled, a pea under the mattress. I had learned to pay attention to this feeling, especially when it came early in the morning. When I sleep my brain churns through the day's events, rearranging them and connecting them in unexpected ways, and culling the detritus. Sometimes there will be a fact, an event, some small observation that can't be filed away but also can't be tossed in the rubbish bin. These tidbits are sent upstairs for further inspection. I ignore them at my peril.

So I remained in bed, flat on my back and statue still. I closed my eyes. Anyone peering through the window would swear I was in deep sleep. I replayed the images of the night before. Brenna howling at the moon (I did not linger here for fear it would derail me). The bright lights and sudden appearance of Nimrod's Chaparral in the dark cove. His inquisitiveness. Brenna's low mock howl from the head. Seeing Nimrod, his boat floating dangerously close to mine. His khaki shorts. His deep sea fishing shirt. Brenna, again, crouched in the tiny head, naked.

The whole episode was jarring, but nothing was amiss. The events all fit into place. I opened my eyes and contemplated the ceiling again. Had I sufficiently inspected whatever it was that had been stuck in my craw? I thought so. Yes. There was nothing else.

I climbed out of my bed and stood before the window, stretching, toe touching, twisting my torso into action. It was Thursday, a fasting day. No poker tonight, no bourbon. I needed the fast, the cleansing.

I turned on the shower to maximum heat and let the steam build while I brushed my teeth. Then I stepped in, pained at first by the sting of hot water, but I let it flow over my head and down my back. After I had washed and scrubbed, and smeared a drop of body wash across my cropped scalp, I turned the water to full cold. It remained hot for a moment, then warmed briefly, then surged icy cold. I caught my breath. I do this sometimes (should be more often) to shock my system and open my pores.

Under the frigid water, my flesh numb, the tiny unresolved nit in my mind came roaring back.

Nimrod said he was an amateur astronomer. I never knew that. He never talked about it at poker, and he never missed a chance to crow about himself. Maybe it was a new hobby?

He was wearing something around his neck. I had thought it was binoculars but they were too bulky. Now I wondered if they could have been special binoculars for stargazing. Was there such a thing? I turned off the cold water and stepped out of the shower to dry myself.

My subconscious mind must have been screaming at me. Then I heard it, finally.

Who would look for stars under a full moon? Who would gaze at distant constellations from a small boat that rocked continuously on the surface of a lake?

No one, that's who. No one who actually cared about stars.

Nimrod was looking at something else. Had he been watching Brenna and me the whole time? Through those special binoculars? Rage welled up inside me.

Gotta talk, I texted Dale.

It was barely 7:30 in the morning. He replied immediately: *Lunch?*

I considered my commitment to fast that day, then replied: *cantina azteca noon.*

I resolved to eat sparingly.

Over coffee I studied the markets and let Lion Oil purr away. I was taking a decidedly cautious stance on options trading in the final months leading up to the election, and I placed no orders even though I was tempted.

The day was shaping up to be hot and humid. I let the boat bake under the sun for a few hours, then made my way down to the dock around ten to clean up. I jumped onto the boat and conducted a quick inspection first.

I had cleaned up surprisingly well the night before - no corks or napkins remained to tell their story.

On instinct I opened the door to the head where Brenna had hidden during Nimrod's inquisition. In the small sink I saw her plastic wine glass, a few drops of golden chardonnay settled in the bottom and ruby lipstick marks on the rim. Again I pictured her huddled here, nude, sitting on the doll toilet lid and turning this wine glass around and around in her hands.

Usually Meagan was the only one to use the head. I mouthed a prayer of gratitude that it was me and not Meagan who found this wine glass.

I covered the boat and raised the lift, then returned to the kitchen with the wine glass. I was washing it when I heard the garage door rumble open. Meagan was home.

"Hi Daddio," she said, breezing into the kitchen. "Whatcha doing?"

"Just cleaning up a bit," I said. I placed the wine glass on the drying rack. Meagan noticed nothing. "How was Maddie's?"

"Good," she said noncommittally. Somedays she was chatty, other days *good* is all I could expect to receive.

"Have a busy school day?" I asked.

"Nightmare," she replied. "I've got a test in fifteen minutes." She opened the freezer and removed a frozen burrito.

"I'm grabbing lunch with Dale today," I told her. "Want anything?"

"Nope," she replied. She took the wine glass from the drying rack, held it up to the light to see that it was clean, and then filled it with cold water from the fridge door. "I'll just have a burrito and glass of water."

If glassware could tell stories.

* * *

I walked into Cantina Azteca at noon and Dale was already seated in our regular booth. In front of him was a fishbowl sized margarita.

"Hola," I said with a tight smile. I still wasn't sure how many of last night's details I would spill to Dale. I resolved not to get a margarita - it would loosen my lips.

"Hola," he replied. "Get yourself a drink and start talking."

I shook my head slightly and dropped into the booth.

A server appeared immediately. Before she could say a word, Dale piped in, "Another margarita, *por favor*." I looked at Dale in protest but he ignored me.

"Please don't tell me you made another naked call," he said. We had been burned badly by naked calls on Tesla and sworn a blood oath (sometimes ignored) to guard and protect one another from their temptation.

Naked call. I cracked a smile. He was closer to the truth than he realized.

My margarita appeared the next instant. Maybe they had half a dozen already made up behind the bar, ice slowly melting.

My resolve weakened and I raised the enormous goblet toward Dale. "Cheers pal," I said. "I'm gonna need some advice today."

"Cheers. You've come to the right place," he replied, smacking his lips.

Dale has always been a good listener. He doesn't interrupt and he offers an attentive array of eyebrow reactions. My ironclad resolve to not eat, not drink and not discuss my sex life dissolved.

I told him everything.

When I finished speaking, his plate was cleared and mine was untouched. I took a gulp from the goblet.

Dale motioned toward my plate. "Cold enchiladas are no good," he said. "Take a bite while you still can."

I broke my fast with a forkful of cheese enchilada, which I actually think tastes better after a bit of cooling.

Dale continued, "Nimrod was not out there last night *because* of you." He paused, then added, "He just happened to stumble upon you."

"Well," I said, looking up from my plate, "his timing was impeccable."

Dale smiled.

"Jack," he said. "If Nimrod wasn't looking at stars, there can only be one other reason he was out on the lake at night with binoculars."

I looked at Dale and shook my head. *Why?*

"He was looking in windows," Dale said matter of factly.

I was incredulous. "A peeping Tom?" I asked.

Dale nodded. He had just handed me the key that unlocked a door.

"That miserable creep," I said. The rage welled up inside me again. "He cruises around in his boat watching people." Most of us leave our window coverings open at night. It's beautiful to look out over the shining black surface of the lake at night, and it provides all the privacy anyone could need.

"It makes sense, doesn't it?" Dale persisted. "Nimrod's always on patrol, looking for violations of his beloved community standards."

Dale's key unlocked a door that led not into a room but to a hallway with many more doors.

"Oh shit," I muttered. "He must have been doing this for years. First he drove his car up and down every street in the neighborhood taking pictures of every nit violation. Now he does it by boat."

Dale nodded soberly.

"That's why most of the pictures he's brought to the board meetings lately have been of people's backyards, not their front yards. He's been taking pictures from his boat."

"Precise-a-mundo," Dale said.

I pushed my half finished plate to the side of the table. "So," I said, trying to fit the pieces together, "Nimrod goes out while it's still light and patrols for community violations, then he stays out after dark to get his jollies peeping in windows."

"That'd be my guess," said Dale. "By now he knows exactly what time of night Mrs. Smith takes her bath and Mrs. Jones does her nude yoga."

"God only knows what he's seen." I think for a moment about my image of the angel that flies over the rooftops of the neighborhood and peers into the sad lives inside.

Dale rested his elbows on the table and covered his face with both hands. After a moment he looked towards me with disbelief. "Jack," he said, "I think I just figured out something else."

I arched an eyebrow, an attempt to imitate Dale. *Yes? What?*

"He takes pictures at night, too," Dale said. "He doesn't just take pictures of people's backyards during the day. He takes pictures of Mrs. Smith and Mrs. Jones, too."

I swallowed. "That would take a hell of a camera," I said.

"Damn right," Dale said. "And you saw it. It was hanging around his neck last night."

Now I'm walking down the secret hallway Dale unlocked and I'm peering into the doors that line it.

"That bulky thing he had on. Those weren't ordinary binoculars."

"I wouldn't think so," Dale said. "I would guess they were military grade night vision binoculars with an integrated digital camera."

Sonofabitch, I thought. "I didn't even know there was such a thing."

"I don't know for sure," said Dale, "but why *wouldn't* there be?" He hesitated a second. "Google it."

I pulled out my iPhone and searched on *military grade night vision binoculars with camera*. There were dozens of results on Amazon, starting at two hundred bucks. This was getting creepier by the second. I handed my phone to Dale so he could see.

"How many laws is that bastard breaking?" I asked.

"Plenty," said Dale. "The real question is whether he takes pictures of minors, and what he does with the pictures."

Nausea swept over me. *Meagan. Had he seen her? Did he have pictures of her?*

"If he has pictures of teenagers on his computer, he'll be in serious trouble," I said.

A terrible realization hit me. Another door on the corridor.

"Dale," I said, "he puts these pictures online. And he probably sells them. Anonymously."

Dale blinked. This was getting worse the more we thought about it.

"Dale," I continued. "He's a radiologist who works out of his home. He sits there in his basement all day looking at images on his computer. Only it's not just X-rays and CT scans he's looking at."

Dale and I looked across the table at one another in silence. *What had we stumbled on?*

"We've got to call the police," Dale said.

"But we need evidence," I replied. "This is just an elaborate theory by two guys drinking jumbo margaritas."

Dale cracked a smile. "Another round?" he asked.

"No," I replied with a grin. "I'm fasting today." I pointed to the half eaten enchiladas on my plate just as the server removed it from the table.

"So how do you propose to collect evidence?" Dale asked after a pause. "Is this just an excuse for you to spend the afternoon browsing porn sites?"

I wasn't sure. I knew there must be websites where people buy and sell illegal porn. And drugs, and fake passports, and credit card numbers. They pay for everything with Bitcoin.

"Dale," I said, "if I even started poking around the Dark Web, I'd probably make a rookie mistake and end up being targeted by the North Koreans."

Dale nodded, "Yep, or at the very least contract a nasty virus, and not the kind a face mask can prevent."

"Is this what the FBI is for?" I asked Dale. "Should we try to find their local field office?"

Dale shook his head. "Yes," he said, then paused. "But this would be chickenshit for them without any evidence or any idea of the scale."

Again we sat in silence, our minds buzzing with margaritas and intrigue.

"Jack," Dale finally said. "Every teenage boy can name the top porn sites. We just need one who's also really, really good with computers." He winked at me, then added, "Know anyone?"

"You must be referring to the mastermind behind Lion Oil," I said with a thin smile.

"He does fit the description," Dale said.

I considered possibilities. "If I call him, it's going to be a very awkward conversation."

"It suits you," Dale said. "You're very awkward."

I slid the tab across the table to Dale. "Fine," I said, "But you're buying lunch."

* * *

I waited until five to text Jimmy. I figured that would be the best window to reach him - his online classes would be over but his evening plans, whatever they were, wouldn't have kicked in yet.

Got a sec to chat? I texted him.

Less than a minute later my phone rang. *"Whazzup, Dad?"* Jimmy asked.

"Jimmy," I began. "Do you know much about the Dark Web?"

"Dark Web or Deep Web?" he replied.

I wasn't sure. "What's the difference?" I asked.

"Well," said Jimmy. "The Deep Web is the regular Internet, just the stuff that doesn't show up on a Google search."

"What would that be?" I asked. I thought everything showed up on Google.

"No, think about it," he said. "Content that sits behind a password would be Deep Web. Like your bank account information."

"Ah ha," I said.

"Even subscriptions, like the Wall Street Journal," Jimmy went on. "You need a password to read those articles. They don't show up on Google searches."

"I see," I said to Jimmy. "Then what's the Dark Web?"

Jimmy paused for a moment. "Probably not where you want to be," he said.

"Okay," I replied, "but what is it?"

"It's a different Internet," Jimmy said. "There are websites, but they don't end in dot com or dot org."

"Okay," I said, processing this news.

"Dark Web sites end in dot *onion*," Jimmy went on.

"Onion?" I asked.

"That's right," Jimmy said. "Onions have layers and layers. You peel an onion, and what do you get?"

"More onion," I said.

"Right!" Jimmy exclaimed. "That's what the Dark Web is like. Information is buried under layers and layers. It's almost impossible to figure out who operates a dot onion site, or even what country they're in."

"That's why the Dark Web is used for illegal activity," I said.

"That's right, Jimmy replied. "You can buy cocaine and child pornography and paid assassins. It's the dark underbelly of the Internet."

"You spend a lot of time in the onion?" I asked. I wasn't sure I wanted to hear the answer.

"Dad, what are you trying to say?" Jimmy asked. He was genuinely indignant. Before I could respond, he continued, "I did a paper on it last year. And then me and another student tried to find onion sites that weren't set up right and accidentally gave away their location."

"That's interesting," I said. "Did you find any?"

"Nope," Jimmy replied. "We only tried for a couple nights. Never could get to the center of the onion."

"No," I mused. "That's the thing about onions."

"Are you gonna tell me what this is all about?" Jimmy asked.

I released a heavy sigh.

"Jimmy," I said. "I think someone here in the neighborhood has been taking pictures at night through people's windows." I hesitated. "You know, from the lake. When you can see right inside people's bathrooms and bedrooms."

"Sounds like something Mr. Nimrod would do," Jimmy said flatly.

The kid is smart.

"I don't want to say anything else right now," I told him. "But it's illegal to be a peeping tom, and it's really illegal if you take pictures and sell them online."

"What a creep," Jimmy said.

"Would you know where to look for pictures like that?" I asked.

Jimmy considered the question. "There's a few places I could check first. There's one called the Empire Market, which is sort of like the eBay of the Dark Web. I might get lucky. I might not."

"Take a look around, son," I said to Jimmy. "See if you can find any pictures that look like they were taken from Lake Cooke."

"Okay Dad, I will," he said. "This might actually be kinda fun."

"Be careful on the Dark Web, Jimmy," I said to him.

"Don't worry, Dad," he replied. "I can cover my tracks pretty well."

We spoke a few minutes about the weather in Boston and his online classes. I wasn't thrilled to be paying full boat tuition so Jimmy could sit in an apartment and attend class online.

"One more thing, Dad," Jimmy said. "Whoever's doing this, Mr. Nimrod or whoever, you need to find out if they have a Bitcoin wallet."

"Why is that?" I asked.

"If this person is selling something on the Dark Web, they're most likely being paid in Bitcoin."

"Okay," I said, following his train of thought. "We could trace the Bitcoin to Nimrod's wallet?"

"So it is Mr. Nimrod!" Jimmy exclaimed.

I couldn't believe I'd let it slip.

"Keep it to yourself, Jimmy. He's innocent until proven guilty."

"I'd love to prove that creep guilty," Jimmy said gleefully.

Then Jimmy continued, "Bitcoin wallets are anonymous, Dad. If someone buys cocaine on the Empire Market, they transfer a certain amount of Bitcoin to an anonymous wallet. They have no idea who owns the wallet."

"So how could we ever know if payments were being sent to Nimrod's wallet?" I asked.

"Well," Jimmy said, "Every Bitcoin wallet has a public address, sort of like an email address. It's a very long number with no *at* sign. You use that address to send Bitcoin to someone. But only the owner of the wallet can take the Bitcoin out."

"Okay," I said, not sure I fully understood.

"Dad," said Jimmy. "Anyone can send an email *to* you, but only you can send an email *from* your account. Bitcoin's the same way."

"So I need to see if Nimrod has a Bitcoin wallet?" I asked.

"That's right," Jimmy said. "And if he does, you need to get its public address. Then I can see if it's the same address that's being paid for nudie photos on Lake Cooke."

"Jimmy, how would I possibly ask Nimrod for his Bitcoin wallet address?" I asked.

"Easy," said Jimmy. "Just tell him you want to send him some Bitcoin. He has to give you his public address to receive it."

"Sure," I said, "but why in the hell would I want to send Bitcoin to Nimrod?"

"I don't know, Dad," Jimmy said cheerfully. "That's your part of the puzzle. My part is to peel the onion and look for some juicy pictures."

"Okay," I said, "I'll work on Nimrod. Call me if you find anything."

I ended the call and leaned back in my office chair. Why would I ever send Bitcoin to Nimrod? I don't even own any Bitcoin.

My phone vibrated. A text from Dale. *poker tonight?*

In that moment, inspiration hit. I arched an eyebrow just like Dale would.

yep i'll be there. seven.

For the first time ever, I was hoping Nimrod would whoop me.

* * *

I stepped into the Men's Lounge a few minutes before seven and was engulfed in a haze of cigar smoke. The opaque curtains were pulled tight. Before my eyes could adjust, I heard my name called.

"Callany." It was Aristotle, in his usual place facing the door. He was always there twenty minutes early. His seat - and it was *his* - commanded the widest view of the room. I think he also liked to position his electric wheelchair discreetly under the table without an audience. Aristotle epitomized dignity.

In my mind an image formed unbidden: Aristotle nude, awkwardly transferring his large sagging form from his wheelchair to the plastic chair in his shower one evening. Outside the wide window of his bathroom on the black surface of Lake Cooke, Nimrod watching, snapping photos, stealing this fine man's dignity. I was filled with rage. And purpose.

"Judge Poe," I replied in salutation. "It smells like a frat house in here."

"That should make you feel right at home, Callany," he replied in his low James Earl Jones tenor.

I approached the bar and greeted Enzo. "Evening Enzo. Blanton's. A good pour, no water."

"Yessir," he replied, in no way acknowledging the deviation from my usual order, which would have been a smaller pour of Woodford, plus water.

I needed to be loose as a goose tonight, at least in hands where Nimrod was signaling strength. It would gall me to lose to him and I needed the undiluted Blanton's to achieve it.

I took my seat next to Aristote and greeted the Sheriff and Zinheiss, who were both already seated. Steve was stacking chips, readying for the buy in.

A moment later the door opened and fluorescent light from the hallway filtered in through the blue smoke. I made out Dale and Nimrod, who entered together. Nimrod wore blue hospital scrubs, a pretentious reminder that he was a doctor, and thoroughly absurd considering he worked from home.

"Evening, gentlemens," Dale said, hailing the room even though I knew his eyes were not adjusted and he couldn't know who he was greeting.

"Evening Dale," Sheriff Steve said gravely.

"Ah," said Dale. "I can see you now." The door closed behind him. "Jack, hello. Darren." Dale greeted his opponents one by one.

Then he faced me. "Ari and I were just discussing how brilliant Mercury has been these past few nights." Dale arched an eyebrow.

"Yes," said Nimrod. "Stunning." He turned to me. "I was actually looking at Mercury last night when I came across Jack here in his new Cobalt."

Dale looked at me in mock surprise. "Jack, you're an amateur astronomer, too?"

Thanks a lot Dale, I thought. I still hadn't cooked up a good explanation for why I was out on the lake at midnight on a Wednesday.

"No," I replied pensively, "but I'm thinking of taking it up."

Steve called the house to order, demanding that everyone get their drinks, take a seat, and buy in for their chips. I slid three one hundred dollar bills across the table and claimed my stack of chips.

For the first hour, the table was tight all around. One hefty bet would cause most of the other players to fold. I was getting bupkis, which suited me just fine. I had come to lose.

Shortly after eight Nimrod bet fifty bucks from an early table position just after the flop. He was signaling strength. The flop turned up Ace Queen, so I put him on a pair of Aces. Everyone folded until the bet reached me.

"Raise," I said, dropping in two fifty dollar chips.

More folds. Nimrod called. Now it was just the two of us, head to head.

Fourth Street came up Queen.

"How much ya got, Jack?" Nimrod asked from across the table.

I counted my short stack of chips.

"Forty," I replied.

"Then I bet forty," said Nimrod with a sneer.

"Fine," I replied. "Call." I pushed my remaining chips to the center of the table and stood.

The River card was a five. No help.

Nimrod flipped his hold cards. Ace, as I had expected, and a Seven.

"Aces and Queens," he said smugly.

I shook my head and mucked my cards. "Pair of nothin," I said with resignation.

Steve looked at me quizzically. This wasn't my usual game play.

"Re-buy Jack?" he asked.

"Sure," I replied, passing him another Benjamin. He slid a new stack of chips to me.

I sat down and tried to act dejected. "I suck," I said to no one in particular. "First I lose a fortune on Bitcoin, and now this."

Nimrod perked up and looked at me. "I didn't know you were into Bitcoin," he said.

"I wasn't until this summer," I replied. "Jimmy got me interested and I bought in at twelve thousand."

"Sucks to be you," said Nimrod. Bitcoin had plunged below ten thousand over the past couple days. Then he added, "I've been since 2017. Bought in way below ten."

"Deal the damn cards, Nimrod," Steve said. "No one wants to hear about your Bitcoins."

Nimrod appeared wounded. "Fine," he said, and dealt the next hand.

An hour later I had polished off four tumblers of straight Blanton's and made two more rebuys into the game. I was down five hundred bucks in poker, and at least a hundred in liquor. I decided that next time Nimrod signaled strength I'd make my move.

That time came on the next hand.

I had twenty dollars in chips, just enough to get myself in trouble. It didn't help matters that I was out of cash. I had brought five hundreds with me to the game and at this point they were all in Sheriff Steve's till.

My hold cards were unimpressive: Jack and Three. No one placed a bet so we got a free flop. It came up Ace, Two, Four.

Suddenly I had a hand, Ace to Four. A Five would give me a straight and nice win. I tried to remind myself I didn't want to win. Today I win by losing.

Aristotle bet ten, others called, then Nimrod raised the bet to one hundred. He was signaling a pair of Aces, or maybe two pair.

When the bet came around to me, I said, "Guys, I want to call but I'm out of cash. Am I good for it."

"Hell no," said Zinheiss with a snicker.

"Eat shit," said Dale.

"Geez," I said in a mock appeal to the Sheriff. "With friends like these, who needs an enema?"

Steve snorted. "He's good for it."

The others folded, leaving Nimrod and me head to head once again. I didn't want to win, but yet I really wanted to win.

The Turn was a Jack, giving me a pair. But it wouldn't be enough if Nimrod had Aces.

"Up a hundred," said Nimrod, coaxing me.

"Call," I said.

I really wanted to see a Five on the River, but that was my old competitive streak at play.

The River came up Six. Bust for me.

"Up two hundred," said Nimrod. His bug eyes were fixed on me.

I knew it was highly unlikely my Jacks would carry the day. If I lost, I would owe Nimrod three-hundred and eighty bucks. On the other hand, a pair of Jacks was decent. It was the second highest pair possible on the table.

I did what any middle aged poker player with four bourbons in his belly would do.

"Raise," I said, "Up another two hundred."

Nimrod was shocked. I hadn't raised after Fourth Street, so why now? He leaned back in his chair and studied me like I was a blurry CT scan.

"You ain't got shit, Callany," he said. "Call."

I flipped my hold card. "Read 'em and weep," I said, revealing my sorry Jacks.

Nimrod turned over his cards: Ace, Six. Two pair with a pair of Aces. He had me.

"Sorry, Callany," he said greedily. "How much does he owe me, Steve?"

Steve pulled the stinking cigar from his mount and looked at the ceiling for a moment. "Ari, the chips on table are yours, and Jack owes you five hundred and eighty."

Dale let out a low whistle.

"I better call it night," I said, rising stiffly.

"You better go to an ATM," Nimrod said. He wasn't kidding either.

This was my moment.

"Nimrod," I said, "Wanna take Bitcoin instead?"

He considered my offer.

"Don't be a fool, Ari," Zinheiss said.

Nimrod ignored him. "Sure," he said. "I'll take Bitcoin."

"How do you do that?" Steve asked.

"Easy," said Nimrod. He took his iPhone from his pocket and opened the Coinbase app. "Jack, I'll text you my wallet address. You transfer six hundred dollars worth of Bitcoin to me by noon tomorrow."

"Six hundred?" asked Steve. I was thinking the same thing.

"Convenience charge," said Nimrod with another sneer.

"Fine," I said with resignation. "I may need Jimmy to help me."

Nimrod pointed an accusing finger at me. "Noon tomorrow." I felt my phone vibrate in my pocket with his text.

I waved at the table and said goodnight. Sympathetic heads nodded toward me, then returned to the table. They would play for another hour or so before Enzo shut them down.

"I'll walk you out," said Dale.

Dale rose and we made our way to the door.

"G'nite, Mr. Callany," Enzo said somberly from the bar. I was a reliable tipper, but tonight I had been drained. A gave Enzo a small salute and shrug of the shoulders.

Nimrod never tipped, so this would not be a banner night for Enzo.

Dale walked me to my car. In the cool night air he turned to face me. "What the hell, Jack?" he asked probingly.

"Dale," I said. "I wanted to lose to Nimrod."

He arched an eyebrow.

"Well then you succeeded grandly."

"I wanted his Bitcoin wallet address."

The other eyebrow arched.

"I'll explain tomorrow," I said to him.

I reached for the handle of my Tesla.

"Jack," Dale said. "Mercury set at eight thirty last night."

I looked at him, mystified. "Huh?"

"Mercury wasn't visible in the night sky last night."

Dale was grinning. "Jack, remember how Nimrod and I were talking about astronomy when we walked in tonight?"

It came back to me. "Ah yes," I said. "Nimrod was crowing about watching Mercury when he found Brenna and me."

Dale nodded. "Nimrod's definitely up to something."

Under the waxing moon, Dale looked the part of the Underwood ham dancing devil. Spontaneously, I hugged him and slapped his back.

300

"And you're definitely not driving in this condition," Dale said when we separated. "Want a lift?"

"Shit. Thanks," I said. "You're right." I looked into the clear night sky. "I'll hoof it home."

* * *

The next morning I woke up early with a splitting headache. I had forgotten to gulp down a few glasses of water when I got home, and the undiluted bourbon in my system had dehydrated my brain to the size of a walnut. I washed my face, not happy with what I saw in the mirror, and walked heavily into the kitchen for water and coffee.

The lights were on in the kitchen and Meagan was filling the blender with frozen berries and protein powder. She looked fresh and clean, a sharp contrast to my hobo shabbiness.

"Morning Daddio," she said brightly.

"Not so loud," I growled in reply.

Meagan leaned back and assessed me. "Let me guess," she said. "You lost all your money in poker and then you and Mr. Dale drank a bottle of bourbon."

I raised my eyebrows. "Does it really show?"

She didn't respond, but instead turned the blender onto high. It sounded like a roaring jet engine, off course and ready to plow into our home and pulverize everything we held dear.

While the blender ran, Meagan contorted her face at me and stuck out her tongue.

God I love this kid!

When the berries and protein powder were sufficiently liquified, she turned off the blender and smiled at me.

"Water, Dad," she said sternly. "Drink. Water. Now."

"Yessir," I replied. I filled a glass at the dispenser in the refrigerator door.

301

"I'm late for class. Bye, Daddio," she said, and turned to go to her room for online classes.

I drained the glass of water, then had another. Then another.

I saw my iPhone on the kitchen counter where I had evidently left it when I got home. There was six percent charge left. Shit. I saw a text from Nimrod - that would be his Bitcoin wallet address, no doubt, and another text from Jimmy sent at four in the morning. *Call me when you get up*, it said.

I took the iPhone back to my bedroom and plugged it to charge. I needed to shower and swallow some black coffee before calling Jimmy.

Thirty minutes later I was feeling better. I had taken a steaming hot shower, then put the water on full cold for three minutes. I donned my uniform of shorts, Birkenstocks and a craft beer shirt (*Wooden Robot*) and went upstairs to my office with a partially charged cell phone.

I called Jimmy and he picked up on the first ring.

"I saw your text," I said when he answered.

"Dad," Jimmy replied. "I've literally been up all night."

"You found something," I said flatly. It was a statement not a question.

"I found a lot," Jimmy said. There was a pause. "A lot."

Suddenly I was fully alert and focused. If my walnut brain was still throbbing, I didn't notice it.

"Allright," I said. "Hit me."

"For one thing, it was easier than I thought it would be," Jimmy began. "I used the Tor Browser to go to Empire Market. There are about ten million porn categories, but I found one called Secret Cameras that looked promising. Lots of different sellers with pictures and videos that were taken in secret."

I had no idea something like this existed. "Like what?" I asked.

"Dad, you really don't want to know." He paused for a moment, then continued. "There are lots of pictures from cameras hidden in bathrooms.

People on the toilet. People in the bathtub. Most of them are not supermodels, I'll tell you that."

"You can watch these videos?" I asked.

"Some you can, some you can't," Jimmy replied. "Some sellers will show half a video and make you pay to download the whole thing. Some of them blur out the private parts and you have to pay to see the clear video."

"So that's what's inside the onion?" I mused.

"That, and a lot more, Dad," Jimmy said. "The onion is not a nice place."

"Did you find anything that looked like Lake Cooke?" I asked Jimmy.

"Yes, but it took almost all night," Jimmy said. "And I can't unsee some of the stuff I saw while I was looking for it."

When you put it that way, there are quite a few things I wish I could unsee.

"Around two this morning I found a seller called *Love Thy Neighbor* in the Secret Cameras section. That's when I hit the jackpot."

"What did you see?" I asked.

"Dad, it was Lake Cooke, for sure. Almost all the pictures were taken at night. Some were obviously taken from a boat because you can see water."

"Okay," I said, ready for more.

"There must be a hundred pictures. I don't know, maybe more. Most of them are pictures of people standing near their windows at night. You know what I mean, Dad? Naked people. Sometimes couples. Sometimes couples in bed with a light on."

"Are you sure it was Lake Cooke?" I asked. "Could you recognize anyone?"

"It was definitely Lake Cooke, Dad," Jimmy said. "I could recognize a few people. I saw Ms. Loving in one picture. And Mrs. Jones." He hesitated, "and Ava Welton."

Ava was David Welton's daughter, the same age as Meagan.

"Were they pictures or videos?" I asked.

"Pictures mostly," Jimmy said. "And most of them had blurring."

I was silent.

"Dad," Jimmy said, "there was one of you."

My spine became rigid and my fight or flight instinct instantly took over. Was it me with Brenna? Had Jimmy seen my indiscretion?

"What was it?" I asked. I was trying to remain calm. My brain was racing through scripts in case I needed them.

"It's you by the pool, Dad," Jimmy said. "I can't tell what time of day, maybe early morning. You're just standing there. Naked. It looks like you're looking right at the camera."

Waves of relief pour over me. Anything is fine except a picture of me with Brenna.

"Naked?" I asked. It was all I could think to say.

"Yes," Jimmy said. "But blurred. You know. Down there."

"I doubt that one will be a big seller," I quipped.

"Uh, no," said Jimmy. "No downloads of that one."

"Did some have a lot of downloads?" I asked.

"Ava's did," he said. "Ava Welton. Probably a dozen downloads. It was a series of about twenty pictures of her getting out of the shower and drying off."

"Geez Jimmy," I said, "did you download them?"

"No!" Jimmy said emphatically. "I could see the thumbnails, and most of them were blurred out. Not all of them."

"Don't download anything, Jimmy," I said to him. "Especially Ava. She's a minor. That would be child pornography."

"I know that, Dad," Jimmy said. "I'm not an idiot."

"Jimmy," I said, "do people have to pay to download the pictures? I mean with the blur removed?"

"Yes, Dad, of course. That's how this thing works."

"How much are they?" asked.

"Well," said Jimmy, "The series of Ava was thirty bucks, but you have to pay in Bitcoin."

I considered this. "How much for the picture of me?" I asked. I hated myself for being curious.

"A dollar, Dad," Jimmy said. He was quiet for a moment. "Don't feel bad. Most of the pictures of men are really cheap. Some are even less than a dollar."

"I'm good with a dollar," I said. Not bad for Mr. Invisible.

"Dad, I got the Bitcoin wallet address for Love Thy Neighbor."

"Tell me," I said, "I'll write it down."

Jimmy carefully spelled out the Bitcoin wallet address. It was thirty-four characters, letters and numbers. Some of the letters were uppercase, some lowercase. The last five were Lty51.

"Why's it so complicated?" I asked Jimmy after we triple checked the address.

"I'm not really sure," said Jimmy. "To make them hard to guess, maybe?"

"Jimmy," I said. "Are you ready for the moment of truth?"

"Really?" Jimmy asked. "Did you get Mr. Nimrod's Bitcoin address already?"

"I sure did," I said. "It cost me six hundred bucks last night at poker, but I got it."

"You told him you wanted to pay with Bitcoin?" Jimmy asked, incredulous.

"Yep," I said. "I worked it into the conversation."

"You're good, Dad," he said. "For a Boomer."

"I'm not a Boomer," I replied.

"Okay," said Jimmy, "Let's hear it."

I opened the text from Nimrod. There were no words, just a long sequence of letters and numbers. The last five were Lty51. I felt my throat catch.

"Jimmy, we have our man," I said quietly.

"That's so cool, Dad," Jimmy said. "We're crypto sleuths."

"You're Sherlock," I said. "I'm just Watson."

"What are you going to do next," Jimmy asked.

"Well," I said. "Before noon today I need to send six hundred dollars in Bitcoin to Nimrod. I have no idea how to do that."

"I can do it for you," Jimmy said. "I'll send him the Bitcoin right now and you transfer six hundred bucks to my bank account."

"Thanks, Jimmy," I said, genuinely grateful to have my son as a partner in this venture. "This is all new ground for me. And it can't be good for Nimrod - selling kiddie porn on the Dark Web."

"No," replied Jimmy, "I wouldn't think so."

"Don't tell anyone about this, Jimmy. Absolutely no one," I cautioned him. "I need to think about this and decide who to call."

"Cool," said Jimmy. "If you don't mind, Dad, I'm going to get to sleep."

"You've earned it, Jimmy," I said. "Sweet dreams."

"Not sure that will be possible," said Jimmy, "but I'll try."

40.

THE DOPPLER EFFECT | 2020

I SHOULD HAVE FELT UNEASY LAST YEAR WHEN LEAP DAY arrived calm and sweet. It is an unusual day, of course, observed only once every four years, unless the year ends in 00, in which case there is no Leap Day, unless the year was divisible by 400, in which case there is a Leap Day after all. Aware of this subtlety (and proud of it), I was chagrined in 2000 when most people simply expected it to be a Leap Year. *No*, I explained to anyone who would listen, *it's only because 2000 is divisible by 400.*

On Leap Day 2000, that rarest of Leap Days (it was a Tuesday), we learned that Diane was pregnant. She may have had inklings before it was official, but she had learned to ignore the telltale signs. We were serving a life sentence for a reckless and unwanted pregnancy ten years earlier.

I was lecturing a cashier about 2000 being divisible by 400 when Diane paid for the pregnancy test. Maybe that's why Jimmy's so damn good at math.

Leap Day last year began with the pink glow of a winter sunrise softly brightening our bedroom and the tangled sheets. Diane was still asleep and I lay quietly watching her form rise and fall. I was at peace, filled with a postcoital calm. We had been intimate the night before, the first time in months. It was a Friday, Jimmy away in college and Meagan at a friend's house. Our quiet date night began with martinis - gin for me, dirty vodka for Diane - and progressed to sushi by the fireplace. Diane surprised me when she ignored the dirty dishes and led me upstairs, where in the darkness she was uncommonly generous.

At seven Diane's iPhone alarm began to play the sound of ocean waves crashing. The waves became progressively louder until she awoke and reached for the device.

"Tennis?" I asked.

"Mmm hmm," she said, looking at her phone screen. "Clinic at eight-thirty."

She rotated her body, now draped in a sexless nightshirt, out of bed and shuffled heavily to the bathroom. I lay quietly watching the sky brighten to yellow. I had no idea this room, this window, would be my home office in less than a month.

While Diane was still in the bathroom, door closed, I climbed out of bed and made my way to Jimmy's bathroom (my backup) and then downstairs to the kitchen. I collected our sushi plates and chopsticks from the hearth and our martini glasses from the coffee table, and began washing them in the kitchen sink.

Diane entered the kitchen thirty minutes later, bulging in her gray and lime green tennis costume, her long gray hair pulled back tight into a ponytail. She filled her Yeti with ice, then snapped open a can of Diet Coke and poured it, fizzing, into the Yeti.

I was at the kitchen table with a cup of black coffee, doom-scrolling on my phone. Most of the articles were hysteria about a virus in China. I had seen this a few years before with SARS and it had amounted to nothing. This would be the same.

Diane did not sit with me at the table, but stood by the counter drinking her soda and eating a protein bar.

"Thanks for cleaning up," she said.

I looked at her for a moment. I was still feeling an afterglow from the night before, but she was plainly back to business.

"Hey," I said. "Thank you." I hesitated, then added, "For our date."

"It was nice," she said. The conversation had reached a cul-de-sac.

"We should do that more often," I added with a weak smile.

"Yeah," Diane replied, and then said, "I love sushi."

I did some mental math. At our current lovemaking tempo, I'd have my next shot sometime in May.

Of course, I was wrong about that, too. It would be September, and it wouldn't be Diane.

She opened a second Diet Coke and poured it into a Yeti. "Bye, Jack," she said. "I'll be back by 1:30. I'm having lunch with Siobhan after clinic."

"Toodaloo," I replied.

And then I was alone at the kitchen table, a quarter cup of coffee remaining, still warm. My morning would be yard work - raking the leaves and accumulated detritus from the beds around our house, taking down a smallish dead tree in the side yard and stacking the segments for firewood.

Before any of that, however, there was the matter of a Leap Day prank, a tradition I had been trying to start but which the family seemed to dismiss. I lifted my coffee mug absently and looked inside for inspiration. Who to target - Diane or Meagan? The key is figuring out who is most uptight about something, finding that foible and then lancing it.

For Diane it's easy - her weight. She hates it, she won't discuss it, and she won't do anything about it. She weighs herself every morning. I hear the cheerful, too loud beep of our bathroom scale when she steps onto it. It's a bluetooth scale that sends the data to Diane's iPhone so she can chart her growing mass. I began to contemplate how I could hack the scale, have it send the wrong data to her phone, add a ten pound surprise to her post tennis weigh in. This had all the hallmarks of solid prank, but it also felt too cruel and, frankly, too hard to figure out technically. I would have to call Jimmy, and then Diane would be pissed at both of us.

I turned my attention to Meagan. It's more fun to prank her, and no marital repercussions to worry about. Her foible was conspicuous and unmistakable, the brand new lime green Jeep she had paid cash for last summer in an astonishing display of how lucrative it can be to have followers on TikTok. Diane and I were simultaneously appalled and impressed when she made her case at the dinner table one evening. She had the money, she had found the vehicle, and after a weak attempt at imparting life lessons, we acquiesced. Meagan adored her Jeep, kept it spotless (to include cleaning the air louvers with Q-tips) and by all accounts was a calm and observant driver.

That sealed it. I opened my laptop at the kitchen table and created a Craigslist ad for her Jeep. For the photo, I Googled *lime green jeep wrangler*, then copied and pasted a prime example from an unsuspecting dealer's lot three states away. Meagan had paid twenty-five thousand for hers, so I listed it for forty-five hundred. As *contact* I listed my email address and Meagan's cell number. That way I was the one confirming the listing but she would be the one getting the calls and texts. *Submitted. Confirmed. Done.* My Leap Day prank was in motion and it was barely nine in the morning.

I spent most of the next hour in the front yard raking the landscaping beds and depositing the dead leaves, sticks and endless sweetgum balls in our large wooded side lot. There was a sharp chill to the morning air, but it was above freezing and warming nicely. The clear sky I had awoken to was beginning to fill with billowy white clouds. It was the kind of day that could break in any direction by the afternoon.

When I finished with the beds, I checked my battery powered chainsaw. The chain was clean and tight and the battery had a full charge - enough to dispatch the tree that would otherwise crack under its own dead weight and rip my gutter off. I checked the bar and chain oil level and saw there was none at all. *Painintheass.* I would have to make a trip to Lowe's before I could get started. That would add thirty minutes at least to my morning yard work module.

I pulled on a ball cap and climbed into my Tesla. One thing I like about Lowe's is you can go there wearing absolutely anything. In the middle of painting the nursery and covered in pink paint drippings? No problem. Covered in sawdust? *No problemo*. It's not Wal-mart, of course, you can't go in your jammies and slippers, but there is no category of DIY attire that is unwelcome at Lowe's. Still, the ball cap adds a touch of respectability.

On the main road between our neighborhood and Lowe's, my iPhone began to play the main riff from *Free Fallin'*. It was Meagan.

"*Hola*," I answered in my best Maria Hinojosa imitation.

"Dad?" Meagan asked.

"*No comprende*," I said.

"Dad, it's not funny," she said.

"It's kind of funny," I replied.

"Dad, I've gotten like a hundred text messages this morning from people who want to buy my Jeep."

Wow, I thought. My prank had taken flight.

"I didn't know you were selling it," I said blankly.

Another call was coming in. "Hang on," I said to Meagan.

I looked at my screen and saw Siobhan Sorcer's name. I declined the call and returned to Meagan.

"I'm not selling it, Dad," she said. "I have no idea why people are calling me."

"Maybe somebody else is selling a jeep and they gave out the wrong number by accident."

Meagan considered this for a moment. "Dad, that would be too weird."

I heard the tone again of another call coming in. It was Siobhan, again. I declined, *again*.

"Somebody must have listed my Jeep for sale and given out my phone number."

I let a few seconds pass while I considered this highly improbable event, then asked, "Why would anyone do that?"

Suddenly the traffic in my lane stopped and cars pulled to the side of the road. I heard the wail of an approaching siren, and then a fire engine coming in the opposite direction roared past me, straddling the double yellow dividing line. An ambulance followed blaring loudly. I waited a moment for the sirens to fade.

"I'm back," I said to Meagan. "The Doppler Effect."

"What?" she asked, disinterested.

"The Doppler Effect." I said. "Have you ever noticed how the sound of a siren changes as it gets closer to you and then passes?"

"Dad, please," Meagan said. "What am I supposed to do about all these texts? Can I call Verizon."

Again, the tone of an incoming call. It was Siobhan calling for the third time.

"Meagan," I said. "Hold on for a sec. Someone is really trying to reach me."

The cars in my lane began moving again and I eased from the curb.

"Siobhan," I said, clicking over to her call. I couldn't mask the hint of irritation.

"Jack!" Her voice was hysterical. "Diane collapsed on the tennis court. We've called 9-1-1."

I took a deep breath. Time slowed. Around me, silence. I saw cars moving but heard nothing. I felt weightless, automated.

"Jack!" Siobhan screamed again.

"I'm coming right now," I said.

Then I added, "Is she okay?" It was a stupid thing to say.

"No, Jack. She's unconscious. She has blood all over her face."

I could hear sirens through the phone. *God*, I thought, *those were for Diane.*

"I'll be there in two minutes," I said.

"Hurry," Siobhan said, ending the call.

At the next light I pulled into the left turn lane and waited for the green arrow. The feeling of weightlessness returned. My heart was racing and yet I felt a certain calmness, like I was floating above myself and outside of time.

God let her be okay, I thought to myself, or maybe whispered. It was as close to a prayer as I had come in a long time.

The arrow turned green and I made a U-turn, retracing my route back to our neighborhood.

I heard *Free Fallin'* playing from what seemed like a great distance. I glanced down at my phone.

"Meagan?" I said when I answered.

She was irritated. "I've had three more texts since you hung up on me," she exclaimed.

"I'm sorry, honey," I said. "Mom's had an accident and I'm driving the tennis courts right now."

"What?" said Meagan. "Is she okay?"

"I don't know," I said. "They called 9-1-1. I'm heading there right now."

I heard Meagan's voice catch in her throat. "I'm coming, too." she said. "Oh God, it'll take me at least twenty minutes to get over there."

"Okay," I replied. "I'll call you when I get there."

The sensation of detachment and silence clung to me as I drove the two miles to our Club. When I arrived, I saw the fire engine and ambulance parked near the tennis courts. There was a police car as well. Red and blue lights were flashing.

I parked my car and opened the door. Sounds washed over me, unintelligible chatter from people, friends of ours, gathered by the gate to the tennis courts.

I was no longer floating, but fully under the pull of gravity.

As I approached the vehicles and the small crowd, Siobhan moved towards me. Her face was twisted.

"Oh Jack," she said. "The paramedics are with her now."

"Tell me what happened," I said. Everything was playing out so quickly I had not even formulated any theories.

"She just collapsed, Jack," Siobhan said. "She was running back to the baseline and she just kept going. She hit the fence and ...."

Siobhan paused, drew a deep breath and whimpered as she released it. I looked intently at Siobhan and nodded. *Go on*, my eyes said.

"She just crumbled to the ground. Her face hit the clay so hard." Siobhan shuddered again.

I walked slowly toward the courts and Siobhan followed.

Through the tall fence with its mesh privacy screen I could see paramedics kneeling around a figure. Two police officers stood near them, watching intently.

The tennis ladies who were gathered near the gate became silent as I approached. *It's Jack*, I heard someone whisper.

They parted as I approached the gate. I felt someone gently touch my back.

As I reached for the handle of the gate, one of the police officers approached from the other side and pushed it open a few inches.

"Are you family?" he asked. I didn't recognize the officer. He was ridiculously young, a child in a black uniform with a holstered gun at his waist. His hat was too large and seemed to be resting on his ears. I could make out the black stubble of crew cut hair.

"I'm the husband," I said. *The husband.* I suppose we drift into the third person when moments become too hot to handle.

"*Mr.* Callany," the officer replied. The emphasis was on *mister.* He had obviously become familiar with *Mrs.* Callany already. "Officer Goodman," he said. "Step inside."

I stepped through the gate and Officer Goodman closed it immediately. He positioned himself between the paramedics and me. I could make out Diane's legs. She was laying on her back.

Officer Goodman extended his hand and offered a noncommittal handshake.

"She's not responsive," he said. "They're trying to bring her around."

"Can I see her?" I asked.

"You should wait here, let them work," he replied.

The paramedics continued to kneel around Diane but I couldn't make out any activity. Officer Goodman gave me a curt nod and walked back to the other police officer, a woman. I stood there awkwardly, twenty feet from my wife, while these strangers performed their act. A paramedic rose and spoke to the two police officers. The female officer spoke into her radio.

I waited.

The other paramedic rose. I could see a light gray blanket had been placed across Diane's feet. One of the paramedics began unfolding the blanket, drawing it up over her legs, then her stomach, then over her face.

I became weak. My knees were suddenly jelly and I thought I might fall over backwards or simply collapse. I wanted to take a step forward but I could not move.

Officer Goodman was next to me. He placed his hand under my elbow to steady me.

"Mr. Callany," he said. "There's been no heartbeat since the paramedics arrived."

He looked at me gravely, waiting a moment for the information to seep in.

"I'm very sorry," he said.

I noticed a zit on the side of his nose. He must have just graduated from high school. Maybe Meagan knew him.

"I need to sit down," I said.

He led me to a small bench under a canopy between two of the courts. I sat, facing away from Diane's body. I took a deep breath.

"What's next?" I asked.

"We need to call a funeral home," Officer Goodman said.

A low trembling moan escaped from my lips as I exhaled. *A funeral home.*

Free Fallin' began to play in my pocket. I knew it might be Meagan so I removed my phone. It was.

"Dad?" I heard her say.

I couldn't speak.

"Dad?" Now she sounded hysterical.

"Meagan," I said, trying to be calm but I could hear my voice tremble.

"Is Mom okay?" she screamed into the phone.

"No," I whispered. "No."

I heard Meagan wail through the phone.

* * *

Fourteen hours later, the horrible Leap Day drew to a close. It was a day that should never have existed in the first place, except that all those extra minutes over the past four years had been piling up and had to be jammed into the calendar somewhere. Otherwise, after a few centuries, Christmas would land in the middle of summer. I'd prefer that, franky. Let the seasons drift slowly across the calendar. Let us swap places with the other hemisphere once every millennium or so. I'd choose that fate in a heartbeat over reliving this one single day.

In a heartbeat. That's an option for people who have one to spare.

I took a seat at the kitchen table and eyed my coffee cup, still there from the morning. A thin film of coffee remained at the bottom. Funny what can happen in the course of drinking a cup of coffee. *There's many a slip 'twixt the cup and the lip*, Oma had said to me. You think you know what's going to happen, but you're wrong. For no particular reason I lifted the cup to my lips and swallowed the remaining drops.

Meagan was in her room, asleep, I hoped. Jimmy would be flying home from Boston tomorrow. Just like when Mom died, and when Dad died, *Death Incorporated* was stealing my waking hours. The funeral home, the announcements, the arrangements. I was only just now, at midnight, able to start *feeling* what had happened.

My mind drifted back through the day. I wanted to find the last absolutely normal moment and savor it. Chatting with Diane in the kitchen. Setting up the prank on Meagan. Raking out the beds. Driving to Lowe's. Meagan's call while I was in the car. Declining Siobhan's call, twice. That would have been it, I supposed. Talking to Meagan and seeing Siobhan's number pop up on my phone.

I rose from the table to fill a tumbler with Woodford and ice, then sat down again. I swirled the ice and stared blankly at the golden liquid coating the clear cubes. I remembered the traffic slowing, cars pulling to the side of the road. Sirens blaring as the fire engine and ambulance barrelled down the middle of the street.

Sirens blaring. They made one kind of shriek as they approached and a different kind as they passed me on their way to Diane's lifeless body. The Doppler Effect, I had told Meagan over the phone. *An increase or decrease in the frequency of sound as the source and observer move toward or away from each other.* A siren always emits the same sound - the same frequency - but when it's moving we hear different frequencies. And guess what? We're always moving. Nothing is ever really truly still, not even the last normal moment of this Leap Day.

41.

EARTH, WIND AND FIRE | 2020

LOOKING BACK ON LAST YEAR, *ANNUS HORRIBILIS* FOR THE whole planet and not least of all me (and Diane), I'm tempted to play God with the extra seconds that had been quietly accumulating over the previous four years. Instead of stapling all of them onto the end of February and fabricating Diane's death day, I would have used half the time to extend the twenty-first of September. There just weren't enough minutes in that day for everything that happened.

I'm not sure what I would have done with the other twelve hours - maybe spread them out evenly between Thanksgiving and Christmas to give a little more time for shopping. Maybe offer them up to the Food and Drug Administration to get a vaccine approved that much sooner.

The twenty-first was a Monday and therefore a fasting day. I began my day early with a cup of black coffee outside, sitting on the stone steps that lead from our terrace down to the pool deck. There would be a Club board meeting tonight, my first *sans* Brenna. It was also two weeks exactly since my meeting with Ms. Reynolds at the US Attorney's office for Western North Carolina, and today was the latest, she said, that I should expect action to be taken in the case of Mr. Ari Nimrod.

After my conversation with Jimmy three Fridays earlier, I sealed my lips on all matters Nimrod. The case we had on him was ironclad but could evaporate instantly. If Nimrod had a hint of suspicion that anyone was onto him, he could erase Love Thy Neighbor from the Dark Web in an instant and move whatever Bitcoin he possessed into a new, untraceable wallet. More than anything, I wanted to lay out the case for Dale and get his advice, but I resolved to fly solo through the next few steps in the process. I couldn't risk Dale making even the most obtuse crack during poker, and beyond that, I didn't want to pull anyone I cared about any closer to the Dark Web and its dark money.

I spent the middle part of that Friday familiarizing myself with the finer points of law enforcement against child pornography and cyber crime. Almost immediately I dismissed the idea of calling the local Lake Cooke police. They were by and large a plump, pimply speed trap gestapo with little experience in serious crimes. A few years earlier Diane's engagement ring had disappeared from her nightstand the same day the pest control guys made their quarterly visit. We turned the house upside down looking for the ring and it was nowhere to be found. Then we called the Lake Cooke police and made our case that the pest control company may have played a role. The two officers, spit shined and armed like bandits, recorded our conversation and scrawled notes in small spiral notepads. Over the course of an hour, they toured our house, drank four Diet Cokes, asked the same three or four questions over and over (*are you sure that's where you left your ring?*) and then finally departed, amiably, with promises to keep us posted. That's the last we ever heard from them.

After dismissing the *shop local* option, I spent some time on the FBI website. *Maybe*, I thought, but they seemed more focused on terrorism. Nimrod was terrorizing our neighborhood alright, but not enough to call out the Hannibal Lecter squadron.

I started Googling news items about convicted child molestors and child pornographers. It only took a few gruesome articles to realize that the

US Attorney's office was where I needed to start. They had two groups that looked promising, the Child Exploitation and Obscenity Section and the Cyber and Intellectual Property Crimes Section. In US government parlance, they were CEOS and CIPCS, though in my fevered mind I kept thinking *CPICS - see pics*. Nimrod had officially gotten under my skin.

I called the local US Attorney's office and to my surprise was speaking with a human being in under a minute. I wanted to report a case of possible child pornography and computer crimes taking place in my neighborhood. I had evidence to share. I was not a quack. I gave them my name, social, vitals and was ready with a stool sample if they needed it.

Please hold, the voice said.

After about two minutes a woman's voice came on the line. "Reynolds," it said.

"Ms. Reynolds?" I asked, unsure of the protocol at this point.

"This is Ms. Reynolds," she replied. The voice was sharp and unhumorous, something I would normally find off putting, but in this situation it was perfect.

None of the information I had given to the first person had made its way to Ms. Reynolds, so I patiently repeated the facts. Ms. Reynolds began asking questions. *What kind of evidence do you have? Do you know the suspect? Are you or a member of your family a victim of this crime?* I did my best to answer without disgorging every detail over the phone.

Finally Ms. Reynolds asked if I could come into the Charlotte office. *Yes, of course.* On Monday afternoon? *Yes, of course.* Please bring whatever evidence you have. *Yessir. I mean, yes ma'am.* (I really did make that mistake).

I called Jimmy late the same afternoon. I hoped that by then he would have caught up on the sleep lost the night before.

"Hey Jimmy," I said. "Catch up on your sleep?"

"Pretty much," he said. "I skipped my classes this morning and slept until about two."

"What classes did you miss?" I ask, ever the parent.

"Dad, don't worry. It's early in the semester."

"I *do* worry," I said.

"Well don't," he replied. "It was just underwater basket weaving."

I reflected for a moment on the tuition checks I was sending to Cambridge, Mass.

I told Jimmy about my conversation with Ms. Reynolds. He listened attentively. The whole situation was becoming very real.

"I need to bring some evidence when I meet her on Monday."

Jimmy thought for a moment.

"I could go back on the Dark Web and take some screen shots," he said.

"Perfect," I replied. "I think that's what she needs. Get screenshots with the thumbnails of Ava. And the ones of me, too." I winced at the thought.

"Will do," said Jimmy. "I'll also get a screenshot of the Bitcoin wallet address."

"Yep," I said, "That's the critical link."

"You'll have them by midnight," Jimmy said. "I'll send all of the pictures as a PDF file."

"You da man, Jimmy," I said.

"*You* da man, Pop," he replied.

"Don't tell a soul," I reminded him.

"Roger," he replied.

"And don't call me Roger."

On the seventh of September I drove into Uptown and parked alongside Romare Bearden Park, the closest I could get to the high rise that houses the US Attorney's office. It was a sparkling day, poised perfectly between summer and fall, and I saw more Charlotteans out and about than I had suspected. Almost all were masked, as was I.

Had I walked into the US Attorney's office wearing a black mask one year earlier, guns would have been drawn. But this year, *ho-hum*.

I checked in with the receptionist on the sixteenth floor, and before I could even sit in one of the naugahyde chairs, Ms. Reynolds appeared. She was my age, maybe older, wearing a Hillary-style pantsuit. Her hair was sensibly short and brownish gray. She wore unflattering black framed glasses straight from a 1950's black and white physics lecture reel.

"Mr. Callany," she said through her cloth mask.

I gave a small salute. She did not offer a hand or elbow, but gave a flinty nod and said, "Come with me please."

We walked past a number of cubicles, mostly unoccupied, and entered a large windowless conference room. A younger man was already seated at the table with no mask on.

"Please have a seat, Mr. Callany," Ms. Reynolds said to me, motioning to the head of the table. She took a seat opposite the young man and we were all suitably spaced from one another.

"You may take your mask off," Reynolds said. "I'm certainly going to."

"Thank you," I replied. I placed a manilla folder on the table in front of me.

"Mr. Callany," Reynolds began, "My name is Maria Reynolds. I'm a senior investigator in the CEOS division." I remembered this, the *Child Exploitation and Obscenity Section*.

"And this is Billy Bland," she continued, motioning toward the young man. "He's with the cyber crimes division." All I could think of was CIPCS, *see pics*.

I nodded in Billy Bland's direction. *That's quite a name to lug around,* I thought to myself.

"I need to inform you that we will record this interview," Reynolds said. At that moment, Bland Billy pressed a button on a small device at the center of the table.

"Fine," I said. "No problem."

Over the next hour, I laid out my case. Nimrod. The years of patrolling the neighborhood for violations of community standards. The color photos he has been bringing to the Club board meetings. How the pictures had gradually changed from front yards to back yards. My encounter with him during the date with Brenna (I left her out of the story). The strange binoculars he was wearing. His story about stargazing. How the bits and pieces hadn't fit together. Jimmy.

"Tell us more about your son, Mr. Callany," Bland asked.

"He's the family computer genius," I said. "He's a sophomore at MIT." Reynolds and Bland glanced at each other.

"I wanted Jimmy to see if Nimrod was selling any pictures on the Internet," I continued. "You know, the Dark Web." I looked at the two of them, but neither gave a reaction.

"I would have no idea how to get on the Dark Web, but I figured Jimmy might," I continued. It would be one thing if Nimrod was just a peeping tom and getting his jollies, but it would be something else entirely if he was taking pictures and selling them."

"Both are illegal," Reynolds said. "But you're right, selling them online is much more serious."

I told them about my call with Jimmy the previous Friday. How he had then stayed up all night. The pictures he found. The prices. I passed my color printouts around the table for the two investigators.

"I was hoping my full monty would be worth more than a dollar," I cracked. Reynolds regarded me but did not smile.

"How can you prove Mr. Nimrod took these pictures?" Bland asked.

I explained how Nimrod had given me the address of his Bitcoin wallet after my poker loss.

"You're playing poker for cash?" Reynolds interrupted.

Oh shit, I thought, I forgot that was illegal. I cleared my throat.

"Just a friendly neighborhood game?" I offered, weakly.

Bland looked at Reynolds and nodded at the recording device. He was doing me a favor, I think.

"Please go on, Mr. Callany," Reynolds said.

I explained how the seller on the Dark Web was accepting payments in Bitcoin, and how the seller's wallet address was identical to the one Nimrod had given me.

Bland perked up. "Can you give me that address?" he asked.

I slid a piece of paper to him. It contained a long Bitcoin wallet address as well as a QR code.

Bland examined the page. "This is good," he said. "Very good."

Reynolds looked at Bland, then at me. "Maybe we should be talking to Jimmy about a summer internship," she said. I caught the hint of a smile.

When I finished making my statement and distributing all the pages I brought with me, Reynolds and Bland peppered with me questions for another hour. Did I have some kind of grudge against Mr. Nimrod? (*Well, yes, I couldn't stand the guy.*) Had I been surfing the Dark Web myself? (*Are you kidding me?*) Questions about my job, my income, my dead wife.

Gratefully, the topic of poker did not come up again.

I was not put off by the questions, but I quickly realized that my little wisecracks were going nowhere. Reynolds and Bland were simply trying to establish my credibility before making a Federal case (literally) out of the Nimrod story.

After two hours Reynolds thanked me and wrapped up the meeting. Bland turned off the recording device.

"What's next?" I asked, as we all stood.

"We've got some work to do on our side," Reynolds told me. "You should hear something from us in two weeks, maybe less."

"Please don't discuss any of this with anyone," Bland added. "Not even your son."

"Of course," I replied.

Reynolds led me back to the reception area and waited with me while I summoned the elevator.

"Nice meeting you, Mr. Callany," she said.

"Nice meeting you, too," I replied. This would have been the juncture when a parting handshake was offered, but not this year.

"And I didn't hear anything about a poker game," she said. Her mask was on and I couldn't tell if she was smiling. It seemed like the lines around her eyes crinkled just a bit.

"Me neither," I said. I was smiling and I think it showed.

⋆ ⋆ ⋆

Two days later, in the early afternoon, my iPhone started chiming from the other side of the kitchen. It was the Facetime chime, and it startled me. No one other than Meagan Facetimed me, and she was in the house, upstairs in her room doing online high school. I walked across the kitchen and saw the name on the screen: Brenna Wilder.

I swiped to answer and her face appeared, filling the screen. She was almost too close, all lips and nose, no broader head context or background.

"Hellooo, Mr. Callany," she said. It was a decent imitation of *Hello, Mrs. Robinson* from a movie I doubted she'd seen and with implications I'm sure she didn't fathom.

"Hellooo, Miss Wilder," I replied in kind.

Now I could see she was driving. She kept looking up from the phone, then back down. The radio was playing loudly.

"Happy anniversary," she said with a playful smirk.

I must have twisted my face in confusion. *What anniversary would that be?*

Before I could answer, she said, "It's our *one week* anniversary! Did you get me something?"

I didn't mean to hesitate, but I did. I was processing her words. *Are we an item now? With anniversaries and gifts? Whatever happened to a good old fashioned fling?*

"Oh silly Jack," she said, "I'm just teasing." She looked up at the road again.

"What's the gift for the one week anniversary, anyway?" I asked. "A paperclip?"

"That's it, yes!" Brenna exclaimed. "I was just flipping through Emily Post and you're right. A paperclip, or anything else from Staples that's under five dollars."

"Brenna," I said, "Are you driving?"

"Yep," she replied, "going to get my nails done."

"You know you really shouldn't use Facetime when you're driving." I said it, then immediately felt like a scold.

"Yes father," she replied. "And you shouldn't drive your boat drunk."

"Fair enough," I said. "Speaking of the boat, we still have a few weeks of nice weather."

I wanted to rewind my words. Maybe there would be another date, maybe not. The intimacy, the adult contact, had been a tonic that night, but the gulf between was wide. I had spoken those words too automatically, out of a sense of protocol, I supposed.

"Totally," she replied. "It was so beautiful out there."

I seldom use the world *totally.*

Wanna take another tour this weekend?" I asked, unable to break protocol. My voice was noncommittal.

Brenna was silent, looking up from her phone at the road. Maybe she was pulling into the nail salon.

At last she spoke. "Um, I have plans this weekend, but maybe another time?"

The words stung, even though I was relieved to hear them. *Plans* meant another guy, and *another time* meant never. I don't know why I even cared. Clearly we were a mismatch, and it bordered on creepy. It was just my inner twenty year old alpha male, hunting and howling.

"Sure, of course," I said. "I need a little extra time to run to Staples anyway."

"You're funny," Brenna said. She had stopped moving now. I think she had parked. "Gotta run."

"Bye," I said.

My screen went dark.

* * *

A week passed uneventfully. Meagan and I palled around on the evenings when she was free, which was only a few. At her suggestion, I bought an air fryer at Costco and we started experimenting with air fried brussel sprouts, french fries and then, when we had gotten our confidence up, chicken wings. They were excellent, and absurdly easy to make. Meagan made a TikTok video of herself doing handstands, and in the final seconds eating an entire lemon pepper chicken wing while standing on her head.

"I think that would make me vomit," I said, when she rolled onto the carpet and stopped recording.

"Me too," she said. "It's amazing what you can do when the camera is rolling."

That made me think of Nimrod and his always rolling camera, and I felt my stomach twist.

More than anything, I wanted to wash down some enchiladas with Dale, but I held off, wanting to honor my commitment to Ms. Reynolds and the Attorney General's office. He texted me a couple times, but I begged off.

On what would've been my two week and two day anniversary with Brenna, she Facetimed me again. It was mid morning and I was in my office, pondering the advice of Lion Oil.

"Hey Jackeroo," she said brightly. "Whatcha doin?"

"I'm thinking about placing a naked put," I said matter-of-factly. I would have attempted a wink, but it was too hard to keep my eyebrows in the frame of the Facetime call.

"Ooh," she said, "sounds naughty."

"It is," I replied, "especially when you rub it down with lion oil."

Brenna made a face and then released a low, sexy growl. Why did I let myself get pulled into all this flirtation that I didn't even want?

"Hey Jack," she said, breaking character, "I need some fatherly advice."

There was that word again, a buzzkill for any stirrings I might be feeling.

"Sure, Brenna, of course," I said. "Whazzup?"

"Um," she began. "Do you remember when we were on the boat and I told you I had interviews last spring in DC and Boston?"

"Yes," I replied. Actually, I had forgotten, but I was hoping the details, if there were any, would come back to me.

"Well I got an offer," she said. Her voice showed excitement, not trepidation. "This afternoon. And they want to know if I can start on Monday."

"Wow," I said. I needed a moment to collect my thoughts. "Six months of radio silence, and now this. Who is it?"

"It's the association of associations, or something like that," she said. "There's an acronym. They want me to run their social media."

"Is the pay decent?" I asked.

"It's great," she replied, "for me anyway. More than twice what I get from the Club."

"I lived in DC for a long time, Brenna," I said to her. "It's a great place, and it's a great city to get started in."

"So you think I should take it?" she asked.

"You sound pretty excited," I replied.

"I am," she said. "I'm sick and tired of waiting to get my life started."

"Then take it," I said. "The great thing about DC is there are tons of opportunities. If the association doesn't work out, you can walk across the street and find another job the same day."

Brenna was quiet.

Finally she said, "Thank you, Jack. You've been awesome." A hesitation, then, "I really mean it."

"Are you literally heading up there this weekend?" I asked.

"Tomorrow," she said. " I have a friend from college who's got a place near Georgetown. She said I could crash with her until I get set up."

"That's perfect," I said. "I spent a lot of time in Georgetown. You're gonna love it."

"I've got to tell Pam," Brenna continued. "Think she'll kill me?"

"No, she'll understand. We all knew the Club was just a placeholder for you. But call her now. She's got a board meeting on Monday and she'll need to make other arrangements."

Brenna was silent again. Then she said, "I guess I won't get to see the rest of the lake for a while."

I smiled. My first thought was to say *it'll always be there for us*, but then I calmly set the dating protocol and faux sentimentality aside.

"Brenna, you'll find other lakes," I said, "and other boat drivers."

She smiled sweetly through Facetime.

"And you can keep your options open, Jack."

Now I smiled back.

"Godspeed, Brenna," I said.

"Back atcha," she replied.

Then the screen was dark again.

I leaned back in my chair and gazed out the window onto the lake. *I guess that was the first breakup of my new single era.*

Meagan called from downstairs, "Daaaaddd…."

I turned my head toward the door and replied, "Yeeessss…."

I heard her running up the stairs toward my office. She was holding a new unopened bag of Oreos.

"Dad," she said breathlessly, "let's air fry some Oreos."

"Brilliant!" I exclaimed. I rose from my chair and we bounded down to the kitchen. My mood rose like a birthday balloon with no string.

* * *

The next Monday morning, during a break from her online classes, Meagan came walking down the hallway from her room to my office blasting *September* by Earth, Wind and Fire on a Bluetooth speaker.

"Hey, that's my music," I said. "Go hang with your own generation."

She paid no attention, but instead started dancing and twirling in front of me. She was adorable. A perfectly normal high school senior trapped in a big empty house with her dad, robbed by an invisible virus. I leaned back in my chair and smiled, watching her.

When the song ended, she sat on the floor.

"Happy twenty-first of September," she said.

"Happy twenty-first of September to you, too," I replied. "Wouldn't you say my music is better than Kanye, or whatever you listen to?"

"Today it is," she said. "I think I'll make a TikTok to this song."

"What will the finale bite be?" I asked.

She looked at the ceiling, ruminating. "Something from the air fryer." She thought some more. "Could you deep fry ice cream?"

"Hmmm," I said. "They used to do it at the Mexican restaurant where I worked in high school. Give it a try."

She stood and gave me an elaborate, fleeting hug. "Love you, Daddio," she said.

"I wanna try that fried ice cream," I called after her as she disappeared down the hall. She had restarted *September* on her speaker.

For me the twenty-first of September was a fasting day, and a Club boarding meeting day. It was a beautiful September day, mild to cool, and I decided to walk the mile to the Club. I arrived about fifteen minutes early to find Pam Loving placing agendas at each seat.

Nimrod was there too, sitting priggishly in one of the chairs along the wall. A small briefcase rested in his lap, no doubt containing large color photos of the latest round of community standards violations. I was dismayed to see him here. Today was two weeks since my meeting at the Attorney General's office and I had been hoping he'd be called in for questioning by now. Maybe he had been, but I hadn't been told anything.

I ignored Nimrod completely and gave a small wave to Pam.

"Howdy Pam," I said. "Can I help with set-up?"

"Hi Jack," she replied. "I think we're all set. Did you hear Brenna left?"

"No," I said, fibbing. *Why would I know anything about Brenna?* "As in, quit?"

"As in, *quit*," Pam confirmed. "Apparently she had applied for a job in DC in the spring and they finally decided they needed her urgently."

"Well, good for her," I said. "She needs to get her life started."

"Yep," said Pam. "We'll muddle through."

Nimrod cleared his throat. "I thought you knew Brenna pretty well," he said.

You bastard, I thought. *Had he seen her on my boat? Had he gotten any pictures?*

"Just from these meetings," I replied nonchalantly, barely glancing at Nimrod.

I decided to end the conversation, at least my side of it.

The other members began to enter and take their seats. Aristotle motored to his place at the table. Pam had removed the chair to make room for his motorized wheelchair. Rick. Siobhan. Two others I was only beginning to know.

Pam called the meeting to order at seven. Her executive report was dismal. The Club had lost a high single digit percentage of its members, presumably due to economic impacts. New memberships so far in the year were at one-third of projected levels. Dining and bar revenues were at half of last year's level, though carry-out business had allowed the Club to keep the chef and one server. Golf and tennis utilization were high, but this didn't add any new revenue above and beyond member dues.

"Dare I utter the word *assessment* again?" asked Rick O'Shea.

"I hope not," Pam replied. "We've delayed all renovation work to preserve capital."

Aristotle, normally silent, uttered, "Read my lips. No. New. Taxes."

There was a chuckle around the table.

After running through the financials in detail and discussing plans, or lack thereof, for the upcoming holidays, Pam said to the board, "The next agenda item is resident input. Are there any resident inputs this evening?"

She looked around the table, careful to avoid making eye contact with Nimrod. This was, of course, the agenda item he had been waiting for. The other board members remained silent or softly shook their heads.

"Okay then," said Pam, hopeful she could move toward adjournment, "there being no resident inputs …."

Nimrod cleared his throat loudly and rose from his chair.

"Ms. Loving," he said, "I would like to speak as a resident."

Pam turned to Nimrod. "Very well, Doctor Nimrod," she said. "You have the floor."

Nimrod laid his attache case on this chair and opened it, withdrawing a small sack of eight by ten photos.

"Ladies and gentlemen of the board," he began. This was more formal than usual. Nimrod had something up his sleeve and he wanted our attention.

He cleared his throat and continued. "My precious family and I have been living under a state of siege and we demand your attention and support."

Several board members shifted uncomfortably. Aristotle peered intently at Nimrod, his old barrister instincts alert.

"Please take a close look at this abomination." With a flourish, he dropped his first photo onto the center of the boardroom table. The members all leaned in to see it.

It was a color photo, taken outdoors in broad sunlight, of a full size Bob's Big Boy statue. The perspective was angled upward, as though the photographer were eye level with Bob's neck. Bob, with his rotund belly and cheerful red and white check overalls, loomed large and oddly sinister. Bob's right hand was raised toward the sky, fist closed except for a beefy middle finger, which stuck defiantly upward.

Rick O'Shea guffawed and then caught himself and looked around sheepishly. Siobhan cleared her throat.

Cyrus had done a remarkable job carving the new hand and attaching it seamlessly to the original statue arm.

"This," said Nimrod, "is what my family must look at every hour of every day. This statue has been placed directly in line with our water view, and it is brightly lit all night long with halogen spotlights." He cleared his throat for emphasis. "The glare from those spotlights keeps Sara and me up all hours of the night."

I removed my cell phone from my pocket, and keeping it out of view of the others, texted Meagan: *Go get Cyrus and have him drive to the Clubhouse. He's got to hear what's going on tonight. Hurry!*

"Ari," Pam said, "what exactly are we looking at here?"

Nimrod turned his head to face Pam. "You are looking at a statue that has been placed in my backyard. It's a disgrace and it violates multiple community standards that have been approved by this board."

"If it's in your backyard," Rick asked, "why are you complaining to us? Just take it down."

Nimrod's face instantly flushed and the vein rose on his high forehead. "It's not mine," he sputtered. "It belongs to Cyrus Bolton, my next door neighbor!"

Nimrod began to place more photos on the boardroom table, walking around behind the seated members and reaching between them to place his photos at intervals.

He spoke as he walked. "You will see in these photos that the shoreline bends around in our cove. My home is situated in just such a way that our sightline to the water crosses a small part of Cyrus Bolton's lot. He has placed this abomination intentionally on that part of his lot so that he barely sees it from his house but we see it from every room."

Siobhan pointed to one of the photos. "And these are the spotlights here?" she asked.

Nimrod craned forward. "Yes," he said. "Three of them. High powered spotlights that shine up on this statue from every angle." He paused. "This statue is over seven feet tall."

Aristotle let out a low whistle and glanced at me.

"Nimod," I piped up. "I'm not aware of any community standard approved by this board that prevents a man from putting an illuminated statue in his backyard."

The vein in Nimrod's forehead began pulsing and he glared at me. "Callany," he said, "are you not familiar with the architectural standards?" He gaped at me in disbelief. "No resident may erect a structure on their property without getting prior approval from the architectural committee." Nimrod was clearly flabbergasted.

I was needling Nimrod, and enjoying it. "Well," I asked, "did he get the approvals?"

"Of course he didn't get the approvals," Nimrod erupted.

Aristotle spoke calmly. "Mr. Bolton does not get any approvals because he's not required to." All eyes turned to the retired judge as he continued, "Mr. Bolton's property lies outside the homeowner's association boundary. In fact, his lot is in the unincorporated area of the county. He can put whatever he wants on his property."

"Come on, Poe," shouted Nimrod. "That's nothing but a technicality. This thing is directly in my sightline." Nimrod looked around the table, seeking a modicum of support. "Come on, you people. He's destroying property values for all of us!"

"You people?" asked Aristotle, arching an eyebrow at Nimrod.

Nimrod was taken aback. "I'm sorry, Mr. Poe," he said meekly. "I just meant, all of you. All of *us*."

Aristotle gave a faint, disapproving shake of his head.

Nimrod's shoulders sagged. "Please," he implored us. "Please help me. This isn't like the other community standards violations. Please help me get this removed."

"And if we don't," asked Siobhan, "I suppose we'll be reading about it in the *Town Herald*?"

Suddenly we heard a commotion coming from the main lobby of the Clubhouse, not far from the Lakeside Room where we sat. There were loud, indistinguishable voices and heavy footfalls. A moment later the door to our room was opened by three men in uniforms emblazoned with US Marshal Service insignia. Behind them stood Maria Reynolds and Billy Bland. At the rear was one of Lake Cooke's finest - I'm almost certain it was Officer Goodman, the man-boy who delivered devastating news to me on Leap Day. All six wore black face masks, compounding the surrealness of the moment.

Pam rose from her chair and leaned forward with her pudgy fingertips pressed into the table. We all followed her gaze to the officials standing in the doorway.

Before Pam could speak, one of the marshals stepped forward and scanned the room. "We're looking for Mr. Ari Nimrod," he said.

We all turned our eyes to Nimrod, who was standing beside the boardroom table holding more photos of Bob's Big Boy.

The marshals followed our gaze and one of them stepped toward Nimrod. Another joined him beside Nimrod while the third and Officer Goodman remained at the door with Reynolds and Bland.

"Ari Nimrod," said the imposing marshal. "I'm placing you under arrest for producing, selling and distributing illegal pornographic images of minors."

There were gasps around the table. Nimrod's face, only moments before a furious red, drained pale and he stepped unsteadily backwards. His mouth hung open.

"You need to come with us … now," the marshal said with conviction.

Nimrod looked around the room frantically, a cornered animal.

"No," said Nimrod. And then he shouted, "NO! This is some kind of mistake." He held up a photo of Bob's Big Boy as though it could somehow exonerate him.

"Mr. Nimrod," Officer Goodman said. His voice was deeper and more commanding than I remember from the tennis courts.

Nimrod motioned to the board. "This is impossible," he said. "These are my neighbors, my friends. They'll tell you. This is a huge mistake." His eyes darted around the room while we all sat motionless.

Color returned to Nimrod's face and the vein protruded once again from his broad, flushed forehead. He skirted around the boardroom table until he was standing behind Aristotle Poe.

"I need your badge numbers … NOW!" Nimrod shouted. "All of you are going to lose your jobs," he continued defiantly.

Two of the marshals approached Nimrod from one side of the board-room table while the third left his post at the door and approached him from the other side.

"Stay away!" screamed Nimrod.

The largest of the marshals sprung suddenly, grabbed Nimrod's neck from behind, and forced his head down onto the boardroom table. Nimrod's left cheek was mashed flat on the table and he looked directly at me, crazed and violent.

Click. Click. One of the marshals had him in handcuffs in a single swift motion. The marshal who had tackled him now pulled him upright from the table and pushed him brusquely around the table and out the door. The other marshals and Officer Goodman followed.

Suddenly the room was silent. Pam remained on her feet, not from a sense of fiduciary duty, but simply because she was gobsmacked and had forgotten she was even standing in the first place. We the board looked at one another in a state of absolute speechlessness.

Maria Reynolds broke the silence. "Mr. Callany," she said, "may I have a word with you?"

All eyes turned toward me as if to say, *Oh God, not him, too!*

"Of course," I mumbled. I stood and approached Ms. Reynolds.

"Step outside, please," she said.

We stepped outside the Lakeside Room and closed the door, leaving Billy Bland behind with the other board members.

I looked across the Clubhouse foyer and saw the flashing lights of two Marshal Service vehicles. Reynolds saw my gaze.

"Want to watch?" she asked, unhooking her face mask and letting it hang from one ear.

I looked at her. "Yeah," I said. "I need to see this."

We walked to the main entrance of the Clubhouse and out the front door. I saw the large marshal push Nimrod into the backseat of the first car and close the door. Nimrod glared at me through the rear window with a murderous gaze.

"I couldn't tell you before we made the arrest," said Ms. Reynolds. She gave me a frank smile. "You did the right thing, and you helped us build an airtight case."

"Thank you," I said. I was still sorting out the events of the past few minutes.

I heard the beeping horn of a golf cart exiting the eighteenth green and driving swiftly towards the Clubhouse entrance. I looked up to see Cyrus in his dilapidated cart. Attached to his roof was the enormous plaster cheeseburger.

Cyrus gave a wide toothless grin and raised a can of Bud Light high into the air. On the seat beside him was Meagan, holding her phone out at arm's length, recording the entire scene.

Reynolds looked at me curiously.

"That's my daughter," I said, grimacing. "The girl, I mean."

"I'm glad it's not the other one," she said.

Cyrus pulled his jalopy alongside the lead US Marshall vehicle and found himself face to face with Nimrod.

"You old perve," Cyrus shouted with glee.

Nimrod was bug-eyed. He craned forward in the back seat and eyed the plaster cheeseburger on the roof of the golf cart, then slowly raised his right hand and gave Cyrus the finger.

Cyrus cackled and took a long, deliberate draw from his beer. Officer Goodman approached Cyrus, shook his head wearily, and told him to either move along or climb into the backseat next to Mr. Nimrod.

"Yes, occifer," growled Cyrus. He shifted his golf cart into gear and rolled forward. Meagan caught it all on video.

"See you at home, Daddio," Meagan said cheerfully as they moved past the entourage.

A moment later the lead car turned on its flashing dash lights and rolled slowly from the parking lot. The second car followed.

I stood with Ms. Reynolds by the Clubhouse entrance, suddenly quiet.

"We went to his home first," she said. "We thought we might catch him at dinner."

I nodded.

"His wife told us he was probably here," she continued.

"He never misses a board meeting," I said. "That's when he displays his handiwork each month."

Ms. Reynolds looked at me probingly.

"You know," I said. "His *photos.* Pictures of all the community standards violations."

"Well," she replied. "That will be coming to an end. Two of our marshals stayed back at his house to confiscate his computer, cameras, thumb drive, all that stuff."

I arched an eyebrow.

"We had a warrant," she said with a frank look.

Billy Bland came through the door and approached us. "Mr. Nimrod on his way?" he asked through his mask.

"Yep," said Ms. Reynolds. "Just departed us a few minutes ago."

She pulled her mask back on and faced Bland, "We need to catch up with them. Ready?"

"Aye, Captain," said Bland.

I extended my elbow in the pandemic approved manner and they each reciprocated.

As they began to walk to their black Suburban, I called after them. "What's gonna happen to him?"

Reynolds half turned her head toward me, then shrugged.

I stood outside the Clubhouse for a few minutes, collecting my thoughts and musing over the events of this most unusual month. *September* came unbidden to my mind.

I walked back into the Lakeside Room to a dozen stunned faces and sat down to tell my story. (*Well, most of it.*)

42.

THE CAT'S MEOW | 2021

IT'S TWO HOURS BEFORE SUNRISE ON THANKSGIVING. MY BODY is craving deep dark slobbering snoring sleep, but my mind is racing like a greyhound at high noon, hind legs impossibly out in front of its head. This day last year was a sorry affair, just Meagan and me and an antisocial virus howling outside the door. We didn't want Jimmy to risk the trip home from Boston, and so the two of us made due with a turkey breast, a box of stuffing and a trembling cylinder of cranberry sauce at the kitchen table. This year will be more like Thanksgivings past, with an actual bird in the oven, hand-made sides, and ten thankful and vaccinated souls gathered around the table, including Jimmy and Meagan, home from Beantown for a long weekend.

I've outsourced a few dishes to guests I trust not to screw them up. Pam Loving agreed to bring the sweet potato casserole and Dale consented to French green beans and butter rolls. That leaves the real business of Thanksgiving to me and two teenagers (well, one has just turned twenty) whose plane landed in Charlotte only about five hours ago and who will probably be sleeping until the crack of noon. I am rising to the occasion, literally.

I stand in the darkness of my bedroom looking through the glass panes of the French doors that open onto my terrace. I see Lake Cooke, still and quiet in the early morning, a few all night dock lights spill onto the surface of the lake. There is no evidence of a rising sun. I move through my morning regimen of stretching and twisting, and then pop off fifty push-ups before I can think of a good reason not to.

As my eyes adjust to the darkness, I make out the frame of an eight by ten photo on the dresser. It's a photo I know well. A close up of Diane's face, flushed and beaming. I took the photo two summers ago after she and Siobhan clinched the 3-0 women's doubles title at our local Davis Cup. The match had gone to a tie breaker and Diane had served the winner. I snapped the picture a few minutes later while she was packing up her tennis bag. When I called her name, she looked up, unposed and genuinely happy. I rediscovered the photo when I was preparing a loop video for her memorial service. It struck me as so authentically *her* that I had it printed and framed. Now she's here on this dark morning, eighteen months gone from my life, watching me warm up my rotator cuffs.

Diane would be amused to know it's not just Dale, but Dale plus three at our table today. He had never come to our place on Thanksgiving. I think he normally celebrates with his brother's family on the other side of the state. This year, new configurations are emerging, along with new seating charts.

Dale left me hanging one night a couple months ago with a comment about having met someone. He walked from my front door to a waiting Uber, turned and briefly arched an eyebrow, then made his proclamation.

"What the hell!" I yelled at him. "Get back in here and start talking."

He shook his head and gave what I can only call a shiteating grin.

"Dale, get back here right this second. I'll pay the driver to wait an hour."

"Go to bed, Jack," he said, climbing into the car.

And then, he was gone.

I stood woozy by the front door. *Well how do you like that?* It was Dale who had been favored by Lady Luck all this time and he never so much as dropped a hint.

I walked back to the kitchen and poured myself a tall glass of water. Carrying the glass with me, I checked that the sliders to the terrace were closed and locked. I stopped to turn off a lamp. That's when I saw what wasn't there: Diane.

The mahogany box I had placed on top of Mr. Hopper was gone.

That fucker, I thought immediately. Dale had come in here and moved Diane while I was waiting for him by the pool with his next bourbon. *Not cool. Not cool at all.*

I looked in a few obvious places. In the cabinets below the bookcases. Under the coffee table. On the opposite bookcase. No sign of her anywhere.

I pulled out my phone and texted Dale: *very funny.*

A moment later he replied: *huh? can't I meet someone?*

My reply: *that's not what I'm talking about and you know it*

Dale: *go to bed call any*

After that he wouldn't reply again.

I had to smile to myself. I had it coming. *Don't get mad, get Steven.* I finished my glass of water and turned in for the night, resolved to find and restore my Diane at first light.

Then, to no avail.

After a welcome solid night of sleep, my reward for finding the perfect ratio of high quality bourbon and water, I searched everywhere for Diane. Dale had been out of my sight for less than five minutes the night before. His radius of cruelty could not have been more than a room or two. I looked on every bookshelf, including behind the books, in every kitchen cabinet, on top of the kitchen cabinets, in the powder room, inside the tank of the toilet (desperation), inside the oven, the microwave and the air fryer. Then under the couch, behind the curtains, under my bed. Literally everywhere. Literally. She was nowhere to be found.

I called Dale, text be damned.

"Morning Jack," he said.

I offered no salutation. "Where the hell did you put Diane?".

No response.

"Dale?!" I prodded, irate.

"Jack, what are you talking about?" he asked finally.

"You moved Diane's ashes last night." I said. "Where did you put them?"

"Jack, I swear to God I didn't touch them." He was quiet for a moment. "Why would I ever do that?"

A wave of doubt rolled through me.

"Dale," I said, "I told you I moved her ashes into the family room as a test to see if they would stay there."

"I remember," Dale said. "You put her box on top of the art book."

"Hopper," I said.

"Huh?" Dale replied.

"Nevermind. Dale, please. Please don't fuck with me."

"I'm not, Jack. I promise."

"If it was a prank, just tell me," I said. "I'm offering full amnesty right now."

"I didn't touch it," Dale said. "I would never do something like that."

He sounded sincere. He was my best friend and he was telling me the truth. I held the phone quietly.

"Dale," I said finally, "this is really weird. You saw the box last night. It was there when we got to my house. After you left, it was gone. There was no one else here."

"You're kind of giving me goosebumps," Dale said.

"It's giving me goosebumps, too, damnit," I replied. After another moment, I said, "Wanna grab lunch? Figure this thing out? Plus, you've got some 'splaining to do."

"Can't today," Dale replied.

This was unusual. Dale never had other plans, especially when a Friday bust-a-gut Mexican lunch was being proposed.

"Plans?" I asked with mock incredulity.

Dale cleared his throat. "I'm going away for a long weekend," he said.

"Your brother's?" I asked. I knew that wasn't where he was going.

"No," he said. "Charleston." After a moment, he added, "with my new … friend."

This was big. Really big. Dale was my best friend and I was hearing about this for the first time.

I cracked a smile. "You old fart," I said. "You've been hiding some big news from me."

"Nobody knows yet, Jack," he said. "I've been wanting to tell you."

"Go ahead," I said.

"It's a little complicated," he replied.

"Is it as complicated as selling naked put options in the money?" I asked.

"It's in that general realm of complexity," he replied. "How's next week for lunch? Wednesday. I'll spill the beans."

"You're killing me, Smalls," I said.

"Cantina. Wednesday. Noon." Dale said.

"Okay," I said. "Have a good weekend. Don't do anything I wouldn't do." I paused, then added, "Loverboy."

I spent the next few days unsettled. I continued to look in every imaginable place for the mahogany box but it was nowhere to be found. Dale was utterly sincere in his denial, but still, he could be inscrutable. He *had been* inscrutable, in fact, hiding his new love interest from me. Was he getting even for my Bumble prank? I had it coming, I really did. But Dale knew that messing with Diane's remains was beyond the pale.

I didn't tell the kids a thing on our regular Sunday afternoon phone calls. How could I? Later Sunday night, just before turning in, I checked Hopper and the dining room again. No sign of her.

Monday morning, the same. Monday night, the same. Tuesday repeat. Wednesday, rinse and repeat. I now had a new ritual in my day, right alongside brushing my teeth and poor man's yoga.

I arrived early at Cantina Azteca on Wednesday only to find Dale already seated in our regular booth and doomscrolling on his phone. There were two margaritas on the table, rimmed in salt. I slid into the booth.

"She's really gone. Vanished." I said.

Dale looked at me blankly. Looking back now, his blank stare greatly bolstered his claims of innocence.

"Dale," I said, looking at him intently. "Diane. She's vanished."

He blinked to attention.

"Diane's remains," he said softly. "I just assumed you'd found 'em by now."

I shook my head.

"Jack," he said. "God's honest truth. I didn't touch the box. You know I would never do that to you."

I looked down, then returned his gaze. I did know that. It just wasn't in Dale's make up to mess with another guy's wife (or her remains).

"I know, Dale," I said softly. "I'm not accusing you. Just updating you. It's really gotten under my skin."

"She'll turn up, Jack," he said sympathetically. "We put away quite a bit of bourbon that night. You may have moved her and completely forgotten about it."

I suppose that could be true. I had been obsessing over the box and whether anything ever moved on its own in my empty house.

A server delivered chips and salsa and took our order.

I looked across the table at Dale. There was a brightness to him. *Popping like popcorn*, as I used to say to the kids.

"Speaking of getting drunk and moving women around," I said, "is there anything you need to tell me?"

A wide smile spread across Dale's face and he nodded his assent.

"It's still pretty new," he said.

I smiled, then took a chip, waiting for him to continue.

"That Friday when you tricked me. Here." He began. "With Jennifer."

"Mmmm, hmmm," I intoned, chip-in-mouth.

"Well," Dale said. "I had a second date that day. That evening. Drinks."

I arched an eyebrow, mimicking Dale's trademark reaction.

He continued, "She was an actual real three-dimensional person."

"Did she have nice conical sections?" I asked.

"You're an ass," he said, smiling. "But yes, she was three D all over."

"Name?" I asked.

He hesitated a moment, then said, "You know her, Jack."

"Really?" I replied. This was a surprise. "A Club lady? A gay divorcee?"

Dale looked at me intently, trying to probe how much or how little I might know. The truth was I knew nothing at all, and I hoped it showed.

"Separated," he said, still waiting for me to ask him outright.

"Pam Loving!" I said gleefully. My eyes lit up.

At that moment the waiter placed two enormous platters of enchiladas and refried beans on the table. The action prevented me from reading Dale's face.

Dale shook his head slowly.

"Jack," he said, "Pam's a bit too three dimensional for my tastes."

I brought my thumb to my chin. "Have you seen Pam lately?" I asked. "She's dropped a lot of weight."

"I haven't," Dale replied. "But good for her."

I gave a little wink and recited a favorite line from Ogden Nash, "Some ladies smoke too much and some ladies drink too much and some ladies pray too much, But all ladies think that they weigh too much."

I received a minimal reaction from Dale.

"Okay, buddy," I said. "Spill it."

Dale lifted an enormous forkful of melty cheese enchilada to his lips. This would buy him time to consider the next clue to offer.

He finished chewing, took a long draw from his margarita, and said to me, "She left her husband last year after he was arrested."

I haven't snarfed food out through a nostril since high school. But it happened when I heard this. I felt the burn of refried beans spread through my sinus cavities.

"Nimrod's wife?" I choked.

Dale gave a crooked smile. "Sara," he said.

I looked at him in disbelief. I knew Sara, sort of. For years I had seen her at the Club and around town. She almost always had their twin girls in tow. Sara was small boned and wispy, and painfully shy. I remember standing in a small circle of people at a party one night and thinking the skin of her neck was translucent.

Sara was an invisible person.

"I'm speechless," I confessed to Dale.

"Jack," he said, "she's really something special. You'd be surprised."

I took a deep breath. If she was important to Dale, then she was important to me. I would just have to rewire part of my circuitry.

"Jack," he went on, "did you know she's published two books of poetry?"

I shook my head.

"She's a Yale grad. English Lit," Dale said.

I continued rewiring.

"Jack, she's had a helluva tough year," Dale said. "Nimrod was an ass to her for years. Never helped with the kids. She had no idea what he was doing down in the basement. She filed for divorce the week he was arrested."

This much I knew. Nimrod had been released on bail with an ankle bracelet but had not returned home. He worked out a plea agreement last fall and was serving a four year sentence at the Marion Correctional Institute in McDowell County.

"How'd you meet?" I asked quietly.

"Bumble," Dale said. "Where else?"

I cracked a smile, then reached across the table and slapped Dale roughly on the shoulder. He beamed.

"Okay," I said, "go on. Is this getting serious?"

"I don't know," Dale said. "It's only been a month. This past weekend was our first time away together."

I arched an eyebrow and Dale arched one back at me, then smiled.

"I'm fifteen years older than her," Dale said. "But we really seem to get each other. You know? I'm an INTJ and so is she. We're both quiet people, but when we're together we can't stop talking."

I found myself reconsidering Sara, reconstructing what I knew about her. Yes she was invisible. Yes she was painfully passive. But she was also striking in a vulnerable Woody Allen sort of way.

I had not given a single thought to Sara or her girls after the Great Nimod Caper. I felt shame wash over me as I sat across from Dale. She had suffered under Nimrod more than anyone, and her reward for loyalty and patience was a heap of humiliation and a one way ticket to single parenthood. Why hadn't I, of all people, been more empathetic? I knew something about loss, but evidently not enough to see beyond my own selfish world.

"I barely know her," I said to Dale. "I should have reached out last year."

Dale gave a small nod.

"I'd like to meet her," I said. "For real. With you. Really get to know her."

"I'd like that, too," Dale said.

* * *

I step from my dark bedroom into the walk-in closet and pull on jeans and a sweatshirt, then into the bathroom where I regard myself in the mirror. At certain angles the skin on my neck seems to sag and I don't like it one bit. I try jutting my lower jaw forward to tighten it up, then worry I'm only making it worse. My eyelids seem to be sagging, too. I'm not aware of any eyelid exercises, but I make a mental note to look on YouTube.

I walk through the foyer into the kitchen and turn on a light. I am quiet. Jimmy and Meagan are upstairs sleeping and they shouldn't be punished for my insomnia.

There's a lot to be done before the crowd descends around noon. I check the turkey, which rests in a Yeti cooler in a bath of icy brine. It looks fine, goose bumpy and cold. I make a cup of black coffee and begin chopping a mound of celery and onions for the stuffing. I will saute these in real butter and herbs until soft and then knead the compote into the pieces of white and whole wheat bread that have been drying in the upside down lid of the turkey roaster for the past three days. The best stuffing is made from stale bread, lovingly pulled into small bits.

When the stuffing begins to feel right, smell right and look right, I wash my hands and walk to the pantry where I have stashed a small bag of Meow Mix. I open it and remove a single brown nibble. Then, using a wooden spoon, I pry a small channel in the moist stuffing, drop the nibble into the channel, then fold it closed again. No one walking by would ever know a small morsel of cat food hid in the belly of the bird.

This act has been a tradition in my family since I was eight years old. On Thanksgiving of that year, I stood with my father in the kitchen one Thanksgiving while he prepared the stuffing.

"Smells good, doesn't it?" my father asked me.

I didn't think it smelled particularly good. I had just fed Jake, our Siamese cat, as I was required to do every morning.

"Not really, Dad," I said. "All I can smell is cat food."

He looked at me with a furrowed brow and then suddenly transformed into Jack Torrance from *The Shining*.

"Bring me the cat food," he said with authority.

I reached under the kitchen sink to retrieve the tupperware container of Meow Mix that I had just replaced moments before.

"Add some to the stuffing," he ordered.

I looked at him in shock. He was still Jack Torrance, his hands deep in the stuffing, which he churned and kneaded.

He nodded again toward the stuffing. "Right on top there," he said.

A devilish grin spread across my face and I shook a generous portion of Meow Mix in the stuffing.

"That's enough," Dad said. He winked at me and continued kneading. "Put that stuff away."

When I returned to his side a moment later, the incriminating bits had been thoroughly blended into the stuffing.

Jack Torrance looked at me menacingly. "Don't tell your mother."

"Yessir," I replied.

"Or your brother."

I nodded.

Hours later when we sat groaning around the dinner table, empty plates before us, my father clinked his wine glass with a knife.

"May I have your attention please," he said. All eyes turned to him.

"Did everyone enjoy their meal today?" he asked.

There were nods and affirmations around the table.

"How about the stuffing?" he asked.

More nods.

"It was one of your best, dear," my mother said. "Did you do something different? More sage?"

"We did do something different this year," my father said. He became Jack Torrance again. "Tell them, Jack."

I looked at my father in horror. He had sworn me to secrecy and now I was thrust onto the stage. I sat in silence, though I'm sure now my face was a map of shame.

My father waited for me to speak, but I said nothing. I couldn't. My jaw was locked.

"Well, everyone," my father began. (I can't remember who was with us that day, but it was more than just the four of us.) "Jack thought it would be a good idea to add Meow Mix to the stuffing."

My brother Brian made an involuntary and loud vomiting sound. My mother's hand went to her mouth. Suddenly there were real groans around the table.

Jack Torrance looked at all of us maniacally, then his eyes settled on my mother.

"Linda," he said, "you just told us it was one of the best."

She began to slowly shake her head. "Is it even safe for humans?" she asked finally.

"We'll find out," my father said gleefully.

What exactly happened next has faded from my memory, but from that year forward - it's now been forty-seven years - I have always seen to it that a single morsel of Meow Mix finds its way into the stuffing. I always wait until the meal is over before announcing it to the assembled guests, though it's no surprise to anyone in the family.

Apparently it's fine for humans.

I finish mixing the stuffing and set it aside. Most of it will go inside Tom Turkey, but some will go around the outside, a bumper between Tom and the roasting pan. It's too early to start the turkey - it will need to go into the oven around ten.

I wash my hands, make a second cup of coffee, and step outside into the cool fall morning. Usually by this time in autumn a fierce storm - residuals of a Gulf Coast hurricane - has ripped through the Carolinas and stripped the trees of their leaves. Not so this year. Fall has been docile and pleasant. Excellent weather for running and walking.

Pam Loving and I have done a fair amount of walking together, in fact. We've become closer over the past few months. I got her interested in fasting, and so we walk together all over the neighborhood on our fasting days. I was happy when she accepted my invitation for today. She doesn't have anyone special right now and her family is mainly on the west coast.

When I walked back into the Lakeside Room at the Club the night Nimrod was arrested, the others were planted in their seats, dumbfounded. Photos of Bob's Big Boy shooting the bird were strewn across the boardroom table. It was Pam, our Chair, who adjourned the meeting and called down to Enzo to bring us a full bottle of tequila and seven glasses.

"None for me," I said, taking my seat. "It's a fasting day."

Aristotle glowered. "You're gonna damn well drink with us, Jack," he said. "And you're gonna sing like a bird."

There were grave nods around the table.

Enzo entered, lined up the glasses on the boardroom table near Pam, and filled each one, setting the half empty bottle ceremoniously before Pam. Rich O'Shea began sliding the glasses down the table.

Pam raised her glass. "I propose a toast," she said, "to Jack Callany, and whatever the hell he did to rid us of Ari Nimrod, and may he spill the beans post haste."

"Hear, hear," uttered Aristotle. Glasses were clinked, shots swallowed. Eyes turned toward me.

And so I did sing like a bird. I reminded everyone about our August meeting, when Nimrod first complained about the statue in Cyrus's backyard. At that point, Bob was still hoisting a plate with a cheeseburger on it and the spotlights had not yet been installed. I recounted my kayak trip to Cyrus's place to see the statue for myself, and how I had seen the fat fist and raised middle finger being carved in his shed. There were murmurs of incredulity.

When I got to the part about my midnight encounter with Nimrod, I told them I hadn't been able to sleep and had decided to take my new boat out - with an aside to Pam, thanking her for selling me Gordon's boat - to see the full moon.

I continued the story, telling them about my suspicions of Nimrod the next day, his stargazing under a full moon, his unusual binoculars, the suddenly dawning theory about what he was really up to.

"What a creep," said Siobhan. "I should've known." There were nods of assent around the table.

Then I told them about the Dark Web. Jimmy. Bitcoin. Losing in poker to Nimrod.

Aristotle narrowed his eyes at this part of the story. "I played with you that night, Jack," he said. "You played like a damn fool."

"I thought you might've been suspicious, Judge," I said to him. "That was the one and only night I've ever wanted to lose."

I concluded my tale with the story of my trip to the US Attorney's office two weeks earlier.

"And now, my friends," I said grandly, "you were all here for the grand finale."

Applause erupted around the table.

"Another round!" shouted Rick.

We finished off the tequila on the second round and I filled in little details in response to the questions that kept coming. After another half hour, Pam collected Nimrod's photos and we rose to say our goodnights.

We moved as a group toward the main entrance to the Club.

"Good night, everyone," Pam said.

Then to me she added, "Walk me out in a minute. I'm going to drop Nimrod's photos off in my office. These will hang on our wall of shame someday."

I waited while Pam took the pictures to her office. She returned in less than a minute.

"The Club board has become a lot more exciting since you joined," Pam said to me.

"Ah yes," I said, "beginning with the first contested election in Club history."

We left the building and walked toward our cars, the last two in the lot.

Pam turned to me and said flatly, "You weren't alone on your boat the night you saw Nimrod."

She had me. I wasn't expecting to hear those words and I had no reply at the ready.

"No," I said softly, shaking my head.

Pam looked hard at me.

"I have a guilty pleasure," she said.

Oh God, I thought. *Don't tell me Pam was out there with binoculars, too.*

I arched an eyebrow. "Yes?"

"I'm on TikTok," she said.

"Then you must see Meagan performing her antics all the time."

Pam nodded. Then she added, "I also follow Brenna."

We stood there looking at each other. Brenna had videoed the lake and the moon, but she had been careful not to include me in the video.

"You think I don't recognize my own boat?" she asked.

I was a deer in the headlights.

Then Pam released an enormous laugh and beamed at me.

"It's okay, Jack," she said. "I just wanted to see your face!"

My tension released and I broke into a smile. "Busted," I shrugged.

'I'm happy for you," Pam said. "Really. You're moving on."

"I guess," I replied. "Yes and no."

Pam moved in for a maskless hug. A friend's hug. A sister's hug. The hug of someone who genuinely cared about me.

We became friends. Met for coffee, then graduated to lunch. It became apparent to me how unhappy and self conscious Pam was about her weight. She talked about it openly. She had tried every diet. It was hard, she had said, living alone with the fridge and no accountability.

I suggested fasting, and at first she said it would be impossible.

"I get so damn hangry," she said to me on one of our walks.

"I did too," I told her. "By the third or fourth day that all stops."

So she did try it. And by the third or fourth day she stopped being so hangry. That's when we started walking together instead of eating together. And that was a year ago. Pam has dropped twenty-five pounds. I wouldn't say she's at her college weight, but she looks great and feels great. We still walk every week on our fasting days. On Monday this week I asked her to join us for Thanksgiving.

"That's a Thursday, Jack," she said. "I'm fasting."

"You're hardcore," I said. "Will you bring a casserole anyway?" I asked.

"How does sweet potato sound?"

"Perfect," I told her. "Thanksgiving's not complete without it. But you have to eat."

* * *

I finish my coffee and return to the kitchen. There's not much food prep I can do at this point, so I decide to set the dining room table. It's been two years since I've sat at this table, and I don't believe I ever set it myself. That was always Diane's dominion, which was fine with me.

I flip on the dining room lights and begin opening the drawers of the sideboard in search of a table cloth and place settings. I find the table cloth neatly folded and place it on the center of the table. In a moment it's fully deployed and with roughly even overhang on all sides. Next I count ten elegant cloth napkins. As I place them around the table, four on each side and one on each end, I begin to think about the seating chart.

I'll take one end of the table, the head, and I'll put Cyrus at the other end. That's partly to honor his senior age, and partly to keep his hands and feet away from my plate.

I've seen more of Cyrus this past year than ever before. He considers himself the hero of the Nimrod story, and me his best supporting actor. He pulls into my driveway at least once each week in his golf cart, which still has a plated cheeseburger on its roof, and for which he is a minor celebrity in these parts. When he had his last remaining teeth pulled last spring, in the month or so before he got his falsies, he stopped by every day for a pity beer and a chance to smack his gums at me. Throughout the summer he brought me baskets of okra and tomatoes from his garden.

Last week Cyrus came careening into my driveway so fast I thought his cart would flip, or at least launch the cheeseburger through sheer centrifugal force. Peaches lurched beside him, paws on the dash and ropes of saliva trailing in the wind.

"Jack!" he shouted from the driveway.

I was in my office upstairs and padded down in sweatpants and slippers to see what the commotion was about.

"Morning Cyrus," I said. It was just after nine.

"Jack," Cyrus erupted, dismissing all greetings and formalities. "Do you know a *motherfucker* named ricochet?"

"Rick?" I asked. "Sure, I've known him a long time."

Cyrus glowered and took a long draw from a can of Bud Lite.

"You tell that *sonabitch* I ain't moving the statue."

"You mean Bob?" I asked.

"Course I mean Bob," he replied testily.

I stepped through the front door and sat on the top step, facing Cyrus. Peaches let out a low, threatening growl.

"Cyrus," I said. "Rick is a realtor. He's trying to sell Nimrod's place."

"You think I don't know that?" Cyrus replied. His eyes were bloodshot but his false teeth, which were still fairly new, were straight and glistening.

"Rick's gonna have a hard time selling that place with a seven foot Bob's Big Boy shooting the bird at everybody who visits the house," I say.

"That statue is on *my* property," Cyrus said defiantly. "And if it wasn't for that thar statue, Nimrod would still be peekin' up girls' skirts."

"True dat, Mr. Bolton," I said with a conciliatory smile.

Cyrus fumed. Peaches showed her substantial pink gums and strained towards me across Cyrus's lap.

"You got a good hold on Peaches there, Cyrus?" I asked.

"What? Peaches?" he asked incredulously. "She wouldn't hurt a fly."

"I know that, Cyrus." I said. "She's just a sweet little puppy. But please hold onto her anyway. I don't want her to fall out of the cheeseburger-mobile and hurt herself."

This time Cyrus flashed a movie star grin, a new (and discordant) look for him.

"Cyrus," I went on. "You might get some very nice neighbors. In fact, you're due some. By the law of averages, you'll never have a neighbor like Nimrod again."

Cyrus looked puzzled. "Law of averages?" he asked.

"It's a true *bona fide* law," I said, prevaricating just a bit. Jimmy, if he were here, would jump in to correct me. "The law says that if the chances of something bad happening are one in a hundred, and then something bad does happen to you, then there's practically no way it will ever happen again."

Cyrus took another swig of Bud Lite and pondered this more a moment.

"So you think I should move Bob?" he asked, chastened.

I drew in a deep breath. It was gratifying how this rough beast respected my advice. I would be careful not to abuse the trust.

I nodded sagely, then said, "Cyrus, you single handedly saved this neighborhood by erecting that statue." He leaned back slightly and beamed, glorying in the praise. "There's no telling how many teenagers and housewives you spared from humiliation by your act of courage. In fact," I paused for dramatic effect, "I wouldn't be surprised if you don't hear from the mayor at some point."

A goofy smile spread across the old man's face. It made me think of the scene in The Wizard of Oz when the Great and Powerful Oz gives the lion a medal for bravery. I make a mental note to speak to the mayor, who is a journeyman poker player and sometimes stops by the Club for punishment on Thursday nights.

"Jack," Cyrus said gravely, "do you think the mayor would want the statue down at City Hall."

Oh God, I thought to myself. *I've taken this too far.*

"I'll ask him about it, Cyrus," I fibbed. "He might have concerns about small children seeing it."

Cyrus nodded. He could see the wisdom in my concern.

"But, Cyrus," I said. "I do think you should move it so Rick O'Shea has a snowball's chance in hell of selling that house."

"Goddammit Jack, you right," Cyrus said with resolve. He concentrated for a moment. "I think I'll put it in my front yard."

I arched an eyebrow.

"You want it to be flipping off everybody who drives down the street? That's not very neighborly."

"No," Cyrus said, reflecting. "No, it's not."

"Maybe you could saw off the middle finger and turn it into a street light."

Cyrus beamed. "Jack, that's a helluva an idea," he exclaimed. "I could electrify it."

"Of course you could," I said with encouragement.

"It'll be done in a week," Cyrus said. "Come on by on Thanksgiving and have a look."

I felt a rush of sentiment when Cyrus said this.

"You have plans for Thanksgiving, Cyrus?" I asked him.

"Nah," he said. Then added, "Well yes, I guess. I'll make some squash from the garden."

"Cyrus," I said with authority. "As of right now, you have plans for Thanksgiving. You're coming here."

He blinked. I think I caught him off guard.

"That's right nice of ya, Jack. Thank ye."

"We take care of our neighbors around here, don't we, Cyrus?" I asked, smiling. The words *Love Thy Neighbor* flashed across my mind, unwelcome.

"We shore do. Yessir," replied Cyrus. "Mind if I bring Peaches?"

He must have seen the blood drain from my face. Cyrus let out a hyena laugh.

"I'm just pulling yore leg, Jack. Peaches'll stay home."

"That might be best, Cyrus," I said. "But I know, she wouldn't hurt a fly."

"Ya got that right," Cyrus said. He turned the key in his golf car, raised the now empty Bud Light can into the air, and motored back onto the street.

* * *

I continue to study the dining room table. I'll have Dale and Sara sit at Cyrus's end of the table, opposite each other. That actually solves the puzzle. I'll put the twins next to their mother and Jimmy and Meagan directly across from the twins. Jimmy will be next to Dale - that's great, they can discuss options trading - and Meagan can keep an eye on the twins.

That leaves two seats. Pam will sit to my left, next to Meagan. And on my right ….

"Morning Daddio," Meagan says to me. She's in fuzzy socks and I have not heard her slip into the room.

"Hey Doll," I say. "Happy Thanksgiving."

She moves in for a sleepy bear hug.

"I thought you'd sleep until noon," I say.

"I'm too excited," she replies. "I love being home. I wanna wake up Jimmy."

"Why don't you hang with me for a while, let him sleep a little more," I say.

"Okay," she says cheerfully. She drops into the chair immediately to the right of where I'll be sitting this afternoon.

I study her for a moment. Funny she chose that chair.

"You're sitting over there today," I say. I point to a seat on the other side of the table.

Meagan makes a pouty face

"I wanna sit next to you," she says.

"I want you between Jimmy and Pam," I tell her. "Across from the twins."

"The twins?" she asks.

I rub my eyes. Where do I begin?

"Come on," I say. "Want some coffee."

"I'd die for some coffee," she replies dramatically.

"Well, my coffee will kill you, alright."

I make a cup for her and we sit together at the kitchen table.

"You know Dale, right?" I ask.

"Uh, no," she says. "Duh!"

"He's met someone," I say.

"Some*one*?" she asks, "or a pair of naughty twins?"

I can't suppress a smile.

"He might like that," I say. "But no. He met someone who's not naughty as far as I know, but who does have a pair of twins. I think they're seven."

"Seven?" Meagan asks. "Both of them?"

I've missed this girl. She has my ridiculous sense of humor.

"You know 'em," I say. "Or at least know *of* them."

Meagan is pensive for a moment.

"The only twins I know around here are the Nimrod girls."

I make no reply but stare into her eyes.

"Oh my God," Meagan shrieks. "Mr. Dale's dating Mrs. Nimrod!"

I take a sip of coffee, then raise both eyebrows as high as I can and nod.

"This is too weird," Meagan says.

"It's new." I say. "New*ish*. Sara Nimrod's a sweet lady and she deserves someone kind."

"How'd they meet?" Meagan asks.

"An app called Bumble," I reply.

"Is it like Tinder?" Meagan asks..

"What do you know about Tinder?" I ask, not really wanting to know the answer.

"I don't live under *Iraq*," she says. It was one of our standing jokes.

"Bumble's for middle-agers. The women call the shots."

"I'll keep that in mind," she replies.

"Tell me about school," I say, redirecting.

Meagan and I sit at the kitchen table for a delightful hour. I hear about Aditi, how her mother calls her every night, seven days a week. I hear about Introduction to Philosophy, the coolest class ever, and Introduction to Psychology, the most fascinating class she's ever taken. The Golden Eagles dance team. Seeing Jimmy at the Head of the Charles. Running up heartbreak hill, the steepest known hill on any marathon route.

My heart is soaring with joy to know her college experience is happening, that she's basking in so many superlatives.

"You slowed down on TikTok," I say to her.

"Yeah," she replies, bored.

"Meagan," I say, "your fans need you. And your sponsors need your fans."

Meagan regards me over the top of her coffee mug. "I've turned down every sponsorship since October."

"Really?" I ask. I'm shocked to hear it.

"I think I'm done," she says to me. "It's so fake."

I nod. It is fake, absolutely fake.

"Will you still eat junk food with me?" I ask, smiling.

"Got some right now?" she asks cheerfully,

We hear Jimmy's heavy footsteps coming down the staircase. He appears in the kitchen tousled headed, dressed in an ancient tee shirt advertising Pi Day 2015 and Harry Potter sweatpants.

He walks directly up to me, locks his eyes onto mine, and asks, "Did you remember the cat food?"

"Does the Pope crap in the woods?" I asked. Another interior joke of mine.

"I don't know what that means," he says.

I look to Meagan for help and she shrugs.

"It's a way of saying yes," I reply. "It means not only yes, but *obviously yes.*"

"What does that have to do with the Pope?" Meagan asks.

I shake my head in dismay.

"Well the important thing is," Jimmy announces. "The stuffing has been prepared in the traditional manner."

I rise from my chair and pull him in for a bear hug.

"Happy Thanksgiving," I say. I step back and regard them both. "I'm so happy to have you both home."

Jimmy makes a coffee and joins us at the kitchen table. He lowers his face into the steam.

"What's new with you, Daddio?" Meagan asks. "Still day trading?"

"Always," I say, smiling. It's been a good month. "In fact, Jimmy," I add, "Mr. Dale will be here this afternoon. Maybe you can finally set him up with his own Lion Oil."

Jimmy emits a noncommittal *mmmm hmmmm.*

"Mr. Dale is bringing Mrs. Nimrod here for Thanksgiving," Meagan blurts.

Jimmy raises his eyes to me, and I explain, one more time, how this came to pass.

"You know," I say. "Life moves along down here, even when you're away."

There is silence for a moment. It's pleasant. Cozy. We are a family again, or at least three-quarters of one.

At last Meagan speaks. "So, Dad. Is your life moving along?"

They both look at me. Is my life moving along, or am I just moping around, lonely, dueling the Noonday Demons and playing the stock market? *Am I dating*, that's what they're really asking.

"I wanna tell you guys something," I say to them. "I've been waiting until you were both home."

"Oh God," Meagan says. "Dad's coming out to us."

"Shut up, Sis," Jimmy says.

They both eye me.

"I've invited someone over today," I say.

"Pam Loving," Meagan shrieks. "Oh my God, I knew it! All that fasting and walking."

"Pam's great, yes," I say. "And she's coming with sweet potato casserole, but that's not who I'm talking about."

Jimmy remains quiet. He gives me space. Meagan charges in head first.

"Is it someone we know?" Meagan asks.

I nod and say, "Yes, you both know her."

"So *it is* a her," Meagan exclaimed. Jimmy gives her a sideways glance.

The week before Labor Day, Siobhan Sorcer had called. I hadn't seen her regularly since my board term at the Club wrapped up earlier in the summer, but she and Doug checked in occasionally, good neighbors, and the attentive former tennis partner of the deceased wife. Siobhan was in a mild panic when she called.

"Dr. Sanders isn't coming back this fall," she said to me. He was the math teacher who worked miracles on math haters at the high school. Jimmy and Meagan both had him and loved him.

Siobhan went on, "Steven is freaking out. He's got Calculus AB and BC this year and they don't have a full time teacher."

Steven was their son, an only child. Jimmy hadn't known him well, but he and Meagan had been in a few classes together. He was a soccer kid, away every weekend for tournaments. I gathered that Steven was good, but not scholarship material.

"I could tutor him," I offered. "Meet a couple nights each week and make sure he's steady on his feet."

I heard Siobhan draw a breath. "Jack, would you ever in a million years consider being a sub?"

"A sub?" I asked. I wasn't following.

"A substitute teacher," she said. "You'd be amazing. Diane always said what a math genius you are. Just for a few weeks, until they hire someone."

In my mind I watched *Ferris Bueller's Day Off* on fast forward. I let out an audible sigh.

"I know the principal, Jack. I could call her," Siobhan entreated.

And so it began. I spent Labor Day weekend relearning differential calculus and drawing up lesson plans that would carry me through a few weeks. Pam took me shopping for some teacher's clothes - craft beer tee shirts and Birkenstocks would get me *dress coded,* as the kids say. On Tuesday morning I was Ben Stein, standing in front of a classroom of juniors and seniors whose hormonal minds had eradicated all math knowledge during the just ended summer.

Jimmy and Meagan looked at me in sheer amazement. "You're teaching math at Lake Cooke?" Meagan asked.

"Are you still teaching, Dad?" Jimmy asked.

"Yes and yes," I replied. "I survived September and the principal asked me to teach out the semester."

"Oh my God," Meagan said again, her favorite refrain. "I can't believe it."

"So who's coming to dinner?" Jimmy asked.

I continued with the story I had been saving up for this moment.

On the Tuesday after Labor Day I met the principal, Ms. Axelrod, at 6:30 in the morning. We pulled into the teacher's parking lot at the same time, and she greeted me warmly. My orientation lasted all of fifteen minutes, during which I was briefly shown my classroom, introduced to the school *resource officer* (an off-duty Lake Cooke cop), and deposited in the teacher's lounge where I helped myself to a cup of overheated thin black coffee from a Mr. Coffee machine that dated to the school's opening in 1979. Alone, I took a seat at the long table and flipped through my lecture notes for the first day.

"Mr. Callany?" a woman said, entering the room. I recognized the face immediately - she was the kids' guidance counselor - but her name eluded me completely. "Hi," she said, extending a hand. "It's Claire. Claire Moonpenny. I was Jimmy and Meagan's guidance counselor."

She was dressed smartly, neat and a bit soldier-like in red slacks, a white blouse, and a navy blazer. Her brown hair was much longer than I remembered. She sat down directly across from me and placed a Starbucks venti on the table.

I rose and shook her hand. "Ms. Moonpenny. What a relief! I don't know another soul here except Ms. Axelrod."

She smiled and sat across from me. "Call me Claire. Please." she said. "And here's a pro tip. Don't drink the coffee in the teachers' lounge." She nodded toward her Starbucks. "My first stop every morning."

We chatted for a few minutes as other teachers came in, said hello, and then dispersed to their classrooms.

"Good luck with the savages," Claire said as we both rose ahead of the bell.

"Can a guidance counselor call the kids savages?" I asked.

"Ask me tomorrow morning after you've survived a day," she replied.

I must be the exception to some rule because I loved my first day of teaching. I decided to abandon my lecture notes and spend the day getting to know my students. I sat on the top of my desk, feet dangling, and asked each student to tell me three things about themselves, one of which had to be a lie. I made a point of memorizing each kid's name as they went around the room. In each class, the introductions began guardedly and ended raucously. After each kid spoke, I called out one of the other kids who had already spoken by name and asked them to guess the lie they had just heard. At the end of each period, my students were buzzing. I had them primed for math, which would commence in earnest the next time we met.

The next morning - it was a Wednesday - I took Claire Moonpenny's advice and drove to the Starbucks. I'm a *grande* guy on the rare occasions I go there, and I take pleasure in calling it a *medium* (that's what we used to call *grande*, back when coffee was less than a buck).

While I waited for my Americano to come up, Claire walked through the door and took her place at the end of the line. After a moment she noticed me and I gave a small salute. A wide smile spread across her face.

"Sit for a minute?" I asked when I had my Americano in hand.

She looked at her watch. "Sure. Yes. That'd be nice."

"That's how it started," I say, looking from Meagan to Jimmy with a sheepish smile.

"Hold on a second while I pick my jaw up off the floor," Meagan says.

Jimmy chimes in. "Dad," he says, nodding. "I liked Ms. Moonpenny. She always remembered me, and she didn't think I was crazy for wanting to go to MIT."

Meagan is still staring at me. Finally she asks, "Dad, are you actually *dating*? Is this serious?"

I had prepared for this. Honestly, it's the real reason I was up so early this morning.

"We're just friends," I say. "At this point." I look at them. "We've been to dinner a few times. We've been hiking almost every weekend this fall. She loves hiking."

"Cool," Meagan says.

I study both of my offspring, then say it. "I think we …." I pause, then continue. "I think we both want to date." I clear my throat. "I told her I wanted to talk with you guys about it first."

There is silence in the kitchen. Then a tear rolls down Meagan's face, but she's starting to smile at the same time.

"Dad," she says. "Of course it's okay for you to date. You're such a great guy. The world can't let you go to waste."

I grin.

Then Jimmy speaks. "Dad, when we had dinner in Boston this summer I told you not to underestimate yourself. I'm not surprised the ladies have come knockin."

My eyes fill, and when I blink a tear rolls down my cheek. Meagan leans in to hug me and then Jimmy wraps his arms around both of us.

"Family cave!" Meagan erupts, muffled by our arms.

When we separate I keep one hand on each of their shoulders. "Thank you. Thank you guys for understanding." I hesitate. "No one will ever replace Mom, but life goes on."

"Dad?" Jimmy asks soberly. "Do we have to call Ms. Moonpenny *mom*?"

Meagan begins to punch Jimmy on his chest and arms. He pulls back in mock defense.

"So she's coming today?" Meagan asks at last. "That's her chair, the one next to yours?"

I nod and give a sideways smile.

"Have you told her about the cat food?" Jimmy asks?

"I will," I say, "when we're done eating."

43.

THANKSGIVING | **2021**

IT'S JUST AFTER 10:00 PM AND I STAND ON THE BACK TERRACE with a tumbler of bourbon. Meagan has gone to her friend Maddie's house and Jimmy is somewhere upstairs watching Netflix or playing a video game. We're a modern family, I suppose. We had a wonderful Thanksgiving dinner and now we've each retired to our separate corners.

There's a chill in the late November air, though it's still what Diane would call *sweater weather*, not full blown coat weather. For Jimmy, now an inveterate Bostonian, it's shorts and tee shirt weather. The bourbon warms me.

It was no surprise that Cyrus arrived first today, at eleven, a full hour early. What was surprising was what he brought - a large casserole dish of fried okra, an even larger dish of sliced squash, expertly seasoned, and two enormous apple pies. All these he claimed to have made himself from the fall production of his garden. The old boy had outdone himself.

The other thing he brought, the biggest surprise of all and also from his backyard, was an enormous painted wooden hand giving the bird.

When I opened the front door for him, still holding a dish towel and not yet ready for guests, Cyrus stood beaming with the obscene hand thrust forward toward me.

"Happy Thanksgiving, Jack!" he said with genuine delight.

"And the same to you, Cyrus," I said heartily. "That's quite a centerpiece! Come on in."

Cyrus stepped into the foyer and Jimmy and Meagan appeared from the kitchen,

"Jimmy, Meagan," I said. "Bring in the dishes from Mr. Bolton's golf cart."

Jimmy grinned broadly at Cyrus. "Hey ya, Mr. Bolton," he said on his way to the golf cart. He turned around on the front steps and shouted back into the house, "What'dya do with Bob?"

Cyrus set the carved hand on the dining room table next to the wicker cornucopia I had brought down from the attic storage.

""I took yore advice, Jack," Cyrus said so that Jimmy and I could both hear. "I moved Bob so he wouldn't bother them realtors no more."

"Where is he now?" Meagan, walking back in with an apple pie in each hand.

Cyrus shoved his hands deep into his pockets and took stock of us. "I moved him to my front yard. Up by the street."

I arched an eyebrow.

Cyrus continued, "I'm gonna cut a hole in his stomach and turn him into a mailbox."

"That's definitely not allowed by community standards," I said, smiling.

"Oh, I'll use an official mailbox," Cyrus said. "I'll mount it right inside Bob's belly."

"What about the right arm?" Jimmy asked. "You gonna put the cheeseburger back up there?"

"Hell no," Cyrus said, indignant. "That's gonna be my streetlight."

I moved the obscene hand to the table in the kitchen. We'd set the pies and other desserts around it. I didn't think it belonged on the dining room table while we ate our Thanksgiving meal. Call me old fashioned.

Dale and Sara arrived next with her twin girls. This was my first direct contact with Sara if you don't include Club socials or grocery store sightings. After greeting Dale and engaging in the ritual handshake and back slap, I turned to face Sara. She gave me a shy smile.

"We meet at last," I said to her.

"Jack Callany," she said, gazing at me steadily. "I don't know whether to kick you or hug you."

I glanced at Dale quickly. There was a twinkle in his eye.

"I have that effect on women," I said to Sara. "Why don't you kick first, then we'll hug?"

She twisted her trunk, windmilled her arms around, and cocked her leg for a walloping field goal kick. The blood must have drained from my face. Immediately she unwound herself and let loose a bright sparkling laugh, then leaned into me for a hug.

"It's been quite a year for us, Jack," she said as she pulled back. "You've certainly changed the direction of my life." She cast a glance at Dale who was grinning.

"Let me take those," I said to Dale, motioning to the green bean casserole and bag of rolls he was carrying. I looked at the twins and said, "Come on girls, let's see if we can find Meagan."

We walked into the kitchen where Meagan was peeling potatoes and Jimmy was doing some dishes. I saw Cyrus through the window on the rear terrace smoking a cigarette.

The twins gravitated toward Meagan and she began to show them how to use the peeler.

Jimmy dried his hands with a dish towel and greeted Dale and Sara.

"Jimmy," Dale said, "I understand you have some software that might be useful to me?"

Jimmy beamed. "Lion Oil, Mr. Dale," he said. "My dad's superpower."

"I know, I know," Dale replied. "He's been gloating over it for a year. Any chance you could hook me up?"

"I'll need ten percent of the upside, Mr. Dale," Jimmy said with a winning smile.

"Sure," Dale replied. "And I assume you'll take ten percent of my losses, too?"

Jimmy looked at me, checkmated.

"Go show him Lion Oil, Jimmy," I said. "Maybe you can link his account."

Dale rubbed his hands together greedily.

Sara and I drifted away from the girls. "I should've come by," I said to her, "a long time ago."

"No," she said quietly. "It's better like this."

She looked at me, then added, "I hadn't been happy for a long time. I had no idea what he was doing, but I knew something was going on."

I nodded.

"You caught him, Jack," Sara said. "Caught him and stopped him."

"Is the divorce complete?" I asked.

She nodded, "All but," she said. "We have a final hearing in December."

"Will Ari be there?" I asked. I didn't know whether felons could leave prison to attend their own divorice decree.

"No," she said quietly. "He's signed everything he needs to sign."

The slider opened and Cyrus walked in grinning.

"Howdy neighbor," he said to her.

"Mr. Bolton," she replied. I couldn't begin to imagine how these two felt about each other.

They regarded each other for a moment, neither offering a handshake.

"I appreciate you moving the statue, Mr. Bolton," Sara said at last.

Cyrus buried his hands in his pockets and rocked back with satisfaction. "Well," he said, "Jack here says you need to sell yore house. No reason I can't do my part to help."

The doorbell rang. I walked to the foyer to see Pam Loving and Claire Moonpenny standing together.

"Hi Claire. Hi Pam," I said cheerfully. "I see you've met."

"Just now," said Pam. "We pulled in at the same time."

I led them to the kitchen, taking Pam's sweet potato casserole and a chocolate pecan pie that Claire had made. I sat Claire's pie on the kitchen table next to Cyrus's apple pies and the carved monstrosity.

"Oh my," said Claire. "That's not a traditional Thanksgiving centerpiece."

Pam let out a laugh. "No," she said, "it certainly isn't, but it's made a few people around here very thankful."

And with that, the spectacular chaos of Thanksgiving Day began. Voices and laughter filled the kitchen. Dale and Jimmy reappeared, speaking in low conspiratorial tones about arbitrage opportunities in the options market. The twins gleefully mashed potatoes under Meagan's less than attentive supervision. Pam and Cyrus struck up a conversation and he offered to take her for a ride in his cheeseburger-mobile (she obliged).

I offered to show Claire around the house.

"Your home is … lovely," she said when we were alone. "I don't think many substitute teachers live like this."

"Thank you," I said. "It feels too big and too lonely most of the time."

I took her upstairs to my office.

"The nerve center," she said. I couldn't tell if she was impressed or disgusted with my bachelor pad furnishings.

"Folding tables from Costco," I told her.

She moved past my desk and computer monitors to look out the window. It was only early afternoon but the sun was nearing the tops of the trees and slanting golden across the surface of Lake Cooke.

"Such a beautiful view," Claire said.

"This used to be the master bedroom," I told her, and then regretted saying it.

She stepped through the French doors and out onto the balcony. I followed.

"Your boat?" she said, pointing to our dock.

"Yep. Pam sold it to me last summer. It was her ex's." I paused. "I'd like to show it to you sometime," I said. "Take you out on the lake. You've been?"

"I'd like that," she said. "It's been a long time."

I stood beside her on the balcony looking out across the lake. We were both silent. Then we both spoke at the same time.

"I'm so glad …," Claire began saying.

"I talked to …," I said at the same time.

We both laughed. It was our rom-com moment.

"Please," I said. "You first."

Claire smiled sweetly. She had a way of looking directly at me while slightly turning her head down. Her eyes were a pale liquid blue.

"I was saying how glad I am that you took over Dr. Sanders' classes." She continued to look at me. "You're very popular, maybe even more than he was."

I smiled. "I like it more than I ever thought I would," I said. "And I have to admit, I like our morning coffee routine, too."

"Me too," Claire softly. Then she asked, "What were you about to say?"

I cleared my throat. "Well," I said, "I talked to Meagan and Jimmy this morning."

I paused and waited. Claire said nothing, but looked at me intently.

"I asked them how they would feel if I started dating."

Claire cocked her head. "Dating in general?" she asked.

"No," I said grinning. "Dating in specific. Their old guidance counselor."

"Hmmm" she said. "Does this *old* guidance counselor know what you're planning?"

"She has no idea," I replied. "But I'm hoping she'd be open to the idea."

"Hmmm," Claire replied demurely.

I moved my face close to Claire's and she tilted her head imperceptibly. I kissed her, softly, on the lips, and then stepped back and met her gaze.

"Dating in specific," she said. "I like that idea."

* * *

Our Thanksgiving feast was a fabulous success. Everyone shouted over everyone else. Wine was drunk and so were people. The turkey, in truth, was too dry but we suffocated it in gravy. The stuffing was savory. Pam's sweet potatoes were exceptional. Cyrus's okra and squash dishes were scraped clean and he smiled proudly at each compliment.

After the meal and the catfood reveal and a walk through the darkening streets of the neighborhood and an endless amount of dish washing and drying and stacking, the guests began to say goodnight. Cyrus fired up the cheeseburger-mobile and waved as he pulled through the drive. Dale and Sara and the twins followed. Then Pam.

At 9:30 I walked Claire to her car.

"Thank you, Jack," she said. "That was wonderful."

"My home hasn't been that full of life in a long time," I replied. "I like this place better when you're here."

She smiled, and in the next instant my hands were on her waist and I was kissing her. Deeply this time. I felt her hands move up my arms and then around my neck in an embrace.

"Is this happening?" I asked.

"I think so," she said, through lips that grazed mine. They were soft and pliable.

"The kids head back to school on Sunday," I said. "Doing anything that evening?"

"You tell me," Claire said.

I smiled at her. "Yes. You are. I'll pick you up at six."

She kissed me again, then slid into her car. I handed her a gleaming empty pie dish.

* * *

Now I jostle my tumbler and listen to the clink of ice cubes. I had been sleepy an hour before, tryptophan coursing through my system, but now I'm wide awake, my mind electric.

Knowing that the kids are nearby, safe and warm and well fed fills me with a sense of peace and order. That feeling is only amplified when I think of seeing Sara and Dale together, and his awkward, loving paternal gestures towards the twins, and then seeing Pam, newly thin, chatting up Cyrus with his too white dentures. For a moment, under this dark November sky, everything feels right with the world.

But the electric feeling does not come from my sense of order, which is calming, but from reliving my kiss with Claire only half an hour before. I haven't had the right kind of kiss in a long time, years really. Diane and I were far past making out. We kissed, of course, but it was usually a peck, or if it was more, it was mapped terrain, comfortable but not electrifying. Then there was Brenna, so unexpected, such a release for me, but her kisses were hard, gum grinding, and she opened her lips too readily. With Brenna kisses were hurried TikTok moments.

When I kissed Claire tonight she seemed to melt. Her lips were soft, nearly but not completely forbidden. She was grateful for my touch, as I was for hers. We know we're not young, and we know the physical progression that will likely unfold between us, but we thrill at the prospect, and being mature, we will not race through it.

That's what makes me electric.

I move to the terrace steps and sit, facing the mirrored black surface of the pool and the lake beyond. I hold the near empty tumbler of bourbon on my knee. Time slows and I feel I have reached the end of something, a chapter, a trial, a fast.

I have also come to the beginning of something. A new career (*really?*) teaching high school. A new relationship (*am I ready?*) with someone who has known loss, who has guided my children throughout high school, and who makes a righteous chocolate pecan pie.

Am I ready for this new beginning, have I earned it? If the past eighteen months have been a time for rebuilding, what have I built? Am I any closer to discerning the prime factors of Jack Callany?

I try to summon the prime factors I've assigned to myself since the summer. *Defiant smart ass* is where I started. Yes, I am those things, even though I'm not sure they're prime factors. *Money obsessed.* Yes, even though I hate that I am. I have enough, more than enough. Claire had been duly impressed by my home here on the lake. *Possessing fortitude and an inventive mind.* Check. I have these qualities, maybe not to an extraordinary degree but enough to distinguish myself in this neighborhood.

A thought arrives unbidden. *There is a way* for a fifty-five year old money obsessed defiant smart ass with fortitude and an inventive mind to redirect these inglorious traits into something positive: teaching. The defiant smart ass must admit himself into an asylum of defiant smart asses, and that would be a high school. Any high school would do. My defiant smart assness has mellowed and matured, but I can sniff out the same quality in others, do fair battle with them, and on a good day help them redirect their energies into something worthwhile. *You can't bullshit a bullshitter*, as the sales reps at American Fiber used to say.

Of course, being a defiant smart ass is necessary but not sufficient to make one a good high school math teacher. A bit of testicular fortitude and an inventive mind help, too.

I turn over *money obsessed* in my mind. It's an unusual prime factor. In some ways I'm not money obsessed at all. I don't really want more stuff. In fact, I don't spend that much money. Rare bourbon is probably my most unjustifiable expense. I don't care to take other people's money (unless there are cards involved). My obsession is more about winning in the stock options game. If I open twenty positions, I want to close all twenty in the black. I don't really care if I make fifty thousand dollars or one thousand dollars on any given position. It just becomes a number in a ledger somewhere. I will probably never even spend all the money anyway. But I like to win the game every single day.

So it's not really *money obsessed*, it's more like *competitive with a touch of gambling addiction*. Boy, it really sounds bad when I put it that way. I picture myself sitting in the dark smokey Men's Lounge year after year, pushing chips to the center of the table and (sometimes) raking them back onto my own pile. I suppose the shoe fits.

Does being *competitive with a touch of gambling addiction* qualify me to be a great teacher? I think I know what the Parent Teachers Association would say about that (if they knew). But, using my inventive mind, I invert the problem. Being a teacher will tame my *competitive with a touch of gambling* animal spirits. I'll be standing in front of a room full of pimply defiant smart asses for every day from 9:30 to 4:00, which is exactly the hours when the markets are open.

During these past three months of substitute teaching, I've had to wean myself from most of the options trading. I admit that I've used Lion

Oil with *Enable Trade Execution* turned ON a few times this fall when I've spotted some slow moving prey, but if I'm being honest with myself, it's not very fun because the competitive element has been solved by AI (thanks a lot, Jimmy.) The truth is, it's been liberating to step away from day trading. The dual monitors, the news ticker, the trading volumes and the Greeks have receded from the foreground of my mind while I've been teaching. It feels, well, healthy.

And anyway, I can still get my competitive kicks with a touch of gambling addiction every Thursday night.

Teaching feels right to me. It's part of what I want to build next. It dovetails nicely with my prime factors, even the less than flattering ones, and in fact it gives me some confidence that I've actually found my right prime factors. I grin inwardly. I can't be too money obsessed if my dream is to be a public school teacher. I make a note to myself to ask Ms. Axelrod if I can take a salary of one dollar a year when I join full time.

I tip the bourbon glass to my lips and drain the final drops, which are mostly water at this point. With the flick of my wrist I toss the remaining ice cubes into the pool and watch them float. There is one final prime factor I need to revisit. Ironically, I may need incompleteness to complete myself.

The Callany Incompleteness Theorem states that Jack Callany is incomplete, ambiguous, fractional and ineffectual without a woman.

Can the theorem be proven? Alone, am I half a person?

I reflect over the many months since Diane has been gone, since *JackandDiane* has ceased to be, and I picture myself in moments alone. I see myself trail running in the state park, jumping over roots and dodging half buried rocks. I am happy in these times, I am not incomplete. I see myself at my desk, pivoting my head between two computer monitors, snatching pennies before the slowly approaching steamroller. I am happy during these times, too.

Then I see myself walking through the empty house in my boxer shorts before bedtime, checking that doors are locked and lights turned off. This feels lonely. I see myself stretching out on the couch after lunch on a sunny Tuesday, surrendering sweetly to a nap, and then jolting myself awake with the fear of Noonday Demons. This feels very lonely. When I see this man on the couch I think, *damn, he is incomplete.*

I am both of these Jacks. Happy to be alone, loping along a trail, and miserable being alone, a lonely diner surrounded by happy chatting couples. Which am I, a lonely particle or a contented wave? Or a happy particle? Is that possible?

These thoughts give way suddenly to Claire. The moment I laid my hands lightly on her hips I felt her shift her weight towards me, perhaps inviting my kiss. Sitting here now, I relive the kiss, I literally feel her lips on my lips, yielding imperceptibly. The recollection makes me electric once again.

I see a truth now, and it's neither good nor bad, simply true. I *am* incomplete without this electric feeling, and it comes only from companionship. I don't know about particles and waves, but I don't think a single particle could ever be a wave. Two particles could, if they chose to. Yes, Claire and I could be a wave.

Diane and I had been a wave, and then for a long time, just two particles. I think we both wanted to see if we could become a wave again. We never got the chance.

Diane, I say softly under my breath. *I love you. Life goes on. Long after the thrill of living is gone. My life goes on and I want your blessing.*

I don't know if you'd call it a prayer.

I unlace my shoes and remove them, placing them on the step next to me. I pull off my socks and lay them across the top of my shoes. I stand and pull off my sweater, then loosen my belt and remove my jeans and boxers. I feel the chill of the November night air on my body.

I walk nude along the side of the pool until I reach the deep end. Facing its full length I curl my toes around the coping. I do not hesitate, but raise my arms like Superman, lean forward, and when gravity has its hold on me, dive.

The water is frigid and stuns my heart and skull. I take an underwater stroke, then break the surface, and swim with long strokes toward the shallow end. I do not acclimate to the cold water. It grows colder with each stroke I take. This pool would quickly and uncaringly drain my life away.

When I reach the shallow end I take giant steps out of the pool and suck in lungfuls of air. My skin is pink and clammy. I have no towel.

Idiot, I think.

I pull on my jeans, then my sweater, and sit shivering uncontrollably for a moment. The soles of my feet are freezing. I dry them quickly with my boxer shorts, then pull on my socks. I've got to get inside to dry my head.

I stand and walk across the terrace. I leave my boxers and shoes and the empty tumbler on the step and remind myself to retrieve them later, before Jimmy and Meagan can discover them. *Dad, you're losing it.*

I open the slider and walk into the glonously warm family room. As I enter my eyes move to the bookcase. There, on top of the Edward Hopper art book, rests a mahogany box.

ABOUT THE AUTHOR

MARK MCDOWELL IS AN ENTREPRENEUR AND INVESTOR WITH a secret passion for literary fiction. His techie career and his writing career are unified by his love of words and storytelling, and his unceasing curiosity about the world and the people around him. Mark lives in North Carolina with his wife and two young adult children, dividing his time between Lake Norman and the Blue Ridge Mountains.

Learn more at www.MarkMcDowellAuthor.com